Strength in Numbers:
A Novel of
Cryptocurrency

Bill Laboon

Dedicated to my dad,
who always asked me:
How are you going to make money with that?

Contents

Chapter 1

Note To The Reader

At the time of this writing, the entire world does not yet run on cryptocurrency. Therefore, I have done my best to make the relative and absolute values of the various cryptocurrencies used in the novel (Bitcoin, Litecoin, Ethereum, Monero, Federal Reserve Tokens) obvious from context. If it is ever not obvious, or you wish to know more specific numbers, you can look up the various conversion rates between them in Appendix A.

Each chapter ends with a short article from *The Econometrician*, an economics-focused newspaper of record, published weekly and known for puns in their headlines. Any resemblance to an actual newspaper is purely coincidental. Note that the articles are from different publication years, and so various political figures and situations will change from article to article. You can tell the date the article was published (in relationship to the story) by looking at the volume and issue information listed. Volume shows which year it was published (with Volume I equal to eighteen years before the events in the story) and issue shows which week (with issue 1 being the first week of the year, issue 2 being the second week, etc.)

I have followed the convention of capitalizing the names of the various cryptocurrencies when referring to the network as a whole (e.g., "Are you on the Bitcoin network?") but using all lowercase letters when referring to units on the networks (e.g., "I sent him one litecoin").

I hope you enjoy this glimpse of the future.

Chapter 2

The Nature of Coin

"Ten bitcoin? Free and clear?"

Phlox repeated it in her mind. Chris was offering to split with her fifty-fifty, but even half of that amount seemed beyond her comprehension. With five bitcoin, she wouldn't have to work at the diner to get through school. She wouldn't have to work ever again, if she didn't feel like it. She could spend the rest of her life reading and writing about reading.

"Slightly more than that, actually," Chris replied. "About ten point oh one four one."

Phlox sighed at the unnecessary precision. Chris was a Computer Science major, after all, and that was not exactly a field where approximation was a virtue. Her chosen field, English literature, was not quite as averse to it. Still, it felt like someone telling her that they had found a ten thousand carat diamond, but then stopping to give the various measuring errors possible. The entire idea was immense, beyond what one person could comprehend. The grandeur could only be spoiled by trying to pin it down.

"Give me a second," said Phlox. "I'm going to get some coffee. This is a little bit much."

Phlox got up and headed to the counter. Nobody was in line. There were only a few people scattered in the coffee shop at 8:00 AM. Mostly students came here, and if there was one thing students did not like to do, it was get up early. Phlox herself had rolled out of bed only ten minutes ago, and had to run to meet Chris. Chris looked like he had been up for a while, but he was insistent that they meet at a time when few others would be around, and refused to mention over email why he wanted to meet.

Now Phlox knew why. What he was talking about what was something beyond life-changing wealth. It had seemed odd that Chris had gotten in touch with her about this. They had gone to elementary and middle school together, but his family had moved away their freshman year of high school. They had left the small Rust Belt town of Amsteco for Ecotopia, one of the new car-free communities springing up the last decade, this one built deep in the hills of Appalachia. They had both ended up at the University of Pittsburgh, and while Phlox considered him a friend, they weren't exactly close.

The heavily tattooed barista raised an eyebrow at Phlox, asking for her order without a word. He was a tall, muscular Indian man, probably a student from one of the many colleges near here. She was slightly intimidated talking to him.

"Large coffee, room for cream, please," Phlox said.

The barista set down a tablet on the counter, then left to fill up a cup. Phlox looked at the tablet, with its "Accepted: Bitcoin and Litecoin" header. Phlox pressed the "Litecoin" button and what looked like a piece of abstract black and white art underneath. The abstract art was, she knew, simply a representation of the address to send her microlites — a QR code. Phlox pulled her sleeve back to expose her watch, tapped in a few numbers to confirm her identity, and scanned the QR code. A few moments later, "Transaction confirmed!" appeared on the screen and a short, happy melody played.

"Here's your coffee," the barista said. "By the way, I love your hoodie!"

"Thanks," said Phlox, a bit embarrassed by the attention. Most people didn't know the picture on it was James Joyce, and she didn't wear it to advertise herself, or modernist literature in general. Occasionally, though, people commented on it.

"Well, you have my attention," Phlox said, returning to her seat. "Whose bitcoin is it? And how did you find it?"

Chris fumbled around in his book bag, and brought out a thick textbook with the title *Cross-Chain Transactions: Fundamental Theories and Applications*. It was illustrated with a photograph of three fancy-looking birds, arranged in a triangle around a fleur-de-lis. At the bottom of the cover was written the author, S. B. Chambers.

"Have you heard of the Chicken Book?" asked Chris.

"I've heard of the chicken dance..." said Phlox.

"It's a weird thing in computer science textbooks. They all seem to have silly nicknames. There's a book on compilers called the Dragon Book, a book on operating systems called the Dinosaur Book, a book on Perl called the Camel Book..."

"Wait, I thought we were talking about computer science, not gems."

"Funny. Perl — P, E, R, L — is a programming language. The Chicken Book is *the* book to cover how to convert one kind of cryptocurrency to another. The author was a major researcher in the field when it was first starting up twenty years ago or so. Anybody in the field would recognize it."

"So what does this have to do with your free bitcoin?"

"The bitcoin belonged to Sam Chambers, the author. It looks like he did some mining in the really early days of bitcoin, when the entire currency was, well, if not worthless, next to worthless. Then he forgot about it."

"It sounds to me like you're talking about stealing it from him."

"He's dead. Died in a boating accident more than fifteen years ago."

"Okay, so you're stealing from his estate."

"Well, he never had any kids. Never even got married. Maybe, *maybe*, ethically, it would be stealing from his relatives, but it hasn't been moved from the original account. As far as the world knows, it's gone. Just another one of the thousands, if not millions, of bitcoin that were lost before cryptocurrency took over the world. Did you ever hear about that guy who left seventy-five hundred bitcoin on a hard drive that he threw out, then spent years digging through trash to find it?"

"Oh yeah, I remember hearing that story, I think. Didn't he find the hard drive but it was smashed and ruined?"

Chris snorted. "Yup. It was like some sort of Greek tragedy, although I'm not sure what sin the gods were punishing him for. Wastefulness, maybe? Throwing too many things away?"

Chris was quiet for a few seconds, as if going through the list of all the sins that the man could have committed that would be worthy of such a punishment. Owning that many bitcoin would make you one of the richest people in the United States, if not the world. To have it and then to have lost it!

"Anyway," continued Chris, "Dr. Chambers actually taught here at Pitt." He opened up the book and showed her the 'About the Author' section in the back, along with the blurb explaining Dr. Chambers' research interest and recent promotion to full professor at the University of Pittsburgh. "I think Carnegie Mellon tried to recruit him away but he never left."

"How do you know about this secret bitcoin that he had? So secret that apparently he forgot about it, or at least didn't mention it in his will?" asked Phlox, taking a sip from her coffee.

"I've been doing research. I wasn't out looking for old stashes of bitcoin, but rather trying to understand why he made some of the assumptions that he made in the Chicken Book. Some have held up really well, but some haven't, especially those that assumed that network latency would not decrease in any sort of superlinear way…"

Phlox's eyes started to glaze over, and she ran her hands through her brown, slightly frizzy hair. The frizziness told her it was going to be humid today.

"That's beside the point, I guess," Chris said, noticing the far-off look in Phlox's eyes. "The point is, the University kept all of his research papers and notes. He was famous enough that they thought somebody might want to write a book on him, although no one has, as far as I can tell. There are a few boxes in the basement of Hillman Library that have everything that was in his office on the day he died. I don't know if anybody besides me has looked through them since that day."

"And you found a note mentioning that he had forgotten that he had enough bitcoin to buy half of Oakland?"

"No, no, not exactly. I found a bitcoin address listed in one of his notebooks, with an arrow pointing to it and labeled 'cold storage (PW)'. I looked up the address on a blockchain explorer and saw that it held slightly over ten bitcoin."

Phlox saw that he was slightly uncomfortable rounding down how much bitcoin was there, but she was thankful for

the effort to not talk like a computer. He swiveled his laptop over to Phlox to show a Bitcoin address on the screen:
1z51uFfD7XY8NLdX7inb1kpVUyLTwtRyP.

"It looked like he was an early miner, and stored some away on
a paper wallet. I mean, maybe 'PW' was a place or a friend of his,
but I'll bet he meant paper wallet."

"Wait, what?"

"You know how the Bitcoin network works, right? It's secured by
specialized computers doing mining work and verifying transactions,
and putting them into blocks. They're all working on a mathematical
problem, and as soon as one solves it, they can add a block to the
chain and get a reward from the network. Back in the early days,
it was fifty bitcoin per mined block. Fewer bitcoin now, but on the
other hand, each bitcoin is worth immensely more."

"And Dr. Chambers bought one of these special computers and
set up a mining business?"

"Well, in those days, you could use a personal computer. It was
something that quite a few of the early cryptocurrency pioneers did."

Phlox nodded. It seemed like something she may have learned
one time, but had not decided to waste any of her neurons on. Money
was money. Her boss gave her some litecoin each week, then she gave
some millilites to her landlord, and some microlites to the barista,
and to anyone else to whom she needed to give money. She was
vaguely aware that there were people keeping the whole system running, but she wondered about them about as often as she wondered
about the technicians on the generators that kept the lights on in
her house.

"He mined for a while, and moved it into cold storage on a paper
wallet. In other words, he printed something out which would allow
him to access the funds."

"Wait," interrupted Phlox. "So it's like a passphrase that I'd
enter to access my litecoin?" Phlox had a few millibits for savings,
but on a day-to-day basis, she really only dealt with Litecoin, like
most of the population of Pittsburgh. Sure, people used bitcoin for
large purchases like houses or fine art, but it was mostly for savings.
Litecoin was used for just buying and selling; the transaction fees
were a fraction of those of Bitcoin. She was relatively certain that
the "Bitcoin" button for buying coffee here had not been used in

years — you'd pay more for the transaction than the coffee itself cost. She couldn't remember a customer ever trying to pay for their waffles in Bitcoin, although she did get asked occasionally if they accepted Monero.

"It's the public and private key of a Bitcoin address. If you have access to that paper, you have everything you need to access the bitcoin stored within it."

Phlox took another big swig of coffee. It had cooled down enough that she didn't have to sip it, and she could use the caffeine. She wasn't used to waking up this early, and the adrenaline from hearing about the vast stash of bitcoin was beginning to fade. Technical details always were a bit of a soporific for her.

"It still feels a little bit wrong," Phlox said. "I mean, people don't just get free money out of the air."

"To be fair," Chris replied, "that's what people said about Bitcoin when it first came out. 'Nobody is going to want your magic Internet money', 'it's not backed by anything real', 'it's just a bunch of numbers, who would trade real money for that'..." By the end, his voice had turned into an imitation of somebody who was just barely intelligent enough to use words with two syllables.

"Ethics aside, as long as we don't steal it from him, we're legally in the clear. Paper wallets are like cash or bearer bonds. Whoever has them, owns them, unless you can prove that they got it in some sort of illicit way. We're not going to do that. You can go look up the cases in the Law Library: *Virginia v. Hiltschmetz*, *Jones v. Gupta*, *California v. Parsons*. It's up to the owner of the cryptocurrency to keep their private key under wraps."

Phlox was still looking a bit concerned, so Chris tried a different tack.

"Think of it as treasure on a shipwreck. I mean like an old shipwreck, from Blackbeard or whomever. If we find the ship and get the treasure, and Blackbeard hasn't been trying to salvage the ship the whole time, it's ours. This treasure dates back to almost the beginning of the Bitcoin blockchain; it's like finding treasure from a Roman ship or something. Maybe a raft that someone made in the Paleolithic age. The laws are pretty clear that it will be ours if we get it. And if nobody finds it, that ten bitcoin is just going to sleep forever with the rest of the lost early bitcoin, just like a ship would rest at the bottom of the sea if we don't pull it up."

Phlox considered this. At a minimum, it was an adventure. She had always lived through adventures vicariously, through books, since she was a small child. Now she could feel the butterflies in her stomach. Was this how Robin Hood felt? Or Beowulf? Or Elizabeth Bennet?

"I'm in!" Phlox exclaimed, a little too loudly. She quickly put her hand over her mouth and felt her cheeks redden. Perhaps thinking about Elizabeth Bennet had made her act a little bit like the protagonist of *Pride and Prejudice*. I should figure out what all this entails first, she thought.

Chris beamed. Phlox knew this had been on his mind for a while, and that he hadn't told anybody else about it. It probably felt great for him to have a partner in crime.

"Just one thing," Phlox said, "why do you need my help? I figure you'd want some other programmer, or a cryptographer, or a soldier of fortune or something. Anything but an English lit major and part-time waitress."

"Well," Chris replied, "you're smart, that's obvious. You also have a different perspective than I do on the problem. Most of my friends are engineering types and are going to think just in terms on numbers. But you'll be able to look at things with fresh eyes. Dr. Chambers was a pretty well-read man; his textbooks are full of quotes from all sorts of authors that I hear you talking about. You think like he thought. Different fields, of course, but there's a similar... vibe, I'd guess you'd say."

He paused momentarily. Now it was Phlox's turn to beam. She wasn't the type to go fishing for compliments, but it was always nice to get them.

"Plus, you live in his old apartment."

"Seriously? He lived in the student-housing wasteland of South Oakland?" Phlox was too surprised by this to realize that the compliments on her intelligence and perspective were probably not the principal reason that Chris emailed her.

"Yeah. South Oakland wasn't quite so bad back then. It would have been a quick walk to work for him, which was probably more

important than a giant yard and, I don't know, granite countertops
or whatever they liked back then."

Phlox thought about the countertops in her own apartment. Every time she or her roommate put something heavier than a cup
down, she thought that they might break. The various stains left by
generations of students had made their own little map of a fantasy
world, Phlox had joked. It was a decent enough place for a student,
but she couldn't imagine an actual *adult* living there.

"You think he kept the paper wallet in the house, then?" Phlox
asked.

"Well, it's possible. More than possible, I think. At a bare minimum, it will allow us to rule it out and then move on to check
somewhere else."

"How do we know we'll find it? Dozens of students must have
lived here since he died. Wait a second... did he die in the house?"

"No.   Boating accident, remember?   Somewhere on the
Youghiogheny River. So, yeah, I mean, that was the house he lived
in, but he didn't die in it."

"Oh. Right. I guess I don't remember any lakes in the basement,
except when it rains. But none of those would be big enough to
drown in. Back to the question... how do we know we'll find it? Or
that it even exists?"

"We don't. That's what makes it an adventure! Wouldn't it be
boring if we knew we were going to find it?"

"I'd be ready to spend much more energy on it if I was sure it
existed in the first place. Some renter may have thrown it away eight
years ago, or it's just a pile of mold in the attic somewhere. Did you
check through all of his notes stored in the library?"

"Of course! It was the first thing I did. It probably hasn't been
very good for my GPA. I've been going down there every morning as
soon as the library opens. I'm positive it's not there. If it were, I'd
be sitting on ten point oh" — a glance from Phlox — "and something
bitcoin already."

Phlox felt energetic, and it seemed like the conversation was becoming more rapid. She took another gulp of coffee, less for the
caffeine and more for something to do other than talk. The conversation felt like it was moving of its own accord, but she wanted to
keep some control over it.

Chris seemed to have felt the need to slow things down as well. He adjusted his thin pince-nez glasses (an affectation Phlox thought he could have done without) and shifted a bit in his seat. He was very obviously thinking, eyes looking skyward, breathing calmly.

"There are a few reasons I think that the paper wallet exists, and that it is in your apartment. First, process of elimination. It wasn't in his office, and both of his parents died years before he did. It's possible he kept it in their old house, but unlikely. It didn't seem like they were particularly close."

Phlox got emotional for a moment. Chris paused, as if something was wrong, but when she quickly comported herself, he continued.

"He could have kept it in a safe deposit box, but he wasn't the sort of person to have lots of valuables and be familiar with putting things in safe deposit boxes. Even if he were, I don't know if he would have even considered it - remember that these bitcoins altogether would be worth, I don't know, a few microbits now, when they were moved to the paper wallet."

Phlox laughed inwardly. It was hard to think of a bitcoin then being worth so much less than even a microbit now.

"Second, I found this note in the back of his notebook. He says he — let me quote it..." Chris trailed off as he fished through the crumpled papers in his backpack. Finally he brought out a photocopy of a notebook page, with part of the page circled with an emphatic red pen. "Here we go... 'Moved cold storage to over the pots.' That was only a week before he died, according to the date on the page. I also found a receipt from a hardware store he was using as a bookmark, dated the morning of the day before he wrote that. He bought spackling paste and a couple of tools; I'll bet he made a secret compartment for his paper wallet."

"Okay, now I see why you wanted me in on this. And thanks for that, by the way. I guess you could have tried to come over and rifle through my kitchen when I wasn't looking."

Chris looked hurt. "It only seemed fair. And besides, if we split fifty-fifty, we're both set for life. I'm not looking for Satoshi's Hoard. Honestly, my life probably would be worse if I had ten bitcoin. I've heard enough stories about lottery winners whose lives are ruined by it. But with five... well, that's more than I'd ever make in my lifetime. But it won't put me into the range of people who have to worry about being assassinated."

"What's Satoshi's Hoard?"

"Satoshi Nakomoto was the person who first invented Bitcoin, and kicked off modern cryptocurrency as we know it. But he disappeared, and with him his entire stash of bitcoin, forever unusable unless someone discovers the private key."

"How much is in it?"

"Not much. A little under a million bitcoin."

Phlox swooned for a second. Again, this seemed like something a teacher told her when she was younger, but it was ancient history and had little to do with life in her town of Amsteco, so she didn't really file it away. A million bitcoin would give him the economy of a nation-state. Not even some silly microstate hiding in the Pyrenees or the Alps, some half-forgotten remnant of a medieval era treaty. No, this would make a single person the equivalent of a China or United States. The rise of cryptocurrency had led to vast wealth for people who got in early, but Satoshi's wealth was too much for her to think about. She changed topics to the just barely comprehensible.

"So we are planning to split the ten bitcoin fifty-fifty..." Phlox paused. The butterflies in her stomach were rapidly transforming into eagles, if not pterosaurs. She felt compelled to add, "...if we do it?"

"Sure. I have a simple smart contract set up and ready to run on Ethereum now. Once we enter the private key here — which we should find on the paper wallet — it will transfer exactly half to me and half to you, minus transaction fees. I've programmed in a pretty high fee to make sure that the transaction goes through as soon as possible. See?" Chris swiveled his laptop and showed her an open window on his computer. It was filled with text and symbols.

"This is all gobbledygook to me."

Chris scribbled an address down on paper, and handed it to Phlox. "Here's a link to the code. You can look at it yourself, have a smart contracts lawyer look at it, whatever. Although I don't recommend you show it to anybody who is not us. It's actually enabled by some of the work that Dr. Chambers did, having one blockchain influence another like that. Once you're ready, just sign it on the network with your watch. I already did. Once we both sign it with our private keys, it will go into effect, and any bitcoin from that address will be evenly split between our two accounts, as soon as someone enters the private key for the original bitcoins."

"What's to stop me from just going back to my apartment, finding the paper wallet, and sending the entire stash to myself?"

"Just your sense of ethics. But I trust you. This is a small thing, but I still remember how you got back an extra five dollar bill from the lunch lady. This was back when people still used paper money, of course. You told Kate, and she was so excited. She wanted to spend it on candy or whatever. You had such a look in your eye, like Kate betrayed you. Then you marched right back to the lunch lady and gave it back."

"Ha!" Phlox said. "If you were to ask me about what I remember about lunch back in middle school, all I could have told you about is the time that one of the teachers yelled at me. Said I was too old to be playing with my food. I was just mixing the whipped cream into the pudding. Still bitter about that after all these years."

Chris nodded in sympathy for this ancient hurt, then continued. "The smart contract does a couple of other things. The Bitcoin network has changed quite a bit since then, there have been a couple of soft forks, but the contract takes care of all of that. It's really all quite simple." Chris adjusted his glasses, pushing them up a bit on his nose. Phlox fidgeted in her chair, and Chris seemed to notice.

"I'm not worried about the contract, Chris." Phlox said with a suddenly determined look. She drained the last few teaspoons of coffee from her cup. "I've just got class soon, and no matter if I'm going to be rich once we find this buried treasure, attendance counts for Dr. Lin."

Chris laughed. "Oh yeah, I had her for French Literature class."

"I'm surprised! Why did you take a course on French literature?"

"Eh, just a 'general education' requirement. I needed some sort of lit class, and it fit my schedule. Still amazes me that you could go through your entire undergraduate career without learning even the rudiments of coding, but heaven forbid that I go through without having read some fiction."

"It makes you well-rounded. Don't complain. I had to take math classes, which aren't really my thing."

"I guess that's true." Chris stood up, picking up his backpack. "And there are some gen eds I really liked. I remember my Early American History class when we got to read letters written by the Founding Fathers. Amazing to see their actual thought processes instead of just what the history books say. So, when can we start the search?"

"How about tomorrow night at six?" Phlox got up and slung her own backpack over a shoulder. "Holly has a night class."

"Who?" asked Chris.

"My roommate. There's no way I could afford a place of my own in Pittsburgh, even in Oakland. We got a really good deal on this one. Maybe the landlord took pity on me. Even if I did have enough money to do it, I don't know if I'd be able to force myself to live so extravagantly. You're from Amsteco, too, you understand."

"Yeah, although things were different when we moved to Ecotopia. It was a pretty bourgeois place, but it was pretty cool being in an entire city without cars. I don't want to bore you too much, though. I know you have to go. Six works for me." Chris said it with the tone that signals that the conversation is over.

He couldn't help himself from expressing one last thought. "Wow... this feels like the start of something big."

"I sure hope so — can you add a guarantee for that in your smart contract?"

"All the perplexities, confusions, and distresses in America arise, not from defects in their constitution or confederation, nor from want of honor or virtue, as much from downright ignorance of the nature of coin, credit, and circulation."
-John Adams, letter to Thomas Jefferson

A COIN Too Far?

An excerpt from an article in The Econometrician, *Volume II, Issue 13*

United States President Xavier Rodriguez was not elected to stay the course. With inflation peaking at 39% last year, and the collapse of the U.S. dollar as the world's reserve currency, the nation's first Democratic Socialist president knew that drastic changes were needed to the way the country operates. Surprisingly, his first major initiative has not been a major public works project, as he campaigned on, but a proposal to have the United States government issue its own cryptocurrency.

The "Currency Origination for the INternet" (COIN) Act will authorize the creation of a new cryptocurrency which can be exchanged directly for U.S. dollars. As more and more transactions move to various blockchains, and trust in the banking system reaching lows not seen since the depths of the Great Depression, this was seen by the Rodriguez administration as the only way to prevent an entire collapse of faith in the dollar. The COIN Act will propose creation of a new blockchain, with dollars being exchangeable for Federal Reserve Tokens (FRTs) at parity. All federal taxes and fees could be paid for by FRTs, and it could be used as legal tender for private transactions as well. The technical specifications are still being worked on, as well as the exchange locations where users could purchase FRTs, but these are expected to be hammered out soon.

The opposition Libertarian party expressed mixed reactions to the bill. Many Libertarians state that they can never support any currency which is backed by the Federal Reserve. Others balk at the cost of introducing a new currency, when there are already several popular ones in use by the majority of the populace. Still others are concerned that having a government-sanctioned cryptocurrency introduces a new monopoly to the system. Even with these misgivings, a majority of Libertarians seem to support the bill. "It's a step in the right direction," said Minority Leader James Polieri (L-CO), "even if it's not as big a step as we may have wanted it to be."

The two major regional parties, the Democrats and Republicans, are united in registering opposition to the bill. However, with only a handful of Representatives and even fewer Senators, their opposition means little. As the constituencies of both of these parties skew older, this could simply be an indication of a previous generation's lack of technical savvy.

With the Democratic Socialists riding high on their first presidential win, the COIN Act looks like it will pass with a large number of bipartisan votes. It remains to be seen whether or not U.S. citizens will give up their bitcoin, litecoin — or even dollars — for the new FRTs.

Chapter 3

Most Simple and Most Ordinary

Phlox opened the door to her apartment and heard the excited screams of her roommate Holly. The yells weren't directed at her, but Phlox recognized them all the same. Some minor goal had been achieved, or a flower looked particularly nice, or she had successfully poured exactly enough almond milk in the cereal bowl to perfectly balance out her shredded wheat. For Holly, there was no such thing as the golden mean when it came to emotions. Anything worth experiencing was worth jubilating over.

"Phloxy lady!" yelled Holly down the stairs as Phlox took off her backpack. Professor Lin not only took attendance, but even counted the number of times you contributed in class. She marked it down in a little notebook on the podium, along with her estimate of how much thought went into the comment or question. It was certainly one way to ensure that her students read Stendahl, but it took quite a bit out of Phlox. She didn't know if she could handle Holly for more than a few minutes, but smiled politely up at her.

"Hey, Hollywood," said Phlox as she trudged up the stairs to their shared apartment. Holly's last name was Wu. The obvious nickname was given to her freshman year, about three minutes after she arrived in Phlox's dorm. Unlike most of the other roommates thrown together on their floor, they had gotten along fabulously, and had lived together ever since.

"Violet's over, so the Flower Garden's got an extra flower today!"

"What's your sister doing here?"

"She just started at Pitt this semester, remember? I'm going to be her tour guide — going to walk backwards around campus and point out the sights!" Holly giggled.

Phlox was at the top of the stairs now, and could see the Wu sisters sitting on the futon in the living room. Phlox had met Violet a few times, so it wouldn't really be polite to just walk into her bedroom, even if it was exactly what she wanted to do. She'd been having second thoughts about the conversation with Chris this morning, and she did her best thinking alone. Or sometimes talking with her Dad, but he was down in Amsteco, and she also couldn't work up the energy to actually pull out her watch and make a call.

"Hi, Phlox," said Violet, with just as much energy as her sister, but only about a hundredth of the amount of confidence. Holly could state, *definitively*, that gravity was not real to a Professor of Physics, and would stick by it if the entire city of Pittsburgh disagreed with her.

"Hey, Violet," responded Phlox. "How's your first semester?"

Violet beamed. "It's great! I keep hearing it's going to get more difficult, but it's so much nicer being able to schedule my time myself. I hated getting up early in high school, and now my earliest class is at eleven."

"What are you taking?" asked Phlox.

"Well, I don't know what I'm going to major in yet, so it's mostly a bunch of gen ed requirements. Intro to Sociology, Calc, Intro to American Lit, Intro to Performance and umm... Intro to Poli Sci."

"Lot of intros there!" said Holly.

"For me, this semester is an intro.. to college!" laughed Violet. Holly joined in laughing at the bad joke. For a moment, Phlox wondered if Holly had "introduced" Violet to some sort of recreational chemical.

"I'm not a big fan of the Lit class," continued Violet, after she calmed down a bit. "Sorry, Phlox! But I think Poli Sci is pretty neat. I'd never really thought about politics. All the talk on TV, Libertarians, Socialists... I don't know, it just never really seemed to have any impact on me. But it's neat to understand why they disagree."

"Well, you know, different strokes and all," said Phlox. "Not everyone loves trudging through *The Last of the Mohicans*."

"I figure freshman year is all for figuring out what you like, you know? It's not like I was able to figure it out in high school."

"True, true," said Holly. "I was always a math nerd, but I thought about dropping it for chemistry for a while when I was a freshman. But I took Intro to Number Theory with Professor Lakes, and I realized that it was what I wanted to do with my life. Now look at me! Literally!" She threw out her hands dramatically to show off her t-shirt. It had all of the digits of the constant e printed on it, in the shape of the letter e.

"I still don't understand why you find that stuff so interesting," said Phlox. "Just changing a bunch of numbers around."

"It's *so much* more than that!" exclaimed Holly. "Everything is mathematics! If you see a raindrop fall, you can map out its trajectory with math. If you send an email to somebody, know how the computers work? Math! Why can't I just spend your litecoin when I want to get a bottle of wine? Math!"

"Well, I could argue that everything is literature," shot back Phlox. "Everyone's life is just a story they're telling to themselves, and sometimes others."

"This is getting a bit deep, and I haven't even taken Intro to Philosophy yet!" chimed in Violet, leading to more giggling. Maybe they had gotten some wine, thought Phlox. Although hopefully with their own litecoin.

"Anyway," said Holly. It was the kind of "anyway" that meant that she wanted to wrap up the conversation. "We're going to get some lunch. Want to join?"

"No thanks," said Phlox. "I think I'm just going to get some reading done. Oh, plus I have an essay I need to finish up for my Russian Lit class this afternoon."

"Okay," said Holly. "See you later!"

"Have fun!" added Violet.

Phlox went into her room and pulled the used copy of *The Death of Ivan Ilyich* off of the cinder-block-and-scrap-wood bookshelves in her room. She could have read it online. Most students did. There were plenty of free text editions on the Internet, or in the library, so purchasing a copy was definitely a luxury. Physical books, though, were an affordable luxury. She never felt like she could get into reading something on a screen. The world was still there, sending words to her. But with an actual book, she didn't feel like she was in the real world anymore. She was entirely in the world created by the ink on the paper. Pixels just did not have that effect on her.

She opened the book, but after a few minutes of scanning the same words over and over again, realized that she wasn't making any progress. She wasn't entering the world of the book, but she was barely in this world. Her mind kept wandering from thought to thought, her eyes wandering from corner to corner of the room. The messy room of a messy student. Messy bed, sheets falling off a cheap mattress. Notebooks crammed with messy handwriting. Just... messiness. It used to drive Holly crazy when they shared a dorm freshman year.

Phlox knew that no reading was going to be done. Her mind just refused to focus. How could it when she might be the recipient of over five bitcoin in a little over twenty-four hours? At first she thought that she would start the search now. She could still share the bitcoin with Chris once she found it. No, though, that still felt like cheating. She had told him they would look for it together.

Phlox thought her conscience would let her get away with thinking about where the paper wallet might be hidden. But it was a gorgeous September day, and the best way to let the mind wander was to let the body wander. She laced up her sneakers, threw her threadbare black backpack over her shoulder, and headed downstairs. There was still over an hour to go before class, more than enough time for a detour through Schenley Park before her afternoon class started.

The sidewalks of South Oakland were teeming with students. It was that special time of the semester where everyone was back from summer break, but the workload hadn't really started to get onerous. Aside from the ones like Phlox, for whom an A- was almost as bad as an F, they had plenty of time on a sunny day to get ice cream, or some pizza, or even a beer. She navigated through the warren of one-way streets that compromised the unofficial student housing section of South Oakland. Sure, there was the occasional non-student here. An old Italian family that had been living here since the days of the steel mills, or a recent graduate who hadn't found housing elsewhere yet, or even the occasional burnout who just liked living in an area where house parties were a regular occurrence. For the most part, though, she walked through a sea of fellow undergraduates.

She passed by the line of people begging along Forbes Avenue, perhaps a dozen or fifteen, ranging from a man and a woman around her age deliberately dressed in dirty outfits, to older men with an air of faded glory, wearing clothes that would not look out of place in an office setting if they weren't so ripped. Perhaps most remarkably to a new observer, one man was wearing a cartoonishly large sombrero. All of them had cardboard signs, pasted with printed-out QR codes along with handwritten messages, heart-breaking or laugh-inducing. "Why lie? I want microlites for beer." "Litecoin Needed For Lung Surgery — GOD BLESS." "Traveling — Broke — Hungry — need some microlites for food." She even saw one person with a Monero code, rare here in Pittsburgh, although she was of course familiar with them from Amsteco. "Jesus says to share with the poor — please share some millimons" encircled the QR code in a half-cursive scrawl.

Phlox had seen most of these people every weekday since she arrived her first day of college, although the man and woman who were supposedly "traveling" were definitely newcomers. Veteran of the South Oakland streets that she was, she walked past without a second glance. A young-looking student — probably a freshman, she thought — was leaning over to give some microlites to a middle-aged man who looked like he had already had a few beers. His sign read "Need 2 bitcoin to hire ninjas."

By the time she got to the Boulevard of the Allies, a ten-minute walk from her home, she had thought of several different places where the paper wallet might be hidden. "Above the pots", the notebook had said. Well, she knew where she and Holly kept the pots (actually, where Holly kept the pots, since much to Holly's chagrin, Phlox's *modus operandi* was to leave the single pot that she used on the burner whenever it was not actually being washed). Dr. Chambers probably used the same spot. There was a new pantry that had been constructed last year, but maybe there used to be a counter in that area?

She was heading past the last stores in South Oakland, head in the clouds. The garishly advertised and neon-bedecked stores did their best to distract her, but they barely merited a second glance. They did their best, though - not a sentence went by without an exclamation point, and no lower-case letters were included. USED CARS - JUST HALF A MICROBIT DOWN! EVERYTHING'S A MILLILITE! IF OUR COMPETITION UNDERSELLS US BY A MICROLITE, WE'LL GIVE YOU A MILLILITE!

Phlox crossed the bridge into Schenley Park, enjoying the crisp air. Somebody was jogging towards her, and she could have sworn that he was looking at her oddly. Maybe it was the James Joyce hoodie. It was hard to tell because he was wearing sunglasses. As he got closer, Phlox was sure that he was looking at her face. Did she know him? She couldn't remember ever seeing him. For a moment, she was afraid, but then he continued running past her. He must have thought that he knew her or something.

Nerves. That's all it was. Despite Chris's assurances, she was worried that she was going to get in some sort of trouble on this treasure hunt. Ten bitcoin don't just disappear. It's not like pirate gold in a kid's book. You don't just forget about enough money to buy twenty houses. You definitely don't hide it in a kitchen above some pots.

Wait. Maybe he hadn't meant pots in term of "pots and pans." Didn't old people sometimes say "pot" to refer to marijuana? It definitely sounded like the kind of slang that you'd hear in a turn-of-the-century movie. So perhaps his "pots" were his stash of drugs? She'd have to talk to Chris about this. This Chambers guy didn't seem like the type to be doing drugs, but Chris would know more about him. She filed it away as another possibility.

She continued through the tunnel under the Boulevard, past the public swimming pool, recently closed for the season, up to the top of the hill. The man who had jogged past her on the bridge had come up through the woods and was once again heading towards her. She could see that he was a bit older, with hair just starting to go grey. He did not seem to be paying any attention to her this time, but something seemed off. There were a few people around, but not many.

Phlox held her watch, rotated the bezel, and called the first person on the list, her dad. If this guy were going to do something, he might think twice if someone knew where she was. Besides, she had been meaning to call her dad. He always had good life advice for her, and she hadn't talked to him since she had come back to Pittsburgh for the semester. Her fear was momentarily washed away by guilt — she always *meant* to call him. She wasn't a bad daughter, just busy! And distracted!

"Hey buttercup," a voice came from the watch.

"Hey Dad," said Phlox. "How's it going?"

The man jogged past her, seemingly paying her no mind. Was she just being paranoid? Oh well, better safe than sorry. And this was as good an excuse as any to get a chance to talk to her dad.

"... and a raccoon got into the garbage last night," she heard a voice say. Oh right, she already was talking to her dad. Or at least he was talking while her mind went off in a hundred different directions. "Took me forever to clean it up. My fault, I shouldn't have left the lid off the can."

"Dad, you know the raccoons are all over the place down there! And you need to lock the lid, too. They can open the lids about as easily as a person can."

"Yeah, yeah, I know, I just forget sometimes. I'm not a college kid like you, taking classes in Advanced Raccoon Deterrence Strategies. How is school treating you this term?"

"Not bad. Lots of reading this semester. I'm already looking forward to my next semester, should be pretty easy. Just two seminars and some fun classes, then I'm out of here."

"You have a plan for what you're doing next?" Phlox knew her dad was concerned about that. He wanted her to make a good living, better than he did. English literature majors right out of university, with nothing on their resume that was not somehow related to food service, were not exactly being fought over by top companies. Her dad didn't know this specifically, but he had picked up that she was worried about her prospects in the job market.

"I've got some ideas, but..." Phlox trailed off. She actually had no ideas. But she thought it might be a good excuse to talk to her dad about some other things, things she didn't want to discuss over the network. She wasn't normally concerned about wiretapping — she didn't even use anything other than the default encryption included on her watch. But this seemed like something that you didn't want to talk about publicly. She continued, "... I was hoping to talk to you about it. Do you mind if I come down tonight?"

"Mind? That'd be great!" he said. "Want to meet up at the Waterfront Saloon?"

Her dad's normal watering hole. It was strange, since he never drank that much, but he went there almost every night the last few years, ever since Phlox had moved to Pittsburgh for school. He'd get a single beer, and nurse it for several hours while reading old paperback science-fiction novels. Well, there were worse ways to spend your time. The graveyards in many of the old mill towns like Amsteco were filled with those who decided to try some new drug to pass the time, and ended up having no more time to pass.

"Sure. Be there around six?"

"Sounds good. Don't worry if you're a little late, I know rush hour's bad up there. See ya, lotus."

"Bye, Dad."

The walk back to Oakland was uneventful, but nice for all of that. A few leaves had started to turn colors. A chipmunk crossed her path. She ambled towards the Cathedral of Learning, the gargantuan forty-story building that dwarfed virtually everything in Oakland. It was easy to see why it was nicknamed "the drunk man's compass." As long as you could see it — and it was darned easy to see — you'd at least be able to get to the center of the university.

Before she could reach that, she had to walk past the life-size statue of a diplodocus in front of the museum. She remembered being scared of it when she was little; it was at least twenty-five feet high and seemed to touch the sky when she was only a tenth of its height. Not that she had grown that much. She was still one of the shortest people she knew. Dinosaur statues had lost the ability to terrify her, though.

As she approached the Cathedral, she thought back to her first introduction to Pitt. She was on a tour of the campus her senior year of high school. Her dad had not been able to join her. Although one of the benefits of him being unemployed was that he normally had plenty of time to attend events like this, he refused to go anywhere near the city. It had been a crisp autumn day as she listened to the tour guide, walking backwards as always, go on about the various restaurants on Forbes Avenue. She couldn't keep her eyes off the forty floors of the Cathedral. The limestone edifice looked like something out of a fantasy novel, and she couldn't help fantasizing about studying inside. She had had plenty of classes there, but it still maintained an air of magic about it in her mind.

She settled into a chair in the back of her Russian lit class. Unlike Dr. Lin, Professor Mikailov did not much care if you asked questions, or answered questions, or even showed up. He stood behind the podium, talking through his massive grey beard in his thick accent, probably giving the same lecture for the sixtieth or seventieth time. Still, Phlox went to every single one of his classes and even paid attention — as much as she could — for the entire class period.

A rustling and a flutter of movement from outside caught her attention. Holly and Violet were looking in at her and waving their hands the only way they knew how, that is, excitedly. Phlox waved back in as low-key a manner as possible which would still be considered polite. If the situation was reversed, she knew that Holly probably would have jumped out of her seat, lecture or no, and rushed to the window.

Even the small wave of Phlox's hand caught Mikailov's eye. He glared at her disapprovingly, but it did not seem to impact a single syllable of his lecture. He continued his monologue of Tolstoy's childhood, and Phlox ignored the blood rushing to her cheeks as she wrote down notes.

Finally the lecture came to an end. "Remember that you are responsible for the Ivan Ilyich essay next class. Until then, have a good day."

Phlox looked at her watch. Ten minutes to four. The class exited with the familiar rustling and mumbling.

She didn't have a car. What student did? Well, maybe occasionally the son of some Bulgarian asteroid mining company founder, or the nephew of some tech employee who had bought some litecoin early on. She did have an account with EthShare, though, so she could rent one for a few hours. Amsteco wasn't more than forty-five minutes away if traffic cooperated with her.

Heading back out into the last vestiges of the sunshine — clouds were rolling in, but her watch told her it would not be raining today — she realized that she had never eaten lunch. There were some food trucks right up the street. They were pretty affordable, only

30 microlites for her favorite, *tofu tikka masala.* She wandered up Bigelow Boulevard to the trucks and ordered some *malai kofta.* She noticed the jogging man from the park at the Chinese food truck next to her. She buried her head in her watch, playing it cool. Who *was* this man?

Her food came after several nervous minutes of waiting. This truck had the best food, but always took forever to make it. Usually this was a trade-off she was willing to make, but had she known that this middle-aged man would be next to her, she would have gone to the Thai food truck a few feet down. Maybe not the best food, but it was ready immediately. As she left with her mango lassi and tofu, she casually looked over her shoulder and noticed the man sitting on a bench near the food trucks. He was apparently paying her no mind.

The Cathedral of Learning had its share of hiding holes, places where she would be able to see around her but someone wouldn't be able to see her. She entered the revolving doors on the ground floor, went up the stairs to the third floor, down to the second floor, then back up to the third floor. Her heart was racing. Not from the stairs — Phlox walked almost everywhere, and the steep hills of Pittsburgh were a workout in and of themselves. Her life had been spent almost entirely within books, and even though it seemed ridiculous, she seemed to be doing things straight out of a spy novel.

Finally, she found an alcove which looked down on the ground floor. Across the hallway was a class that was in-session, and the students were facing toward the door. The heavy wooden door was propped open, and she could see the bored looks on the students' faces. If there was any commotion, chances were at least one of them would notice it. She sat down at the table, laid out her food and began to eat.

The food was delicious as always, but her brain was not letting her really enjoy it. She scarfed down the food quickly and cleaned up the alcove. She jumped down the heavy stone stairs down to the ground floor and walked back up to Fifth Avenue. Very soon, she saw the EthShare station on Fifth Avenue. It was a collection of small electric cars, all with the distinctive EthShare logo on the hood, along with a small black and grey pedestal on the sidewalk.

This was not the first time she had taken an EthShare car, but driving was not something that she did very often. Virtually everything she needed was within walking distance (at least, walking distance for her, which was a radius of about four miles from her apartment). If she ever needed to go somewhere in the city that was too far to walk, she could request one of the innumerable self-driving EthShare cars. Sadly, their range was limited to the city of Pittsburgh. Amsteco was definitely not in their local memory.

She walked over to the pedestal, and deftly entered various parameters: how long she wanted the car for, what distance she planned to drive it, her authorization code, and others. It only took a few seconds. Nothing bothered her more than standing in line while some person tried to deal with the interface. Read up a bit before using it, people! She then placed her watch against the pedestal to authenticate herself.

All over the Ethereum network, on computers all over the world, bits shifted, ones becoming zeroes and zeroes becoming ones. These were the result of the smart contract that she had signed via the watch. The contract was smart because it was self-reinforcing. If she violated the parameters of the contract, by driving erratically, or taking the car to a location she wasn't authorized to do so, or whatever, the car would pull itself over to the side and stop. She would then have to communicate with EthShare Customer Support to either request a pickup or explain why she had violated the terms of the contract.

She was more than free to look at the code behind the contract. That was the way to make it legally binding, make sure that anyone was free to see what they were agreeing to. However, like most people, she didn't understand the code or the legalese associated with it. She clicked the "I agree" button.

The screen displayed "Please enter car in location 2 — license plate ETHDR192." She hopped in the car as its seat moved up and mirrors automatically adjusted themselves to her profile's settings. Her account with EthShare knew a plethora of information about her, down to her height and preferred music stations. All of this was stored — compressed and encrypted, of course — on the Ethereum blockchain.

With the sun just starting to retreat behind the hills, Phlox started her drive to Amsteco.

"Ivan Ilyich's life had been most simple and most ordinary and there-fore most terrible."
-Leo Tolstoy, *The Death of Ivan Ilyich*

The Golden Black and Gold

An excerpt from an article in The Econometrician, *Volume XIII, Issue 28*

The City of Pittsburgh has long been known for its industry. From its early days as a glass-making powerhouse, to when its steel production helped the Allies win World War II, to its early 20th-century revival from "eds and meds", it has been the steel buckle on what became known as the Rust Belt. Nowadays, however, it is probably best known as home to some of the best computer security researchers in the world. As the economy of the United States, and most of the developed world, grows more heavily reliant on cryptocur-rency, Pittsburgh has become the epicenter of a worldwide boom.

Real estate prices in ritzy districts such as Squirrel Hill and Shadyside now rival those in San Francisco or London. Your cor-respondent was unable to find any houses in either of these neigh-borhoods for sale on Ethbroker for under 1.02 bitcoin (8.83 litecoin / 1,934,000 Federal Reserve Tokens). The unemployment rate is one of the lowest in the nation. Construction of new office space is an omnipresent sight (much to the chagrin of commuters, who must navigate the narrow roads of the city choked with scaffolding and cranes).

Peter Czakowski, mayor of the city, credits a focus on the var-ious universities in the city, especially Carnegie Mellon University and the University of Pittsburgh. Additionally, the City Council has provided numerous tax breaks to tech companies to be started or relocate here. A massive network of bike lanes championed by the mayor's predecessor has had the city called "the Amsterdam of

Appalachia." This has encouraged migration of creative types, especially as individual car ownership in the United States continues to decline to rates not seen since the Great Depression.

There are those who hold that this economic growth is leaving many behind, however. While the city was long-known for affordable homes, even during the turn-of-the-century housing boom, now there are few apartments available to rent at a price affordable to someone making minimum wage. Smaller cities and towns near Pittsburgh have seen a "brain drain" as few young people wish to stay in them when an economic powerhouse is such a short drive away.

A new group is trying to bring these issues to the attention of others. Tech Is Strangling Pittsburgh (TISP), has grown to over 50 members, according to co-founder Ezekiel Krupp. "We need a way to ensure that the economic growth seen by the top one percent is seen by all," states Mr. Krupp. "While engineers, cryptoeconomists, and tech company CEOs have been treated very well by the city, what about the other 99%?" Their founding document includes numerous measures, including a call for a 50% additional tax on all tech companies to finance public works and a "citizens' council" which would have the power to ban any tech company from the city if they encourage gentrification.

Chapter 4

Would I Were In An Alehouse

Despite her dad's warning, rush hour traffic was not that bad. The weather was nice enough that most people were cycling, a much more efficient use of the streets. The majority of cars that were on the road were self-driving, following extremely efficient traffic patterns. She was soon through the Liberty Tunnels which led to the South Hills, and driving down Route 51 towards Amsteco.

Amsteco could have once been considered a small city or large town. It was a company town, even in name, which was a shortened version of "American Steel Company." Nowadays, there were still a few stretches of strip malls and businesses, but American Steel had long ago shut down the Amsteco Mill Works, the beating heart of the town. The outskirts of Amsteco were mostly deserted, broken-down houses, or empty lots where houses had been torn down. The houses that remained occupied, mostly closer to the central business district, were generally not in great shape. Infrequently, an older person sat on a front porch, watching the light traffic. Phlox imagined them mostly as retirees, pensioners, people who were born in Amsteco and never left, and didn't want to leave now just because their children had. They would stay here until their pensions from working in the coke plant ended, or their lives did.

The Waterfront Saloon was located, at its name implied, right on the banks of the Monongahela River. Driving the point home further, it was on River Road. The back windows looked down over a bluff that led right to the brownish water. Despite the unappetizing look of the water, it was actually in much better shape than Phlox remembered from her childhood. One of the benefits of the loss of heavy industry in the Monongahela Valley was the drastic reduction in pollution going into the river. The toll it took on the people who lived along its banks, however, was striking.

River Road had always been part of the "commercial" part of town, since people weren't very interested in building houses there. Living close to the river also meant living closer to the coke plant, along with all of the rotten-egg aromas that it had produced. Not that the river didn't produce its own share of smells. At least those smells were usually organic, even if they were from fish dying from hydrogen sulfide emissions. These days, only a few shops were open on the main drag. Boarded-up storefronts outnumbered open businesses by at least a two-to-one ratio. Besides the Waterfront Saloon, Phlox saw two other bars, a laundromat, and an auto body shop, all with garish neon lights advertising their wares.

She pulled the car into the parking lot. The sign directing guests to parking was notably understated, a spray-painted piece of wood that simply said "PARK." The parking lot was technically paved, but was in such need of repair that it looked more like gravel. A few other cars were there, most at least twenty years old and all gas-burners. Her electric car had plenty of charge, but she wondered where she would charge up if she had to. The on-board electronics would, of course, warn her if she was getting anywhere close to not being able to bring the car back to the city. The smart contract she had signed when she rented the car would automatically see to that.

Parking the car, and being sure to engage the security system to maximum, she walked over to the entrance. It was quiet here, unlike the city. No cars were heading down River Road, nobody was yelling out of windows, there weren't even any people walking down the street. In the distance, she could see a couple holding hands and sitting on the stoop of a closed restaurant. Other than that, she seemed to be all alone in Amsteco. Her feet crunching on the rocks of the parking lot, along with the occasional newly-fallen leaf, sounded loud in her ears.

Opening the door to the Waterfront, she was struck by the sudden noise. It must have been well-insulated to keep in the old country music that was blasting from a stereo system. She didn't know the song, but knew it was the kind of country her dad called "outlaw country" — songs about running from the law, spending nights in prison, a sheriff gloating over a man's upcoming hanging. It had always seemed depressing to her. She didn't know why her dad listened to it. He didn't understand why she liked depressing books, though, and she wasn't sure she could explain it to him.

She saw him sitting at one of the large wooden booths along the back of the bar, absentmindedly fiddling with his watch. Not using it, or even wearing it, just spinning it around in his hands. A brown bottle of cheap beer was in front of him, although it looked barely touched, and an old science fiction paperback was resting on the table, a napkin acting as a bookmark. It was rare to see her dad without a book. She was always sad that he hadn't had a chance to go to college. He would have been an excellent student.

None of the other booths were occupied. In the other corner, a few older men, men who looked like they had tough lives, were playing darts. At the bar itself, the middle-aged blonde bartender was pouring pale yellow beer into a stein from one of two taps. Besides Phlox, she was the youngest one here. The mixed crowd of men and women sitting on stools around the bar mostly stared sullenly down at their glasses, listening to the music.

Her dad was dressed in what she thought of as "Dad Standard Uniform", jeans and a black t-shirt, with his red flannel crumpled on the seat next to him. With the flannel off, she could see his full sleeves of tattoos. She had joked with him about them when she was younger, as they consisted mostly of flames, snakes, dice, and more of what she called "stuff that teenage boys think is cool." When she turned sixteen, though, he had transformed the handle of a knife and most of a skeleton into a beautiful set of pale blue phlox flowers, as pale blue as her eyes. She had never joked with him about the tattoos again.

"Hey dad," she said, giving him a magnificent hug. It was nice to embrace him, reminding her of dark nights watching storms together on their back porch. He had put on a little weight since then, but he was still svelte compared to the other people in the bar. Something about Amsteco seemed to just infuse people with weight. At five feet two inches, and weighing barely over 100 pounds, Phlox felt almost obnoxiously tiny.

"Buttercup!" he yelled over the music. It was an old joke, calling her by the name of different flowers, but she didn't mind. "Want a beer?"

She looked up at the cardboard sign above the bar. Written on it with a marker was once written "Monero or Cash ONLY" but somebody had come along and struck a line through the last two words. Now it read "Monero or GTFO."

"What's that?"

"Monero?" her dad answered. "It's an anonymous currency, doesn't let the whole world know that you've gotten some money. Especially Uncle Sam. You're not going to find many places down here that want people to know how much money they have."

"No, no," answered Phlox. "I know what Monero is. What's git-fo?"

Her dad laughed. "It's old slang for 'get the fuck out.' I don't know, there was a whole craze for abbreviations like that when I was younger. We didn't have the time to type back then, I guess."

"Ohhhh..." said Phlox. "Let me get it, Dad. I don't think I've ever actually bought you a beer."

"That is very nice of you," said her dad, not even making a hint of protest. He chugged down the beer that was in front of him, surprisingly fast considering that it had been full. He smiled, obviously proud of himself.

"I know you hate the city, but you'd fit right in with the frats at Pitt." Phlox smiled.

Phlox and her dad talked for a while about what had been happening in Amsteco the last few years. Most of the big stories were people's children leaving. Occasionally, though, some current event reminded her dad of a story of Phlox's mother. She had died from a car crash when Phlox was six, only a year after she had married Phlox's dad. The driver was drunk, and blood tests showed a variety of synthetic drugs in his bloodstream. Her biological father had died of a heroin overdose only a few weeks after Phlox's mom found out that she was pregnant. According to the stories her dad had told Phlox, her mom had never even known he was using until she came home one day to find him cold in the bathroom, a needle sticking out of his arm.

John Tseretelli, the man sitting across from her, was the only father Phlox had ever known. She knew that he hadn't come into Mom's life until she was three or four, but she couldn't remember a time when he was not around. Mom had met him at the diner where she worked, or so Phlox remembered being told. He was visiting from Indiana, but fell in love with her mom and ended up staying in Amsteco.

John had had trouble holding down a job, but not due to any maliciousness. He just couldn't focus. He'd be hired to stock shelves, and the manager would find him trying to fix a broken-down toilet in the break room. He'd mow a lawn and go right through a hedge, telling the owner that he was thinking about something else. Mom never minded. His heart was in the right place, and he doted on both his wife and Phlox. And Mom had had a steady job working for the diner, and made good money in tips, more than enough to get by.

Life got a little bit harder after Mom died. Despite feelers from a few single Amsteco women, he never re-married, or even really dated anybody else. They never went hungry, and Phlox always had enough clothes, but nobody would have mistaken their family for well-off.

Phlox went up to the bar. The bartender looked at her, almost like a challenge. Her hooded eyes had crow's feet, the crow's feet themselves having crow's feet. She could see the dark roots showing under the bright blonde dye job. "What'll it be, sweetie?" she said, although the "sweetie" seemed more condescending than endearing.

"Umm..." started Phlox. "Two beers, please. Whatever's on tap."

"You got it," said the bartender. "You dahn here from the city? Sahnds like it."

Her accent — classic Western Pennsylvania "yinzer" — contrasted strikingly with the seemingly accentless English her father spoke. He was from the Midwest, and spoke like it. The Midwest was pretty close to a "standard American accent," and despite their very different lives, her dad sounded more like one of her professors than any of the people here in the bar.

Phlox had heard somewhere that a Pittsburgh-area accent was one of the worst to have in academia. It sounded uneducated, with its "ow" sounds flattened to "ah", and constant dropping of "to be", as in "the car needs washed." However, it wasn't well-known outside of the area, so hiring managers didn't realize it was just a dialect. Even though Pittsburgh was becoming one of the top tech centers in the world, its local accent was still not recognized. Professionals and academics tended to have any localized speech ground down, leading to a near-universal "professional" accent. Phlox herself had worked to eliminate any vestiges of her own accent, even though she had a head start growing up with John.

"Yeah, just visiting my dad," replied Phlox.

"You're John's kid!" exclaimed the bartender, finishing the pour. "I've heard so much abaht you. Studyin' up there in Pittsburgh!"

"Yeah..." Phlox wasn't sure what to say.

"That'll be eighty-six micromons, hon. Monero only." She tapped the sign above her head, then brought out a tablet with a QR code.

"One second," said Phlox, as she fiddled with her watch's wallet. Did it even have Monero integration? When she lived down here, of course she had a Monero wallet. You couldn't buy a stick of gum here without one. But the stores in Pittsburgh kept all of their transactions aboveboard, almost always using Litecoin, or occasionally Bitcoin if you were buying some expensive jewelry or something.

Finally. Her wallet did have a setting for Monero, although she had to pay some extra fees to shift her litecoin over. It was just a few nanolites, but still, she was a student. Every bit of money lost meant that much less ramen, rice and beans for the month. She paid the bartender, rounding up to 100 micromons to include a tip.

She brought over the two steins of beer to the table and gently set them down. How do those barmaids in the pictures and movies carry a half a dozen at a time? Maybe she should amend her exercise regimen to more than "walking and occasionally carrying a particularly thick book."

"Are you thinking of changing majors?" asked her dad. "You seemed a little... I don't know.. pensive when you called."

"No, not really." said Phlox, decisively.

"Shakespeare's got that much of a hold on you, huh?"

"Well, my focus is on modernist literature, not so much the Elizabethan era..."

"Sooo..." interrupted her dad. "Late Shakespeare?"

"Ha. Ha. Ha." said Phlox sarcastically, emphasizing each individual "ha" to let her dad know how bad his dad joke was. She knew he couldn't really help himself. "I do love Shakespeare. But I wanted to come to ask your advice. Like, life advice."

"I don't know if you want to hear any life advice from me, petunia." Her dad looked more than a little pensive himself. "About the only things I've done right in my life were marry your mother and raise you."

"That's more than enough, dad. You were always a great father." Out of touch with the singer on the stereo singing about raisin' Hell and raisin' Cain, Phlox felt a heavy weight in her heart as she realized how much she meant it. It couldn't have been easy raising her by himself. Her mom's sisters had helped out occasionally, but they had their own lives. He had sacrificed so much for her.

"Thanks, lilac." He took a sip of beer and composed himself. "So what's the situation?"

Phlox filled him in on everything that she and Chris had discussed that morning. Was it only this morning? It seemed so long ago.

"I don't know." her dad said. "I wouldn't want to get involved. Nobody just loses ten bitcoin. And don't you think the government's going to have something to say if a college student starts walking around with an account full of bitcoin?"

"Chris says it's legal," replied Phlox. "As long as we didn't do anything illegal to get the private key. And looking around in my own apartment doesn't really seem illegal."

"Legal, schmegal," said her dad. "It's going to raise a lot of questions. It's going to bring a lot of attention down on you, if anybody's watching the blockchain. Which they probably are."

It was easy to forget that all transactions on the Bitcoin blockchain were publicly visible. Addresses were pseudonymous, identified only by a string of characters representing an extremely large number. In the city, this wasn't a big deal. People just didn't care if somebody spent vast resources to determine that a particular person bought a coffee at a particular time. Of course, it came up from time to time, in police dramas and the like, where somebody was able to prove at the last minute that the defendant *could not* have been the murderer since the blockchain showed that she was buying toys for orphans at the time. But here in the small towns of

Western Pennsylvania, only a few miles from the first shots of the Whiskey Rebellion, tax avoidance had become an art form.

"From an account of a man who's been dead for almost two decades?" Phlox asked.

"What if whoever killed this Dr. Chambers has a smart contract that will notify them as soon as anybody moves the bitcoin?" her dad replied.

"He wasn't killed. He died in a boating accident. And if anybody did kill him, why would they keep watching his accounts for twenty years?"

"I don't know. You hear of stranger things happening."

"It just doesn't seem likely. Ten bitcoin just wasn't that much money back in those days. If anybody was so interested in it, they probably would have just set up their own mining operation then. Or just bought bitcoin back when it took ten thousand to buy a pizza."

"Well, okay, let's think about this ethically, then. Aren't you taking somebody else's property?"

"The way I see it, it's like finding out that somebody left some gold coins in your house. I'm pretty sure that after such a long time, morally, it's covered under the legal precedent of *Finders v. Keepers.*"

"You're stealing from everyone else who holds bitcoin, though," replied her dad. "You're adding some bitcoin into circulation. Isn't that reducing everybody's else holdings by a tiny amount?"

"Hmm..." said Phlox. This was an ethical dilemma, but she loved this game, and she knew her dad did, as well. "Does that mean that gold miners are unethical for reducing the cost of gold held by others? Besides, right now that bitcoin is doing nobody any good. When Chris and I have it, we'll spend it. Grow the economy. Honestly, I thought you'd be all for this."

"I have all I need," said her dad. "And I thought you did, too. But if you and Chris need this for something... wait, is Chris your beau? Is it for a wedding or something?"

"We're not anything, and there are no wedding bells on the horizon for me." Phlox said, and meant it.

"Hey!" said her dad. "No need to get upset. You just never talk with me about boys, that's all."

"I love you, Dad. I'll tell you if I get a boyfriend. Chris and I are... well, I'd say *just friends*, but not even that. Long-term acquaintances, maybe."

"You trust him, though?"

Phlox thought it over. "Yes. I do."

"I never could stop you from doing something you really wanted to do, hyacinth. But I really think you shouldn't go looking for it. It just seems like you're asking for trouble. You've got it made! You're going to have a college degree soon! You know what I would have given to have the chance to go to college?"

"It's a degree in English lit, Dad!" Phlox exclaimed, suddenly emotional again. "I'll work like a dog for another ten years, getting paid less than minimum wage, just to get a chance to apply for jobs in my field. Then the chances of me actually getting a job are about the same as getting hit by lightning. And what am I going to do with that if I can't get a job in academia?"

Her dad's eyes were a little wet. She knew that he couldn't stand thinking of her as anything but the smartest girl in Amsteco, one who was destined to go on and do great things. He also knew, deep in his bones, what it was like to not be able to get or keep a job.

"You do what you need to do," her dad said. "I'll support you no matter what. But don't get your hopes up on this. Even if it isn't a bad thing to look for this old wallet, who knows if it's still there? Or that you'll be able to find it?"

"I know, Dad. Thanks for talking." Phlox got up, leaned over, and hugged her dad. "I'll be careful, and I won't get my hopes up. I need some adventure in my life, though, I think. Too much reading and not enough doing."

John smiled. "Suppose I can't argue with that. Thanks for the beer. You okay to drive?"

Phlox looked down at her stein of beer, which was well over three-quarters full. "Yeah, pretty sure that I can handle a few teaspoons of beer."

Outside the window, storm clouds were covering the moon. There was an ineffable sense that it was going to rain even without any visible clues. The air felt different, heavier, more still.

"I've got to hurry and return the car," Phlox said, looking at her watch. "Contract says I've only got an hour to go. Should be good, but never know if there's traffic."

"Come down again, soon, lily," said her dad. "It's always nice to see you in person."

As she headed back to her car, a few raindrops started to fall. Yet she walked only slowly back to the EthShare car. Into each life, some rain must fall, and trying to rush through often only made it worse.

"Would I were in an alehouse in London! I would give all my fame for a pot of ale, and safety."
-William Shakespeare, *Henry V*

The Law in Black and White, Or 1's and 0's?

An excerpt from an article in The Econometrician, *Volume II, Issue 11*

With the massive growth in so-called "smart contracts", or contracts written in code which enforce themselves without an outside arbiter, work for lawyers has been decreasing. A case to be tried before the United States Supreme Court this session, *Connecticut v. EthShare*, may signal a turnaround in the employment opportunities of that noble profession.

A smart contract is a bit of self-executing computer code, running on a trusted network such as Ethereum. For example, if you purchased an automobile with credit recently, the dealership most likely had you cryptographically sign a document in which you agreed to pay so much money per month until the loan was paid off. Until a few years ago, a variety of computer systems, paperwork, and, yes, lawyers were necessary to assure the smooth functioning of this system. If you reneged on the contract, by not paying the lender, for example, it was a complicated and drawn-out process to resolve what should happen based on the contract. This process consisted of using the courts to determine that the contract had been violated, and if the violator of the contract was not cooperative, finding the violator and the car. There is even a now-dwindling occupation of "repo man" who "re-possess" vehicles of those who violated their contracts. This often involves such cloak-and-dagger schemes as tracking down the vehicle's location via surveillance and breaking into it in the dead of night to recover it for the lender.

With a smart contract, such situations are a thing of the past. The smart contract can simply be set to automatically deduct a certain amount of money from an account on an ongoing basis, and warn the user if there is not enough money in the account to cover the payment. It may even specify that a certain amount of money must always remain in the account. If the lendee tries to abscond with the vehicle, or stops making payments, a simple device connected to the car can disable the car as well as broadcast its location. This device is removed once the payments have completed; if a malicious user tries to remove it early, without the cryptographic signature of the company, the car simply fails to start.

Economists estimate that the cost of contract compliance could be reduced by 61% to 83% by moving to smart contracts, depending on the industry and, as always, the economist. All mainstream economists agree that, from an efficiency perspective, economic output for countries which implement smart contracts would measurably rise

What happens when something goes wrong with a smart contract? There are ways for traditional contracts to be nullified, modified, or arbitrated through the court system. They can also protect people from "unconscionable" contracts, such as charging usurious interest rates. Many of these protections are unavailable with a smart contract, or at least may happen too late to offer any real protection to the signer of the contract. Leaving the human out of the loop in understanding how a contract is executed may lead to situations which have clearly been considered unlawful in the past, with no recourse to the signers of said contract.

The code for a contract may also be faulty. If the smart contract software contains a defect that allows a user to not pay the lender for the car, and the lendee takes advantage of that defect, should the lender have a legal remedy? After all, smart contract code is publicly available to be viewed, and both sides agreed to follow the results of the code. Is the code law, even if it leads to manifestly ludicrous situations such as obtaining a car for free?

The case before the Supreme Court touches upon this directly. The State of Connecticut had set up a fund for state employees to use EthShare self-driving cars in Hartford. According to the state Attorney-General, negotiations between EthShare and the state included a provision to cap the amount that could be spent in a single month by employees. Neither side disputes that these conversations took place. However, the code for the shared smart contract, while having a function which checked to see if the cap had been exceeded, did not actually stop state employees from using the system even if it had been. It simply sent an email to a government employee, at an email address which was specified in the smart contract. When that employee left the service of the government, nobody read these emails recording these cost overruns.

This soon led to exorbitant costs — well over ten times the amount of the cap for months on end — as employees took advantage of the new EthShare cars. The cash-strapped state government insists that all money above the cap should be returned. Attorneys for the state have already lost both their initial case and their appeal. Analysts were pleasantly surprised when the Supreme Court then granted a writ of certiorari to hear the case.

The current tack is to argue that smart contracts should not, and cannot, be the source of the law itself. That is, computer code cannot be legally binding, and that a plain reading of the contract would give a very different result than what actually occurred. This is a question that has been haunting the world of smart contracts in general, and Ethereum specifically, since its inception.

Chapter 5

The Ruler of Forms

The next morning, Phlox woke up feeling more refreshed than she usually did. She knew that she would be working at the diner this morning, but even that didn't dull her spirits. Somehow, having to clean up dishes and be sickeningly sweet to customers for a few millilites doesn't weigh on you quite as much when you imagined yourself not needing to do so in the near future. Phlox had never been the type to play the lottery, or even understand the people who did. She felt like she could understand them now.

She put on her Priscilla's polo shirt and slacks, the most dressed up she had been since the last time she had gone into work. The entire time she was getting ready, her mind wasn't on brushing teeth, or putting on deodorant, or finding her shoes. She imagined the moment that she saw that she had over five bitcoin in her account. It was probably ten times as much as her dad had seen, altogether, in his life. He was against her looking for it now, but he'd change his tune when she could buy him a new car to replace his old clunker.

A glance at the clock showed that she was running late, not that this was anything out of the ordinary for her. Holly wasn't up yet, or at least Phlox hadn't heard her screaming with excitement over the fact that a bird landed on her windowsill, so she assumed she was still asleep. Phlox quickly threw on her James Joyce hoodie and ran down the squeaky stairs as unsqueakily as she could.

As she opened the door, she noticed an older woman across the dirty street, leaning against the front railing on a porch. About 35,

Phlox guessed, and well-dressed. The woman would have stuck out in South Oakland even with just those two characteristics, but even more strangely, she was reading a newspaper. Phlox didn't even know where she would have bought a newspaper. Phlox loved to read physical books, and found reading a screen for too long to be slightly nauseating. Still, though. The whole concept of printing out yesterday's news, delivering it to various places, and then people buying it for a non-trivial amount of money, only to throw it away or put it at the bottom of their birdcage by the next morning... it seemed like such a wasteful and ridiculous thing to do. Some people still did it, though, at least enough to keep the industry going. People were weird.

Moving a bit more quickly than could be called "walking", Phlox headed to Priscilla's Diner, a popular spot on campus, famous for their waffles. It wasn't unusual to see a group of students recovering from an all-night study session with some giant waffles smothered in maple syrup. Phlox studiously avoided the earliest shift, from 4:00 AM to 8:00 AM. She had never woken up before 4:00 AM and as far as she was concerned, would like to keep it that way for the rest of her life.

The walls of Priscilla's were covered in artwork, from Studio Arts students of years gone by, from kids with crayons, from estate sales of old South Oakland residents. It was a cacophony of styles, frames, and levels of quality, but for all of that, it had a homey feel to it. It wasn't an antiseptic restaurant chain's idea of inoffensive art, but a hodgepodge continually fed by the community.

Thanks to Phlox's quick gait, she had arrived a few minutes before her starting time. The diner was only a quarter full, and not yet loud. Any students who had pulled all-nighters were gone by now, and any other students who would be coming in wouldn't be here for another few hours. Right now, the place was dominated by people getting off their shifts at the hospital. Priscilla's had an ebb and flow all its own, as regular as the tides. Phlox had worked there for two years and felt that she could tell the time within twenty minutes just by looking at which customers were there.

Gloria came out from the back. Gloria liked to joke that she was Phlox's exact opposite — outgoing, blonde, tall, heavy-set. Also, although she would never note this fact, pushing sixty and in total denial of it. Balancing a tray of waffles, bananas, and coffee, she caught Phlox's eye.

"Hey hon," said Gloria. "Do you think you can get table six for me? I know it's my section but Henry never showed up this morning so I'm a bit overloaded."

"Sure," replied Phlox. Henry was a great worker... when he showed up. The manager, Georgette, had threatened him numerous times, but somehow he always skirted the edge of being fired without actually falling into it.

Looking over at table six, she saw that it was the jogging man from yesterday. He was wearing a well-fitting suit today, and playing with his watch. Phlox swallowed down the nervousness she felt and walked over to the table.

"Hello," said Phlox, then followed up with the classic waitress line that supposedly brought in the most tips. "I'll be taking care of you today."

"Hello, Phlox." said the man. Butterflies in her stomach, which had been sleeping while she played the role of waitress, repeating lines she had used thousands of times before, suddenly and angrily awakened. How did he know her name? Then she remembered the plastic name tag on her chest, pinned securely onto the polo shirt.

"Can I get you something to drink, or are you ready to order?"

"I'll have a coffee, and..." the man scanned the menu. He wasn't a regular. The menu was only a single page, and probably the most-memorized text in South Oakland. He sounded out slowly, "... the Waffle Heap Extraordinaire."

"You got it," Phlox said, smiling widely, playing the role of the waitress. "I'll be right back with your coffee."

As she went to put the order back in, she felt eyes on her back. Against her better judgment, she turned around, thinking it would put her mind to rest. Maybe someone was just checking her out. Sure, checking out her boyish frame in oh-so-sexy slacks and an ill-fitting polo shirt. When you picture a *femme fatale*, you definitely think of them wearing an ill-fitting polo shirt.

The jogging man was looking down at his watch, but there was somebody looking at her. Somebody new sitting at table eight, her section, in front of the windows. It was the newspaper-reading woman that was across from her house earlier this morning. She was still reading the newspaper, although she had set it down in front of her on the table. Bad idea, thought Phlox. We try to keep the tables clean, but that newspaper's going to be glued down by maple syrup in five minutes.

Phlox entered the order for coffee and the Waffle Heap Extraordinaire (three waffles: one strawberry, one blueberry, and one apricot, all covered in whipped cream), then came out to talk with the woman. Now that Phlox had a chance to see her up-close, she realized that the woman was wearing a full business suit. Her dark hair showed the occasional gray root, but it didn't make her look old, just a bit distinguished. She had on thick glasses, but they accentuated her almond-shaped eyes. She wore just enough makeup to be noticeable, along with delicate jewelry that was noticeable without being dazzling. She looked like somebody who had some bitcoin and used it to make sure that she looked "professionally elegant."

"Hello," she said briskly, before Phlox had a chance to do her waitress spiel. "I'll have a glass of orange juice and a short stack of pancakes."

"You know, if you've never been here, we're famous for our waffles..." On her first day, Phlox had been instructed to always try to get the customers to order waffles. Higher margins.

"No, thank you," said the woman. "Just the pancakes. And orange juice."

The woman looked back down at her paper. The conversation was clearly over and Phlox had been dismissed.

More customers soon came in, and Phlox was too busy taking orders and delivering food to think much about the man and the woman. But every time she noticed them, those butterflies in her stomach came bursting out of their chrysalises. They didn't do anything that aroused suspicion, and both left good tips — 60 microlites each. Exactly.

The rest of the morning was a blur of caffeinated beverages, and various combinations of batter, fruit and syrup. Waitressing was a good job if you were trying to distract yourself from anxiety. There was always something to do and it always should have been done five minutes ago. Phlox didn't even notice that her shift was ending until Gloria pointed up to the clock. Gloria would be here for a while longer, as she was always taking over people's shifts.

Phlox headed back towards her apartment on Atwood Street, carrying one of the major perks of her job — free waffles. The sun was high in the sky, and a group of pigeons were cooing merrily, excitedly pecking at the remains of some student's pizza on the sidewalk. Her Greek Philosophy class was meeting in half an hour, but she was going to skip. There was no way that she was going to be able to pay attention, and besides, she had forgotten to do the reading on Pythagoras.

Heading up the stairs to her apartment, she heard the now-unmistakable sound of the Wu sisters talking, perhaps yelling. There really wasn't that much difference in volume between the two. As she rounded the corner at the top, she saw that Violet was wearing a bright red shirt with a picture of Che Guevara on it. She was using her hands an awful lot to try to explain something to Holly.

"Hey Phlox!" said Holly, seemingly anxious to get out of this conversation. "Violet's a communist now."

"I thought you said you didn't really follow politics?" asked Phlox.

"There was a meeting last night!" explained Violet. "I never realized how little class consciousness we have here in the States! By the end of the night, I understood that a proletarian revolution is not only just, but inevitable."

"They certainly were persuasive," said Phlox.

"I know! I've been *trying* to get Holly to see past the errors of her petty bourgeois ways, but she doesn't want to listen to me. Have you ever read the Communist Manifesto?"

"Uhh, no, but it's on my to-read list." Actually, Phlox had read it, way back in high school, but she really did not want to discuss politics right now.

"You really should! I think I have a copy in my backpack..." Violet eagerly reached deep into her backpack and began shuffling around papers. Holly seemed relieved that her evangelism had a new target and was enjoying the peace.

"No, that's okay, I think I have a copy somewhere."

"Well," Violet continued, zipping up her backpack, "if you ever change your mind, I've got a copy right here! Or maybe at home. Somewhere! Oh, I've got to go. There's a rally tonight I want to prepare for!"

After Violet left, Holly let out a sigh and gave a knowing look at Phlox.. "Freshmen, eh?"

"Yeah... I guess I can't judge too much, though. You remember what I was like as a freshman."

"Didn't you just wear black all the time? It's not like you were calling for a dictatorship of the proletariat."

"Maybe wearing black was my way of expressing nihilism, the purest of all political philosophies."

"Ha!" Holly laughed, half seriously and half sarcastically.

"I have a question for you," said Phlox, changing the subject. "But it might take a while for you to answer. Do you have some time?"

"Sure! I don't have class until this evening. And it's just Postwar American History. Never got that gen ed out of the way..."

"Do you know how you were saying that cryptocurrency is all math? Could you explain it to me? Just at a high level. Like, is each bitcoin a certain number or something?"

"Whoa, no, no, no!" exclaimed Holly. "You're thinking about it all wrong. Let me think back to my Intro to Number Theory days. I learned some good analogies there." Holly closed her eyes for a few moments, then opened up a notebook to an empty page.

"First off, let's pretend that the bitcoin already exists. We'll talk about where it comes from later. So... imagine a giant room full of safety deposit boxes. It's not really infinite *per se*, but so large that it may as well be for our purposes. You can always get a new box with a new address and key."

"Okay, I'm with you so far. So each box is like my wallet?"

"Your wallet is just a collection of keys to some number of boxes. That's how you can have a checking and savings account, for instance. But all you have are keys to the boxes. The actual boxes are all on the network itself."

Phlox nodded. So far, so understandable.

"As long as someone knows the address of your box, they can send you bitcoin, or litecoin, or whatever. It's like our mailbox downstairs. There's a one-way hole at the top of the box; people can put mail in, but nobody can get it out unless they have the key. Same idea — people can slide bitcoin in if they know the address, but to get it out and put it someone else's box, they need the key. That's why it's called a 'private key.' "

"Ahh, so the key is just like a secret password?"

"Kind of," said Holly. "There's actually a mathematical relationship between the address and the private key. Do you know about one-way functions?"

"I know about one-way streets..."

"It's actually a similar idea!" said Holly, as if she had never heard the phrase before. It was easy to see why she was a good teaching assistant. "Here, take this. You need to do some math by hand. No calculators. Don't worry, it's easy." She handed Phlox the notebook and a pencil.

"Good," said Phlox. "I haven't even had a math class in the last two years."

"Okay," said Holly. "What's 3.6 cubed?"

"That's easy. Three point six times three point six times three point six." She wrote down the numbers, and scribbled for about a minute. "Forty six point six five six."

"Okay," said Holly, with a bit of an evil grin. "Now what's the cube root of 74.088?"

Phlox stood dumbfounded for a few moments. She wasn't even sure how to start this one. Finally, she thought, 74 is a little less than twice 46. Maybe one and a half times 46. So maybe 1.5 * 3.6? She did the multiplication on paper — 5.4. Let's see, 5.4 * 5.4 * 5.4, that's 157.464. Way too high. Maybe it was just a little bit more than 3.6, then... 3.8 * 3.8 * 3.8 is, hmm, 54.872. Well, now she knew it was some number greater than 3.8 but less than 5.4. Maybe 4.5?

"Time's up!" said Holly. "But I wasn't really expecting you to finish. The answer is 4.2. The idea is that the two operations are mirror images of each other, but going in one direction — cubing — is much easier than the other — getting the cube root."

"I get that, but what does it have to do with the boxes?"

"Imagine each address is the cubed number. The private key to access it is the cube root. Now, the difficulty differential is way, way, way higher than just cubing versus cube root. It's one of those things where going one way is so much more difficult than the other direction that you could have all of the computers in the world working on it until the sun burns out, and you still wouldn't be able to calculate it. But as long as you know the secret key, it's trivial."

"But what's *inside* the boxes? Certain numbers?"

"Nothing, really," Holly said. "The boxes are imaginary, and so are the units. And actually, the data isn't stored on the blockchain as boxes, but we can talk about that in a minute. But we can just say that a box has 100 units of... something. It's up to a human to look at it and give it meaning, like 'I will give you a potato if you put 1 microbit into this box'. The numbers themselves only mean something because so many humans *agree* that they have meaning."

"Sure," Phlox said. "It's just like my GPA. If I get an A in all my classes this semester, then my GPA goes up. But it's not like there are actual items going into my GPA to make it go up. It's just a... representation number, I guess you could say. And the only people that care about it are grad schools. If I am going to watch a movie, they don't care about my GPA, because it's just some value that's useful in certain circumstances."

"Exactly! But to get back to the original question — you have the idea that two numbers are important — the address and your private key? And that you can always put money into somebody's box if you know the address, but you need the private key to move money away from it?"

"Yes." Phlox said. It was relatively simple; she just had never looked into it deeply before.

"The blockchain contains a list of all transactions ever made on the network. So it can calculate that Joe gave you 7 millibits last year, and Jack gave you 2 millibits yesterday, and you gave John 4 millibits this morning, thus giving you access to 7 + 2 - 4 millibits, or, umm, 5 millibits. The boxes are a way of thinking about it, but the network just contains a list of which addresses have sent what amount of bitcoin or litecoin to other ones."

"So it's kind of like when I'm checking out of my shift at Priscilla's, and I can see that the customers gave me, say 50 millilites altogether, and I gave back 10 millilites in change. Then the diner itself ends up with 40 millilites."

"Exactly!" Holly said again. It was probably a habit that she had picked up when teaching to encourage students working on a difficult problem. "Imagine that writ large. Every transaction ever made on bitcoin, from when Satoshi Nakomoto first put Bitcoin online until now, is out there on the network. That's the blockchain."

"Well, why can't I just go in and change the blockchain to say that someone gave me a hundred bitcoin?"

"Two reasons. First, nobody else on the network will accept your transaction without knowing the private key of the account it came from. And second, there are only certain transactions that can create bitcoin. I guess we should talk about where bitcoin comes from. Miners are constantly working to package up valid — and only valid, they check — transactions into blocks, which get added to the blockchain. Whichever miner does this first also gets to create a certain amount of the currency as a reward. They also get any transaction fees from transactions on that block, which incentivizes them to validate as many valid transactions as possible."

"So that's what miners are doing! I just kind of assumed they were just magically making money."

"Nope. Without miners, the network would have just a teeny-tiny fraction of the amount of security we have now. They are the ones who are doing the work of ensuring that everybody else follows the rules."

"So what's to stop the miners from cheating and give themselves more?"

"Cryptocurrency is decentralized. They could stop playing by the rules, but nobody else would recognize their blocks as valid. They'd end up living in some alternate universe of cryptocurrency. Lots of time and energy would be spent, which would have to be paid for, but they'd be doing useless calculations. Nobody else would recognize their blocks as valid and they'd just waste money."

"Oh, neat. Everyone's incentivized to play by the rules, because if you don't, people can just ignore you. And you're stuck wasting electricity to just figure out cube roots or whatever."

"Right. If you don't follow the rules, nobody trusts your transactions. And it's super-easy to check that somebody's following the rules. Theoretically, the same computing resources that the miners use to secure the network could also be used to try to break it. One of the genius things that Satoshi Nakomoto did when designing the system was to make sure that for any given amount of computing power, you would make more money mining than trying to cheat it."

Phlox rubbed her temples, and brushed her back behind her ears. "Thanks, Holly. That was interesting. But I don't think that my brain can take any more right now. Just to make sure I understand — as long as I know the address and the private key, I can access the money in that account?"

"Yeah, that's all your wallet is doing for you. You could write down the numbers on paper, though, or even memorize them if you had a good memory. You'd then be able to access it whenever you wanted."

"Thanks, Holly," Phlox said. "I appreciate it."

"No problem!" said Holly. "It's good to know about this stuff. Our country does run on the almighty coin. Oh God, I don't sound like Violet, do I?"

Phlox laughed. "Don't worry, I'll let you know if you do. Just don't start an uprising against the bourgeoisie while I'm trying to sleep."

A buzz filled the air, and Holly glanced at her watch. "Oh shoot," she said, uncharacteristically quietly. "My mom's calling. I should take this."

"Yeah, no problem," said Phlox, and headed to her room. She half-heartedly picked up some books that were on the floor, and made her bed. Or at least, put the sheets and blankets mostly on top of the bed. That should count as "making it." It was just going to get messed up again when she went to sleep that night. Good enough. She still had a few hours before Chris came over to start looking for the paper wallet. She grabbed the copy of *The Death of Ivan Ilyich* off the bookshelf — that she had just put up! cleaning is so inefficient! — and started to read.

"Number is the ruler of forms and ideas, and is the cause of gods and daemons."
-Iamblichus (quoting Pythagoras), *Life of Pythagoras*

A Clique of Cryptocurrency Carnegies?

An excerpt from an article in The Econometrician, *Volume V, Issue 16*

Andrew Carnegie was not known to be a kind-hearted business-man. In fact, the history of the American steel industry — and related industries — of the late 19th and early 20th centuries is chock-a-block with tales of his running roughshod over competitors. This was how he became one of the richest men in the world at the time. However, upon retirement, Mr. Carnegie donated the major-ity of his fortune to a variety of programs to elevate humanity, such as the Carnegie Endowment for International Peace, four museums, and over 3,000 Carnegie libraries.

History repeats itself. The first generation of the "crypto-wealthy" are starting to retire, many of them rich beyond the wildest dreams of their often-nerdy youth. Many of these young people even matric-ulated at a school founded and funded by Mr. Carnegie, Carnegie Mellon University. As befits their background, however, these "Bit-coin barons" are donating to very different projects than the titans of the Industrial Age.

Liu "Louie" Han, who set up one of the first large-scale mining operations, has recently pledged over 90% of his fortune to longevity research. Bjorn Hammarskjold, whose company has marketed several solutions to make blockchains resistant to quantum computing, has created the Hammarskjold Foundation which focuses on a single issue in theoretical computer science, the "P versus NP Problem." Sam Audley was an early adopter of Bitcoin who stored approximately 1,000 bitcoin on his hard drive, then promptly forgot about them. Discovering them later in life, he was instantly one of the wealthiest people in his city. Mr. Audley immediately put 999 of them into a trust to develop "the most perfect programming language as can be imagined."

Most striking, perhaps, has been the massive investment in space exploration. Little needs to be said about the Musk Colonies on Mars, or Moonbase Prime, but at least five different asteroid mining ventures have been funded by those whose fortunes come primarily from the cryptocurrency boom. Nina Valdez has provided over seventy-five percent of the operating costs of the upcoming Stardust expedition to Proxima Centauri, our closest stellar neighbor. Much of Roger Lee's wealth has gone to his new startup which aims to provide affordable vacations to low Earth orbit.

Chapter 6

The Usual Trick

At around 5:30, Phlox put down her book, then headed to the kitchen to start looking for something to eat. The refrigerator was mostly bare, but it did have peanut butter and jelly. That could work if there were some crackers. Opening the cupboard and rifling through the packages of ramen, canned vegetables, and the occasional candy bar, she found some graham crackers. They weren't even stale. Today was a good day.

While eating her graham cracker PB & J and a banana, she absentmindedly checked her email. Nothing good. There's never any good email, she thought. It's either work for me to do, or something to delete.

A knock at the door told her Chris was here. Glancing at the corner of her watch, she saw that it was 5:58. He could wait a minute. She checked herself out in the mirror to make sure that no peanut butter, jelly, or cracker fragments had ended up on her t-shirt or jeans. She was less worried about what Chris might think than that her Virginia Woolf t-shirt might acquire an edible patina, however slight. It was difficult to find t-shirts that looked good on her and fit well. The ones that did fit, she cherished.

Any longer and Chris might start wondering if he had the right house. She went down the steps quickly but deliberately, and opened the door to the waning light and the large figure of Chris. He had definitely gained weight since they were kids, although Phlox felt like that may have been better than her situation. She sometimes felt that she had barely grown since middle school.

"Hey," Chris said to Phlox, already in the process of slipping off his battered orange backpack. When the backpack was younger, it was bright enough that it could have kept him from being shot in the woods by a deer hunter. Now it was a pale imitation of its former self, threadbare in more than a few places.

"Hey Chris," Phlox smiled, excited, giddy even, although she was doing her best to keep her emotions under control. The inner glow that she was feeling came through, though. "I just realized that it's dinner time... did you eat yet?"

"Yeah, yeah," Chris said, distracted. "I stopped at Bob's with a friend of mine from my Theory of Algorithms class. We were working all morning on a proof of..." — Phlox zoned out for a while — "...turned out that solution was not Pareto-optimal..." — Phlox smiled again, weakly, her brain miles away — "...but we could re-use a lemma that we had already proven for another problem!"

"Sounds like quite an adventure," Phlox said, "but I have to say that I am ready and raring to go find this paper wallet!"

"Let's go, then!" Chris said and waltzed through the door. Literally, he seemed to dance in. He was excited for the search, too, thought Phlox.

As they walked up the stairs to the apartment, Phlox felt slightly embarrassed by the various smudges on the walls, the paint flaking off in corners, the piles of shoes left in the foyer. Then again, she was a college student. What college student re-paints drywall? Wait, was it made of drywall? She wasn't really sure what drywall was, but she was pretty sure she'd heard her dad talk about hanging it. Well, whatever it was, she wasn't going to paint it. Or put her shoes on a shoe tree.

Phlox was still trying to remember exactly what drywall was — something to keep water off of the walls, she decided — when they reached the shared living room at the top of the stairs. "Nice place," said Chris as he looked around. Off to one side were Phlox's and Holly's bedrooms — Phlox's door open, Holly's closed. Holly's door had a collection of bright, rainbow-colored letters, arranged neatly, reading HOLLY, along with a dry-erase board below it. Phlox's was unadorned.

A relatively large and long kitchen, open to the living room, was across from their bedrooms. The appliances looked to be at least thirty or forty years old, and banged and scuffed from generations of short-term residents' daily lives. A closet and a bathroom rounded off that area of the living room, and the apartment as a whole.

"So this was Dr. Chambers' place," said Chris. "He made quite a few references to it. I think the kitchen and bathroom were both in the same places, and he used your room for a home lab and office space. His bedroom was Holly's room."

"Makes sense," said Phlox. "Her room is a bit bigger. She pays an extra few millilites a month for the privilege."

"I guess we should start in the kitchen, though, eh?" said Chris. "The note did say that the cold storage was 'above the pots.' I was thinking, though, it might not be a paper wallet. He usually referred to paper wallets as PWs, and he specifically wrote cold storage for this. It might be a hardware wallet."

"Like an old watch?"

"No, not exactly," Chris explained. "Think of it as a really specialized small computer, but all that it does is act as a wallet. Doesn't do anything else, so it has less of an attack surface than a 'full' computer. It's a secure way of handling cryptocurrency, a bit more convenient than a paper wallet, and only slightly less secure."

"Do you think it would work after all these years?"

"Possibly. Or if we could figure out the seed, we could reproduce it ourselves."

"What? How?"

"Well, remember that everything a computer does is absolutely deterministic. There's no room for chance."

"But I know that there are games you can play that have randomness. I've heard about Ethereum Roulette at the casinos. That wouldn't be very profitable for the casinos if people could figure out what the next number is. Or when my dad plays chess against the AI opponent on his watch, it doesn't always make the same move."

"Sure," said Chris. "Computers can *act* as though they're making random numbers. But in order to fake it, they need to get some outside 'seed' and run an algorithm on it to make it seem even more random."

"I don't understand. And I don't see what this has to do with restoring hardware wallets."

"Okay, let me explain the first part first. Bring up the calculator on your watch." He waited a moment while Phlox did so. But it was only a moment — calculating something on your watch was a task that she, along with virtually every member of her generation, had been doing since she was just starting to walk.

"Now," continued Chris, "a computer is really just a more complicated version of a calculator. If I ask you to give me a series of random numbers on the calculator, what would you do?"

"Close my eyes and mash the buttons a bit, I guess."

"Uh-uh, that's you — the user — making random numbers. How can you give instructions to the calculator to do it?"

Phlox shrugged.

"It's impossible," Chris continued. "You need to give it something to start with. A really simple example is a clock. Let's imagine a simple dice game on your computer, like craps. You need a random number from 1 to 6 to be the result of your die roll."

"Right. You need two of them, actually."

"Well, the concept is the same as with one, you can just repeat it if you need two. So one thing you can do is look at the seconds hand on the clock, and look at the 'tens' column of the number it is pointing to. For example, at 15 seconds, the 'tens' column is 1, at 33 seconds, it's 3, at 4 seconds, it's 0."

"Yeah, but then you can only get numbers from 0 to 5."

"Right, but you can just make an algorithm to add one to any result you get and then you have a number from 1 to 6."

"Oh, cool." It really wasn't that cool, she thought, but it was interesting.

"The number from the clock is the 'seed' for our random number generator. You can see that any result in our algorithm results from the seed. The algorithms used for actual programs are much more complex, of course, but it's the same idea. You can create an infinite amount of data, but it's all entirely determined by the seed."

"I get that, but how do we reproduce a computer like a hardware wallet just by knowing a seed?"

"The manufacturers of the hardware wallets knew that they couldn't last forever. They needed a way to reproduce the data that was on them exactly, so that if your hardware wallet broke, you could still get the private keys. You understand how those work, right?"

"Sure. The private key is a number that's related to the address, and allows you access to the money stored in that address."

Chris looked impressed. "Exactly! And a hardware wallet generates these private keys for you. But, as we already talked about, computers follow a deterministic process to calculate seemingly random numbers. Given the seed, we can follow the algorithm and re-do it exactly. Just like if I told you that the seed of our random number generator is 12, you can take the 1 from the 'tens' column, add one to it, and get the result 2. On a much bigger scale, of course."

"So you can reproduce the entire hardware wallet, as long as you know the seed? And since it will generate the same private keys, the new hardware wallet will have access to the same accounts as the original one did."

"Right! As long as you know the seed, you can calculate the private keys, just as if you had the original hardware wallet. The seed is usually twenty-four words from a particular set of words."

"Why exactly twenty-four words? Don't you need a number for the seed?"

Chris sighed, but just slightly. "You can think of a list of words as a number. For example, if I told you the words 'one two seven', you would know that I really mean the number one hundred and twenty-seven."

"Yeah, but those are just words that represent numbers. You're saying it can be other words like 'fade' or 'fatal'."

"It's just a longer list of possible" — he air quoted with his hands — "numbers than one, two, three. There's 2,048 possibilities, instead of just ten. You could think of the first word in the list as zero, the second as one, et cetera, all the way until you get to two-thousand-and-forty-seven. Just replace each one of those numbers with a word instead, since people usually find it easier to remember 'slice' rather than 1,628."

Phlox frowned. "That seems like it would be easy for someone else to just guess. Or have a computer keep guessing until it's able to construct a wallet."

Chris shook his head. "Nope. It may not seem like it, but the numbers involved are mind-boggling. There's a list of 2,048 possible words, and 24 words. The possible number of combinations is 2,048 to the 24th power. That's about the same number of atoms as exist in the visible universe. You could have all the computers in the world trying to crack a hardware wallet, and chances are the sun would die before they found it."

"Weird. Holly used the same analogy about the sun dying when she was explaining keys to me."

Chris smiled. "I guess nerds have a common fear of astronomical happenings." He was enjoying himself. He probably should have been a teaching assistant, too, but Phlox knew that he liked his internship.

He continued his lecture. "If it's a hardware wallet, we're either going to have to reproduce it or figure out the PIN for it. But let's cross that bridge when we come to it. Maybe we'll luck out and it will just be a paper wallet. Those just have the private key printed on them."

"Well, no time like the present to find out," Phlox said, getting up.

The rest of the evening was spent examining every nook and cranny in the kitchen. First they looked in the cupboard, over the sink, near the stove, anywhere that pots might have been stored by Dr. Chambers. Then they looked through places that were less likely to be used for storing pots, such as under the sink. Finally, they looked at places that they couldn't imagine could be used to store pots. Perhaps they couldn't fathom the alien mind of an adult academic, though, for whom storing pots along the floorboards might be a perfectly normal thing to do.

Around 8:30, Phlox looked over at Chris, who was looking up at the ceiling and thinking. They had already examined the ceiling closely, including taking the cover off of the light and unscrewing the light fitting.

"It's not here," he said. "I was so sure..."

"Maybe it's somewhere else in the house," Phlox said.

"Where else would you store pots, under your bed?" Chris asked. He looked deflated. His hopes were probably as high as Phlox's had been, but his life had mostly been going well. He had left Amsteco, after all, and was looking to be on a trajectory to a good career as a software developer. Phlox was more used to disappointment in her life, which gave her the strength to deal with little setbacks like this. Little setbacks like thinking you were about to get five bitcoin and then, in the next moment, having them evaporate.

"I was thinking," Phlox said. "My dad still uses lots of old slang. Isn't 'pots' what our parents called marijuana? Maybe he had a stash of it somewhere? If it was illegal back then, he probably had a good hiding spot for it, which would also be a good hiding spot for the wallet."

"Good thinking!" Chris was almost jumping for joy. Hope had returned. "Where would you hide drugs in the house? Now I regret not doing drugs when I was in high school. Hiding 'pots' from my parents might have given me good insight into this."

"I'm not sure," Phlox replied. "But let's think about it tomorrow. Holly will be home from night class soon, and I've got a paper to write up."

"Tomorrow it is, then," he said, oddly formally. "Even if we didn't find it tonight, it was a good time hanging out with you."

"You, too," said Phlox off-handedly. "Oh, tomorrow won't work. I've got an engagement." She echoed his slightly more formal tone.

Downcast, Chris replied, "Oh... with whom?"

"There's a French meet-up I go to every Thursday," said Phlox. "It's my turn to bring the crêpes."

"Oh!" Chris exclaimed, seemingly visibly relieved. "How about Friday night, then? We could have dinner at my place. Do you like Indian?"

"Sure," Phlox said. That would at least mean she wouldn't have to worry about figuring out food that day. "Sounds good. I don't mean to be rude, but I do have like eight more pages to write, so..."

"Oh yeah, yeah, see you Friday," Chris said, and quickly headed down the stairs. As he was about to open the door, he called out over his shoulder, "good luck on the paper!"

From the bottom of the stairs, Phlox heard the unmistakable sounds of the Wu sisters talking and giggling. As they arrived at the top of the stairs, Holly gave her a knowing grin, while Violet smiled to herself. Violet was now wearing ripped jeans, a too-tight tank top which was, if possible, even more ripped than her jeans. A circled 'A' for anarchy was crudely drawn with red paint across the chest.

"Heeeeey Phlox..." said Holly with a wink. "Who was that sneaking out the door with a big grin on his face?"

"Just my friend Chris," said Phlox. "Emphasis on the word 'friend.' I know what you're thinking. And that is *not* the reason he's grinning."

"Well, he's happy about something, all right," said Violet. "And I know what guys get happy about."

The sisters giggled again, but Phlox wasn't sure what to say. For some reason, she didn't want to tell them about the search for the hardware wallet. Adventures in books were always secret. And now she wasn't reading about an adventure, she was having one. It just seemed right to keep it quiet. Although maybe deep down, Phlox was worried that Holly would demand a share of the bitcoin, since it was in their apartment and she paid the rent, too.

Phlox decided the best tack was to change subjects. "Why the change in clothes, Violet?"

Holly rolled her eyes. "Violet went to some sort of communist meeting, and by the end of the evening met someone from the Kropotkin wing. I guess now she's an anarchist!"

"Anarcho-communist!" corrected Violet. "The Marxist-Leninist style of right-wing communism inevitably leads to a shallow bureaucracy tyrannizing people's souls. We believe that people can cooperate in societies without a government breathing down their neck, without the rigid planned economies of traditional Marxist dogma..."

"Save the report for your poli sci class, Violet," Holly said. "I've got a whole coffee cup full of topology homework tonight... or maybe a doughnut full!" Holly laughed a bit at her own joke, then looked around to blank faces. "Sorry! Topology joke! I swear it's hilarious if you're taking a topology class!"

Phlox and Violet looked at each other and raised their eyebrows almost in sync.

"Shut up!" said Holly. "And yes, I know you haven't actually said anything."

Phlox yawned. "Yeah, I've got a paper to write myself. Speaking of coffee cups, I'm going to lock myself in my room with a cup of coffee and won't come out until I've got another six pages on Tolstoy typed up."

"You two don't get a chance to do anything fun, huh?" said Violet. "I am not looking forward to being a senior. As for me, I've got a copy of *The Conquest of Bread* that is just itching to be read tonight!"

"We all have our ideas of fun, don't we?" asked Holly, rhetorically. It was obvious that any idea of fun that she had did not involve reading Russian political philosophy. "Have a good night!"

After Violet left, the house quieted down considerably. The only noises were the rhythmic tapping of keys from Phlox's room and the background scratching of pencil against paper in Holly's. This solemn silence was punctuated only with the occasional expletive, gasp, expression of delight, curse, roar of rage, declaration of eternal vengeance against the gods of logic, sigh, scream to the heavens, or general grumble from Holly. These didn't happen more than once every ten or fifteen seconds, though, which counted as a quiet night for Holly.

These various noises had trailed off considerably around midnight, so Phlox assumed Holly had gone to sleep. That was at least forty-five minutes ago; Phlox wasn't always so slow at writing papers, but she hadn't been able to keep her mind on her work. The threat of a poor grade kept her at it, though.

Phlox crept out of her room to the kitchen, site of so much searching that evening. She poured herself some cereal and almond milk and thought about what Violet and Holly were teasing her about. She hoped she wasn't leading Chris on. Oh no, he was going to get her dinner, wasn't he? He needed to be disabused of the notion that Friday night was going to be a date.

Well, the oldest trick in the book was to pretend to have a boyfriend, right? Boyfriend might be a bit much, but maybe someone she was dating? In a different country? No, too unbelievable. Phlox had never left the United States. At a different school? An image formed in her mind, a person that Chris could imagine her dating that was definitely not Chris. A music major. Bagpipes. You can study bagpipes at Carnegie Mellon. It was totally believable. Skin tanned brown from spending too much time outside playing bagpipes to the robins in the park. Oh Lance, how many times must I tell you to put on sunscreen? But of course he wouldn't listen. He was a rebel, which was part of the reason she found herself falling for him.

Phlox sighed and returned to reality. This was a fun adventure, but it wasn't supposed to be a romance novel.

"She had done the usual trick – been nice. She would never know him. He would never know her. Human relations were all like that..."
-Virginia Woolf, *To The Lighthouse*

Goodbye To All That Paper

An excerpt from an article in The Econometrician, *Volume I, Issue 31*

This past week, the Rothbardian Republic of Venezuela has officially become the latest country to move all official transactions to cryptocurrency, removing any reliance on traditional fiat currency. It joins Switzerland, Singapore, and of course Estonia, all of which have seen dramatic inflows of capital and foreign investment since the switch. In the last several years of ever-worsening global inflation, this so-called "Estonian option" has been seriously considered in almost every country around the globe.

Although it is the first state in the Western Hemisphere to remove itself entirely from fiat currency, it is certainly not the only one where cryptocurrency is used more often than state-issued money. According to *Econometrician Economic Report* estimates, Argentina, Chile, and Brazil already conduct a majority of day-to-day business using cryptocurrency. In both Ecuador and Bolivia, it is believed to be approximately fifty-fifty. It was only a matter of time before one of these countries bit the bullet and joined the growing list of countries who have removed government from the business of minting currency.

Jerry Gray, lame duck President of the United States, has insisted that the United States will not be among them. In a speech this week, he condemned the use of cryptocurrency, calling out Bitcoin and Monero specifically. "There is nothing, nothing at all, that cryptocurrency can do that a traditional payment processor does not do.

At least, nothing that is legal and aboveboard. The United States government will continue to monitor the Bitcoin, Monero, and other networks for malfeasance. The United States dollar shall continue to be a beacon of strength for the entire world."

Those words may not mean much, with a growing percentage of United States commerce being handled by cryptocurrencies, and incoming president Xavier Rodriguez being a noted proponent of Bitcoin. Although Bitcoin and Litecoin have been handling the lion's share of this, other "altcoins" such as Monero are handling a larger percentage of commerce in recent months. Estimates have put usage of cryptocurrencies other than Bitcoin, Litecoin, or Ethereum (the "Big Three") at approximately 12% of all cryptocurrency usage in the United States. Savings accounts at traditional banks continue to offer an average of less than 1% interest annually, while inflation is eroding the power of the U.S. dollar at double-digit percentage rates. The futures for all cryptocurrencies which are "inflation-proof" by virtue of having a mathematically limited number of coins is looking bright.

Chapter 7

Which Satan Supposedly Relished

Phlox awoke to reflected sunlight streaming through her window. After a few moments of grogginess, she realized that she had never set her alarm clock after staying up late last night to finish the Tolstoy paper. She could still make it to work on time as long as she skipped breakfast. Slipping on a pair of khakis, she examined her Priscilla's polo shirt. There were a few splotches of syrup along the bottom, but if she tucked it in, they wouldn't be noticeable. Better than ironing her other shirt, which was technically clean but lying on a floor in a heap, along with most of her other clothes. Ironing would take much more time than she had this morning.

Behind the bathroom door, Phlox could hear Holly's normal morning routine. This usually entailed yelling at the toothpaste for falling off her toothbrush, excited chirps of merriment that her deodorant was still there, animated discussions with herself on the correct temperature of the water coming out of the faucet, and the like. Phlox knocked on the door.

"Hey, Holly," she said, a bit chagrined. "Do you mind if I just grab my toothbrush and whatnot? I have to get to Priscilla's."

"Sure, sure," replied Holly. Phlox opened the door to see Holly wearing only her bright purple towel wrapped around her. Her black hair was slicked back and held in place in a ponytail. None of this was unexpected, but one thing was. Her left shoulder seemed to be dyed a bright red.

"What the..." said Phlox.

"What?" said Holly. "Oh, it's just red paint. Violet and her friend were making paint bombs to lob against... I don't know, some statue or something. Some of it just spilled on me when she hugged me."

"Must be interesting, having a sister," said Phlox, "but I've got to go. I slept in."

"Have fun!" yelled Holly, and went back to making delighted noises that there was still plenty of toilet paper on the roll.

Phlox bounded down the stairs and out the door onto the sidewalk. There were no weird women reading newspapers today, which was good. It looked like someone had felt the need to vomit right in front of their door, which was bad. At least it was supposed to rain again today, so hopefully it would soon be on its way to the sewers.

She walked quickly — not quite running — the four blocks to Priscilla's, and opened the door with seconds to spare. She saw Henry taking care of a middle-aged couple seated in the corner, and Gloria heading over to hand her a notebook for taking orders. The place was packed today.

"Hey, hon," said Gloria. "Guess what, Henry actually came in on time this morning!"

"Huzzah," said Phlox, catching her breath. "It'll be great to have the help."

The morning was an almost-undifferentiated whirl of customer comings and goings. Was it homecoming weekend or something? There seemed to be more older people than should be here at this time of day. One of them even did the Awful Waffle Challenge, a somewhat famous contest to eat a massive (and massively burnt) waffle covered in whipped cream. It had always seemed faintly ridiculous to Phlox, if not outright stupid. Still, not a day went by that somebody didn't decide that they wanted to have their name etched in the halls of Priscilla's Valhalla as one who had slain the Awful Waffle and consequently had their 250 microlites refunded. The fact that they had gotten something for free outweighed the fact that what they gotten was a giant, burnt waffle.

She noticed that one table wasn't getting up, though. The well-dressed middle-aged couple in Henry's section had been nursing their coffee and orange juice for over an hour. Upon closer inspection, they were the same man and woman that she had seen yesterday, although this time they were sitting together. This was strange. She couldn't imagine anybody's waistline could stay smaller than a hula hoop if they ate at Priscilla's for breakfast every day.

A ringing at the door indicated new customers coming in. Usually the hostess would seat them, and so Phlox didn't pay the bell any mind. It was only during the real off-hours that a hostess wasn't working. Since her mind was already distracted by the well-dressed couple, though, Phlox's eyes darted involuntarily towards the door, only to see Chris entering.

A sudden rush of emotions enveloped Phlox. Excitement — was there some news on the hidden bitcoin wallet? Fear — was all of this, even the wallet, just a ploy to stalk her? Uneasiness — was she going to have to come up with some sort of way to let him down easily? Her mind went back to Lance, the imaginary love interest she had created last night, and she tried to think of a way to casually drop him into a conversation with Chris.

Then she noticed that Chris had opened the door for a girl who looked like the dictionary definition of "fiery redhead", if the dictionary included phrases and not just individual words. She had what Shakespeare would have called "alabaster skin," freckles sprinkled all over her face and shoulders, and a very Irish-looking face. She was wearing a strapless floral sundress for which the weather seemed to be a little too cool, showing off her hourglass figure.

"Thanks," the red-headed woman said to Chris as she stepped through the entryway, a slight blush showing on her cheeks. She was so pale, though, that blood anywhere near her cheeks left them looking as bright as the coral lipstick she was wearing.

Phlox felt a little embarrassed by her wrinkled khakis and dirty shirt. This girl with Chris looked elegant, sophisticated. She tried to ignore them and paid close attention to her customers.

"Phlox!" she heard Chris saying, "I forgot you worked here."

"Yeah," said Phlox, "it's a living."

"Oh, let me introduce you two," continued Chris, "Vera, this is Phlox. We go back to middle school."

"Nice to meet you," said Vera, in a way that made it clear that it was anything but nice to meet Phlox. She edged almost imperceptibly closer to Chris.

"I'd love to stay and chat, but..." Phlox motioned around the hustle and bustle around her.

"Of course, I'll see you tomorrow," said Chris, to a slightly wounded and angry look from Vera.

Vera and Chris enjoyed a long breakfast, although thankfully they ended up sitting in Henry's section. Phlox kept hearing Vera's laugh in response to some witticism on Chris's part, the kind of laugh that goes along with touching someone's arm and looking deep into their eyes for just a moment too long. Definitely the honeymoon phase of whatever kind of relationship they were in.

The older couple continued to drink and talk. It sounded like some sort of conversation about business, as it was sprinkled with acronyms like ROI and PE ratios. She was unfamiliar with those acronyms, but they didn't seem to be technical acronyms, and they didn't look military, so she assumed that the conversation was about business. What else could it be?

When Phlox's shift was over, her eyelids were heavy, but so was her Litecoin wallet. Besides being busy, there were quite a few good tippers today. A brief conversation with one family let her know that there was some sort of event for parents of freshman students today. She played up a persona of "just a hard-working student working hard to get through college." The persona was essentially the truth, but it never hurt to play it up a bit. Parents who saw her as their surrogate daughter for the course of a meal — maybe even an improved, harder-working version — Emily, why can't you be more like her? — would probably be inclined to tip more. Phlox had been in the waitressing game for long enough to know these little psychological tricks.

On the way out the door, she saw that Vera and Chris were not far in front of her on Forbes Avenue. She decided to take a slightly more roundabout way home to avoid them.

When she arrived at her house, it was silent, which meant, sure as one of her mathematical theorems, that Holly wasn't home. She pulled off her polo shirt, which had gotten enough syrup on it that it was definitely going to need a wash. She took a moment to remember which pile was the dirty pile of clothes and threw it on the top, along with her khakis, which despite having survived the Sisyphean

ordeal of syrup avoidance rather well, could also probably stand to
be cleaned. She threw on a fresh pair of jeans from the clean pile and
a light red (not pink, as she had explained numerous times to people)
t-shirt. The look was completed with her James Joyce hoodie. Truly,
this was the next fashion trend straight from Milan.

Phlox had printed out her paper, entitled *A Pacifist Reading of
Tolstoy's The Death of Ivan Ilyich*, last night. She was quite proud
of it; she thought that it was a unique take on the novel. Tolstoy
was a known pacifist and a Christian anarchist, but the focus of this
particular book wasn't on either of those aspects of his life philosophy.
Still, she had been able to tease out some subtle themes. She just
hoped that Violet didn't see it, or she'd probably become a Christian
anarchist herself.

With the paper tucked away securely in her backpack, she
headed to her Russian Lit class, eating a plain waffle from one hand.
Syrup and fruit were actually overkill if you had a good waffle. And
Priscilla's waffles were good waffles. Along the way, she noticed a
splash of red near the Cathedral. Half-hidden amongst the bushes,
there was an old bronze sundial which commemorated the War of
1812. It was one of the oldest pieces of the University still standing.
Phlox knew all of this because she had spent a good portion of her
freshman year exploring nooks and crannies on the campus, usually
followed by some Internet research on whatever she found.

The sundial was covered in fresh red paint. A sign was hanging
from it, made of cardboard and hastily attached with packing tape.
Scrawled across it with a black marker were the words "JAMES
MADISON — BLOOD IS ON YOUR HANDS! THE TREATY OF
GHENT WAS A TRAVESTY! THE COLONIES NEED TO RE-
TURN TO THE BRITISH CROWN!" She thought back to the red
paint that she saw on Violet's shoulder this morning. It did look to
be the same shade, but Phlox could not, for the life of her, think of
why Violet would be defacing a monument to a war that was close
to two and a half centuries over.

Shaking her head, she headed to class to turn the paper in. She
was early. The instructor wasn't there yet, and there were only a few
students, most of whom looked tired from staying up too late writing
their paper, and all of whom were looking down at their watches. She
wondered idly what people had done with their free time before they

had a device to amuse them whenever they were bored. She set the paper down on the desk and joined the crowd, sitting near the back windows, and stared down at her own watch.

Phlox decided to check out her currency accounts. Rent would be due soon — her share was just under five millilites. Exactly 4,975 microlites, if Chris were talking about it. Holly paid a little bit more — 5,025 microlites — thanks to her larger room. In her account, she had slightly over seven millilites, and a paycheck coming in today. By law, payment had to be in Federal Reserve Tokens, but these were almost instantly converted to litecoin by almost anyone in Pittsburgh. She had heard rumors that FRTs were used if you were going to buy a house or take over a business, but for her, and for most people, they were just the weird currency that you got paid in and had to convert some of your savings back to once per year to pay taxes.

Looking up, Phlox noticed Lawrence walking into the classroom. Lawrence's and Phlox's paths crossed regularly, as he was a fellow English lit major. They had actually met the very first night of college, at a freshman dorm icebreaker. They were in that weird sort of relationship where you never actually make plans to see the other one, but somehow you always do.

He sat down next to Phlox and set his beige canvas messenger bag on the desk. The top flap fell open, exposing the various books inside: *Atlas Shrugged*, *Infinite Jest*, and *The Illuminatus! Trilogy*. All unread, of course. Lawrence seemed to enjoy being an English literature major more than actually reading literature in English.

Lawrence took off his scarf (for which the weather was much too warm), and started a monologue with Phlox. It was classic Lawrence. Phlox listened stoically.

"What did you think of the paper? I feel like there were quite a few parables" — he meant parallels, Phlox knew — " to *Fight Club*, about the inevitable uselessness of striving for something better, *especially* something in this corporate world. I mean, we're only on this Earth for so long, you know? I don't want to be chasing the almighty bitcoin my whole life. Have you ever read *On The Road*? By Kerouac? There was someone who really knew what it was like to take life and really, you know, suck the juice out of it. I think that's a quote from him, actually. Maybe it was in *Dharma Bums*...?"

He continued on for another few minutes, but at this point he was the only one listening. Despite his vehemence, Phlox knew that approximately thirty seconds after graduating, realizing that there was no way that he'd be getting into grad school, and looking at his student loan balance, he'd be right there with the rest of the rats in the rat race, chasing that once-accursed almighty bitcoin. She didn't harbor any illusions that there wasn't a good chance she'd be the next rat over, but consoled herself with the thought that she might put that off for a few years by getting a doctorate.

Luckily, Professor Mikailov had entered the room, which caused Lawrence's voice to gradually trail off, and a Russian-accented voice to start up, talking about something slightly more interesting than what Burroughs *really* meant in *Junky*.

Only slightly more interesting, though. Phlox worked on various doodles — including one she was quite proud of, a collection of ladybugs climbing a vine — and half-listened to Mikailov's monotone. Out the window, she saw Chris and Vera on the Cathedral lawn, intense looks on both of their faces. Occasionally Vera would touch his arm and laugh.

Suddenly, Phlox panicked for a moment — did she sign her paper before turning it in? All essays had to have been signed by private key. This was usually as simple as running the function on her word processor — literally any word processor with a version released in the last five years had it installed. The hash of the paper, signed with a key known only to her, was then appended to the end. This would look like a long string of random letters and numbers, but was actually a representation of a hash of what she wrote that could only be created by someone who had access to the same private key she used to pay her tuition. The professor — or more likely, his grading assistant — could then run their watch over it, performing some optical character recognition, and could then verify the result against her public key stored with the university. This proved that she wrote the paper, or at least that she was there to sign it... or was dumb enough to lend someone her private key.

Then Phlox remembered seeing that somewhere in the middle of the long string of characters that made up the cryptographic signature was the sequence P10HX, which looked kind of like her name (if you squinted). She breathed a sigh of relief. The paper was turned in appropriately, Chris wouldn't be bothering her with unwanted romantic advances (judging from the fact that when he looked at Vera, his eyes almost seemed to be turning into hearts and popping out of their sockets like an old cartoon), and she was on her way to recovering the modern equivalent of buried pirate treasure. It was a good life.

"She was a woman with red hair and green eyes — the traits which Satan supposedly relished most in mortal females."
-Robert Shea and Robert Anton Wilson, *The Illuminatus! Trilogy*

ID, You D, We All D

An excerpt from an article in The Econometrician, *Volume XVI, Issue 41*

This past month has not been good for traditional repositories of governmental data. The Social Security Administration, in the United States, and the Department of Work and Pensions, in the United Kingdom, admitted that they had recently been targets of a sophisticated hacking scheme. Both organizations have announced that any data stored on their servers was most likely compromised by an unknown actor. Accusations have flown, with suspects as diverse as the Russian Federation, the Earth Liberation Front, and a shadowy hacking collective known as 4DaLulz.

As virtually all citizens of both countries have either a Social Security number (U.S.) or a National Insurance number (U.K.), this has been a historic breach in terms of number of people affected by a data breach. Well over 350 million people can no longer assume that their work, tax, and salary histories are private. Rumors are already swirling that sites on the Dark Web are offering salary histories for individuals for a few millimons.

Libertarians in the United States have been especially vociferous in condemning the fact that so much of this information was stored in one place. "This is merely another example of the dangers of centralized data storage," Brad Smith, junior Senator from Montana, said. "But if you are going to store it, it should at least be protected. The fact that this data was on a publicly accessible network, unencrypted, is just gross negligence."

Several unique identification schemes are already popular on the Ethereum network. These have the benefit of being cryptographically secure by design, decentralized, and ensuring that only the specific data that the owner would like to share will be shared. The minority Democratic Socialists have already announced that a party platform plank for the next Presidential election will be creating a similar scheme to act as the official replacement for the Social Security number. The Libertarians, meanwhile, have continued to hold that the best way to determine which unique identification scheme to use should be left to the free market.

Chapter 8

Infinitely Outdone

Phlox took a big bite of her *tofu tikka masala* and looked across the table at Chris. The living room in Chris's apartment doubled as a dining room. It was a strange combination. There was a table which was probably quite expensive twenty or thirty years ago in the center of the room. Along each of three sides of the table, there was a chair, none of which matched any of the others. On the fourth side, there was a couch, which leaned back against the off-white walls.

"So… is Vera, like, your girlfriend?" She had wanted to bring it up a little more subtly, but hadn't been able to figure out a way to do so. Oh well, sometimes the direct approach was best.

Chris blushed. "I mean, we just met, but…" he stammered awkwardly.

Phlox felt it was her duty to remove any potential awkwardness and made sure that she was smiling. "So, how'd you meet?"

"It was the strangest thing!" said Chris, excitedly. "I was heading home from your place the other night when I rounded the corner on Forbes — you know, where the ice cream store is? — and I bumped into her. She had been staring down at her watch, you know how it is."

He barely waited for her nonverbal assent that she did, in fact, know how it was. "We both said 'excuse me', and it turned out that she was having trouble getting her Litecoin balance to show on her wallet. I helped her and we got to talking about how she really wanted some ice cream, but didn't think she was going to be able to get any because of her stupid wallet, and none of her friends were around. It turned out that she had just turned off auto-sync, so she wasn't seeing her actual account balance. It only took me two seconds to fix.

"She insisted on treating me to ice cream, and we ended up talking for hours over cones. Strawberry for her, vanilla for me. I know it sounds weird, but we had such a connection... I feel like I can talk to her about anything, and it's not awkward. I don't always have that with everyone."

"Yeah, I know the feeling," Phlox said. She opened her mouth to say more but was suddenly interrupted by rustling in the kitchen.

"I thought your roommate was out tonight?" continued Phlox.

"So did I," Chris said, "I haven't seen him since yesterday." He called out, "Brian?"

A tall, almost impossibly gaunt man entered the room, presumably Brian. He needed a haircut, badly, and his blond hair was speckled with something that looked like dirt. She was pretty sure that she saw at least one twig, perhaps two, sticking out of it. From head to toe, he was wearing a camouflage uniform that hung on him like a toga.

All of this was relatively normal. What definitely was not normal was that in each one of his hands he held a one-gallon container of soy sauce.

"Chris!" he said with a frenetic, barely controlled energy. "Do you know where the duct tape is? Oh." He noticed Phlox. "Hi, I'm Brian, nice to meet you."

"Hi, I'm Phlox, nice to meet —" Brian interrupted her with what looked like a well-practiced formal bow.

"Hate to meet and run, but I'm in a rush," said Brian. "Late, late, late."

"What are you doing?" asked Phlox.

"It's usually better not to ask," Chris chimed in, *sotto voce*.

"Secret plan..." said Brian mysteriously, and suddenly seemed to spot something outside the window. "Right! I forgot! I put the duct tape next to the ducts! I'll see you Monday!"

Brian left so quickly that Phlox wasn't entirely sure that he wasn't a hallucination from the spicy food.

"Told you my roommate was weird," said Chris, finishing off a samosa.

"Remind me never to complain about Holly again," said Phlox. "So, are you and Vera going to go on another date? I mean, you already had breakfast together..."

"Oh yeah," Chris said. "We're going to head over to the museum together on Sunday afternoon. She's an art history major, did I tell you that? Focus on Impressionism."

"Chris," Phlox said, sounding serious. "What color are her eyes?"

"Green," Chris replied, "Can you believe it? Red hair and green eyes... well, I guess maybe kind of hazel? Dark green."

He had it bad. Definitely. Any man who knew the color of a woman's eyes a day after meeting her had it very bad.

"But let's talk about bitcoin. Get down to brass bitcoin, if you will." Phlox groaned at his horrible pun. "Any thoughts?"

"I think that our best bet is that, despite our feeling that he wasn't a drug user, he must have hid it with his drugs, his 'pots.' " Phlox made air quotes around "pots" — why was slang from the previous generation always so weird? "That means it could be anywhere in the apartment."

"I hope it's not in Holly's room," Chris said. "But do you think you could come up with a reason to look in there if necessary?"

"Sure," said Phlox. "I don't know what it would be, but I could come up with something."

"Great," said Chris, "but let's wait to do that room until last." He seemed a little nervous.

"I'd think you'd want to try it first," said Phlox. "If that was his bedroom, then that seems like a really good place to hide anything that needed to be hidden."

"If I'm honest," said Chris, "Holly scares me a little."

Phlox stifled a grin. She could see how the overbearing Holly, talking a mile a minute, could have intimidated shy Chris after talking to him for only one of those minutes.

Chris grabbed his backpack, which was stuffed to the zipper with papers, binders, folders, and books. It contained all of the information he had on Dr. Chambers: notes, pictures, anything he could find.

"Let's get to it, then," said Phlox. "Holly's out at some going-away party. One of her math friends graduated this summer and just got a job doing forensic cryptoanalysis."

"I feel like Captain Ahab," said Chris, as he locked up his apartment. "Every spare minute I've been obsessed with finding my white whale. Except he at least knew that Moby Dick was out there, even if he was hiding. We're looking for something that may not even exist. Are we wasting our time?"

"Well," said Phlox, pensively, "I could think of worse ways to waste time. I mean, most people are filling their spare time with something that isn't exactly useful. Chess, drawing, video games... at least the search is something real, even if what we're looking for is not. Not to get too existential."

On the walk over to her apartment, Phlox realized how cold the nights were getting. This was the first night of the season that it was actually *cold* and not just chilly. She wished she were wearing something more than a t-shirt and a hoodie. This was long-sleeved shirt and hoodie weather.

The streets were abuzz with the normal post-dinner activity in a college area. A neon sign advertised "ONE SLICE — 10 MICRO-LITES — WHOLE PIE — 65 MICROLITES — HIGHEST QUAL-ITY" and numerous students were taking advantage of the cheap pizza prices. Phlox wondered how high a quality the pizza could be at those prices, unless the pizza shop was running some sort of odd, pizza-focused charity and selling to poor students for less than the cost of production. The only Marxist pizza shop in existence, perhaps.

As they walked over, Phlox found her mind wandering. "So who was this guy who came up with the whole idea of cryptocurrency? Satoshi Nakomoto?"

Chris looked like he was going to start a long monologue, then thought better of it. "There's a long history of people trying to make digital currency. Back at the end of last century, during a period in the 90s called the 'dot-com boom' — I know it's a silly name — there were a few attempts. But all of them relied on some sort of central-ized registrar to avoid the 'double-spend problem.' Making sure that one person didn't try to spend the same money twice, basically.

"Then this paper came out of nowhere which detailed an incredible solution, by Satoshi Nakomoto. It all came together in one paper which explained proof of work, mining, determining the valid chain, everything. None of the ideas by themselves were that revolutionary, but he was the first person to put them all together. *That* was revolutionary."

"So where is Satoshi Nakomoto now? I've heard you talk about Satoshi's Hoard, but only as a reference to some unimaginable amount of bitcoin."

"That's just it. Nobody knows where he is, or who he is. Or even that Satoshi was a he, and not a she, or a they. They only communicated online, never in person, and suddenly stopped doing even that only a few years after Bitcoin started up."

Soon they found themselves back at the stoop of Phlox's place, Phlox herself looking through her backpack for her keys. Just then, though, Holly and Violet erupted through the front door. Holly was dressed up more than usual, wearing a scarlet tank top and black slacks. Her shoulder no longer seemed to be smudged with red paint. Violet was wearing a slightly ruffled blouse and a modest ankle-length skirt.

"Hey Phlox!" said Holly, giving her a significant look indicating that she knew exactly why Phlox and Chris were coming to the apartment when they both knew that it would be empty.

"Hey Holly," replied Phlox, pointedly rolling her eyes to Holly's unspoken accusation. "You off to your party?"

"Yup," said Holly, "No thanks to Little Miss Takes Forever To Pick Out A Dress, here."

"All of yours are too short!" Violet quickly said. "It's important that as a subject of His Royal Highness, I show, you know, like, decorum."

Phlox's and Chris's eyebrows found themselves raised involuntarily. "A subject?" asked Chris.

"Violet has determined that the American Revolution was really just treason against King George," explained Holly, exaggerated patience in her voice. "She thinks that technically we are" — and at this point she switched to a ridiculous American imitation of a British accent — "subjects of the British Empire and owe allegiance to the Crown."

"You're a monarchist?" asked Chris.

"It only stands to reason," said Violet, "that a well-established and hereditary monarchy will lead to better outcomes for its subjects. After all, who is going to care about the long-term stability of a nation more than someone whose children will inherit it? Democracy inevitably leads to short-term thinking, as well as appeasing the crowds at the expense —"

"You can explain it to him tomorrow," interrupted Holly. "We don't want to be late for Prisha's party. I'm sure you will find lots of people there who want to hear your theories on which states belong to which dukes or whatever."

The Wu sisters headed down Atwood Street to the party. Phlox and Chris could hear them chatting until they were almost a block away, even after entering the foyer of the apartment.

"Shall we start?" asked Phlox once they reached the top of the stairs.

They spent over an hour looking throughout the apartment for any sign of a disturbed wall. Phlox even went into Holly's room, although she felt kind of bad about it. It didn't matter, though. They didn't find anything at all.

They both sat down on the futon in the living room. Chris sighed in an overwrought, affected manner.

"I guess that's it," he said, and sighed once more for good measure. "I had been fantasizing about taking Vera to Paris... maybe Rome..."

Inwardly, Phlox scoffed at how Chris had already incorporated Vera into major parts of his life plan a few days after meeting her. Outwardly, her body language only expressed sympathy.

"Let's not give up yet. It's not even 8:30!" said Phlox. "How about we look through the pictures again."

Chris looked deflated, but he wasn't quite ready to give up, either. He went over to his backpack, which he had thrown down absentmindedly against the wall when he had first come in. He took out a thick blue folder from his backpack and brought it back over to the futon, spreading out the sheaf of printed-out pictures on the table in front of them.

Most of the pictures were of various grad students or Dr. Chambers' office at the school. Only about a dozen of the pictures were from the house itself. There was a picture from a party of some kind, where numerous academic types were drinking wine in the kitchen. Another was a picture of his cheap-looking couch, covered in papers. Showing off how much he had graded at the end of the semester, perhaps? Another was a picture of a sad-eyed man — not Dr. Chambers — looking up from soldering a circuit board. Oddly, there didn't seem to be any pictures of Dr. Chambers himself, but then again, he would have been behind the camera.

"I've looked at so many pictures taken by him," said Phlox. "It's almost like I know him in real life, even if I haven't seen him."

"Yeah, I know the feeling," said Chris. "It's like he's an old friend at this point."

Phlox pulled out a picture that was a close-up of one side of Dr. Chambers' desk. It seemed odd. She examined it closely, squinting at it to try to get some more detail from grainy picture. "What are these things over on the corner of the desk, under the light switch?"

Chris took off his glasses and squinted at the black and white picture along with Phlox. Such a stupid fad of that generation, using advanced CCD technology which could distinguish millions of different colors to take faded monochrome pictures.

"Looks like electronic components," said Chris. "Old-school big ones. Resistors, capacitors... potentiometers... Oh my God!"

"What is it?" asked Phlox, unsure why Chris was so excited.

"The top drawer here is filled with potentiometers," explained Chris. "Pots! Above the pots! Pots was just an abbreviation for potentiometers!"

Chris grabbed a flat head screwdriver from his backpack and went into Phlox's room. Ordinarily he would have asked permission to go into her room, but he didn't even think about it. Phlox followed him in, taking a second to remember to breathe.

He gently unscrewed the light switch, and let the ancient yellowed plastic fall to the ground. It was obvious that the space behind the light switch was slightly larger than the cover. It was dusty inside, but there was a relatively clean looking piece of paper folded up in a small inlet next to the light switch itself.

"The paper wallet!" exclaimed Chris.

He reached into the crevice with trembling hands and pulled out the paper. It looked like a regular piece of office paper, folded up into quarters. Chris and Phlox looked at each other, hearts racing. It was real!

Chris unfolded the paper as they both stared down at it, mouths slightly open with anticipation. Then a sudden shock as they both realized that instead of a private Bitcoin key, the paper had only two words printed on it in pen.

"CHICKEN. ALGORITHM."

"[T]here is no folly of the beast of the earth which is not infinitely outdone by the madness of men."
-Herman Melville, *Moby-Dick, or, The Whale*

Playing With Toy Block(chain)s

An excerpt from an article in The Econometrician, *Volume XIV, Issue 25*

As blockchain technology has become an essential part of the global economy, virtually all major universities offer at least one course in blockchain technology. Some academic institutions have gone beyond offering just courses in cryptocurrency. In the United States alone, there are at least thirty universities which offer degrees or certificates in cryptoeconomics, over fifty universities which offer a major in blockchain development, and Northeastern Wyoming Agricultural College even offers a certificate in Blockchain Technology Applied to Animal Husbandry. Maintaining an immutable, easily-checked record of a calf's ancestors, secured with a hash of their DNA, has been invaluable in tracking genetic disorders, proving and transferring ownership, and scheduling breeding.

While some high schools have also offered elective courses or clubs related to blockchain technology, Amaranth Elementary School in Colorado is believed to be the first to introduce grammar school students to the fundamentals of cryptocurrency. Students in first grade (approximately six years old) work on understanding hashing, cryptography, and distributed consensus. This is done through age-appropriate games, analogies, and occasional worksheets.

"Students who do not understand blockchain are at a significant disadvantage in life," says Principal Sandy Chen. "Although there have been some problems as we determine the exact capabilities of elementary students to understand these concepts, we believe that it is never too early to start teaching students how their money works."

Several parents disagree with Principal Chen. "Students at this age are not prepared for the complexities of cryptographic currency," says a father of two students at Amaranth Elementary, who asked to remain anonymous. "Whatever happened to the three R's? I think we need to focus on basic math, reading age-appropriate books, and learning to write. At this age, anything else is just too advanced."

However, most parents are willing to give Principal Chen's ideas a shot. "It can't hurt," says Yolanda Vazquez, mother of three Amaranth Elementary students, "I'm happy that our school is trying out new things. I wouldn't want my children to be learning the same concepts and ideas that people did in the nineteenth century. Perhaps the concepts are too advanced, but at least the school is not resting on its laurels."

Chapter 9

Dark and Bright

The next morning, Phlox didn't get out of bed until 11 o'clock. That was late, even for her.

That most certainly did not mean, however, that she slept until 11. She did sleep in until 9, but spent the next two hours alternating between staring at the ceiling and playing around with her watch. The paper they had found the night before, that she thought was going to be the end of her not-very-epic quest, seemed to just be a short collection of gibberish.

She and Chris had spent a few minutes of puzzling over what the CHICKEN ALGORITHM might be. Phlox had mocked Chris for not knowing what was obviously a very common algorithm — what kind of computer science curriculum was the university running? After some searches on the Internet proved fruitless, though, she had to admit that it wasn't the name of any kind of common algorithm. They had both lacked the energy to continue their research any further. Assuming that the CHICKEN ALGORITHM was real, it would still be around in the morning. Chris had quickly texted Vera and then told Phlox that he was leaving to meet her at his apartment.

Groggily arising and pouring herself a bowl of cereal, Phlox heard the voice of Violet Wu at the door. She seemed to be involved in an intense conversation with another woman with a deep voice. Just as Phlox was finishing the last of her shredded wheat, the door opened and Violet bounded up the stairs to the living room.

She was wearing all black — black jeans and a shiny black top, giving a bit of a cyberpunk air about her. It was a stark contrast to her outfit yesterday, but then again, Violet Wu's middle name could be "stark contrast." Throwing her backpack down on the couch, she walked into the kitchen where Phlox was rinsing off her bowl in the sink.

"Hey Phlox," she said. "Have you seen Holly anywhere?"

"No," replied Phlox, "and I'm sure I would have heard her if she was around. I haven't seen her since I woke up."

"She was hanging out with this girl at the party last night," said Violet. "I ended up leaving and she barely deigned to say good-bye! I swear it was like she was in a trance! I was just passing by with my friend and figured I'd check in with her, make sure that she didn't go join a cult or something."

"What were they talking about?"

"I don't know, something about Bitcoin. Are there any Bitcoin cults?" Violet paused momentarily — about as long as she ever paused in conversation — and wrinkled her nose in a manner which indicated that she was definitely considering the notion. "I don't think so. No Bitcoin cults — one less thing to worry about."

Phlox's heart skipped a beat. Trying not to show any sign that something was amiss, she asked, "What did the girl she was talking to look like? It wasn't a middle-aged blonde woman, was it?" Damn it. Way to make yourself look suspicious, Phlox, she thought to herself.

Violet didn't seem to notice. "No, she was around our age. Really red hair and lots of freckles. I think her name started with a V. Valerie or Veronica or Vivian, something like that."

"Vera?"

"Maybe. I'm pretty sure it wasn't Violet, I would have remembered that. Whoever she was, she seemed to just be grilling Holly about blockchains, and recovering bitcoin that hasn't been used in years. It seemed kind of dry to me, but I guess she was enjoying herself."

A few more beats were skipped by Phlox's heart. Did Chris mention something to Vera? This whole adventure was supposed to be a secret, but men are generally not very good at keeping secrets from women. Especially ones on whom they had impossibly huge crushes.

Violet was busy looking around in Holly's room to try to ascertain her whereabouts, so Phlox texted Chris a message: "Did you tell Vera about the PW?" She saw almost instantly that it had been read, but after a few minutes of waiting, there was no response. Stupid men. What if Vera convinced him not to share the bitcoin hidden behind the CHICKEN ALGORITHM? A little batting of her green eyes and some well-timed swooshes of her hair and he'd be putty in her hands. She's probably already got him reading her his private keys like one of Lord Byron's poems, interspersed with odes to her eyes like emeralds and hair like the purest fire...

It took her a few moments to realize that Violet was saying something to her.

"Sorry, what?"

"I was just saying that there's no need to worry," said Violet. "Holly was here this morning. Her watch is plugged in, but she had it on her last night. So I guess she wasn't brainwashed to join a Bitcoin cult! Maybe she went out for a long run or something."

"Oh..." said Phlox. She wasn't the type of person who kept close tabs on where her roommate might be spending her time. It made her a bit uncomfortable that Violet apparently was that type, but they were sisters. Maybe that's just how sisters interacted, at least in their family. As an only child, it was a bit of a mystery to her how siblings were supposed to interact.

Violet seemed to be waiting for more of a response, but Phlox's mind was not really focused on the conversation. She could feel the bitcoin slipping through her metaphorical fingers and anger that Chris seemed to be aiding and abetting the loss.

"I guess I'll go," said Violet. "Trish is waiting for me."

"Trish?" asked Phlox.

"She's my next-door neighbor at the dorm! Oh, you'd like her, she's really fun. We're going to play frisbee golf over at Schenley Park with some of her friends from over at Carnegie Mellon University."

"You know everybody just calls it CMU, right?"

"Well, whatever, from the college across the way. Tell Holly I said hi!"

Just as Violet turned to leave, the door opened with a bang and they both heard Holly taking off her shoes and grumbling under her breath.

"Holly!" exclaimed Violet.

"Violet," said Holly, "what are you doing here? And why is Trish sitting on our stoop? I assume the two things are related."

"We're just going to play frisbee golf," said Violet. "I know you don't like her, but —"

"Don't like her!" said Holly, her voice rising. "That's putting it mildly! And I already had to see her all last night, you two wouldn't stop talking..."

"She was the only person I knew there! And you were talking to that red-headed girl for, like, hours! I thought she had hypnotized you!"

Phlox thought this would be a good time to excuse herself. Apparently this was also part of sibling relationships, at least those siblings who ended up at the same college. She gave silent thanks that she was an only child and headed into her room to catch up on some Russian Lit reading.

Her brain seemed to be holding her cortex at gunpoint, though, making her think about what the CHICKEN ALGORITHM could be. She thought of it as all-caps, just as it was written on the paper. Maybe it was the algorithm to produce the public and private key pair?

An algorithm was just a series of steps to produce some result. What if the CHICKEN ALGORITHM was just how the key could be reproduced? For example, let's assume that the key was something like ABABABAB..., and the CHICKEN ALGORITHM was just "repeat A and B until you have created enough characters for a private key"? It would be an easier way of writing down the private key and would also be more resistant to typos. If you wrote down ACABABAB... instead of ABABABAB..., the key would be useless. But if you wrote down CHICBEN ALGORITHM, it would still be good enough to reproduce the key.

This seemed like a promising lead, but she'd have to ask Chris. Assuming he could tear himself away from Vera for five minutes, of course. The real question still was, what was the CHICKEN ALGORITHM? She had tried doing some more searches in the morning on her watch, but the only things she could find were some papers from various agricultural colleges discussing how to increase egg yields.

She was still thinking about this when the yelling in the living room subsided, and Violet left under what seemed like reasonably good terms. Holly walked in to Phlox's room and sighed loudly, a clear indication that she wanted to talk. Phlox looked up and gave her silent assent.

"Wow, what was that all about?" asked Phlox.

"Violet was in quite the mood last night," answered Holly, "telling everybody who would listen — and a few who wouldn't — about how democracy is incompatible with freedom, and that only a strong monarch can solve the problems we see in the Rust Belt, that life would be much better if Pennsylvania were returned to the ancestors of William Penn, et cetera, et cetera, et friggin' cetera."

"I guess you didn't stick around to hear her discourse?"

"Heck no. It was a *party*, I *talked* to people! She was upset that I wasn't part of her one-woman crusade to bring down modern liberal democracy. I think she took it as me abandoning her, though. I mean, I feel bad, but I had friends there, too. And then of all the people at the party she ended up spending time with Trish!"

"Who's Trish? Violet said she was her next-door neighbor in her dorm."

"Next door neighbor, yeah, and horrible human being. Tricia Macmullen went to high school with us. She was one of the popular kids in our high school and... ugh. She's just not a good person."

"What happened?" Phlox didn't want to push, but she was curious and Holly wasn't really the type to keep things bottled up. She just seemed so angry that her words were having a bit of trouble getting out.

"She hated all of my friends in the Math Club, called us nerds. She's only a year younger than me, you know — she's a freshman now but only because she went off on some grand European trip for a while. I think her parents are both vice-presidents of some corporation. One day the six of us in the Math Club walked in to the classroom we held competitions in and saw some sort of contraption on a desk in the middle of the room.

"Our first thought was that it was some sort of bomb. It looked like a beer keg with some wires on it. Before we thought to call somebody, it started shooting rancid milk all over us and the room. Something like seventy gallons of disgusting-smelling milk was sprayed all over us, our clothes, our papers, everything. Ruined my favorite shoes, I had to throw them away. We ran out of the classroom and Trish and her friends were all pointing and laughing at us."

"Why milk?"

"I don't know, something about math and milk starting with M. I still don't understand it. Of course the teachers didn't care, said it was just a prank, let it go. But we couldn't use the room for days while they cleaned it out. Our high school was mostly concerned about getting students out the door with a diploma without getting — or causing — too many black eyes along the way. Math Club was the only place I really felt like I was getting an education, and Trish ruined it for me. But now Violet thinks she's the coolest." Holly rolled her eyes.

"Maybe she's changed?"

Red-hot fire erupted in Holly's eyes. "I don't care. I can't forgive her. Well, maybe I could, but she hasn't even asked for forgiveness. Every time I see her she acts like we're best friends just because we saw each other in the halls back at Sterrett High. Maybe she learned how to be nice in Switzerland, like it was a secret hidden high up in the Alps and guarded by old watchmakers, but I haven't seen any evidence of it."

Phlox nodded in understanding. She'd never had rancid milk sprayed on her, but Amsteco Area High School had a similar distribution of popular students and not-so-popular students, and similar relations between them. As a book-loving introvert, Phlox was definitely not in the popular group. Luckily, though, she was mostly ignored instead of being a target.

"I can't believe she ended up living right next to your sister," said Phlox. She wasn't sure if Holly wanted to keep talking, but then she remembered that Holly always liked to talk. "Quite a coincidence."

"Coincidence my ass! She e-mailed Violet when she heard that she was applying here and they signed up to live in the same building."

"Oh. I can see why you're upset with her, then."

"Yeah, but what can you do?" asked Holly. "Who knows, maybe I'm being the unreasonable one. Maybe Trish has changed. How are things with you? Oh, did I tell you I met Chris's... uhh... paramour, I guess? She seems nice. Really interested in the mathematics underlying blockchain technology."

I'll bet, thought Phlox, especially when she thinks she's going to be getting a fortune in it soon.

Holly, as she usually did, took the momentary silence of Phlox as the go-ahead to keep talking. "She was asking me some interesting theoretical questions about information density. Like how you could get a bitcoin private key just based on a few words."

"Isn't she an art history major?" asked Phlox. "That sounds pretty deep."

"It's simple!" exclaimed Holly, and Phlox could have sworn she saw her somehow physically transform into teaching assistant mode. "It's exactly how the built-in hardware wallet on any watch made in the last ten years works!" She went into her room and came back with a notebook and a pencil.

"So," continued Holly, "let's first talk about randomness. You know computers don't really *do* randomness, right?"

"Sure, Chris told me about it. Computers use a 'seed value' to start with, and then run an algorithm on it to get different 'pseudo-random' values — I think that's the term, right? Numbers that seem random but aren't really because you can reproduce the sequence if you know the seed?"

"Exactly," said Holly, beaming, "so as long as we know the seed, and we have the algorithm to determine numbers from it, we can make a much longer sequence. Say we have a really horrible pseudo-random number generator. It just increments the value by one each time. So if our seed is 5, the sequence is 6, 7, 8, 9, et cetera. Got it?"

"Sure."

"Let's call that the 'increment algorithm'. Let's also assume we have a password — or key — of 5 numbers. If we know the seed is 7, and that I am using the increment algorithm, and I need 5 numbers in total for my key, then I know the key is 7 - 8 - 9 - 10 - 11."

"Do all of these algorithms need a seed? Could I just say, use the X algorithm, and it will generate some sequence of numbers?" The paper just said "CHICKEN ALGORITHM." It didn't have any additional numbers written on it.

"Sure, there are all kind of sequences and algorithms that have a predetermined seed, but these will always produce the same values. The most famous sequence is called the Fibonacci sequence. This always starts with 0 and 1, and then you calculate the rest of it by successively adding the last two numbers together. Like so: 0 and 1 is 1, then 1 and 1 is 2, then 2 and 1 is 3, then 2 and 3 is 5, et cetera. The sequence itself is 0, 1, 1, 2, 3, 5, and so forth. If I know that someone is using the Fibonacci sequence, I don't need you to tell me the seed. It always starts with 0 and 1.

"Imagine doing this but with a more complicated algorithm and a bigger seed. You can specify a very long and hard-to-guess key using a really small seed value. Usually this is a sequence of words, which are transformed behind the scenes into numbers. Humans find it easier to remember, say, 'gold stamp' than nine billion sixteen million four hundred thousand and seventy-two."

"So the passphrase you enter when you get a new watch is just acting as a seed to generate a long sequence of numbers?"

"Sure, that's why it's so long! If you ever lose your watch or get a new one, as long as you enter the same passphrase, you'll end up with the same key. Just like if you enter five into the 'increment algorithm', you'll always get 6 - 7 - 8 - 9 - 10. But 6 - 7 - 8 - 9 - 10 is going to be much more secure than 5 all by itself. The longer the key, the harder it is to crack, generally speaking. Just like using a password of 'a' is really easy to guess, just by trying out all the different possibilities, but 'a912qb' is going to be more difficult."

"Hmm... interesting." Phlox thought for a moment. "Have you ever heard of the chicken algorithm?"

Holly laughed sharply. "No, what is it?"

"I just heard the term. I thought maybe you'd know what it was."

"No, definitely not. What was the context?"

"I can't remember now, just someone using a chicken algorithm."

"Never heard of it, sorry. Why is an English major like you so interested in all of this?"

"Oh..." said Phlox, thinking quickly. "I'm actually English lit, remember. I was actually thinking about writing a novel. About the time when we were kids and everyone started moving over to Bitcoin and Litecoin."

"Neat! I can't write to save my life. My lowest grade in college was when I had to take a creative writing course for my gen ed requirements. I hope it all turns out well!"

"Me, too," said Phlox. "Me, too."

"She walks in beauty, like the night
Of cloudless climes and starry skies;
And all that's best of dark and bright
Meet in her aspect and her eyes..."
-Lord Byron, "She Walks In Beauty"

The Persistence of Memory

An excerpt from an article in The Econometrician, *Volume IX, Issue 11*

Blockchain technology has caused fundamental shifts in all areas of the economy, mostly for the better. Payment processing takes a fraction of the time and energy that it once did. Smart contracts have dramatically reduced the number of lawyers necessary for the ordering of society, freeing them to do other tasks. Sending money to relatives across the world is now just as easy as handing money to somebody standing next to you. All of these are possible through blockchain technology, which acts as an immutable ledger on which anybody can view and verify transactions as legitimate.

There are certainly privacy drawbacks to having every transaction ever conducted on the blockchain be stored for all time (or at least as long as the coin is in use — many of the early altcoins and forks of Bitcoin/Litecoin have already disappeared entirely). While this is less of a concern with Monero and other privacy-centered cryptocurrencies, the burgeoning use of pseudonymous, and not anonymous, currencies like Bitcoin and Litecoin means that more and more transactions are being publicly recorded.

"What would happen if somebody purchased something that is currently legal, but is outlawed later?" asks Dr. Tyler Stilton, a professor at the University of New Amsterdam School of Law. "In the United States, of course, there are restrictions on passing *ex post facto* laws. That is, one cannot pass a law which retroactively criminalized the act of buying something. However, the government — or anyone else looking at the blockchain — may be able to determine what was purchased based on date of purchase, amount of currency spent, and other factors. It would then be a ready-made list of people for the government to check on, even if the purchase itself was not illegal at the time."

Even assuming that there are no legal issues at play, some worry that the personal privacy implications of storing this data on blockchain are worrying. "Would you want a potential employer to know what kinds of places you spent money when you were a teenager?" Dr. Stilton asks. "Just as our generation had to learn that embarrassing images and social media posts will live forever on the Internet, this new generation will have to learn that all of your purchases will also, in a sense, live forever. All it takes is sufficient analysis of the blockchain."

Blockchain analysis is already big business. Economists analyze the blockchain to calculate the current velocity of money (that is, how often it is changing hands), the level of inflation or deflation, and a myriad of other statistics. Smart trading contracts analyze transactions in order to better enact arbitrage between exchanges and currencies to keep values more stable. Investors use it to determine that corporate cash inflows and outflows match what is stated on their annual reports. While it is generally not yet economically feasible to track individuals' transactions, the triad of ever-increasing computing power, ever more purchases on the blockchain, and ever more data-hungry corporations and states mean that this future is closer than we may think.

Chapter 10

A Clue To Men's Characters

The sun streamed down on Phlox later that afternoon. She was wearing a plain white t-shirt and jeans, sitting in the grass under a tree in the park. Her backpack was situated against the tree so as to make it a relatively comfortable chair, although she could feel the straps against her back a bit.

The day had warmed considerably, and she was taking advantage of it. In one hand she held a battered copy of *Atlas Shrugged*. Lawrence had insisted she borrow his copy, and she was a bit tired of reading massive tomes from Russian authors translated into English. Instead, she was reading a massive tome from a Russian author that was originally written in English.

It was probably the last warm day in Pittsburgh this year, Phlox thought. The Cathedral of Learning was almost sparkling in the distance, lording over the other buildings in South Oakland. There were a few fluffy cumulus clouds in the sky, but just enough to add a little spice and ease the boredom of a blank blue sky.

Her watch buzzed, and she looked down to see a text from Chris. She knew that in the old days, texts were sent unencrypted. After a few scandals that arose from this — including one that brought down a Secretary of State, the CEO of a major telecommunications company, and several famous actors — it was absolutely unheard of not to communicate with client-side encryption. She thanked her lucky stars for this encryption as she stared at Chris's text.

"Sorry couldn't talk earlier, out with Vera. Can we talk about the bitcoin?"

Phlox knew it. Vera had talked Chris into splitting the bitcoin with her. Deep in her heart, it suddenly seemed impossible to deny.

She wanted to reprimand him for talking about it at all over the network. Sure, it was encrypted, but it wasn't unknown for someone to break into people's watches. Watches nowadays were pretty secure, but no system was totally secure. And if her watch were compromised, then mentioning any more details would just draw more attention to her.

Then again, if he had already talked about it with Vera, what were a few hackers and federal agents added to the mix?

She decided that it couldn't hurt to be a little circumspect. She set her book down on the grass and texted back. "Sure. Can we meet at your place in twenty minutes?"

It only took a few seconds for the response to show up, "yeah." Phlox tossed the book haphazardly into the bottom of the backpack, zipped it up, and slung it over her shoulder. It was an almost twenty-minute walk from the park to Chris's apartment, and she spent most of it silently fuming. A block away from his apartment, though, a sudden thought came to her based on her conversation with Violet this morning.

What if the chicken algorithm, instead of providing the key directly, was used to indirectly generate the list of words? With the Fibonacci sequence, for instance, instead of using 1, 1, 2, 3, 5, etc. as the values, you could pick out the first word in the book, then the first word again, then the second, third, fifth, etc.? If you could fit them into a book somehow, it would be just like generating the words necessary to act as the seed for the hardware wallet in your watch.

She was still mulling this over when she found herself at Chris's front door. Before she could knock, Brian came rushing out the door. Despite the heat, he had a sweatshirt on, and a heavy coat slung over his shoulders. Attached to the coat with binder clips or something were a hat and gloves. In one of his hands was a large container, labeled "BULK SOY SAUCE — FOR SALE TO RESTAURANTS

ONLY." His demeanor was about as manic as the last time she had seen him.

"Phlox, right? How's it going?" he asked, pausing on the porch momentarily. He was fidgeting, though, as if talking to her was the polite and socially acceptable course of action, but he really needed to be someplace else five minutes ago.

"Yeah, Brian, how are you?" she responded.

"Great, great, great..." he started, and then trailed off. "You haven't seen any ice cream trucks around here, have you?"

"What? No. It's October."

"Right!" Brian smacked himself on the forehead in an exaggerated manner. "They mostly come out during the summer. Mostly."

Phlox stared at him, absolutely at a loss.

"Well, Chris is inside, but I have to go," said Brian, and then lifted up the jug of soy sauce. "Do you know how expensive this stuff is? Paid ninety-eight microlites, and that was after haggling for half an hour. Have a good one!"

Phlox started to say something, but Brian took off down the street, walking at a rate of speed about equivalent to a jog by anybody else. Phlox's staring continued until he disappeared around a corner. Brian had politely left the door open for her to go in, but it had closed in the meantime. She knocked.

Chris arrived at the door looking a bit tired, and wearing the same clothes as he was last night. He seemed happy to see her.

"Phlox!" he said, "Come on in. I think — think! — I have good news."

Phlox was taken aback — she was sure that he was going to shamefacedly tell her that he was planning on taking the bitcoin and move to Tahiti with Vera. No, Tahiti's climate would be too much for Vera's pale skin. Maybe Iceland.

Entering the apartment, she noticed some of the notes from Chris's collection of Chambers paraphernalia lying on the floor. The three books of his were stacked on the coffee table.

"I think I know what the chicken algorithm is!"

"Did Vera tell you?" Oops. She meant to only think that.

"Vera? She doesn't know anything about this. We said we were going to keep it a secret. You haven't been telling people about it, have you?"

Phlox could tell that he wasn't lying. She felt foolish. Chris was apparently not a bad guy, after all. But what did that say about her when, on the flimsiest of pretexts, she thought that he would go behind her back?

"No, but I thought you had. I'm sorry. Holly ended up meeting Vera, and she kept asking questions about recovering keys. I just assumed that you were talking to her about it."

"Phlox, word of honor, I haven't told her a thing about it. Last night, we drove all the way out to Amsteco because she wanted to see where I grew up, and we found an all-night bowling alley. Turns out she is not a half-bad bowler; she was on her high school bowling team! We stayed up the entire night and I dropped her off at her place this morning. The entire time I didn't breathe a word about any kind of cryptocurrency, or Dr. Chambers, or reconstructing keys. I saw your text but I absolutely had to take a nap after that and figured we could talk later today."

"Why was Vera talking to Holly about keys, then? I mean, she's an Art History major, right?"

"She's smart!" Chris protested. "She has, you know, varied interests. Maybe she's just curious about how all of this works. But unless she's been snooping around my papers or hacking my watch or something, there's no way she knows about these bitcoin."

Phlox was still suspicious of Vera, and the way that she seemed to have a hold on Chris's heart after just a few days, but it seemed that Chris really believed that this was all just some sort of big coincidence. She decided that pressing the matter would only make things awkward between them, and moved on.

"So... you've discovered what this famous chicken algorithm is? Found something in your 'Intro to Comp Sci' notebook from freshman year?"

"I think so!" Chris got noticeably more excited. "Brian actually gave me the idea. He was singing Christmas songs this morning in the shower..."

Phlox had a confused expression on her face, so Chris stopped to explain. "He was really loud. I wasn't, like, in there with him or anything." He waited for affirmation from Phlox that yes, this was a perfectly normal thing, everyone gets inspiration from their roommate singing Christmas songs in the shower in early October.

Just an ordinary guy thing to do. Yet no note of affirmation was forthcoming.

"I don't know *why* he was singing Christmas songs. Or..." — he insisted, sensing the next query — "why he was carrying out a big container of soy sauce out the door. That's just, like, Brian."

"Fair enough," said Phlox. "I don't always understand my room-mate, either."

"Brian was singing that song about the Christmas presents... you know, on the first day the singer gives his true love a partridge in a pear tree, then the second two turtle doves, et cetera."

"No idea what you're talking about. I think you should sing it."

Chris's cheeks reddened. "Ha ha. It's obviously a very simple incremental algorithm. Every iteration adds one to the number. If we know the seed, we can then calculate out the full private and public keys."

"That's funny, I happen to know the incremental algorithm! Holly explained it to me before when I was asking how to generate longer numbers from a smaller value."

"Well, isn't Holly a discrete math TA? It's a really easy example for explaining algorithms, I'm not surprised. I think the chicken algorithm is just the incremental algorithm!"

"Why would Dr. Chambers call it the chicken algorithm, then? Why not just 'the incremental algorithm'?"

"Check it out!" Chris pulled out the three books of Dr. Chambers and placed them, one after the other on the coffee table in front of Phlox.

The cover of the first book, *A Friendly Introduction to Hashing Algorithms*, showed a forest scene. The moon was just barely visible, along with a large number of stars. In the center was a large tree with a kind of fruit. Pears. Nestled in a crook of the tree, barely visible, was some sort of bird — was that a partridge? Phlox knew from the depths of her elementary school memories that the partridge was the state bird of Pennsylvania. She should know what one looked like, but she just didn't see them all that often, or ever, in Pittsburgh.

A thick paperback in the middle had the title *Understanding Blockchain Transactions*. There was some sort of complex arabesque design in the center, with two birds looking across at each other. She looked closely. They looked similar to the peace doves she had seen on the banners of protesters, but with dark stripes on them. Her ornithology chops were definitely not up to par, but they certainly could be turtle doves.

The final book, *Cross-Chain Transactions: Fundamental Theories and Applications*, which Chris had shown her in the coffee shop last week, had three chickens and a fleur-de-lis in the middle, set against a deep scarlet background. Chickens... they weren't roosters... thus, they were hens! Three French hens!

"Remember I told you that the textbook was called the Chicken Book? That has to mean something. He must have called it that. At first I thought it was some sort of obscure Litecoin reference — for some reason chickens are associated with it. I don't know the details, people were weird about cryptocurrency back then. But it obviously means that the algorithm should be applied to the words in the book.

"You know how you can use words to make a seed? Like when you get a new watch? I'll bet that we can use the words in here and somehow increment the values, and we can generate a wallet. The formula for doing it is public domain and hasn't been changed in forever. We just need to figure out where to start, then take the first, second, third, words after that."

Phlox leafed through the thick book with dismay. There had to be at least a hundred thousand words there. Minimum. That was a hundred thousand different combinations of 24 words to try. And who knew if they were going to be in the right order? Or that Chris's idea was correct in the first place?

"Okay," Phlox finally said, after thinking for a few moments. "I'll grant you the fact that referencing something called the Chicken Book and the chicken algorithm seems to be more than coincidence. So it's probably some words in this book. But we're not even sure that the chicken algorithm *is* the incremental algorithm. Maybe he meant chicken dash algorithm, like, use the algorithm in the Chicken Book? And we just don't know what algorithm it is? How long would it take to check all the different possibilities of words?"

"Hmm," said Chris, opening up his laptop and bringing up his Emacs text editor. Phlox knew the name of the editor because he talked about it constantly, and Phlox found it amazing that anyone could love a text editor that much. For her own writing, she used whatever was lying around. But she did know that one of the things that Chris loved about it was that basically every function known to mankind was somewhere in it. He once showed her what the current date was in the French Republican Calendar with some minor movements of his fingers.

Chris pressed a few buttons and entered a few figures, then pressed his hands to his temples.

"Well," he said, "assuming the book has about 100,000 words — which I grant is probably an underestimate, although there are quite a few equations which take up room but not many words — and that the wallet has twenty-four words for its initializing seed — there's a total number of possible word combinations of one point six times ten to the ninety-sixth power."

"Is that... that sounds like a lot." Phlox realized she was looking down at the table. She looked up at Chris for confirmation.

"Yeah. It's a one, and a six, and ninety-five zeros after that. I don't even know what number would be called." He pressed a few keys on the computer. "Huh. An untrigintillion. Neat. Oh, and we need to make sure we get them in the right order. Let's see... 24... permutations... set size 24... hmm, so for each of those sets of words we'd need to try six point two times ten to the twenty-third power. That's only a few sextillion permutations to try for each of the untrigintillion possible word choices."

"We'd better hope that we picked the right algorithm, then. There was no starting number. Maybe he knew what the starting number would be? Were there any numbers that were special to him?"

"Maybe his birthday. Or the year he got his Ph.D. It's not like he played the lottery or anything and I could find lucky numbers amongst the lottery ticket stubs."

"Let's just try from the beginning of each of the chapters. Wait, how many chapters are there?" Phlox grabbed the book and flipped through to the end.

"Twenty-four!" she yelled excitedly. "And we need twenty-four words! It must be the first word of the first chapter, second word of the second chapter, and so on!"

"Let's try it!" Chris accepted the book from Phlox's outstretched hand. He had a program running on his laptop which could re-create a wallet given the seed, then check on the network to see the balance of bitcoin stored by it. He slowly went through the book, confirming with Phlox that he had entered the correct word after each one. He then had her look over the final list, glowing in green letters on a black background. The screen reminded Phlox of an old movie about computers, when they were strange hulking monstrosities instead of small gadgets on everybody's wrists.

Finally, Chris looked up at Phlox and smiled. "Ready?" he asked. Phlox nodded and Chris pressed the enter key.

The computer worked for a few seconds, showing undecipherable gibberish on the screen. Phlox definitely saw a "0.00000000" balance listed amongst the hieroglyphics, though.

"No dice," she said.

"No dice," Chris agreed. "But maybe he did it in reverse order, or something. Or maybe he used a zero-based indexing scheme? Or the chapter titles are counted as words?"

They spent another hour trying various combinations, but to no avail. Finally, Phlox leaned back on the couch, stretched her arms back toward the wall, and yawned dramatically.

"I just can't do this anymore," she said. "I need a break — do you mind if I go for a walk for a bit and clear my head? I feel like we're on the right path, but we're missing something."

"Yeah, I need to use the bathroom anyway. You can leave the door unlocked and just walk back in. It won't lock by itself if you don't press the button."

"Thanks," Phlox said and bounded out the door. Despite the failures of the last hour, she felt good. Maybe they weren't making progress that could be directly measured, but they were finding out lots of ways that it wasn't working. That had to count for something.

She decided to make a loop around the block. The streets were relatively full — people were out enjoying the sunshine. Along the streets were the occasional pizza box or empty beer bottle, and commonly a disgusting dark stain — mute testimony to somebody who had had more fun the night before than their stomach was able to handle. The litter and the biological results of reverse peristalsis couldn't bring her down, though. The sun was shining on her, a feeling she always enjoyed. She could even feel it on her shoulders a bit through her t-shirt.

The blocks in South Oakland were rather large. It took her about ten minutes to circle one. When she got back to Chris's house and stepped in, she was surprised to see the red hair and bare, freckled back of Vera. At first Phlox was embarrassed, thinking she had just stepped in to a very private moment between Vera and Chris. As it turned out, though, Vera just had on some sort of strapless, backless black dress which, with the dark room, drew her eyes to her exposed pale skin.

Before Chris could say a word, Vera turned around, an accusatory look in her eye.

"Oh, Chris, it's your friend," she said icily.

"Hi, it's Phlox, yeah," stammered Phlox. She knew she had no reason to be nervous, but Vera's green eyes felt like they were boring a hole right to her soul.

"I was just helping Phlox with some homework," lied Chris, but it sounded unconvincing even to Phlox. He was a horrible liar. Probably a good thing in terms of ethics and living a good life, but a bad thing right now. "She's taking a discrete math course for her 'logical thinking' gen ed. See?"

Chris picked his laptop up from the coffee table and showed her an Emacs screen filled with calculations.

Vera ignored it. "Yeah, well, I was going to go to the art museum. There's a really fabulous display of Impressionists that's only happening for another week. I was hoping you'd come with me but I guess you two are busy. Don't worry, I'll see myself out." She turned around, somewhat stiffly and formally, and headed outside.

"Vera, wait!" cried Chris and chased her through the front door. The door slammed shut behind him, and Phlox could hear low murmurs as they discussed something on the front porch of the apartment. She considered leaving, but the only way was through the front door, and she just could not bring herself to head through the gauntlet that surely awaited her on the other side.

After what seemed like an eternity, but was probably more like two minutes, Chris opened the door and came back inside. He slumped down onto the couch, looking despondent.

"So..." started Phlox, but was immediately interrupted.

"I don't want to talk about it." Chris said. He then proceeded to talk about it.

"I mean, I should be happy, right? Vera's gorgeous and cultured. Who else would wear a dress like that just to go to the museum? And I've always had a thing for redheads. And she's interested enough in me to be jealous! I mean, in high school, I would have basically considered this paradise."

"Sure..." said Phlox, and was once again interrupted.

"But I have other friends, you know. I mean, not just you. What if she thinks I'm into Brian because we're sitting around the living room one night playing cards? Is this really what I have to look forward to?"

"Well, I..." tried Phlox one more time.

"But maybe I'm not seeing things from her point of view. She stopped by, thinking that we would do something together, and I'm here with another woman. Or at least, another woman comes strolling into the house without knocking. Would I be jealous if I went to her place and one of her guy friends came walking in? Actually, I've never been to her house. I like to think that I wouldn't be jealous. But I don't know. Maybe I would be."

Phlox waited for more words, but none seemed to be forthcoming. She looked around at the darkened room — the blinds were drawn, as usual, so that there wouldn't be any glare on the computer screen.

"Nothing to be done about it now," said Phlox. She was generally pragmatic if the situation didn't involve her emotionally. "I could go for some ice cream. How about we go get some and keep working on this at my place? Holly and Violet are both there, in case Vera stops by. Plus, I'll bet a change of scenery would keep your mind off things."

"Vera would probably just think all three of you were trying to woo me," Chris said, but he did look like he wanted to get moving. He gathered the papers, books, and his laptop into his threadbare backpack and went to the door.

The sun was just starting to go down, sending long shadows across the streets, but it was still warm outside. It was a quick walk to the ice cream store, as Chris's apartment was right off of Forbes Avenue. They headed down the main street of Oakland together, past a shop announcing "Bitcoin for gold! Trade your gold for COLD, HARD CRYPTOCURRENCY!"

Surprisingly for a warm, sunny day, there were only two people in front of them in line at Joe and Bobby's Ice Cream. Less than ten minutes after leaving Chris's place, Phlox was opening the door to her own apartment, proudly holding a rocky road cone, bedecked with various additional sprinkles and cookie crumbs. Chris, to Phlox's chagrin, had picked vanilla. Given literally any other option, why would somebody pick vanilla?

They set up shop on the living room floor, Chris manning the computer, Phlox reading off words according to the variations of the simple incremental algorithm they thought up. Holly and Violet, as promised, were around, but both were working on homework in the kitchen. This meant that they were pretty quiet; generally they only said something out loud every fifteen or twenty seconds, and the volume was less than the radio turned to maximum volume. This was considered peace when the Wu sisters were around.

They had been working for only fifteen minutes when Phlox suddenly stood up, midway through double-checking some words in the Chicken Book.

"Chris — we're doing this all wrong!" she exclaimed.

"What? What do you mean?"

"The song! I should have insisted that you sing it! Then we would have realized!"

"Realized what?"

"The song doesn't increment at all! Not really! Chambers was a computer nerd like you — don't look so hurt, computer nerds run the world nowadays — he would have wanted to follow the song exactly as sung." Phlox cleared her throat and began to sing "The Twelve Days of Christmas":

On the first day of Christmas, my true love gave to me...
A partridge in a pear tree.
On the second day of Christmas, my true love gave to me...
Two turtle doves,
and a partridge in a pear tree.
On the third day of Christmas, my true love gave to me...
Three French hens,
Two turtle doves,
and a partridge in a pear tree.

"The progression is 1... 2, 1... 3, 2, 1. I don't know what you'd call it, pseudo-incremental. But I know you Comp Sci types, you always want to be exact. I feel like I know Dr. Chambers. He'd follow the song precisely."

"Okay," said Chris, "that actually makes sense. So... first word of the first chapter, second word of the second chapter, then the first word of the third chapter, et cetera?"

"Let's try it." Phlox opened the textbook and started reading off the appropriate words to Chris.

Chris entered the words and Phlox looked over his shoulder to ensure that they were correct. Just as he was about to press enter, the Wu sisters sauntered into the room.

"Hey you two!" yelled Holly. "We're going to head out for pizza, want to come?"

Chris exhaled. "No, thanks. We're working on a project. Besides, we just had ice cream."

"Have fun!" said Violet.

As the two left the building, Chris and Phlox looked at each other. "I've got a good feeling about -"

He was interrupted by Holly, right outside the door, loudly and rhetorically asking "Is that guy wheeling arund a barrel of soy sauce?" to nobody in particular.

They both rolled their eyes. Brian had apparently upped his game. Turning his attention back to the computer, Chris pressed enter and green characters filled the black screen on his laptop. Phlox stared at the last line.

TOTAL BALANCE: 10.0141391 btc

"Holy sh..." Chris said, and stopped himself. Even at this moment, the internal mom in his head was berating him for swearing.

Phlox was speechless. It was almost too much to believe it was real. Ten bitcoin, free and clear, just like he had promised... was it only last week that this had started?

"Let me run the smart contract," said Chris. "Your addresses and mine are already loaded."

He typed a few more commands in, and Phlox watched as line after line scroll past. Chris was mumbling to himself.

"Just waiting for confirmations on the Ethereum and Bitcoin networks now. Okay, looks like the code has executed on Ethereum... gas consumed, looks good. Transaction fees on Bitcoin are always so high... ugh... ehh, couple of microbits, not bad. Okay, I see it in the transaction pool. Should be official and irreversible inside the hour."

He looked up, eyes shining. They had both just become richer than they had ever dreamed.

"I had a good feeling about today," said Phlox. "I didn't want to say anything earlier and jinx it, but I bought a bottle of champagne. Sparkling wine, technically. I can't afford real cha — oh, actually, I guess now I can! But sparkling wine will do, right?"

Phlox grabbed two plastic cups from the kitchen as Chris continued to stare at the screen. She popped the cork, giggling a little as the drink foamed out. It felt almost unreal, as if she was floating on air. She didn't realize how much the specter of poverty had been haunting her soul, and it was suddenly lifted. The world was shining despite the darkness of the evening, even before she had had a sip of alcohol.

They clinked their cups together, which made a surprisingly cheap-sounding noise — amazing how much you can tell from a clink, thought Phlox — and each downed half the cup in a second. Chris's eyes were distracted by something on the screen.

"First block!" said Chris. "Our transaction is on the blockchain! Generally, it's considered absolutely secure once we're six blocks deep. Average is about ten minutes per block, so in an hour we should be in the clear."

"What are you going to tell Vera?" asked Phlox.

"Nothing yet. But she's good at getting me to tell her things. She's a great listener, which usually makes me a great talker. I hope she's not still angry at me." Chris got up and looked out the window.

"Chris, Vera seems great and all, but you just made FIVE... WHOLE... BITCOIN. You can probably go back and buy the entire town of Amsteco if you want. Now is *not* the time to be thinking about a little tiff. She'll get over it, I know."

"What if she went over to my house and I wasn't there, though? She'll think I'm —"

"Chris." Phlox said seriously, then couldn't help laughing at his frowning face. "She'll text you. She's probably just at the museum, thinking about how ridiculous your whole fight was."

Phlox realized that Chris was not nearly as giddy as she was. Finding this bitcoin meant that she was avoiding some major financial difficulties. For him, though, almost done on his journey to be a software engineer, this had just moved his life expectations from "comfortably well-off" to "rich." More important to him was keeping the girl that he was obviously crazy about. Phlox decided not to be so hard on him. That was easy when she felt like a schoolgirl the day before summer vacation who suddenly realized that *this summer will last forever.*

"So what are you going to do with your share?" asked Chris, without looking away from the window. Phlox fought the urge to tell him that Vera would not be floating down the alley to see him.

"Not sure," she replied out loud. "I mean, I had a feeling I'd get it, but it never seemed *really* real. I'm mostly interested in getting my PhD in English lit without having to, you know, eat discarded bagels from the sewer to save money. Wait, why would a bagel be in a sewer? So, uhh, yeah. How about you?"

"I guess I'm not sure either," he said. "I've wanted to be a software engineer as long as I can remember. Maybe I'll work on some open-source projects. Be a coding nomad for a while. I've always wanted to see Moonbase Prime, ever since I was in high school. I mean, pretty much everyone in the software world who grew up on science fiction wants to go to the first lunar colony."

A change shot over Chris's face, as though he has just remembered something important. "Vera's from Colorado, maybe we'll head out West..."

Phlox felt as though she were physically holding down her pupils to keep her eyes from rolling. This kind of one-track mind was fine in a nineteenth-century romance but it just felt awkward to hear it in reality.

They talked for a while about what they might do with the bitcoin, critiquing each other's plans and suggesting improvements. Chris seemed amazed that, given the opportunity to do whatever she wanted, Phlox would stay in school. Phlox seemed amazed that every single plan that Chris came up with also somehow involved doing whatever Vera wanted to do, preferably leaving the planet with her in the process.

Finally, exactly fifty-six minutes after the initial smart contract executed, Chris announced that the bitcoin was secure in their accounts. It was included in six blocks of the blockchain. Trying to move it now without their private keys would take truly immense amounts of computing power, beyond any nation-state's known abilities.

"It's official," Chris said. He flipped his wrist with a flourish, looked down at his watch, and a grin grew on his face, so wide that he looked like a cartoon character. He quickly tapped the screen a few times.

"Look," he said to Phlox, showing her his watch.

Phlox read the text from Vera: "i am so sorry :(i shouldn't say this, but i really like you and i got jealous. can i come over?" Chris had replied: "of course. see you soon."

"Nights don't get much better than this," said Chris, and started packing his papers and books into his backpack.

Phlox was just resigning herself to a night of drinking the rest of the bottle of wine alone, and fantasizing about her newfound wealth, when she heard a knock at the door. Holly must have locked herself out when she and Violet left. She was a whiz at mathematics, but also had the classic mathematics major absent-mindedness. Phlox headed down the stairs and opened the door.

To her utter surprise, it was her father. Phlox's euphoria died away instantly. Her dad had a look on his face as grim as the day he told her that her mother had died. He had obviously been in a hurry to get here — the adrenaline coursing through his veins was palpable. His eyes had a steel glint, the left corner of his lips had a twitch, and, most worryingly, his hip had a holster with a heavy-looking revolver in it.

"Phlox, I *told* you not to take my money."

"Let me give you a tip on a clue to men's characters: the man who damns money has obtained it dishonorably; the man who respects it has earned it."
-Ayn Rand, *Atlas Shrugged*

A Helping Golem?

An excerpt from an article in The Econometrician, *Volume XV, Issue 4*

In Jewish mythology, a golem is a being made from clay which, although created to protect its owner, ended up having to be destroyed after causing even more damage. However, a cryptographic golem may have just protected humanity from a great threat — colorectal cancer.

The Golem project allows people to sell their spare computing power to those who need it. Although there were previous networks which allowed large-scale problems to be tackled by idle computers, the users of these systems were not compensated, leaving only Good Samaritans joining them. When people were paid to have their spare cycles available, a computational network was formed which dwarfed any individual supercomputer or supercomputing cluster. Even better, as millions of people joined the network, the cost per cycle became incredibly cheap. Computational biologists, especially, found that this cheap source of calculation was ideal for developing drugs.

After a massive number of computations performed in parallel, analyzing correlations and simulating drug interactions, the Massive Colorectal Adenoma Drug Search (MCADS) project reported last year that it had achieved a possible breakthrough in colorectal cancer research. According to simulations, the same relatively simple cocktail of molecules was hypothesized to treat several different varieties of colorectal cancer. It did so using a novel, completely unexpected way of blocking expression of the cyclooxygenase-2 (COX-2) enzyme. Although numerous researchers had noted the correlation of overexpression of COX-2 with carcinogenesis, this was the first way to minimize its expression without causing even more dangerous side effects.

A recent Phase II trial was ended prematurely, with control group patients receiving the actual drugs, after the results were too promising to ignore. "Of the thirty-nine patients in the test group, thirty-eight showed complete or almost complete remission of their cancer within two months," said Dr. Robert Jackson, principal investigator of the MCADS study. "This is to be compared with partial remission in only four of the forty patients in the control group. It would have been unconscionable to continue treating the control group patients with the classic treatment when the results were so unambiguous."

MCADS researchers note that this drug cocktail — which will be open-sourced and is estimated to cost approximately 12 millilites per course of treatment — does not treat every type of colorectal cancer, although it is effective against over 95% of known cases. They emphasize that this drug is specifically formulated to treat colorectal cancer and should not be seen as a panacea for cancer in general. However, COX-2 overexpression is common in several kinds of cancer, and this may point to promising strategies for treating them as well.

"We could not have done this without the Golem project," states Dr. Jackson. "When I was a grad student, I would have done anything for my entire university to have the computing power now available to almost any researcher willing to pay a few millilites."

Chapter 11

In Secret Places

John rushed up the stairs to the apartment, motioning Phlox to follow him. He was clearly upset.

At the top of the stairs, Phlox could hear Chris gasp as an unknown man with a sidearm entered the living room.

"Is anyone else here, Phlox?" her dad called down to her as she ascended the stairs.

"No, it's just me and Chris," she said. "Holly's out with her sister. What's going on?"

"We need to go *now*," he said. Looking around the room, his eyes landed on the other person in the room. "You must be Chris. I'm John — Phlox's dad. You seem like a clever fellow. Clever, but dumb. Why would you post a smart contract on the Ethereum blockchain with the address of the bitcoins you were taking? Dumb, dumb, dumb."

John looked over at Phlox, still wearing her white t-shirt and jeans.

"Phlox, go through your closet and pick out something you don't ever wear. The more unlike your normal hoodie attire, the better. Chris, sorry, but you're going to have to wear this." John threw a dusty flannel shirt at him. It looked to be about a size too small for his large frame.

"Are... are..." Chris was having trouble with his words. "Are you going to kill us?"

"What?" John said, taken aback. "I'm doing my best to save

you! Which I wouldn't need to do if you had practiced a modicum
of operational security!"

Phlox came back into the room, carrying a scarlet taffeta blob
around her forearm. "I found my old prom dress, that's pretty different, right?"

"That's my girl," John said. "Put on some make-up too. The
more made-up, the better. Chris, you should put some on, too. But
you have to hurry! Don't worry if it's not perfect."

Phlox headed back to her room. At that moment, Chris's watch
buzzed, and he instinctively looked down at it.

"I'm going to need you to take the batteries out of that," said
John. "Can't risk it."

"Okay, let me text my... girlfriend... first..." said Chris.

"No can do," said John. "You need to take out the batteries now.
Maybe you can talk to her later."

"But she's coming to my place!" protested Chris. "She just
texted that she'd be there in ten minutes! And she's already angry
with me, well, she's probably angry at Phlox, she's just jealous —"

"Sorry," said John definitively, cutting off Chris's rambling.
"Take out the batteries and put on the shirt."

Trembling a bit, Chris did as he was told. As he was buttoning
up the flannel, Phlox sashayed out of her bedroom, wearing what
a high school student might think was elegant. Tight-fitting taffeta
hugged her body, with a silky, transparent outer layer making it look
a little more conservative. Ruffles and curls and bows rampaged from
her knees to a single shoulder. There were even rhinestones speckled
across her torso. Phlox had trouble wearing it without rolling her
eyes at herself. At least I shaved my legs today, she thought.

"Aww, you look beautiful, buttercup," said her dad. "Now remember, lots of make up. Whatever kind you don't normally wear.
Try to make yourself look as different as possible."

Phlox obediently headed to the bathroom to put on purple eye-
liner, bright red blush, and whatever else she could find at the bottom
of her makeup bag. She didn't know what was going on, exactly, but
her dad seemed so sure — and commanding — that it just seemed
the prudent thing to listen to him.

"When you're done in there, head to your room and get your
toiletries together," said her dad. "Along with some clothes for a

trip. Chris, I didn't know your size, but I brought some clothes for you. Got a spare toothbrush, too."

"Wait, I can't head back to my apartment?" Chris asked.

"No. First, your girlfriend will be there, and honestly you're lucky I'm bringing you along. We're not going to bring her as well. Second, we've got to get out of here A - S - A - F - P. Phlox! You almost done?"

Phlox came out of the bathroom, a vision in smudged cherry-red lipstick and green eyeshadow. It seemed like a fog suddenly lifted from her brain and she wondered why she was doing all of this just based on her dad's commands. Innate filial piety? And what did he mean by *his* money?

"Dad, what's the situation here? The money belongs to an old professor here at Pitt, who has been dead for, like, fifteen years."

"Seventeen years next month," said John. "Boating accident. I remember it well. It was hell getting enough teeth taken out so that they'd be sure to be found by the forensic analysts."

"You're Sam Chambers?" asked Chris incredulously.

"Yup. At least, I used to be. You didn't think it was a bit of a coincidence that Phlox's apartment — which I helped you to get, daisy, remember? — just so happened to be where Dr. Chambers lived?"

"I didn't think that Dr. Chambers would be covered in tattoos," said Chris. "But then again I never could find any good pictures of him."

"Pictures of me are hard to come by," agreed John, "and age has done a good job of masking my features for people who did know me then. Not to mention, most people don't see a former professor underneath all these god-awful tattoos. But look, we need to go. There's a reason I faked my own death; it wasn't just to experience the joy of multiple tooth extraction. And you two are mixed up in it now."

Phlox and Chris looked at each other. If they weren't so nervous, they probably would have laughed at their costumes. Chris looked like a lumberjack wearing his younger brother's clothes and Phlox like she was heading to the Spring Formal at Clown College. As it was, though, they didn't say anything. They grabbed their backpacks —

Phlox's filled with clothes, Chris's with his computer, textbooks, and paper — and headed down the stairs.

Outside, John's old car was waiting in front of a fire hydrant. Even with the reduced number of cars owned by students these days, finding an actual parking spot in South Oakland within a kilometer or so of one's apartment during the school year was about as likely as winning the lottery. There was a backpack in the back seat, and an old cassette player on the front seat, but other than that the car seemed pristine, albeit shabby. The faux leather seats were ripped, and there were even what appeared to be cigarette burns in a few places.

"We'll be safer once we get out of the city," explained John as they piled in — Chris riding shotgun, Phlox sitting behind him in the back seat. "Red light cameras they installed in Pittsburgh, ehh, about a decade ago, also have face and body recognition algorithms programmed into them. Not a hundred percent sure how effective they are but I figure that it can't hurt to do what we can to throw them off the scent with that makeup. Outside of the city, though, we should be good. Feds can barely afford to keep robbers off the road, let alone install face recognition cameras."

As they headed down Atwood Street to the main thoroughfare out of Oakland, Forbes Avenue, Phlox thought she could hear sirens. Shifting her body to look behind her, causing squeaks from the sixty-year old seats, she noticed several police cars pulling up in front of her house. Hearing the squeaks, Chris looked back as well, and gasped.

"Just in time," said John, "just in time. You two have no idea how close you cut it. Or what a world of hurt you would be in right now if I hadn't come."

"It's not illegal!" Chris said. "I mean, even if you are still alive, it's found money. *Virginia v. Hiltschmetz*! *Jones v. Gupta*! All the cases agree. It was up to you to keep your key secure and you hid it in your book like some sort of riddle out of a children's book."

"All true," agreed John. "But it makes about fuck-all of difference to those folks."

Traffic seemed heavy for this late in the evening on a Sunday. They had stopped at a red light. Outside, Phlox saw Violet and Holly walking down the sidewalk with a few other assorted men and women. Violet looked over briefly, but Phlox was pretty sure that she didn't recognize her in the dark with that amount of make-up on. Even if she did, she probably wouldn't have believed her eyes that Phlox ever would wear that much make-up or a ball gown.

It seemed like they had been stopped for a while. Phlox looked down the road to see police had set up a roadblock. They were shining flashlights into each car before waving it on. Occasionally, they would question the driver for a minute or two.

"Oh jeez," said Chris.

"It's okay," said John. "We're just not going to drive out of Oakland right now."

He pulled down one of the innumerable side roads and miraculously found a parking space after only a few minutes of searching. He got out of the car, motioning for the others to stay put, and deposited all of their backpacks in the trunk.

"Here we are, just a man and his son escorting his sister to a date," said John. "They're definitely not going to expect us to try to leave on foot. We have to make them think we're already gone; we'll come back and get the car tomorrow. Oakland's a major thruway, they're not going to keep it closed tomorrow for rush hour, even to find you. Wouldn't matter if you were serial killers, the cars have to get through, right?

"We'll hide out somewhere this evening. Remember, no spending money, though, not even for the vending machines. There's basically no Monero support here in the city. Using some of your bitcoin or litecoin is pretty much the same as shouting 'here I am.' As long as we don't draw attention to ourselves, it should be easy to sneak out in the morning along with the rest of the commuters."

"I have an idea," said Chris. "There's an abandoned church two blocks down. There were some punks who used to live there in some sort of anarchist commune a few years ago. I remember that there's a cellar door through the back that takes you down into a kind of living room."

"You hung out with punks?" asked Phlox, somewhat impressed in spite of herself. It was pretty unlike the Chris she knew.

"Freshman year, I had an identity crisis," explained Chris. "Don't act like you never had one."

"I guess I was kind of goth for a while," admitted Phlox, "but I never wanted to wear any make-up. Kind of ironic I'm reminiscing about that tonight, I suppose."

"Let's try it," said John.

The church itself was easy to find. It was somewhat imposing among the rows of cheap student housing, but not exactly grand. Made of yellow brick, its walls were speckled with graffiti. The lot itself was overgrown and Phlox saw numerous beer bottles and other detritus in the front yard. The main door was barred shut and a NO TRESPASSING sign was conspicuously posted on it. Several windows, plain and stained glass, were arranged in a line across the front, all of which had cracks or missing fragments.

Chris led them around the side of the church, where the grass was trampled down a bit. The trail seemed to lead right to the rear entrance.

I hope nobody else has started living here, thought Phlox.

Fortunately, though, the trail swerved away from the back of the church and onto another street. It was probably just being used as a shortcut between the two streets by students heading to class. Chris pushed on through the knee-high grass towards the cellar door, dodging the occasional plastic bottle, with Phlox and John following.

The cellar door was starting to rot away, but it still provided a good seal. It looked as though it hadn't been opened — or even looked at — in years. A few candy bar wrappers were on top of it. A heavy-looking combination lock was attached to some sort of deadbolt mechanism. Phlox felt her heart sink before she realized that the mechanism itself was no longer attached to the rest of the door.

Chris pulled the door open and tentatively went down the stairs. He stooped and looked around, then, satisfied, motioned for the other two to come down. Phlox brushed away cobwebs as she descended.

They found themselves in a large semi-finished basement. It was partially lit by the light from streetlights filtering through small, high, dust-covered windows. Along the far wall was a bookshelf with heavy-looking books, next to some stairs heading up. Near it was an old-fashioned desk with an unplugged green lamp on it, along with a teetering pile of what appeared to be the same book. All of this looked to be original, from the time the church was originally occupied.

Closer to the stairs they had come down were the remains of the punk living quarters. Three couches, none matching in size, shape, or color, clustered around a coffee table. A Bible was holding up one of the legs to steady the table, which seemed a bit sacriligeous to Phlox. A makeshift set of shelves, made of planks of wood and concrete cinder blocks, took up most of the wall nearest them. There were a few personal care products on it, combs and half-empty bottles of toothpaste and the like, along with a significant number of empty beer bottles. Cheap beer, Phlox noticed, but she didn't expect punks in an anarchist commune to be beer snobs.

In the corner were two smaller rooms. One seemed to be simply used for storage, and was filled with moldering cardboard boxes. The other was a surprisingly sizable bathroom, with a toilet, sink, and even a shower. Water was dripping from the faucet, and the toilet even looked serviceable after flushing it a few times.

Everything was covered in a thick shroud of dust. It looked like decades since anyone had last been here, although they knew that it had been only a few years at most.

"This looks like a good place to lie low for the night," said John. "They'll have to assume that we got away or that you all are at a friend's house." He half-heartedly dusted off one of couches and slumped down in it. The other two followed his lead.

"Alright, I need some answers — who are *they*, exactly?" asked Chris. "The police? The government?"

"I wish I could give you an exact answer to that," said John. "They're definitely affiliated with the government, or have friends there. Whoever they are, they're the reason that I went to such lengths to disappear seventeen years ago. I saw that you have my textbooks — wonder where the royalties are going to now? You know that I was researching cryptocurrency. I was an early adopter, mining back when you could use a regular CPU, not even a GPU..."

He stopped as Phlox had a far-off look in her eyes, although Chris was still looking at him expectantly. To Phlox, it was just her dad telling boring technical details, but to Chris, one of his idols had just come back from the dead to lecture him on one of his favorite topics.

"Anyway," continued John, "I joined the faculty here at Pitt just as Bitcoin was starting to go parabolic, right before people stopped trusting paper money. Remember the curse 'may you live in interesting times?' Those were some *really* interesting times. You have no idea how much everything was hacked — there used to be places called credit reporting agencies that gathered and reported economic data on virtually everyone in the United States operating aboveboard —"

"Wait — that was legal?" Chris asked. "There were no data protections?"

"Ha! Legal, yes. Ethical, no. And when they were inevitably hacked —"

"I'm sorry," interrupted Chris, "I'm just having trouble wrapping my mind around this. People signed up to be monitored?"

"No, no, no," answered John. "These companies basically spied on everyone in the United States, and if you wanted a loan, a bank would ask them about your economic history."

"That sounds like some sort of dystopian science-fiction novel," said Chris.

"People didn't care much about security back then," explained John. "I mean, most people kept their most private email unencrypted on a large company's server. Strange times. One of these credit reporting companies got hacked, leaked the entire database full of credit card numbers and personal information — salary, savings, previous loans, that kind of thing — out onto the web."

"Why would it matter if people got their credit card numbers?" asked Phlox. "I mean, I give five people my litecoin address every day. Were they worried that people would send them money?"

"Oh lilac," said John, "this number acted as both your private and public key. Anyone who had it could charge your account money, but to spend money you had to give companies that number. And how much you were charged wasn't really controlled by you. If you wanted to buy something, you basically gave the company access to your account and asked them, 'could you take a hundred dollars from my account?' and trusted them not to take a thousand. It was a pretty common occurrence for a restaurant to charge you thirty dollars for a twenty-dollar diner, for example, especially if they thought you had had too much to drink and wouldn't remember to check the next morning. Individual banks spent tens of millions of dollars — that's dozens and dozens of bitcoin — annually on algorithms which would try to detect fraudulent use."

"*Seriously?*" Phlox was incredulous. "Dad, I hate to say it, but your generation was not very bright."

"Don't I know it," said John. "But I was trying to move us away from that. The entire financial system then was held together with chewing gum and duct tape. There were quite a few people trying to let the world know, but we were mostly ignored until the Big Hack. In those days, people would often just let companies store their credit card numbers online for convenience. Not long after the credit reporting agency got hacked, several large e-commerce sites all got hacked in a single week, which threw the fraud detection algorithms into a tizzy. You're too young to remember this, but for a few days, virtually everyone in the country spent all their free time canceling their credit cards and trying to get new ones. Of course, in most cases this had to be done by an actual person at the bank, and there just weren't enough employees to keep up with demand. My memories of the time include everyone I knew walking around with a phone to their ear, on hold with a customer service representative, waiting to get new cards."

Phlox and Chris both shook their heads, feeling like they were listening to a scary story around a campfire, but one in which all of the characters, for some unexplained reason, had had lobotomies.

John continued his story. "There were quite a few people in those days who talked about 'hyperbitcoinization' — a time hyperinflation would cause more and more people to transition to cryptocurrency. Surprisingly to many of us, the catalyst for hyperbitcoinization wasn't inflation — inflation hasn't been great, but not too bad the last twenty years — but the fact that nobody with regular money could *spend* it. Banks couldn't trust anyone trying to withdraw money, credit cards were worthless when the numbers were easier to find online than the weather, and businesses started putting up roadblocks to buying after half their orders were retroactively canceled because someone had stolen the card they had used to buy things with. The economy of the country was starting to grind to a halt.

"But people looked around and saw that people were buying things with bitcoin — and to a lesser extent litecoin, ether, monero, a couple of other currencies — and there was a flood of people who joined in. The people like me, who had felt like voices screaming in the wilderness, were amazed. I remember those days, thinking that the revolution had finally come, people were waking up to the benefits of using bitcoin.

"There were those hurt by this move to cryptocurrency, though. People who didn't want others to have access to the same alternatives that they had. People who found themselves holding piles of suddenly worthless fiat."

"Hold on," said Chris, "I want to hear this but I also really, really need to use the bathroom."

Chris got up and headed to the bathroom, closing the door somewhat dramatically.

"I guess I owe you thanks, Dad," said Phlox. "How did you know to come and get us?"

"Because your friend Chris is too trusting," replied her dad. "He put up a smart contract on the Ethereum network that would fairly split the bitcoin in a specific account between you and him. All well and good, but remember that anything you do on the Ethereum network is copied to the blockchain and anybody who can view the blockchain can also view the contracts on it."

"Oh right! It's a distributed blockchain, so it's distributed to anyone running an Ethereum node."

"Exactly. Unlike Chris, I am not trusting, especially after you said you were going to go after that bitcoin. I had my own system which inspected the Bitcoin and Ethereum blockchains, as well as checking that nothing on major blockchains referenced any of the addresses where I still have bitcoin. Entirely local, entirely passive, basically untraceable. It just sat there watching to see if anybody did anything with the bitcoin. Chris broadcast out to whomever was listening that he was on the trail for it. And last time somebody came looking for my bitcoin, soon after, they tried to kill me."

They heard the flush of the toilet and some washing of hands, and Chris came out running his wet hands through his hair.

"There's no soap," he said, "so hopefully nobody here is a germophobe. Other than that, though, everything seems to work."

"Glad to hear it," said John. "As I was saying, around this time the economy was starting to seize up. Nobody trusted anything. I remember hearing reports on the news, go out and shop, use up any paper money you have... it was surreal. The president at that time was absolutely clueless about what was going on and how to stop it. There weren't really any senators or mayors or anyone who knew, either.

"A bunch of us cryptocurrency folk got out ahead of it and tried to explain, and for the first time people really listened. I was one of the people on television, on the internet, explaining how to transition over to this new economy. And that made me enemies.

"One of my friends, Mitesh, who actually helped me set up my first mining rig years before, dropped dead. Heart attack, supposedly. It struck me as odd, though — he was only forty-five, worked out every morning, ate healthily, even occasionally ran marathons.

"I was sad, but not suspicious... until another... ahh... friend, Jane, who was an Ethereum expert, told me that she had seen people following her home to her apartment. The same people, over and over again. She bought a pistol — and she was not the type to do so, kind of a hippie type. I mean, she was a Democratic Socialist before they became one of the big political parties. She told me that if anything happened to her, it would not be an accident. Two days later, her car went off the Birmingham Bridge."

Chris and Phlox stared at John. Chris, because he probably still couldn't believe that Dr. Chambers was alive; Phlox, because she couldn't believe her mild-mannered dad had been involved in some sort of plot where people were murdered.

"Did you know Satoshi Nakomoto? Was he one of the ones who was killed?" asked Chris.

John smiled. "No. Nobody knows who he is. I wish I had met him. Or maybe I did but never knew it. He's a mysterious figure, for sure."

"Even at this point, I didn't really think that they were going to come after me. These had to be coincidences. Then, one morning, I noticed two men in suits watching me. I wandered down the streets of South Oakland, even going through some short cuts between buildings that nobody ever took besides me and a few students, and they were definitely keeping an eye on me. I went back to my place, grabbed some clothes and whatnot, then hopped in my car and just started driving. I had no idea what I was going to do, but I knew that if I stuck around Pittsburgh I'd meet the same fate as Mitesh and Jane.

"Whoever was watching me didn't do a great job. I'm not going to pretend that I was a criminal mastermind and gave them the slip thanks to my unparalleled action-movie skills. I did escape, but just because I got lucky. Eventually, I ended up in Amsteco. I'd never been there, and it didn't seem like a place I would ever go, which of course made it a perfect place to go.

"I figured I would stay in the Towne Motel for a few nights. I actually had a bundle of paper money on me, and they seemed desperate for cash. Most people only had credit cards, and the banks were still having trouble getting their systems back online. Sitting down in that cheap hotel room, I figured out my plan. I would head out of America, to Costa Rica. I have a smattering of Spanish from an undergraduate study abroad in Tegucigulpa. If these people were going to leave the country to look for me, they were probably going to head there, or at least somewhere in Honduras. But while I was studying at the university there, I remembered hearing from some of my fellow students how nice Costa Rica was, so it seemed as good a destination as any.

"Of course, things didn't turn out that way. I had taken to getting my dinner at Rocky's Diner, right next door to the Towne Motel. Of course, I was trying to stay a bit underground, but a man's got to eat. There was a beautiful waitress there with striking blue eyes — Phlox's mom. We ended up talking every night, late into the night, over coffee and cherry pie. After a few nights of that, I couldn't imagine leaving her if I didn't have to.

"The more I thought about it, the more I thought that Amsteco would be a great place to hide. Hide in plain sight, as it were, less than an hour from Pittsburgh, but in a run-down steel town that everybody else was leaving. I still don't know what your mom was doing there, Phlox, or why she stayed, but I'm glad she did.

"It was a whirlwind romance. She knew who I really was, and she didn't care. We really did love each other. She brought me to the dentist who pulled out my teeth. She helped me arrange the wreck of 'my' boat and scatter 'my' remains. She even helped pick out all of the tattoos that I got immediately afterwards. I still remember telling the tattoo artist, 'just put on whatever you can do the fastest.' Ended up being lots of things that teenagers think are cool, and then regret as soon as they turn twenty."

"So that's why you have such cheesy tattoos!" exclaimed Phlox. "I thought you just didn't have any taste."

John smiled. "If I had any taste, I wouldn't have gotten any tattoos. But I was more concerned about blending in in Amsteco than in impressing my four-year-old adopted daughter.

"Alright," he concluded. "I think that's it for story time. I'm beat."

"Wait!" cried out Chris. "I've got some questions..."

"Not now — let's just try to get a good night's sleep." concluded John. "I'm sure you're exhausted. I know I am. Then again, I've got thirty years or so on you two. We've got a long car ride ahead of us tomorrow, there will be plenty of time to talk."

Despite those thirty extra years, Phlox felt like she could barely keep her eyes open. With three couches, they each were looking forward to a relatively comfortable night. They had all just settled down, using some of their extra clothes as blankets and the sides of the couches as pillows, when Phlox heard a door creak open upstairs, and a woman's voice call out:

"Chris?"

"Am I a God at hand, saith the Lord, and not a God afar off? Can any hide himself in secret places that I shall not see him? saith the Lord."
-The Holy Bible, King James Version, Jeremiah 23:23-24

High Up in the Trillion-Aire

An excerpt from an article in The Econometrician, *Volume XVI, Issue 21*

It will come as no surprise to anyone that the rise of cryptocurrency has fattened the accounts of many individuals, especially those who came in early to the boom. What may surprise people is exactly how lopsided the distribution of major cryptocurrencies such as Bitcoin and Litecoin are. In fact, they may have already given birth to the world's first trillionaire, measured in United States Federal Reserve Tokens.

According to research done by *The Econometrician*, at least one address (1Cdey7yCMMNckZW1AiBHwbggxJCCJXdNCk) which belongs to an individual person (not an exchange or corporation) contains a total of over 310,000 bitcoin. This is the second-highest amount of bitcoin to be stored in one address, after Satoshi's Hoard, the 980,000 bitcoin held in the account of the mysterious originator of Bitcoin, Satoshi Nakomoto.

Blockchain analysis by a firm hired by this newspaper has correlated several Ethereum and Litecoin addresses with this account. Together, these place this person's total net worth in cryptocurrency at the equivalent of slightly over one trillion FRTs. Of course, there may be corresponding debts which reduce the actual wealth of this person to well below this value, but conversely, this person may hold other kinds of wealth such as stocks, traditional (non-blockchain-enumerated) bonds, or real estate.

Although our staff were able to correlate all of these accounts, they were unable to determine with any precision who this mysterious trillionaire might be. This is in stark contrast to earlier "rich lists" which magazines compiled. In those days, it was simple to know who would be on it, but estimating their net worth was difficult. Conversely, it is now relatively easy to know how much this entity is worth, but difficult to know who it is.

Whoever it may be, they are emblematic of a trend of increasing wealth centralization. One common measure of inequality used by economists is the Gini coefficient. Under this index, an entirely communal society — where everybody has the exact same net worth — would have a Gini coefficient of 0. A dictatorship where only one person has all of the net worth would be considered 1. The current Gini coefficient of the Bitcoin ecosystem is 0.81, of Ethereum 0.792, and of Litecoin 0.769. Any of these values dwarf the Gini values of the economy of any country in the world twenty years ago.

While undoubtedly raising the standard of living for almost all people in the world, serious questions are being raised by policy analysts about how this massive inequality will impact our economy and way of life. There are those who argue that this will allow greater power over politicians by a smaller and smaller class of "crypto-elite."

Others note that the level of technological change and economic growth have been unprecedented over the last several years, and that the wealth of these "crypto-barons" has been trickling down. No matter which side you side with, however, the fact remains that the economy of the world is changing dramatically compared to the last century.

Chapter 12

The First Time As Tragedy

It took Phlox only a moment to recognize the voice as belonging to Vera. It took her a moment longer to realize that there should be no way that Vera would know that they are there, and oh yeah, that they were all currently on the run from people trying to kill them. She shot an angry glance, through mascara-smudged eyes, at Chris. Chris opened his mouth to defend himself.

Before anything else could happen, John put one finger up to his lips in the universal "be quiet" motion, and with his other hand, covered Chris's mouth. He grabbed his backpack, pointed at the others' backpacks, then made another motion towards the door. The intent was clear — grab their stuff and get out of here. With the amount of disturbed dust, it was going to be impossible to deny that somebody was there. But if all of their clothes were gone, at least Vera — or whoever she was with — might think that it was just some random squatters that she had scared off.

They could hear the floorboards above them squeak as Vera wandered through the empty pews. With John in the lead, they quietly crept across the dirty concrete floor to the stairs leading to the cellar door. It was impossible to see if anybody was on the other side, Phlox knew. There was no other option, though. They would have to hope that whoever was looking for them didn't know about this back door.

John carefully and slowly reached out a hand toward the door, groping in the darkness and finding what he was looking for. Slowly twisting the handle, he opened the door and stepped up. Bracing himself for the inevitable capture, he looked around the lot behind the church.

Just overgrown grass and litter.

He motioned for Phlox and Chris to follow him, Phlox carefully closing the door behind her. With the ambient light filtering in through the open door, it would be obvious to whoever went in the basement that there was a door there. Without it, people might have to spend valuable minutes looking for how someone could get out. Those minutes might be the difference between getting away and getting caught.

They left via the back lot, hugging the sad-looking city trees that ringed it. The streetlights didn't cast much light back here, but you wouldn't need night vision goggles to see somebody. Looking down at the red taffeta, which kept making crinkly noises which seemed to echo in her ears, Phlox regretted not wearing a camouflage dress to prom. She actually had considered it, back when she was a Rebellious High School Student, but it had seemed like too much work. None of the stores around Amsteco had them off the rack, and she hadn't really felt like ordering one or making one herself.

Finding themselves in the far south of South Oakland, they looked down over the cliff which led to Greenfield. A single road, barely wide enough for two lanes, clung to its side.

"Look," whispered Phlox, "the police don't have a checkpoint here. They must have just focused on the main roads."

"We're lucky that nobody can afford good police coverage nowadays," said John. "If this happened when I was a kid, the cops would have covered that house, they'd have barricaded all of Oakland, and we'd all be in jail right now. One of the benefits of the collapse of federal authority, I guess."

"So the question is, how do we get back to the car?" said Chris.

John and Phlox shot him a look.

"I think the question really is, how did your girlfriend know to look for us in an abandoned church?" asked Phlox.

"We'll discuss this later," said John. "I'll bring the car back around here. I've gone seventeen years without being recognized, I think I can last another seventeen minutes. Keep an eye out, I'll pull up in front of that bush."

Phlox and Chris hid in a narrow alleyway between two of the houses. Both houses looked as though they had long been split into multiple apartments for students to rent out. Their porches were covered in signs that read "students live here" to anyone familiar with the species: empty pizza boxes, disgusting couches, and empty bottles of beer. Luckily, both also seemed to be devoid of light. The students living there had either called it an early night (early for students, that is) or were out somewhere else.

"So how *did* Vera know where we were, Chris?" said Phlox, once her dad was safely away.

"I... I texted her." admitted Chris. "While I was in the bathroom. I didn't say where we were, though, just that I was sorry I couldn't meet up tonight due to an emergency."

"Chris..." said Phlox, slowly. "We... are... on... the... run. There are people out there who want to kill us because of that bitcoin. They are allied with the police, who apparently have a manhunt which has shut down half of Oakland looking for us. And you go texting someone because you just can't imagine a life where her brows are furrowed and her green eyes angry when she thinks of you."

"I didn't say where we were!" protested Chris.

"Be quiet," said Phlox. "The last thing we need is somebody to come out from one of these apartments, angry about someone waking them up. Or worse, calling the police because of it."

They stood there quietly for a few more minutes, Phlox letting Chris know through her body language that she was quite irritated. John's car pulled up, and Chris and Phlox jumped in, as if it were just an EthShare car coming to take them out for an event.

Down they rode, anxiously scanning for signs of police presence on the back road out of Oakland. But there wasn't even a sign of another car the entire ride down the hill. For the second time tonight, they had been able to escape through an unnoticed rear exit.

They drove for another twenty minutes without a word, all of them too filled with nervous energy to speak, constantly looking at other cars on the road and waiting for a siren to start up. Every shadow looked like a sniper, every abandoned car in someone's yard a tank, every house a barracks ready to open up with soldiers. But they drove on, these images only in their minds and not a reflection of reality.

The clock on the dash showed that it was 1:00 AM as they crossed the Monongahela River, which marked the southern boundary of the city. As they headed out of Pittsburgh, into the northern reaches of Baldwin, Phlox looked back at the Cathedral of Learning, still just barely visible above the greenish-grey hills.

"I guess I won't be seeing the Cathedral anytime soon," she said.

"Probably not," agreed her dad.

"So, Chris," John continued, "want to tell us how your girlfriend tracked us down?"

"I have no idea!" protested Chris, who seemed like he had been hoping that everybody had just forgotten why they were driving instead of sleeping right now. "I admit it, I texted her. I shouldn't have, but I did."

John stared at the road and said nothing, which compelled Chris to say more.

"I'm sorry. I really am. I just... I really felt like I was starting to love her." In the backseat, Phlox rolled her eyes. "Okay, I mean, I know we only met, but she's beautiful. She's exactly what I ever wanted in a woman." Phlox was not sure if it was medically safe for her eyes to roll back any further, so she tried her best to freeze them in place. "And she was so interested in everything I had to say, we could talk for hours and she'd just listen to me..."

"A good listener, huh?" John said. "Yeah. Most prostitutes are."

"Prostitute?" asked Phlox and Chris simultaneously.

"Maybe a spy, maybe an agent, but probably just some prostitute they hired to keep an eye on you. I am sure she's not the Art History major you think she is. Phlox, what does this Vera look like?"

"Bright red hair," said Phlox, "lots of freckles, really... voluptuous, I guess you could say. And prone to wearing dresses, at least every time I've seen her."

"Mmm-hmm," said John. "And Chris, ever do any Internet searches for 'curvaceous redheads' or 'models with freckles'?"

Chris didn't reply, but his angry silence spoke volumes.

"My guess," said John, "is that whoever these people were, they knew exactly the type of woman you'd fall for, at least physically. Maybe mentally, too, depending on how much they researched you.

Even if they didn't, it's easy enough to make a guy think that you think he's amazing. You've already shown that you don't really do security well, so they were probably tapping your home internet connection for a while. After that, it would be pretty simple to find someone who was your own personal Aphrodite, pay her a few millilites a day to keep her eye on you, maybe put a tracking device on your watch... DAMN IT."

Phlox took her eyes off the road momentarily to look at her father. He had the look of someone cursing himself for a fool.

"Alright, dahlia, you mind driving for a bit?" John asked. It was the kind of question that was really a statement. Her dad pulled over to the shoulder of the road and they switched places. Phlox moved the seat forward and the wheel down, and started the car back up.

"Of course," John said, once they were safely driving again. "You turned on your watch in the bathroom. It doesn't even matter that you texted her. She knew you were there, and may not have noticed that you didn't mention your location in the text. Her job is to keep an eye on you and she was going to lose her bounty. But that means that we have to get rid of your watch. Now."

Chris looked as though somebody had just suggested that they throw his baby out the window.

"Look," explained John, "did you ever leave your watch in a place that Vera had physical access to it? If so, it's probably as good as compromised. And that means that we're trackable. And *that* means that — absolute best case scenario — you're spending several years trying to convince a jury that you didn't actually steal those bitcoins. Worst case scenario, you're tortured to death until you reveal your private key."

Chris went pale. He fiddled with the clasp, took off the watch, and handed it John, his hands shaking. John examined it, turning it over, running hands over the smooth sides of it.

"Doesn't seem to be anything physical. Must be software. Probably a key-logger on there, as well, so you won't want to re-use any of your passwords. Thank goodness watches come with built-in hardware wallets nowadays. You never directly enter the real private key, so we should be safe as long as we can re-construct it with your passphrase.

"My first thought was to try to wipe it, but they're probably expecting that. It's been years since I've had to deal with this kind of stuff, maybe whatever malware they installed could survive a formatting of the disk. Or even display a fake GUI which makes it seem like it's being formatted. Can't really trust anything at this point, not unless I got an oscilloscope and started looking at the voltages directly..."

Phlox had started to zone out. Her dad always was a bit absent-minded and it seemed like he would be rambling for a bit longer. She suddenly realized that his habit of producing monologues instead of dialogues probably came from his days lecturing college classes. So many of her dad's little quirks were starting make sense after tonight's revelations.

"Phlox!" John said — to Phlox's mind completely out of nowhere, although she had a vague, almost-subconscious feeling that he'd been trying to get her attention for a while — "pull over, we need gas."

Off to the right of the road, there was an old gas station with its lights on. A store open so late at night was a relative rarity in the countryside, which had depopulated by quite a bit, especially in the last decade. Phlox remembered hearing about hyperurbanization in her Intro to Urban Studies class freshman year. This is where in many developing countries, cities became the only places that were economically viable to live. The United States had been rapidly progressing towards that stage, as her home town of Amsteco — not large enough to be a city, especially after the steel mills shut down — bore witness.

The gas station being here was even more odd since gasoline-powered cars were, if not exactly uncommon, definitely outnumbered by electric cars. Her dad had always seemed like a relic to her for refusing to buy cars created more recently than twenty or thirty years ago. He insisted that he didn't trust all of the electronics in the newer ones.

Pulling into the gas station, Phlox looked up at the brightly-lit sign advertising MUELLER BROS. SERVICE STATION, along with the price of fuels. There were two grades of gasoline — advertised at 98.2 and 112.3 micromons per gallon for regular and premium, respectively — and diesel for 89.8 micromons. Below the sign listing the prices was another sign, this one written by hand. It informed customers that LITECOIN TRANSACTIONS MUST BE PROCESSED AT COUNTER.

A tired-looking old man sat in a small building behind bullet-proof glass, surrounded by cheap candy, soda, and probably some illegal stimulants under the counter that he'd sell for the right price. If the cashier wasn't automated away by a short Ethereum script and an auto-dispenser, it was probably because he was providing some service that the owners did not want publicly known. The cashier's elbow was resting on the shelf, hand pressed against a scraggly white beard, propping his head up. He didn't seem to be doing anything, just staring at the few cars going by on the state highway. Most of the cars drove with the eerie politeness and grace that marked them as self-driving, so he didn't even get the occasional stimulus of a honking horn. Phlox wondered how one could survive being that bored.

There were no other cars, but a self-driving tractor-trailer was in front of them at one of the pumps marked DIESEL. The truck was tethered to the side of the pump, the nozzle noisily pushing fuel into the tank. Phlox was a bit surprised — most long-haul trucks were not only self-driving but electric nowadays, bought and controlled via smart contracts on Ethereum, with only the occasional human help during loading and unloading. This was one of the old-fashioned self-drivers, first generation. John was unperturbed. He got out of the car, told Phlox to fill it up with regular, and nonchalantly walked over to the truck.

After a bit of fiddling, Phlox figured out how to open the gas tank and operate the pump. Once again she had to convert a few millilites to millimons, as she did not really want to head up to the counter and talk to the creepy old man behind the glass. She was more than willing to pay a few nanolites in transaction fees for that. Suddenly she realized that she was using her Litecoin address and this transaction would soon be broadcast over the blockchain. She panicked but didn't want to show it — besides, her dad did tell her to fill it up, right? How else was she supposed to do that if she couldn't use the money that she had?

Looking over at the truck, Phlox saw that the faded letters on the back were advertising "Bubbly-Bub Soda," which she had never heard of. Maybe it was a local brand? She wasn't much of a soda drinker, so maybe it was huge and she was culturally illiterate in terms of soda. Or "pop", as most of her friends in Amsteco and Pittsburgh called it. Her dad had always called it "soda" so that's how she learned it, but she always felt like a little bit of an outsider when she called it that.

John seemed to inspect the back of the truck for a minute, then went over to talk to the scary cashier as the gas continued to dispense. The cashier's demeanor and body language were at first very suspicious, but quickly turned to somewhat-less-suspicious. He was probably right to be suspicious of a heavily-tattooed man coming up to talk to him in the middle of the night. There wasn't nearly as much law presence on the highways, or even small towns, as in the cities, nowadays. More and more government was localized, and news stories of people being kidnapped, or worse, while driving long distances were becoming increasingly common.

Phlox realized that the cashier was looking past her dad and directly at her, and she was suddenly very conscious of the fact that she was still wearing her red taffeta prom dress, although she had washed off the smudged make-up — or at least most of it — during a bathroom break an hour or so back. She could only imagine what was going through the cashier's mind as he looked at a skinny girl fueling a car from the last century in the middle of the night, dressed up as if she were going to the Homecoming Gala.

Her dad and the cashier went behind the truck together, John pointing up to the top of it and explaining something, who was nodding along. Phlox couldn't hear the words, but her dad sounded like he was convincing the cashier of something — and quite effectively. Chris was still in the car, staring off into the distance, a much younger version of the cashier behind the counter before John has spoken to him.

Finally, the pump turned itself off, just as John and the cashier were shaking hands and apparently wishing each other well. The truck, with its larger fuel tank, was still being filled, and the cashier went over to inspect the progress on the gas pump. John walked back over to his own car as Phlox was messing with the gas pump to ensure that it had in fact turned off and registered her payment. Why the heck were these things so complicated? Maybe that's why nobody in Pittsburgh used gas-powered vehicles anymore.

"Let's roll," her dad said to her. "I can drive for a while." He stretched his arms above his head. "This has been a long night. But no rest for the weary."

As they entered the car, Chris, resting comfortably in the back, looked at them both quizzically. After the doors closed, John finally felt comfortable explaining what happened.

"That truck's heading to Louisville, Tennessee, heading down 64. Deadheading after a trip to lovely Charleston, West Virginia."

"What's deadheading?" asked Chris.

"Driving empty. Look how high up the trailer is, nothing is loaded. It just delivered a truckload of soda a few miles up the road near Charleston, but isn't taking anything back. Which means that it is unlikely to be hassled at any weigh stations, not that there are that many around these days, but still. Good for us."

"Wait, why good for us?" asked Phlox.

"Because it is now also carrying Chris's watch on his bumper. If Vera — or whoever she is working with — is still tracking his watch, they are going to go to Tennessee, which is most definitively where we are not going. I told the cashier that I used to drive commercial — which is true, thank goodness for all those odd jobs I did — and noticed that the rear fairing was developing a crack. I was just friendly, told him he should report it, because it was hurting the fuel efficiency. Cashiers get rewarded for reporting things like that. So I probably just made him a millilite or so.

"Then of course, he wanted to chat a bit. Being a gas station cashier is a lonely job, especially when there aren't many human-driven vehicles out there. Self-driving trucks absolutely gutted the trucking industry, lot of friends of mine — and his — got hurt by that. Used to be trucking meant a hard but good job. That guy's 68 years old, can you believe it? He used to be an owner-operator when he was in his twenties, so he knows that lowered fuel efficiency from a rear fairing means that the company is losing money. While we were talking and he wasn't paying attention to my hands, I stuck the watch on the back of the truck."

Phlox realized that at some point during her dad's explanation, they had started driving again, curving through the mountainous West Virginia landscape.

They took turns sleeping and driving, with no adventures other than wondering what kinds of snacks might be available at the next gas station, until the afternoon of the next day.

Awakening from a deep sleep — or at least as deep a sleep as one could have in the backseat of a fifty-year old car bumping down the poorly-maintained highways of the twenty-first century United States — Phlox looked out the window to see that they had just come to a stop in a sparsely-populated parking lot. She could see a few pickup trucks, all with significant rust issues, and a dumpster labeled "PRIVATE PROPERTY OF AMARYLLIS MOTEL — CUSTOMER USE ONLY!" A sign — which looked like it might not look too shabby when lit up at night, but during the day just looked sad — advertised the motel with rates "as low as 890 micromons / night!"

"Welcome to Amaryllis, South Carolina, rose," said her dad, even in these circumstances unable to resist continuing his dad-joke of calling her by the name of different flowers. "Our home away from home for a while. Not sure how long, exactly. Long enough for us to get a good night's sleep and plan our next move."

There didn't seem to be much to the town of Amaryllis. Besides the motel, there were a few houses all with yards which, to her Pittsburgh eyes, seemed incredibly large. The houses themselves were not new, but they looked generally well-maintained. In front of one of the larger houses, Phlox could see two little blonde girls, about kindergarten age, manning a lemonade stand, advertising the drink for 5 micromons per glass. Across the street from the hotel was a small strip mall with a convenience store, some sort of hunting supply store, a Chinese buffet, and a hair salon. The street itself was only two lanes; it was probably a main thoroughfare a hundred years ago, but now only the occasional pickup or tractor-trailed rattled over it.

"The name of the town seemed like a good omen, at least for you," John said to Phlox. "And I figure Chris can pick up some new clothes and a new watch while we're here."

At the mention of his name, Chris, who had been quietly snoring in the front passenger seat, awoke. He looked around groggily, looked as thought he was going to ask a question, then apparently realized that he was not quite awake enough to articulate one.

"Let's all get separate rooms, my treat," John said. "I think we all deserve some alone time. Not that you all weren't lovely company."

They grabbed their backpacks from the trunk of the car and headed into the lobby of the hotel. It looked like pictures Phlox had seen from the era of the Vietnam War. Weird colors, shag carpeting, wood paneling on the walls. A sleepy-looking, heavyset woman with old-fashioned hair that was not just grey, but entirely white, was standing behind the counter, playing with her watch. She had an irritated expression on her face. Her clothes looked as though they had once been fashionable, making their current lack of fashion all the more blatant.

"Welcome to the Amaryllis Motel," she said, looking up from the watch, her cheery voice belying her depressing looks. "Can I help you?"

"We need three rooms for the night," said John. "And do you have any specials if we're going to be around for a few days?"

"Y'all here for the sewage festival?"

"Uhh... yeah," said John, wondering what a sewage festival could possibly be.

"Ten percent discount for that," said the woman, "but we don't do long-term rates unless you're here at least a week. And much as I love my town, I don't know if there's enough to keep you here for that long after the convention's over."

"It does seem like a nice town, but you're right, we do have to get back to work afterwards. Boss won't be happy if we don't show up."

"So... three days, right?" she said, smiling. John nodded in affirmation. The lady started pecking out commands on the point-of-sale terminal. "Let's see... 890 micromons, three days, three rooms, convention discount... that will be 7.209 millimons."

John unlocked his watch and initiated a transaction, placing it against the QR code on the front of the terminal. A few seconds later, his watch chirped a tune, and a moment after that, the terminal made a similar noise. The woman behind the counter looked pleased at herself for making a sale.

"Rooms 104, 105, and 106 are on your account, and EthHotel is showing me that the reservations are active on the network. They're on the first floor — turn right going out the door and you can't miss them. Check-out time is 10:00 AM your last morning. Do you need your private keys printed out?"

"Sure," said John, "sometimes I head out without my watch. All my moments are senior moments anymore."

"I hear you," said the cashier, smiling. "Just last week I put a carton of milk in the cupboard. Didn't find out until the next day. Brand new carton, too. That was 50 micromons well spent." She printed out a set of three small papers with QR codes on them. "Just hold these up to the reader on the door and it should be just like using your watch. It's a bit old-school, but it works."

As they exited back into the warm late afternoon air, Phlox inwardly thanked her dad that they were fleeing south and not north. She had replaced her prom dress with jeans and a lime-green t-shirt which was just slightly too small on her. After all, she tried to get clothes which she didn't wear much, and shirts that didn't fit were certainly in that category. Now, though, it seemed as if it were ever-so-slightly cutting the circulation in her torso and she was itching — literally and figuratively — to put on something a bit looser.

After making some brief plans to meet up later that evening, if they were awake, they all retired to their separate rooms, each putting a DO NOT DISTURB sign on the door. Phlox wished she could add a few exclamation points to the end of it.

She entered the room and looked around. An old television was resting on a scuffed chest of drawers, with a laminated sheet next to it explaining which number corresponded with which channel. The queen-sized bed was similarly serviceable, but not ornate, and had definitely seen better days. A nightstand next to the bed did not match the chest of drawers. The lamp and alarm clock on it looked relatively new. A window next to the door looked out on the parking lot. Phlox closed the blinds to block any prying eyes.

After unpacking a bit, she headed into the door on her right, entering a clean but spartan bathroom. She pulled off the too-tight t-shirt, feeling much better now that it wasn't constricting the circulation around her upper arms. She started up the shower and to her surprise, it was almost immediately hot. Things weren't exactly luxurious, but they weren't all bad at the Amaryllis Motel!

The shower felt amazing. Phlox wasn't the type to bathe religiously every day, but over the last twenty-four hours she'd slathered makeup on her face, rested on a dusty couch whose previous owner was an anarchist commune, and napped off and on in a car. After getting all of that road grime off of her, she felt clean for the first time since leaving her apartment in Pittsburgh.

After drying off — and finding a large t-shirt and jogging pants in her backpack to use for pajamas — she got under the covers and looked at the alarm clock. The digital readout read 5:25 PM. She considered reading for a little bit — she was pretty sure that she had some of her Russian Literature books in the front pocket of her book bag, and maybe a few others. Just then a wave of sleepiness hit, apparently brought on by the feeling of a blanket on top of her. She realized that her hair was still wet and would probably look a little odd in the morning, but she was too tired to do anything about it. Closing her eyes, she was out within seconds.

"Hegel remarks somewhere that all great world-historic facts and personages appear, so to speak, twice. He forgot to add: the first time as tragedy, the second time as farce."
-Karl Marx, *The Eighteenth Brumaire of Louis Bonaparte*

Not Worth The Paper It's Not Printed On

An excerpt from an article in The Econometrician, *Volume XIX, Issue 21*

Last week's announcement that the government of South Sudan was shutting down its paper money presses, marking the last country in Africa to do so, certainly seemed like a momentous day. In the capital city of Juba, children played on the streets with the equivalent of hundreds of millibits worth of paper currency, all marked with a purple "VOID" message making it no longer legal tender. Estimates are that at least 63% of economic transactions in the country were already being handled exclusively by cryptocurrency, and the announcement came as a surprise to very few people.

Your correspondent visited Malakal, South Sudan's "second city," and found that virtually every store and kiosk accepted a variety of cryptocurrencies directly, mostly Litecoin and Monero, although there was a strong showing of several other currencies. The majority of shopkeepers thought that the shuttering of the money presses would be a non-event for them. "Who uses paper money these days?" asks Gabriel Kir, who runs a small fruit stand near Upper Nile University. "Perhaps brigands or the elderly who do not understand the modern world. But even my grandfather, who is eighty years old, buys his *kisra* bread with litecoin."

This leaves only a handful of nations who have refused to join the modern cryptocurrency-backed economic system, including Myanmar, the Democratic People's Republic of Korea, and East Timor. Even in those countries, of course, much economic activity is recorded on various blockchains. It just may be technically illegal to do so.

Numismatists may groan as their favorite collectors' item is no longer being produced, but as economists, we must greet the end of paper money with delight. Analyzing economic data has become exponentially easier. The danger of hyperinflation is now almost nil, although to be fair, the danger of deflation has increased significantly. Cross-border exchange of paper currency was a complex process, even when digitized, which often took days instead of minutes. Paper money was often used to support the most heinous of crimes, and was subject to counterfeiting on a vast scale.

In retrospect, it is amazing how long it took for nations to reduce their dependency on such an outmoded system of currency. Indeed, it has been over thirty years since the first major cryptocurrency, Bitcoin, entered the world stage. On the other hand, old habits die hard. History is full of examples of politicians refusing to bow to inevitable change, often with disastrous results. We should be thankful that it took only a few decades for nations to come around to an obviously superior monetary system.

Chapter 13

Eternal Lie

Phlox awoke in darkness. Well, almost darkness — a little artificial light crept out from under the blinds, and the alarm clock on the nightstand sent out some of its own. It read 4:45 AM. She realized that she had slept through the night, almost eleven hours straight. She didn't even remember dreaming.

She felt around on the nightstand for her watch, and soon found it and opened it up. This was her normal morning routine and she did it unthinkingly. Her dad assured her that modern messaging protocols were generally secure, unless somebody had physical access to the device. These weren't the days of telnet when nobody secured data over the network.

Scrolling through her new messages, she felt a pang of nostalgia seeing that she had received several from Holly, all on a theme. Holly's messages contained about as many exclamation points as her voice.

"Phlox! Where are you? The police were over and kept asking about you!"

"Phlox! Are you OK? I'm worried! I miss you!"

"Phlox! PLEASE MESSAGE ME! LET ME KNOW YOU'RE ALIVE!"

For a few moments, Phlox considered sending back a quick missive, just to let Holly know that she wasn't dead in a ditch somewhere. But only for a few moments. The less information that anyone else had about her whereabouts, the better. Besides, Holly, goody-two-shoes that she was, would probably take any information about Phlox right to the police to help in their "search" for her.

Phlox did miss Holly. And Violet, confused freshman that she was. Even Lawrence, a bit. It was just weird thinking that she might not see any of them ever again. It hadn't really sunk in, but it was starting to do so. Just a little bit, just around the edges, but she could feel the pain creeping in, and she saw it getting worse.

To keep her mind off of it, Phlox looked through her backpack to see if she had any good books worth reading, but nothing grabbed her. Lawrence's copy of *Atlas Shrugged*, Dostoevsky's *The Idiot*, *The Collected Poems of Alexander Pushkin*... why didn't she think to throw in something light-hearted? She didn't feel like dealing with anything serious at this point.

Could she get breakfast? She vaguely remembered that the hotel advertised a continental breakfast starting at 6:00 AM, but she still had a ways to go before then. Wandering out into the parking lot, still wearing jogging pants and a too-large t-shirt, she found an all-in-one vending machine. Pressing a few buttons and putting her watch up to the its payment scanner, she sent over a few micromons for two protein bars — one chocolate, one vanilla — and some watery-looking coffee.

Phlox sat down on the curb of the parking lot, unwrapped the chocolate protein bar, and drank some of the coffee. Yeah, definitely watery. Looking out at the dark road, entirely barren of vehicles at this hour, she wondered what she could do when her brain did not want to read.

That's when she remembered the television in the room. She had never been a big fan of TV, at least not in the last ten years or so. When she was a kid, though, she loved watching old television shows after her dad had gone to bed. Black and white shows, from her grandparents' or great-grandparents' time. The world on the television seemed like such a different age, full of positivity and hope. It felt, in a weird sort of way, sacred. But mostly it felt exciting since she wasn't supposed to be up that late.

She went back into to her room and turned on the old TV. Flicking through the channels, she found them to be not nearly as exciting as the late-night television she remembered from her youth. A few cartoons... some commercials selling objects she wasn't sure anyone would ever actually want (a painting of a fish that could recognize people walking by and calling out their names, a pizza cutter which could analyze your pizza-cutting skills and suggest improvements via an app, a toilet which doubled as a cryptocurrency miner, with excess heat being used to warm up the seat)... an old police drama. She finally gave up and watched the local 5 o'clock news, which was just starting. She spent a few seconds admiring the chiseled jaw of one of the reporters, and the looks of the generically blonde woman sitting next to him. Both had hair that looked like it would stay in place even if they were sitting in a Category 5 hurricane.

"Troubling news out of Tennessee today," said the TV anchorman. "Sheriff's deputies are searching for clues related to possible terrorism outside of Louisville. Local affiliate station WX9B has the details." At this point, the imagery on the scene switched away from the well-coiffed man to the Bubbly-Bub Soda truck that they had seen at the gas station, illuminated by streetlights. It was stopped on the side of a highway, with several police cars, lights flashing, behind it. In the foreground, an African-American woman, as professionally attractive as the two news anchors and wearing a green business suit, was looking somberly into the camera.

"Bubbly-Bub soda is a Louisville institution, known to many here not only for their seven delicious flavors, but also the company's volunteer work and sponsoring of various baseball teams," the woman said. "Little did the neighbors know that one of their trucks was apparently being used by radical anarchists and terrorists. Police say that they received an anonymous tip that equipment was hidden on this truck to jam the metropolitan area data networks in such a way that may have caused all Bitcoin and Litecoin transactions to be impossible."

The TV screen filled up with the face of a mustachioed old man wearing a police uniform. A chevron at the bottom of the screen announced him as "Sheriff Rex Slate."

"We have taken several suspects into custody and questioned numerous persons of interest. There does not seem to be any imminent danger to any resident of Louisville. Your transactions are safe and we foresee no interruption to them. We want to thank whoever provided the anonymous tip, as well as remind everyone to remain vigilant. If you see something, say something."

The original anchorman was back on screen, hair still perfectly in place, and continued his monologue. "In local news, the Amaryllis Sewage Festival starts today..."

Phlox, who had been about halfway done eating the second protein bar, felt that her jaw had dropped at some point and this realization made her also drop the remaining bar off the side of the bed. She picked it up off the floor, closed her jaw (which surprisingly, was a conscious decision) and went over to her dad's room. There were no lights on that she could see, but she didn't care.

A few knocks and she heard some fumbling behind the door. Her bleary-eyed dad opened the door. Phlox started to talk before he could say anything.

"Dad! Remember the truck you put Chris's watch on last night? I just saw it on the news!"

"Calm down, come inside."

John's room was spartan — there was some sort of horror book by H.P. Lovecraft on the table, and the bed sheets were slightly rumpled, but other than that there did not seem to be a single sign other than his actual presence that somebody was staying here. Phlox sat on a cushioned chair, which did not have a counterpart in her own room. She explained what she saw on the news earlier.

To her surprise, John looked relieved. "On balance, this is actually good news," he explained. "Let's think through it. They now know for sure that Chris escaped their little trap in Pittsburgh, and they know that we were near Charleston. I assume they'll question the cashier, and know that we three were together, and the approximate make and model of our car. I can't imagine that he would have thought to write down our license plate or anything. Still, we should trade in the car as soon as we can. You used Litecoin at the pump, but you converted to moneroj first, right?" Phlox nodded. "We should assume, then, that they'll be able to do some forensic analysis on Litecoin transactions and trace it to you. That's not a certainty, but let's assume it for now."

"All of that seems... not good."

"Well, sure, it's not *ideal*. And in retrospect, I should have given you my watch to use. But this is a game of information, and they've actually given us more information than we've given them. We now know that they were tracking Chris's watch. We know what they did to get it. We know that our little trap worked and we might be able to do something similar again in the future. We know that they are most likely *not* tracking your watch, or they would have been here already. That's all really good. We should probably get rid of your watch, though, just in case they find a way. I'm not up on the latest zero-day exploits. I should have thought of all of this sooner. Guess I'm getting rusty."

Phlox wordlessly started taking the battery out of her watch, while John continued thinking through the ramifications of the truck's "arrest."

"I think our best bet is actually to stay here, lay low for a while. The fewer transactions we make, the better. They're also probably going to assume that we are heading as far away as we can. It would feel psychologically safer. We're checked in here under alternate names, as well. Thank goodness that I made a few fake IDs when Ethereum-based identification services were first getting big."

"Wait, what's my name?" asked Phlox.

"Wanda Cuturpa. I'm Chester Hammock, and Chris is Jack Thistledop."

"Wanda Cuturpa?" Phlox looked at her hands. Were these the hands of someone named *Wanda Cuturpa*?

Realizing that Phlox was not a huge fan of the name, her dad tried to explain. "Long story, but I couldn't just give people arbitrary names. Early on, there was a bug on some identity services that allowed names with certain hashes to be created without proper identification. I took advantage of that and some number-crunching to create false identities just in case I needed them. I tried to make names that at least looked somewhat reasonable. If memory serves, most of the names that would have worked were things like Mxlr Plrk and the like. These alternate egos have been doing some things over the last few years on an automated basis. They should look like any other person here in Amaryllis for the Sewage Festival."

"So I guess we're just going to hang out here for now?"

"Sure. Just blend in, go to bed early, sleep late. The second part, at least, shouldn't be a hard part for you." Her dad smiled.

Phlox laughed. "I guess not. Although I'm wide-awake now. I slept for eleven hours!"

"Well, it's almost time for breakfast, if you want to join me. We'll let Chris sleep in a bit longer. We were up late last night."

"We? What were you two doing?"

"Neither of could get to sleep, so we went over to the Chinese buffet across the street. Really good sesame tofu, by the way, you should try it. He's not a bad kid. I was kind of harsh on him yesterday, but in my defense, he did almost cause you two to get arrested... or worse. He just didn't realize what he was getting into, which makes sense. I didn't either, I guess.

"We talked for a long time about the early days of cryptocurrency. Kind of weird to think how long ago it was, and how out of the game I am. I've been keeping up with developments, but there's only so much one can do. And each year in that world is like a decade in any other field, so I must seem like Gauss or Darwin freshly arisen from the grave to him. Sad that people are still tracking me down even when I'm in my heavenly home."

Phlox's expression grew grave and she looked right into her father's eyes. "Dad? Why *are* they after you? Or at least why do you think they're after you?"

John looked crestfallen. "I wish I could give you a solid answer, tulip. I really do. But I only have theories. My first guess was that it was revenge. When cryptocurrencies took over the world, there were a lot of people who lost a lot of money. I was one of the key instigators, from their point of view, in bringing people away from fiat money — that is, paper money backed by the government.

"But revenge doesn't keep people motivated for almost twenty years. At least not at this level. My other guess is that they want to destroy the crypto-economy, or at least control it like they used to control the fiat economy. I'm not sure why they would think that getting me would help them to do that, though.

"My final guess — and the one I personally think is most likely to be true — is that they're just after my money. Maybe they don't have any ideological dog in this fight. They just want what I have."

"For ten bitcoin, they'd do all this, or, I guess, a little over ten?" She found herself saying. Chris's precision had rubbed off on her a bit, apparently. "That's enough for a person or two to live in luxury, but..."

John laughed. "Oh Phlox! Not the ten bitcoin you found! I was just mining that for a contest I was going to do for the book. First person to figure it out would have gotten all that had been mined to that address. So the longer it took for someone to find it, the bigger the prize got. Oh man, I was so excited for that contest. Made it all super-top-secret, hid some hints in my apartment to get into the flavor of it... oh, good memories. But no, they don't care about that.

"Spread out over a few accounts, I've got around 11,000 bitcoin. Not to mention significant amounts of moneroj, some lites, and ether. Probably a few coins floating around on other chains that I've forgotten about."

Phlox's jaw dropped for the second time this morning. She had gotten used to the fact that her dad used to be a professor — after all, despite the silly tattoos and blue-collar looks, he had always seemed smart to her. To suddenly realize that her dad — the man who couldn't hold down a job as a store clerk — was one of the richest people in the United States was, to put it mildly, difficult to believe.

"I didn't want you to know," explained her dad, "I'd seen too many kids ruined by their parents' wealth, and I certainly didn't get into cryptocurrency to get wealthy. I didn't even *want* to be wealthy. I never met a happy rich person, and I met quite a few back when I was a professor.

"I decided that I'd just help you behind the scenes. Didn't you ever wonder how you got that apartment so cheap? And how you ended up in the same place that I used to live? I knew the landlord — still the same old Italian guy as when I lived there, although of course he didn't recognize me. I talked to him for you, said I wanted to help out my daughter, said I'd give him a little bit of extra on top of the rent each month but not to let you know. Not to mention that leaving it sit was a better choice from an operational security standpoint. I emptied a few of my alternate Bitcoin wallets that nobody knew about to moneroj and have just been mostly living on that. Do you have any idea how *boring* most jobs are? Just couldn't force myself to do it every day, especially when I could just dip into the savings."

Phlox found herself angry at her dad. "You've been helping me out behind the scenes? I thought that I was doing all of this hard work! And now you tell me that you've been pulling strings for me this whole time?"

"You were doing it on your own, buttercup. I was just trying to help out a little."

"I wish you would have told me! I thought I was independent and strong... and capable... but now you're telling me that someone was behind the curtains helping me along. This is on top of the fact that over the last forty-eight hours, I discovered that my dad is some kind of mega-rich cryptocurrency researcher instead of the guy who never seemed to hold on to a job for more than a few weeks. So you can imagine that I'm feeling a little betrayed right now!"

"Phlox, I was just trying to help. Do you know how rough the world is out there? It's not like when I was a kid..." John trailed off, not knowing what to say.

"Dad, I understand that you were trying to help. I really do. But I had an image of myself — that even though I was born in a blue-collar family, in a decaying old steel town, I was able to get to University and support myself. But with lots of hard work, I did it. Me.

"Now that image has just been destroyed, or at least damaged. And even worse, it's happening now, when suddenly I don't have my friends to talk to, and we're on the run from some sort of shadowy agency who is working with police in multiple states. Can you see why I might be a little, you know, emotionally fragile and upset?"

John looked at the floor. "You're right. I'm sorry, Phlox. I should have been upfront with you."

Phlox gave her dad a long hug. He did mean well, and she knew it.

"One more question," said Phlox. "Why do you keep saying 'moneroj' instead of 'monero?'"

"Because that's the correct pluralization!" her dad said. "It's how you pluralize words in Esperanto, and monero is the Esperanto word for 'coin.' Just because the rest of the world Americanizes it doesn't mean that I have to, as well."

"Oh," said Phlox. Apparently she had hit a sore spot.

"Anyway," said John, "I don't know about you but all of this truth-telling and light etymology has given me an appetite. Want to head over to the lobby for breakfast?"

Her earlier vending machine meal had left her filled up, but Phlox was in the mood for some more coffee. Hopefully better than the stuff that she had gotten earlier. She actually wanted to spend a little bit more time talking this whole situation out, but her dad never had been any good at that kind of talk. An apology and a hug — and he did seem remorseful — was going to be all she could get out of him for now.

The sun seemed to be just coming up over the slight hills to the east, not quite enough to light the way by itself, but there were some streetlights running. Plus, of course, the light coming from inside the lobby. As they entered, Phlox noticed the same older woman that was there last night was still behind the counter. She did seem to be wearing a different outfit, though, a loud purple blouse that she definitely would have remembered. The lady smiled at them as they entered.

A small buffet service had been brought out and placed against the wall, and Phlox noticed that there was a small alcove — not quite another room — that had some tables. Apparently the lobby doubled as the cafeteria. There wasn't much of a variety of foods — a selection of cereals, some danishes and muffins individually wrapped in cellophane, a few pieces of fruit. There was, however, what looked to be home-brewed coffee, some hot water and tea bags, and a selection of juices. Phlox poured herself some coffee while her dad loaded up on danishes, an apple, and some tea. As nobody else was there, they were able to pick what they both presumed to be the choicest table, right next to the east-facing window, so they could watch the sun rise.

"So what's our plan for the day?" asked Phlox.

"Maybe we'll head to this sewage festival everybody's so excited about. At some point I want to swap out our car, something as different as possible from the one I have now. I'm probably going to do that myself, though. They must have gotten some sort of details from the gas station attendant about our car, and one thing he'd certainly remember is that there was a younger woman wearing a dress with me. But mostly we're going to just lay low."

"Well, luckily I have some books in my bag. Or I can acquaint myself with the television stations here, pick up some local flavor."

"That's my girl. It's probably going to be boring for a while, so you should be prepared for that. We're just killing time for now. Oh, speaking of killing, if you see Chris, don't make fun of his clothes. I think he's a bit sensitive about them."

As if on cue, Chris came in the door of the lobby. Despite her father's warning, Phlox almost burst out laughing. Chris had always looked like the consummate nerd, with his Trotsky-esque glasses and his t-shirts which almost invariably had some sort of inside computer science joke or reference. Things like 'there are 10 kinds of people in the world — those who know binary and those who do not.'

This morning, though, he had on a woodland camouflage t-shirt with a silhouette picture of a buck with a target drawn on it. In bright orange letters, it read "I'D RATHER BE HUNTING." His pants were also camouflage. A bright orange jacket was hanging loosely off his large frame. The pince-nez glasses remained.

Chris grabbed some corn flakes and milk, poured himself some coffee, and sat down at the table with Phlox and John. Phlox smiled but kept her thoughts to herself.

"Don't say anything," said Chris. "The hunting supply store was the only place that was open last night, unless I wanted to dress myself in empty potato chip bags from the convenience store. Not to mention, I could say some things about the fashion statement that was your dress yesterday, Phlox."

Phlox continued her silence, worried that if she opened her mouth the slightest bit, a torrent of snark would come out. Chris ate a few spoonfuls of corn flakes and stared at Phlox, daring her to say something.

John interrupted the silent showdown between the two.

"Here's the plan for today. I'm going to head out for a new car. Phlox, you should get a new watch at some point today. There are a few for sale over at the convenience store. Nothing fancy, but they'll give you some way to continue to function in the economy. Other than that, just hang out in your rooms, watch TV, read, whatever. Don't check your messages, definitely don't respond to any messages... actually, just try to stay off your watch unless you need to make a purchase.

"On that note, I gave you both some centimons last night. Don't use anything but moneroj out here, even if you have the option. This isn't Pittsburgh, you'll stick out like a sore thumb if you ask to use your lites. It will make you memorable, which is exactly what we don't want. It will also just make it that much easier to track you, although swapping watches should make their job at least a little more difficult.

"So... I'll be gone a few hours. We'll head out somewhere besides the buffet for lunch. Wouldn't make sense to make ourselves too known by showing up at the same restaurant too often. Although I guess that's how I met Phlox's mom, so it's not always a bad plan."

They finished up their breakfast, chatting amiably, and everyone headed back to their rooms. All of them felt like having some alone time. Phlox found that she just couldn't concentrate on any of her books, which was a novelty to her. Usually reading was her go-to method of relaxation. She found that she had had a kind of mental crash — her brain just refused to focus. Finding a few reruns of shows she remembered watching as a kid, she settled under the blankets and turned off her mind for a while.

The next few days passed slowly, for both Phlox and Chris. They read and watched television, or occasionally played gin rummy or canasta using some packs of cards Phlox bought from the convenience store. Phlox had to teach Chris how to play canasta, but all they had was time. John, who had long been used to killing time, did not seem nearly as put out by their little layover. He wasn't really sure where to go to next, or if there even was a "next." Perhaps the best bet was to just settle down in Amaryllis just like he had settled down in Amsteco.

On the morning of the third day, Phlox knocked on her dad's door.

"Come in," she heard, muffled. The door wasn't locked and she let herself in.

Her dad was lying on his bed, reading the thick collection of Lovecraft stories. Phlox suddenly got a flashback to when she was young, maybe seven years old, watching her dad read on the porch swing in the late afternoon. She remembered thinking how boring his books must be, so thick and with so few pictures. She wondered then if she would like long, boring books without pictures when she got old. Obviously, she did.

John put the book down on the nightstand, sticking a scrap piece of paper to mark his place. He had always thought that fancy bookmarks were the silliest use of money that one could imagine, the ultimate Veblen good. People bought them to show off, not to actually store one's place in a book. He had informed Phlox of this many times when she was growing up, many more times than she had ever needed to hear, in her opinion.

When she was younger, Phlox thought that this hatred of expensive bookmarks was because he was cheap, or just poor. She knew that her family wasn't rich growing up, but it didn't bother her; it was just the way things were. Some people were rich, and some were poor, and some were in the middle. Sure, she would have liked to have been rich, but being upset about it would be like being upset that the Monongahela River was wet.

Now that she knew that her dad was sitting on more than a fortune's worth of bitcoin — at least several hundred fortunes, she reckoned — her memories were shaded by the fact that her dad had been playing a part. It was a part into which he had sunk his whole soul, but it was still a part. He had been play-acting at being poor. She saw why he did it, but still felt a little bit of... resentment? Some feeling she wasn't quite sure of. It was as though he had been faking being like her.

"What's up, sunflower?" asked her dad, and Phlox realized that she had been lost in thought.

"I..." start Phlox, then realized she wasn't exactly sure what she wanted to say. "I wanted to hear you talk about Mom." She realized after saying it that it was not what she wanted to talk about. She wanted to know why he stuck around Amstexo, why he hid his money all of this time, why he didn't flee the country, why he stayed and raised Phlox... but all of this was proximal to his feelings about her mom.

John sat up and looked deep into Phlox's blue eyes. "Your mother was wonderful, Phlox. I fell in love with her about two seconds after she poured me my first coffee. She was nothing like anyone I'd ever met before."

"That's all really generic, though, Dad. What made you give up your entire life for her? And for me? You could have gone to Tahiti or Monaco or wherever. You had the money — I mean, you still have the money — and it probably would have been safer for you. Ninety percent of the people in Amsteco would give their right arm to get out, and there you were coming in. I'm glad you did it, of course, but I don't understand it."

Sighing, John rubbed the bridge of his nose. "I don't know if I *can* explain it. I was never an English lit major like you, remember. Computer science professors aren't really known for eloquence.

"Your mom didn't really know who I was. At all. Even so, from the very first, she treated me like I was the funniest person in the world, the smartest person in the world, just the apple of her eye. Even with all that, she was never, you know, fawning over me. She just seemed interested in me as a person. See, now that I'm saying this, it sounds like she was just stroking my ego — but that wasn't it at all."

John adjusted his body so that he still sitting on the bed, but also leaning against the wall, as if he needed the extra support to keep him upright through this emotional talk. Phlox sat down on the chair across from him.

"All I can say is that I felt a connection with her that I had never felt before. As though we belonged together, even before I was able to consciously admit it. It seemed *right*. And once I moved in, and we got married, I thought that this is it, I was going to be happy and safe for the rest of my life. And I didn't need to go to Tahiti to do it. Your mom and I did a really thorough job of 'killing' Sam Chambers and creating John Tseretelli, and for seventeen years nobody questioned the official story.

"When that bastard driver killed her, I didn't know what to do with myself. But I knew what I had to do with you. You were my responsibility, and I knew the safest thing to do was just stay where we were. And I did. I tried to give you as many advantages as I could without letting you know the real story and putting you in danger.

"But you were my purpose, Phlox. I felt that, in a way, my life was over, except in the sense that I could help you start out yours. All of the research I had done, the money I had made, all of it seemed empty compared to doing what I could to help you grow up. And if I'm being honest, looking at you and what you've accomplished, I have to say I did a pretty good job."

Phlox felt like she was going to cry. Emotions were washing over her like waves. But she held back. Hugging her dad, a few tears escaped, but only a few.

John's watch buzzed angrily.

"That's weird," he said, "I didn't think anybody knew this number."

He unlocked the watch and stared at the screen for a few moments. He looked up from his watch silently, ashen-faced, staring into the distance.

"Dad? What's wrong?" asked Phlox, concerned.

"Remember my friend Mitesh? Fellow cryptocurrency miner who died of a heart attack?"

"Sure. He's one of the reasons you went into hiding in the first place."

"Well, he just messaged me."

"It was of this place that Abdul Alhazred the mad poet dreamed on the night before he sang his unexplainable couplet:
'That is not dead which can eternal lie,
And with strange aeons even death may die.' "
-H.P. Lovecraft, *The Nameless City*

Go Register, Young Man

An excerpt from an article in The Econometrician, *Volume IV, Issue 9*

A common problem for developing countries historically has been the lack of property registration of real estate. A business owner may want to put up his building as collateral, for example, but not be able to prove to the bank that he or she is the rightful owner. Scams, where people sold property to which they did not own the rights, were common. Even in the United States, rarely considered a 'developing country', virtually all buyers of real estate, until recently, bought 'title insurance' — a protection against the possibility that somebody else could claim all or part of one's property.

This problem is rapidly becoming one for the history books. Traditional title insurance companies in the United States are facing the same problem that travel agents faced in the last century — their profession has been outsourced and can now be easily handled by individual consumers. By registering property on the blockchain, using one of several compatible dapps ("distributed applications") currently running on Ethereum, buyers and sellers can rest assured that the property that they think they own is actually owned by them. Expensive lawsuits and title research have given way to a quick check of the blockchain.

Expanding the number of people who have legitimate claim to the property on which they live has had a massive impact on the economies of countries that have moved their title registration to the blockchain. While this has been less noticeable in the United States, the nations of Central America have shown a dramatic uptick in their gross domestic product which economists have almost unanimously attributed to more people both owning property and being able to borrow against it. While a few have called it a bubble or a 'sugar rush,' the consensus amongst both traditional economists and crypto-economists is that this is actually leading to a more stable economy for all of these countries.

There is now talk of implementing automatic enforcement and payment of property taxes, property transfer and exploration, transfer of mineral rights and royalties, and other real estate-related matters on the blockchain. Registration is merely the first step on the way to a better path to dealing with the complexities of real estate ownership.

Chapter 14

Nothing Behind Me

"Are you sure it's him and not somebody playing a trick on you?" asked Phlox.

"Hard to be a hundred percent certain," said John, "but it's signed with his private key. And it reads like him. If it's not Mitesh, it's a pretty good mimic."

"What did he say?"

Unclasping his watch and handing it over to Phlox, John got up and started pacing around the room. Phlox read:

" 'John' — Great job hiding all these years... I thought you were the only one of us who had actually died... but now it looks like you're getting sloppy, because I found you... and if I can find you, they can, too... you've got to get out of the country and meet me where we always said we would go. -Mitesh"

She handed back the watch to her dad without a word. "Mitesh always was a big fan of ellipses. I made fun of him for it constantly. It was funny, because he could have been a copy editor — he'd take one look at my papers and spot the grammatical issues immediately. Then in his messages, there was never a single period where three would do. It was always stream-of-consciousness rambling. Just like this message."

"Where did you always say that you should go?" asked Phlox.

"No idea. I don't remember us ever talking about leaving Pittsburgh. It was — still is — the place to be for cryptocurrency research."

"Can't you just message him back and ask him to, you know, clarify a bit?"

"Nope. Sent one-way. No address to reply to. He's right, though. If he found us, others can. I just wish I knew where he was, so I could figure out which direction to start driving."

"So I should start packing? And let Chris know?"

"Yeah. Let's meet back here when you're done and I'll think about what to do in the meantime."

Phlox left the room and headed out into the bright, sunny day. Despite it being the middle of October, the weather in South Carolina was beautiful. Even this early in the season, most Pittsburgh days were overcast embodiments of living greyness. The fields around Amaryllis looked like a movie, sunshine soaking into the pores of the houses, the streets, the grass.

Putting these capital-R Romantic images to rest in the back of her mind, Phlox knocked on Chris's door. He opened the door quickly, so quickly that she wondered if he had been waiting for her. But then she realized that he had been sitting in a chair right up against the door. He had probably heard her approach.

"Hey, Phlox. What's going on?"

"We've got to get going. Not sure where yet, but —" she slipped into a bad imitation of a spy — "our position's been compromised. Dad got a message from a friend. Looks like we're leaving the United States, I think."

"Wait, what? I have to tell my parents... or at least my mom."

"You know, you're an adult now. You don't have to tell her every single time you flee the country."

"Ha," Chris said flatly. "I do want to let her know that I'm safe in case the police come to the house asking about me. My dad probably wouldn't care, but she would."

"Let's wait until we're safely away. I'm also ignoring messages from my friends now."

"Okay, fine, she is a bit controlling anyways. Give me a few minutes to get ready, though. We've had more free time than we've ever had in our lives the last few days and I still wasn't able to keep my room clean."

Phlox smiled and sighed. "Well, here we go again, fugitives. I guess I'm never going to know, now."

"Know what?" asked Chris.

"What the heck your roommate was doing with all of that soy sauce. Seriously, it's still bothering me."

Chris laughed and turned around. Phlox caught a glimpse of him leaning over to pick up some of his clothes from the ground. His backpack was lying next to his bed, some textbooks splayed out beside it. She felt bad for him. At least her backpack contained some fiction. He was stuck with her dad's old textbooks on cryptocurrency.

Surprisingly, her room was pretty clean. Besides her toothbrush and deodorant and a few other toiletries on the bathroom sink, and a t-shirt and towel drying on a rack, there wasn't much to pick up. She had spent a little bit of time each day putting things away. There wasn't much else to do.

Saying a quick and silent goodbye to the room that had been her home the last three days, she headed to the door. She felt a little like a butterfly emerging from its chrysalis, ready to face whatever the world had to throw at her. It was a feeling she rarely had when she was in school, when it felt like no matter how well she had done, the next class could have been the end of her. She yearned for adventure but also dreaded it. But now she felt like the protagonist in a Kerouac novel, ready to *live* and not caring much about what came after that.

Her dad was already waiting for her when she went outside. Chris was only a minute or two behind.

"I already checked out," John said. "We're just going to be another group of people who visited Amaryllis for the sewage festival and left immediately afterward."

"What is the sewage festival?" asked Chris.

"I looked it up. It's about as exciting as you'd think. Apparently somebody who lived here invented biosynthetic methane extraction. Don't worry, I didn't know what it was either, but it apparently allowed sewage treatment plants to run with net positive energy usage. And now they celebrate this guy's life. I mean, there are worse people to celebrate."

They loaded up the new car, backpacks in the trunk, John driving, Chris riding shotgun, Phlox stretching out her legs in the back. That would be something that neither John nor Chris could do. Phlox was thankful for the gift of being short. The car wasn't bad, but it was small. It actually looked kind of cool from the outside — a sort of sparkling yet burnt orange. It was built about two decades ago, but seemed to be in relatively good shape. Better shape than the car that John had just traded in.

"You should have seen the guy who sold this to me," said John as they left the parking lot. "He couldn't have weighed less than three hundred pounds, with a belt buckle that probably weighed fifteen pounds itself. I kept acting like I wanted to deal in Litecoin, he said he'd take 5% off if I paid in Monero. Ha! Shouldn't matter, since the car's in the name of Chester Hammock, but I'm sure not going to give anyone some other possible way of tracking me down."

"How much was it?" asked Chris.

"Thirty millimons, plus a little over four for tax, title, and fees. Not bad."

They soon found themselves driving down Route 301 south, with the non-drivers mostly watching the other vehicles. As expected, most of the other cars on the road were self-driving. Highways were perfect for this kind of thing. City driving, you had to deal with pedestrians, cars stopping to park, numerous traffic lights, and a million other issues. Highways were usually simple, barring accidents, which had become much rarer thanks to the lack of error-prone humans navigating them.

All around them, in their own little bubbles, other lives went on. Kids were playing video games on their watches, adults were napping, many people were singing along to songs in their own self-contained bubbles. They drove for hours, stopping only for snacks and bathroom breaks, but few others paid any attention to their car.

"You know what might be nice?" asked John. "Camping tonight. I honestly thought we were going to have to do some camping, so I have a tent in the back, and I just saw a sign advertising a campground. Might be fun!"

"Hmmm..." said Chris, but Phlox overruled his hesitation with a quick "yes!" She hadn't been camping in years, but it was something that she had fond memories of when she was a kid. It was a vacation that fit in with her dad's illusory poverty when she was growing up. They would head out to the woods around Amsteco, find a clearing, and set up camp for the night. They would sit around the campfire, her dad making up silly stories just for her. Stories about everybody in her school turning into a duck; or a group of companies manufacturing so much ice cream that it covered a whole town; or knights who rode on giant turtles to save a princess but were always too slow and by the time they got there the princess had saved herself. She would sit and eat roasted marshmallows and listen to stories of worlds that her dad made up just for her. Those stories were always more special to her than any mass-produced book.

"It's settled, then!" said John, ignoring Chris's further under-powered protests and taking the exit for Old River Road. Almost immediately, they found themselves surrounded by tall trees on ei-ther side of the road, and a much-reduced number of fellow travelers. There was a combination gas station and diner, probably mostly serving people heading off into the forest here.

"Let's get some real food here before we get into the woods," said Chris. "We should at least pick up some supplies."

"I've got some old military rations in the trunk," said John, but with Chris's sinking heart almost visible, changed his mind. "But you're right, we may as well save those. It's almost dinner time. And it looks like there's a little grocery store there, too — maybe they'll have marshmallows."

Pulling into the parking lot, they felt tiny. The diner — adver-tising itself as The Palmetto Grille — was surrounded by tall trees which seemed to form a solid wall around it. You could see that humanity had just taken a chunk out of the forest here, and given half a chance, the rest of the forest was ready to reclaim it. Phlox thought it felt ominous, like the trees were brooding, watching the humans encroach on territory that was rightfully theirs.

John didn't seem to notice, though. He seemed to be in high spirits as he headed towards the door. Chris was a bit slower, not looking forward to spending a night on the ground.

A bell jingled when they opened the door, and a young blonde woman walked over to them, grabbing some menus from next to the register. Her hair was held back by a kerchief, and she was wearing a pink polo shirt, apparently the uniform here. Phlox nodded in recognition at the outfit, remembering her own syrup-spattered polo shirts from Priscilla's. She was a little bit astonished at someone younger than her working here. The hostess must have been in high school. She was even wearing braces.

"Three?" she asked, despite her youth seeming to have this whole hostessing thing down pat.

"Yep, booth if you got one," replied John.

The hostess — whose name tag identified her as Molly — led them to a corner booth, John sitting in the middle.

"Your server will be with you in a minute," Molly said, and sauntered off toward the kitchen.

The restaurant was busy, but not crowded, populated mostly by what looked to be local families. The menu was standard diner fare, with which Phlox was well-acquainted. She glanced around, half-expecting to see a familiar face. Seeing none, however, she studied the menu, just as Chris and John were doing.

"Maybe it's just the fact that we're going camping," said Phlox, "but I think I'm going to get apple-walnut pancakes. It just feels like the right time for pancakes."

"I'm thinking lasagna," said John.

"Dad!" said Phlox, pointing to the menu. "The menu says BREAKFAST SERVED ALL DAY. That's code for 'order breakfast food.' Trust me, this is my area of expertise."

"Fine," he responded, peering at the menu. "I'll get one of these... uhh... raisin bagel breakfast sandwiches."

"That's better."

Chris looked up from his menu. "Well, since Phlox knows the secret code, I guess I'll get French toast. Plain."

At that moment, a waitress came up to the table, if anything younger than the hostess and even more blonde, wearing an identical pink polo shirt. "Hi, my name is Melissa, and I'll be taking care of you today. Just to let you know, we've got a special today on peach pie, 85 micromons a slice. Can I start you off with some drinks?"

"We're ready to order food, too, if you don't mind," said John, and they gave the orders — Chris emphasizing that he wanted plain French toast, no syrup, no butter — along with coffee for everyone.

"You got it," said Melissa, writing down their orders quickly, then turning around briskly and professionally. Phlox was impressed. Did the school system down here teach serving tables in kindergarten?

She glanced over at Chris, who had a bit of a far-off look in his eye as he stared across the room. Following his gaze, she saw that his eyes rested upon a middle-aged woman with dark red hair. She had on round glasses that gave her face a bit of an owlish look. Her dark blue slacks and a white blouse made her look somewhat more professional than most of the people here, who were dressed pretty casually. She seemed to be just a little overweight, but the kind of overweight that came from being comfortable with your body rather than being unhealthy. She was sitting by herself and just settling in.

Phlox decided that the most appropriate thing to do at this moment was embarrass Chris. "Okay, we get it, you like redheads, you almost got us killed over it. But you don't have to get moon-eyed over every one you see."

"It's not that," said Chris, although his face did seem to redden slightly. "*She* seemed to be checking *us* out. I saw her come in, see us, and ask to be seated over there. Right across from us."

"And why did you even notice her coming in?" asked Phlox, knowing at some level that she was being a bit mischievous, but also wound up by the knowledge of pancakes soon to come, and thus unable to fight the urge to bring up mischief.

"I'm sure it's nothing, Chris," said John, without looking over at the woman. He gave a quick glare to Phlox to let her know that hers was an unfruitful line of conversation. "I remember when I first came to Amsteco and thought every person I saw was coming to get me. A little paranoia is natural. But no matter who they are, these people can't have every diner in the country staked out."

"Yeah, you're probably right," said Chris.

Their food came relatively soon after that. Phlox had proven that she knew her stuff when it came to picking out diner food — everything was good. They didn't dilly-dally afterwards, though.

"We'd better get a move on," said John. "The sun goes down pretty early this time of year, and I do not want to be putting up a tent in the dark."

Phlox noticed that the middle-aged redhead was still sitting at the table across from them, absent-mindedly playing with her food. She wasn't sure exactly what the food was, but it looked like some form of pasta. Definitely not breakfast food. Amateur.

Her dad treated them to dinner. She could get used to this. Of course, she did have five bitcoin in her account, so she was technically wealthy. But with it unsafe to access for now, did it really count? It didn't matter. It was nice to have someone pay for you, no matter how much money you had sitting around.

By the time they left the Palmetto Grille, daylight was definitely on the wane. It wasn't even twilight yet, but the shadows were getting longer. The surface of Old River Road soon turned from pavement into pea gravel. The trees continued to loom menacingly, right off the shoulder of the road, broken only by the occasional run-off stream, and ever-rarer side roads with names like Hodler's Hollow Lane and Lee's Bluff Junction. They drove for a good twenty minutes without seeing any further signs for the campground.

The road was almost empty; they hadn't seen a car in at least ten minutes. Still, the road looked to be clear and well-maintained, even if it wasn't paved or well-traveled. It wasn't likely to end in a clearing or an abandoned mine.

"Are you sure we're heading in the right direction?" said Chris, looking at his watch. "I don't see any campgrounds on the map around here."

"Maybe we missed a turn?" asked Phlox.

"I don't think so," said John. "I've been looking."

The day was just starting to turn into twilight. If they had been in a meadow or on the highway at this time, it probably would not have seemed like it. Here, though, with the trees surrounding them, it was as if they were in a ditch or culvert, seeing only the last bits of sunlight reflecting off the top of the trees to their east. *Alpenglow*, Phlox remembered, was the word for it. When sunlight hit the top of the mountains and could be seen in the dark valleys below. The trees appeared to be turning black as the daylight faded.

Abruptly, Phlox squinted as a bright white light seemed to surround them. She realized it was headlights coming from behind. A large truck speeding down the road? An impatient driver flashing their high beams? Someone out deer spotting with their million-candlepower flashlight?

Whoever it was, they were gaining on the car, and didn't seem to be slowing down. John started to pull over to the side of the road, though there wasn't much of a shoulder. As he did, the vehicle behind them — which Phlox could now see was some sort of large truck — slowed down as well, following him over to the side. It was obviously after them.

"Damn it," said John, and floored the car, kicking off with a plume of gravel. The truck — no, it was a motor home, Phlox saw — slowly started to accelerate behind them. Their car was made for fuel economy, not speed. The motor home seemed to be souped up, as it was having no trouble keeping up with the smaller car. It wasn't quite able to overtake it, though.

The road they were on was relatively straight, a gash across the conifer forests of South Carolina. Whenever there was a turn, though, John took it sharp, hoping that the motor home, with its higher center of gravity, would tip over. No luck, though. It kept following them, remorselessly.

After what seemed like forever, but could not have been more than a few minutes, two orange signs, festooned with lights blinking arrhythmically, announced ROAD ENDS — 1000 FEET and DANGER — BRIDGE OUT. The motor home was right behind them, driving in the middle of the road. John reached down into the center console, feeling for his revolver.

There was a bit of a grassy area around the road, with several more signs warning drivers that the ROAD ENDS in 500 FEET and that were was DANGER because the BRIDGE was OUT. John decided that this was his only chance.

"Hold on!" he yelled, as he jerked the wheel violently to the right, and then the left, rear tires peeling out, spraying gravel and dirt as he attempted to turn around 180 degrees in the small amount of space available to him. If he could just get to the side of the motor home before it had a chance to realize what he had done...

No luck. The motor home had swung itself around sideways, blocking the road. With the trees so close, there was no way around it, at least not in a car. John slammed on the brakes. With a squeal, the car came to a stop about twenty feet from the front of their pursuer.

The motor home sat there, implacable, imperturbable, lights shining sideways into the dark forest. Phlox wondered what they could do. Behind them, she could see the remains of a concrete bridge abutment, with no bridge behind it. It looked like a drop of at least fifty feet. They could take their chances running into the woods, but they were far from civilization. How long could they last out here?

Finally, John made a decision for them. Grabbing his revolver and slowly placing it into the holster around his hip, he opened the car door.

"You two stay here, don't move, be quiet," his shaky voice betraying his nervousness. "If anything happens, run. Try to find the campsite and we'll meet there."

As he exited the car, Phlox saw the red-headed woman from the Palmetto Grille stick her head out from the motor home. She was saying something, but it was lost in the noise of the engine. John stared at her, holding up a hand to protect his eyes from the light. Finally, the engine cut out and the woman yelled.

"Sam Chambers!"

"Nothing behind me, everything ahead of me, as is ever so on the road."
-Jack Kerouac, *On The Road*

Palms Without Grease

An excerpt from an article in The Econometrician, *Volume VI, Issue 41*

Although commentators often derided Bitcoin and other cryptocurrencies as tools used for crime and illicit trade, a new study from the University of Northeast Anglia, published in the *Journal of Political Economics* this month, states that the adoption of cryptocurrency in a country is inversely correlated with the amount of corruption in that country. The correlation was a strong one — so strong, in fact, that initially the authors themselves did not believe it.

While the early days of cryptocurrency did indeed see its use in online "dark markets" which often did sell items such as illegal drugs forbidden by most governments, it was soon realized that forensic blockchain analysis could track down users of these marketplaces — and even more easily, their owners. Progressive governments soon realized that the radical transparency of the blockchain, where everybody can see all transactions being made, could be a tool to increase the amount of light on their own interactions.

With more and more government business being conducted on the blockchain, transparency has increased remarkably. No longer can a bureaucrat tell a user that they are missing some paperwork, which could be overlooked by said bureaucrat for a "service fee." With the rise of smart contracts for most common government interactions, there often is not even a person in the loop to ask for a bribe.

It is often said that sunlight is the best disinfectant. By providing governmental records which are both secure from tampering and provide proof of payment, this sunlight is applied to governmental workings almost automatically. Corruption, as measured by a variety of indicators, has been on a dramatic decline worldwide for the last four years. While correlation is not causation, this most recent work provides additional evidence that cryptocurrency adoption is the decisive factor.

Bribery and other government corruption has been estimated to cost the global economy over 800,000 bitcoin (approximately 1.4 trillion Federal Reserve Tokens) annually. This is in addition to the personal misery caused by dishonest government officials and the lack of trust engendered in authority by corruption. However, with continued adoption of automated, decentralized, trustless systems, trust may be restored in our governing bodies.

Chapter 15

Enough to Live

Phlox found that she was holding her breath. In front of her, she could see Chris frozen in place as well. John stared at the woman, squinting against the light given off by the motor home, trying to see who she was. She did not seem to be threatening them, just standing there, as if she expected to be recognized.

"Sorry, I guess you're going by Chester Hammock now. And I assume Wanda Cuturpa and Jack Thistledop are in the car with you."

John continued to stare for another moment before he could gather his wits. He had been prepared to act as a decoy, do what he could to give the kids a chance to make a run for it. But the red-headed woman was not playing by the script he was expecting.

"Jeez, I expected more of a welcome than that, Sam. Chester. Whatever."

Deep in his brain, a connection between some neurons occurred.

"Jane? Jane Virgil?"

The woman smiled and got out of the motor home. She was still wearing the slacks and blouse that Phlox had seen her wearing at the Palmetto Grille, but with knee-high boots over them. Not dressy boots — boots made for walking in mud. Coupled with the rest of her outfit, they seemed incongruous.

"Jane Virgil it is. Oh, Sam, it is so good to see you!" she exclaimed, hugging John.

"It's John now."

"Actually it's Chester, if the records at the Amaryllis Motel are anything to go by. But I guess that was the best you could do with that old hashing bug. It's how we found you, by the way. Who else would still be taking advantage of the Hollins-Babatunde collision forcing algorithm? That brought back memories."

John still seemed wary of her, although she seemed not the least fazed by his suspicion.

"Nice tattoos, by the way. I didn't even recognize you in the restaurant. I knew you were there somewhere, though. Once I figured out that you were in Amaryllis, I came as fast as I could, then tracked your car from there."

"How... how did you track our car?"

"Mr. Thistledop there really needs to learn some better opsec."

"Damn it, Chris!" John yelled. "Come out of the car!"

Chris, looking sheepish, opened the door and slowly walked over to where Jane and John were talking. Phlox decided to follow, partially out of curiosity, but also because of a deeply buried subliminal response to her dad's command. Hearing that voice, for a second, she felt like a little girl about to get grounded.

"Don't worry," said Jane, "it wasn't really his fault. The watch he bought was running an old version of the Ethereum client, leaked his location and allowed me to associate it with the account checked in to the motel. After that, just made a GUI interface to track his IP and the rest was history." She smiled, looking pleased with herself.

To her surprise, Phlox saw her dad laughing a hearty belly laugh, transforming into a creature about twenty times as relaxed as he was a few moments ago.

"You have no idea how long it's been since I've heard that reference. Nice. So what's the situation? And why didn't you just send me a message like Mitesh instead of running us down in the middle of a South Carolina forest? Or just asked around for us at the restaurant like a normal person?"

"Mitesh sent you a message?" she asked. "Idiot! No wonder you got spooked and left the hotel so soon. He should have known that I was on my way!"

"Are you and Mitesh working together, or something?" asked Phlox.

"Ahh, you are Wanda, I presume?" responded Jane.

"This is my daughter, Phlox," interrupted John, "and Mr. Thistledop over there is Chris. They're both students at our old school."

"You stuck around Pittsburgh!" said Jane, shocked. "Then had a daughter! Quite a brave man, on both fronts. But I guess they would have expected you to leave, and leave alone. Lots of game theory there... but we don't really have time for that. We should get going. I can't imagine that many people are going to be heading ten miles down a dead end road to a washed-out bridge this evening, but still, the ones who do might be asking lots of questions. There's an RV park two more exits down the highway, we can stay there tonight."

"Wait!" said Phlox. "Then what? Is there a plan?"

"There's a plan, but it's going to take a bit of explaining. Have I ever led you wrong, Sam? Err... John?" Jane looked deep into John's eyes, the slightest bit of pleading there.

"No. Jane always knows what she's talking about." He paused for a second, gathering his wits, then shaking his head in disbelief. "Jane Virgil. I thought you went off the Birmingham Bridge. Has *anyone* in my life actually ever died?"

Quickly realizing how insensitive this was to Phlox — and to himself, making memories which had had plenty of scar tissue on them newly raw — he changed topics.

"Jane was one of the early Ethereum adopters," explained John. "She told me it was going to be big, and I didn't listen to her. I thought that it was another wanna-be Bitcoin, with a slightly better scripting language..."

"Slightly!" interrupted Jane. "Ethereum's scripting language is Turing-complete. How could EthShare be possible using Bitcoin's Script? Or 99% of all of the other things it's doing now? Stack-based language... sheesh. There's a reason that Forth never took off..."

"True," said John, "but look at all of the security flaws that caused. How much ether was lost in the DAO hack? The multi-sig issues? The Krambotzki Collapse?"

"Mostly ameliorated with formal verification and strongly-typed languages, without reducing the expressiveness of the core language. Besides, if you want to talk about lost coins, we could discuss how many bitcoin were goxxed..."

"No idea what you're arguing about, here," said Phlox, cognizant of the fact that she was the only one of the four here without a technical background. Chris seemed to be following the conversation, but too timid to make any of his own opinions known. "No idea whatsoever, which is fine, but could we do it somewhere that is, you know, not in the middle of the road?"

"You're right, lavender," said John. "We can argue the strengths of our preferred coins, or altcoins..." — Jane glowered at him — "or whatever later. You drove so far to get us, what's the next step?"

"As I was trying to explain before you started bringing up old flame wars," said Jane, "we can spend the night at the Limehouse RV Park. I looked into it. It's cheap, it's near, they take Monero. We'll be close to the Georgia border, and they're not keen on anonymous cryptocurrency over there. Still a bunch of old Republicans there that never went Libertarian, looking askance at crypto in general. I've even heard that there are some towns in the mountains that use old paper money and gold coins, passing them around from person to person. Those bills must be disgusting by now. At least you can wash off gold coins."

"Oh yeah," said Chris. "Georgia and Mississippi, the two states where it's illegal to use Monero. Forgot about them."

"Right. Any anonymous cryptocurrency, technically, although it's certainly not stopping people from using it under the table, believe you me. We're going to have to go through there, though, to get to Florida, and I don't want to draw any undue attention to ourselves while we're passing through. So we'll get you some gas in the morning and I'll plug in at the RV park tonight. No way I'm going to risk a Bitcoin or Litecoin transaction along the way. Barring any unforeseen difficulties, we'll easily get to Florida tomorrow."

"What's in Florida?" asked Phlox.

"The next step," Jane answered, cryptically. "The less you know right now, the better. Just to be on the safe side. But don't worry, I bet you're going to enjoy the ride I scheduled. It's high time I took the same ride."

They got back into their car and followed Jane back onto the highway, noticing a sign for the campground that they had missed along the way. The RV park wasn't hard to find, and they were there within half an hour. Paying the attendant a half a millimon each for the night, they found two spaces right next to each other. John was a little upset about paying the same price for a spot as Jane when he wouldn't be using the charger or other hookups for the spot, but then realized it wasn't worth making a fuss about.

After getting themselves sorted out, they headed over to Jane's RV. John knocked on the door, and after a vague but affirmative response from within, they all walked in.

The grey walls of Jane's RV were covered in monochromatic pictures, apparently drawn with a black sharpie. They were mostly fantasy scenes: knights battling ogres, dragons breathing flame and wizards looking up menacingly from glowing orbs. The occasional cat or landscape broke the monotony, and Phlox was particularly intrigued by a flying saucer with three friendly-looking aliens waving to a passing asteroid.

The RV was a small model, with a tiny kitchen and bathroom. There were two couches that faced each other, light blue and artificial-looking, covered in the kind of material that fast-food restaurants used to allow easy cleaning. Despite the unorganized riot of pictures on the walls, it was remarkably uncluttered, but obviously lived in. Jane had gotten the hookup working, and they could hear the far-off whine of the batteries charging, along with the sloshing of potable water coming in and waste water being removed.

"Anyone want chocolates?" Jane asked, bringing out a shiny golden box from a small cupboard. "I don't know about you, but I could use a treat after all of that."

They all accepted, Phlox and John grabbing one at random, Chris studying the legend on the top of the box for a solid minute before deciding on a plain milk chocolate. Phlox once again silently judged her friend for his unadventurous taste buds as she bit into her truffle with orange nougat.

"Well, now that we're all here, can you let us know what's going on?" asked John.

"Oh, John, you never were one for small talk." said Jane, shaking her head slightly. "Aren't you curious what I've been doing for the last... what? Eighteen years?"

"Seventeen, by my count. I assume the same thing I was doing. Lying low. But you did it in an RV."

Jane smiled, and in her smile Phlox could see that there was more to the history of her dad and Jane than he was letting on.

"Of course. But unlike you, I've managed to stay in touch with the rest of the Old Bolsheviks."

"The Old Bolsheviks?" asked Phlox. She knew from her Russian Lit class that these were the people who had joined the Bolshevik — soon to be Communist — Party before the Russian Revolution. Virtually all of them who didn't have the good sense to die soon afterward were executed by Joseph Stalin.

"That's what we call ourselves. Kind of an ironic in-joke, since most of us were — are — pretty staunch capitalists. Although there may be a few heterodox Trotskyites or anarcho-syndicalists. We don't talk much about politics.

"We were the ones who were into cryptocurrency in the early days, helped it along, helped it grow. Your dad was one of us, although he was working on the academic side of things and I was on the professional side." She glanced over meaningfully at John. "Still amazed you have a kid, by the way. I was... pretty sure that you didn't want to start a family."

"Things change. People change." John said it in a tone that made it clear that nothing more would be forthcoming about his personal feelings on the matter.

"Anywho," continued Jane, letting that conversational tangent drop, "The New Guard came up, started kicking us out. The price on exchanges went up so quickly —"

"What's an exchange?" asked Chris, interrupting.

"Places where you could *exchange* paper money for Bitcoin or Litecoin or whatever," explained John. "There was a long period of time when that was the way that most people got into cryptocurrency. They'd get their paychecks in fiat, send some of it to an exchange, and get an equivalent amount of whatever coin they wanted. Think of it as a primitive version of how you shift between coins now."

"As I was saying, the price went up so quickly that the relatively small amounts of coin that we had were suddenly worth more than we had ever dreamed." Jane sighed. "At first we were elated. Just like the real Old Bolsheviks were excited in 1917, not knowing what was to come.

"We were targeted extensively. The big banks started buying huge amounts of bitcoin, trying to get in on it. This only drove the price higher, and soon it was worth the time of state actors to come after us. As their economy collapsed, I can't really blame them. They thought they'd grab a few of us who had a few thousand bitcoin apiece, and would be able to jump-start things. What's a couple of deaths and robberies compared to the misery caused by an ongoing recession?"

"Ever the utilitarian," John said, looking at Jane. " 'The needs of the many outweigh the needs of the few.' Even when you're talking about people who are trying to kill us."

Jane shrugged. "I never did understand your worldview. I think you even lent me that Kant book. What was it? *Groundhogs and the Metals of Mortals?*"

"*Groundwork for the Metaphysics of Morals*. The problem is that thinking of everything from a utilitarian perspective means that you can justify anything if you think it's for the greater good. Torturing someone because you think that it will save a trillion people from itchy pajamas."

Phlox was excited to see the conversation heading in this direction, although she wanted to argue on behalf of virtue ethics. She had taken an Ethics class and it had made her think seriously about switching her major to Philosophy. Jane, sadly, seemed uninterested in taking the conversation into that direction.

"Whatever, it doesn't matter if it's right or wrong at this point. They did it, end of story. They came after us, one at a time, all over the world. Word got around that people who were known to have bitcoin or be involved in the cryptocurrency world were not safe. Some joined their governments, or 'voluntarily' gave up their coin for the greater good. But we heard stories... never online, never on a forum... about those who didn't cooperate. And we got out, so that we wouldn't be found with an ice pick in our skull."

"Nobody wants to be Trotsky 2.0," Phlox chimed in.

"Good job getting the reference, sweetie," said Jane, sounding sarcastic but also looking pleased that the next generation was learning their history. "Seems like your dad got the hint, too, although he didn't let us know. Most of us Old Bolsheviks have been living underground, as they say. Assumed identities. Not bringing attention to ourselves. We watched cryptocurrency take over the world, as we predicted, but we weren't part of that world like we thought we would be."

She leaned back on the couch and reached for another chocolate.

"So where is everybody else? Mitesh? Asim? Pat?" asked John.

"Satoshi Nakomoto?" Chris chimed in.

Jane gave him a sideways glance. "Nobody knows where Satoshi is. The man invented the technology that changed the entire world, then disappeared. But that was before my time. I'm not as old as John, here."

"I didn't know him, either. I remember writing a message to him on a forum, but he didn't respond. I wasn't a big deal then. Not a big deal now, either, I guess. But there were a few years in between where I was at least a medium-sized deal."

"Oh, you'll always be a big deal to me," said Jane with a wink. "Everyone I know got away, eventually, although most of them spent some time living underground like you and me. Can't speak of Satoshi, but it wouldn't have surprised me if he was just the earliest. He always did seem to be a few steps ahead of the rest of the world. The people I know, they just got bored with living a life constantly in hiding, like some kind of cockroach, and went away. Can't say that I blame them."

"Away where?"

"Didn't Mitesh tell you? Where we always said we would end up. But to get there, we've got to get out of the country. That means heading South, down to the tip of Florida. Miami. Still a big port down there, should be easy to slip through with everyone else."

"What, are we going to hide on a cargo ship?" asked Phlox.

"Cargo!" exclaimed Jane. "I think I'm a little past the age where I'd want to hide on a cargo ship. Sounds like it would have been a fun adventure when I was your age, I guess. But I'd much prefer taking a cruise. Swim a bit, maybe do some snorkeling, eat more than we should at the buffet. Some of those ships have 24-hour buffets, can you believe it?"

Phlox and Chris looked at each other. Neither of them had ever been on a cruise ship. They were used mostly by the wealthy, the crypto-barons, CEOs, or ones who aspired to those positions. Phlox's vacations had consisted almost entirely of camping and swimming in

Lake Erie, and Chris's were similar, although usually at higher-end campgrounds or motels.

Misconstruing the look on Phlox's face, Jane consoled her. "Oh, cruises are great fun. John would probably say that they're boring." John grunted an assent. "Not nearly as boring as sitting around on a cargo ship, though, I'll bet."

She showed her watch to the others. It was displaying a kitschy advertisement for a trip aboard a ship called the *Angel Princess*. Phlox held her tongue about how cheesy the name was. "I've already found a ship that does a loop around the Caribbean. Havana, Kingston, Caracas, Belize City, then back to Miami. We'll have a day to kill, if my estimates are right. Maybe we can go visit Ernest Hemingway's house while we're close to the Florida Keys. I've always wanted to see it."

Phlox's opinion of Jane went up a few notches, even though Hemingway wasn't exactly her favorite author. If she were honest with herself, she was really finding Jane impressive. Smart, independent woman who kept chocolate at the ready? That more than made up for the first impression of her as a woman who didn't even know to order breakfast at a place that advertised 24-hour breakfasts. Her dad seemed to have some sort of grudge against her, though, but also appeared to be outweighed by the mutual respect, if not exactly friendship, between them.

"We'll get off at Caracas," Jane continued, "It might raise some eyebrows, but it happens. We'll just have to act like we're the type that doesn't care about the expense of missing half of a cruise." She looked down at the tattoos covering John's arms. "This will be easier for some of us than others. We could just slip out like thieves in the night, but that would look suspicious. And we do not want to be suspicious. Maybe we could just pretend to be a family, out to see the Caribbean after their kids graduated from college? What do you say, Sam... I mean, John?"

"That's not going to be our cover story."

Jane laughed off the serious tone in John's voice. "Have it your way! I'm just trying to help! Venezuela is great, from what I hear from Alejandro — John, you remember Alejandro, I'm sure. We still talk. Venezuela is the first country to try something approaching anarcho-capitalism. Certainly hasn't done any favors for the inequality there, sadly, but the economy for the top twenty or thirty percent has been on fire for the last few years.

"There's a small Old Bolshevik presence down there, Alejandro among them, near Caracas. They already know we're coming and they'll set something up for us, including a safe house for a few days."

"We're moving to Venezuela?" asked Chris.

"It's just a stopping-off point. Venezuela is perfect for it. You know how a mixer works?"

Chris nodded, but Phlox interrupted. "I don't. What's a mixer?"

"If you want to hide where your bitcoin or litecoin came from, you could make a transaction to a mixing address along with a bunch of other people doing the same thing. The coins are split up and sent to different addresses, making it hard for anyone doing analysis of the blockchain to follow where these bitcoin came from. Really handy for money laundering, like if you had some bitcoin lying around that came to you courtesy of some ransomware you wrote. Of course, nowadays, if you really care about this kind of thing, you'd just use Monero.

"Venezuela has absolutely minimal entry and exit requirements. Part of their constitution. It's brought in lots of investment, and a few unsavory characters. But because of this minimal tracking, it's an excellent way for us to 'launder' ourselves. We're entering under assumed names, and we'll leave under different assumed names, and by law, not even our assumed names will be stored for more than... two weeks, I think. If we really wanted to confuse people, we could head in and out a few times, using different assumed names and coming in from different border crossings. I think we'll be fine with our current plan, though."

John nodded. "Not a bad idea. I'm more worried about leaving Miami, though. We're going to have to clear U.S. customs, which means using the same identities that we used at the Amaryllis Motel. If you could find us, then it seems possible that they can. Not to mention they'll have us right where they want us, even if they figure it out a few days later. We're certainly not going to be able to swim away if they send some police to the ship via helicopter."

"Oh, John! Always the pragmatist! You forget that I am also capable of planning. Of being conniving, even! Or at least clever."

She opened a drawer and pulled out a thick, green notebook, of a kind Phlox was quite familiar with, used for taking notes in class. Like the walls, it was covered in doodles and pictures drawn in stark black outlines, with occasional cross-hatching to show darkness. Jane flipped through the pages, mumbling to herself until she found what she was looking for.

"Ah! Here we go! See, Jack, that Hollins-Babatunde issue is yesterday's news. If you spent more time studying Ethereum instead of being such a Bitcoin maximalist, it should have been obvious. It was fixed shortly after you used it, if my blockchain analysis is correct —"

"Spare me the evangelizing. I know you love your Ethereum."

Jane smiled. "Oh, indeed. You're right, though, it's irrelevant. I have my own zero-days — Phlox, that just means a security flaw that isn't yet publicly known — that as far as I can tell, aren't being used by anyone except me. I have a few identities we can take advantage of.

"Meanwhile, your pals — alter egos, I guess would be a better way to say it — Chester, Wanda, and Jack, are going to go on a little adventure near Mobile, Alabama. I've got a server physically located there, and a well-encrypted and hidden connection to it. It's going to have you three doing all kinds of actions there. If anyone is monitoring the Ethereum blockchain for you, it will be like a searchlight flooding the area. I'll set off the fire alarm just as we're leaving. If anyone is looking for you, they're going to be heading to a different state."

She handed the notebook to John, pointing to the bottom of the page, which Phlox could see was covered in words and symbols. "I've pseudocoded it out there. Didn't want to do anything even remotely online until I was ready to deliver the payload. What do you think?"

John and Chris looked at the notebook. After a few minutes, John looked at Jane. "No complaints here. But I was never an Ethereum developer. You know the virtual machine better than I do."

"I hate to jinx it, but it's pretty simple. I wasn't trying to do anything tricky. The tricky parts are getting the communication channel to the server in Mobile, which is already set up. I've been using it for years without a problem."

Phlox yawned, in spite of herself.

"All right..." said Jane, signaling the end of the conversation. "What do you say we call it a night? We'll leave bright and early tomorrow morning, get you all fueled up. There's a gas station slash convenience store across the road, that way." She motioned out the windows.

"Phlox, do you want to stay here? I've got two fold-out beds. Might be more comfortable. And this way the guys can have their guy time and talk about guns or fighting or whatever guys talk about."

John rolled his eyes — Phlox thought that he looked very Phlox-like in that moment. "I'm fine with that if she is."

"Oh, splendid! We can drink hot cocoa and braid each others' hair and talk about which boy at school is the cutest." The sarcasm positively dripped off each word. Although Jane did seem to be the type to like hot cocoa, Phlox couldn't imagine her businesslike hair in pigtails.

Phlox was secretly delighted to be spending more time with Jane. She had a similar sense of humor as her own. She was glad that some people kept it as they got older.

After grabbing her backpack and folding out the bed from the couch in Jane's RV, Phlox got ready for bed. Finally, teeth brushed, face washed, and her t-shirt and jogging pants version of pajamas on, she laid down. There was only one pillow, sadly, but she made do with her backpack stuffed full of the rest of her clothes. Jane spent a few more minutes getting ready for bed, putting some sort of cream on her face first, but was soon turning off the light and lying down.

"So, Phlox," said Jane. "Tell me what you want to know about your dad."

"What?"

"Oh, come *on*. You have to be curious about something in his past. You're not going to find a better person to ask than me."

"Why not?"

"We were dating for years! Then he dumped me. Well, it was partly my fault, I guess. I gave him an ultimatum and he didn't take it. I said it was time to settle down, that I wasn't getting any younger. He said he wasn't ready."

Phlox gasped. It wasn't so much that her dad had dated Jane — if Phlox were into women, Jane was the type of woman she'd be into — but rather that her dad had dated anyone besides her mom. After her death, as far as Phlox knew, he never even looked at another woman in any sort of romantic way.

"He was a good man, he always treated me right. I regretted laying it down like that many times over the next few years. That was a long time ago, though."

"How did you two meet?"

Jane inhaled deeply. "I had heard about Sam a few times before we met. He had written a few papers and was known around the Pittsburgh blockchain community. One night, we got into an argument at a meetup about whether ASIC resistance was a good or bad thing in a cryptocurrency. Oh, don't worry about the specifics, it doesn't matter. I ended up asking him to continue the talk over drinks. Twenty-four hours later, I told my best friend that I was going to marry him.

"Of course, that didn't happen. Not quite. But we were together for almost four years before he walked out, hands in his pockets, hangdog expression, saying he just didn't feel ready the way I felt ready. Your mom's a lucky lady."

That stung. "No, she's not. She's dead. Car crash. Drunk driver."

"Oh, honey," said Jane softly. "I'm so sorry. I was rude. I shouldn't have brought this up."

"It's okay. I was six. And it's nice to hear about my dad when he was young. He never talked much about the time before he met my mom. When I was a kid, I had all these theories... he was a spy, or something. He didn't tell me that he used to be Sam Chambers until just a few days ago."

"I feel horrible. You're going through a lot right now, this has to be difficult. Did you want any hot chocolate? I'm actually not good at braiding hair, but I'll try if it makes you feel better."

"No, I'm fine." Despite the little bit of frost in their interactions now, Phlox could see why her dad had liked Jane. The sarcastic outer shell and the caring inner core. "I think I'm just going to get some sleep, now, though. It's been a long day."

"Yeah. For you and me both."

"But it is good that we do not have to try to kill the sun or the moon or the stars. It is enough to live on the sea and kill our true brothers."
-Ernest Hemingway, *The Old Man and the Sea*

Building a Business, Block by Blockchain

An excerpt from an article in The Econometrician, *Volume I, Issue 44*

Old Ethereum hands remember the DAO (the Decentralized Autonomous Organization) as a debacle in the early days of that platform, when a minor coding error led to the loss of numerous ether to an unknown adversary, as well as a contentious hard fork in the blockchain. Even with that history, DAOs — companies whose governing mechanisms, or even operating decisions, are entirely controlled by software –– are making a comeback in a big way. Safer programming languages, more advanced software design techniques and tools, and a better understanding of the limitations of the blockchain have led to a resurgence in the idea after a years-long "DAO winter."

Several smaller DAOs have been deployed over the last few years, controlling payouts for real estate investment trusts, pipeline rentals, and even royalty revenue from selling digital books. This last week saw the first listing of a DAO, Delta-V Technologies, on an American stock exchange. "Having minor decisions made by an artificial intelligence, and automatically implemented through the DAO command structure, allows our executives to focus on more strategic issues," notes Lin Han, the COO of Delta-V. "A decade ago, I would have been on call twenty-four hours a day. This was not only an unfair burden on upper-level management, but also resulted in poor decision-making. Nobody can think strategically on two hours of sleep."

Others in industry are more wary of ceding so much control to what amounts to a piece of software. Janet Beard, CTO of CalCore

Steel, says that while she trusts the code on the robots in her company's mills, business decisions are qualitatively different. "The business world is effectively played on an infinite board," she says, "and there are no rules that you have that will never be broken. Whenever you think that you have figured out the rules to your industry, some upstart is going to try a different approach and eat your lunch. This is the reason that you have human managers, because they are not slaves to an algorithm."

Chapter 16

The Person They Conceal

Sunlight creeping in through the window blinds woke Phlox up. Groggily realizing where she was, she looked over to the other foldout bed. Jane sprawled out over the small expanse of the mattress, a stark contrast to Phlox's preferred sleeping position of scrunching up into the fetal position.

Feeling restless and not wanting to awaken Jane, Phlox threw on a hoodie and her shoes, and tiptoed out the door of the RV. The sun was just barely creeping over the horizon, and its burning through the fog gave the other RVs a soft, almost magical, glow. She stared at the fog and stretched her arms and back. It was overcast, and something about the way the fog clung to the ground made her think that it was going to stay that way for a while.

Just then, she noticed that she was not alone. Chris was sitting on one of the fallen logs which separated the parking spots. He was watching the cars go past on the road, facing away from the sun.

"Hey, Chris," said Phlox quietly, sitting down next to him.

"Hey," he said. "Is Jane as big a snorer as your dad?"

"Ha! No, she was quiet as a mouse. Sorry, I should have warned you about the snoring. I used to fall asleep with the TV on because I could hear him even though he was all the way in his room."

Chris continued to stare out at the cars. Something seemed to be weighing on his mind, but he was having trouble putting it into words.

"Did you know that Jane and my dad used to date? She told me last night. That's so weird, meeting someone besides my mom —"

Chris stopped her. "Phlox... are you sure we know what's going on?"

"What do you mean?"

Chris shifted, uncomfortable. He was clearly planning out a difficult conversation in his head.

"I know it's your dad and all, but hear me out. What proof do we have that any of this is real? Let's say that this was anyone else but John, and I told you that someone came to the door with a gun, ordered us out, and drove away just as the police were pulling up to the door? Told us not to communicate with any of our friends? Made sure we were untraceable? And then met up with a woman on a dark and deserted road and made plans to take us all to Venezuela? Doesn't that sound the slightest bit... off?"

Phlox thought for a moment. "I mean, yeah, it's unusual. But so is finding ten bitcoin hiding in an apartment in South Oakland. The last couple of weeks have been unusual."

"I'm worried that *we're the bad guys*, or at least that we're not really the good guys. Think about it. We're on the run from the police. We're using stolen identities. We're about to lie to customs officials about who we are and head into the most lawless part of South America. I mean, maybe your dad did something really horrible and that's why the police are after him. Not because they're jealous of his bitcoin stash."

Phlox's mind reeled — and her body, almost, as well. She steadied herself against the log. Could her dad be a murderer or something? Could the discovery of the bitcoins and their sudden departure all have been some sort of excuse to leave Pennsylvania?

"What about Jane, though?" asked Phlox. "And the rest of the Old Bolsheviks? That seems to corroborate his story, at least in broad outline."

"I thought about that. But we only have Jane's word and your dad's that these Old Bolsheviks exist. One message on his watch from someone named Mitesh, that's the only proof your dad has provided. Did you even check that that message *was* signed with Mitesh's private key like your dad says it was? If not, it's easily forged. Faking an unsigned message is freshman-level stuff. I'll admit that Jane seems real enough, but maybe they were partners in the crime. Like Bonnie and Clyde."

"And how about Vera tracking us down to that church that first night? How could she have done that if she wasn't somehow tracking you or your watch?"

Chris looked down at the ground. "I told her about how I used to hang out there when I was a freshman. Maybe when I wasn't at my house, she thought that I might have gone there."

"I don't know, Chris. I can't even imagine it. My dad has always been one of the kindest people I know. I just can't picture it."

"He kept the truth about who he was your whole life, Phlox. You didn't find out his real name until, what, five days ago? He didn't tell you about his history with Jane. What else might he be hiding?"

"He kept his identity a secret to keep me safe. And him safe, too, of course. But I certainly wouldn't have been in better shape if he got rounded up and taken away from me. He had to keep it a secret to protect me. Makes sense to me that he wouldn't tell a little kid that their dad was in hiding from some sort of shadowy cabal. I'd probably do the same thing."

"Just like they won't tell us our ultimate destination? We're adults, too, Phlox. We deserve to know where we're going, and why. All of this spy novel stuff, fake identities, meetings with secret societies, car chases, encounters on lonely roads... it just all seems fishy."

"Maybe it does, but I'll trust my dad to the moon and back. He's given up so much for me. I owe him that much." Phlox had a thought. "Besides, what about him putting your watch on that Bubbly-Bub truck at the gas station? The truck got pulled over by the police the next day."

"Your dad put *something* on the truck. Would you swear under oath that it was my watch and nothing else?"

Phlox didn't have an answer for him. She had been fiddling with the gas pump at the time, and trying to avoid eye contact with anyone while wearing her prom dress. She stared off at the slowly-developing traffic on the road. Finally, Chris broke the silence.

"Besides, maybe the police have been looking for us. Maybe they did track down my watch, but because they were looking for us. Maybe we've been kidnapped and we don't even know it."

"I think they would have said something about that on the news."

"Maybe. Well, I'll play along for now. I don't know if I have a choice at this point. I'm going to keep my eyes open, though. You should, too."

"I will. I always do. Well, except when I'm sleeping. Do you want to head over to the store and see if we can get a snack? I am 100% positive that Jane's got something for us to eat somewhere in the RV, but I'm not going to root around in her cupboards."

Chris responded wordlessly by getting up. They crossed the parking lot, half filled with RVs, watching their long shadows, barely visible through the lightening fog, stretch across the pavement. There weren't many cars on the two-lane road that stood between them and the gas station, but enough that they had to wait a bit before crossing.

The convenience store, as expected, only accepted Monero. They had wandered around for while, finally settling on some bottled iced coffee and a raspberry and cream cheese danish for Phlox, and a plain cake doughnut with a cup of water for Chris. They also grabbed a couple various bagged snacks for John and Jane, for whenever they got up. The trip had not exactly led to healthy eating habits for any of them, but such was life on the road.

They were wandering over the grassy shoulder of the road — surprisingly well-kept and mostly weed-free — when they saw that Jane and John were up. They were sitting next to each other on the same log that Phlox and Chris were sitting on earlier, deep in conversation. John was wearing the same clothes that he had on yesterday, whereas Jane was wearing a camisole and flannel pants, with a shawl around her shoulders. *Professional pajamas*, thought Phlox. They quickly stopped talking when the two approached.

"Good morning, early birds," said Jane. "Guess the two geezers needed more shut-eye than you. We don't recover like we used to."

"Good morning yourself," said Phlox. "It really is a good morning. Clean air, warm sun… I feel like a million bits."

John seemed to still be in the slightly dour mood that he'd been in since first seeing Jane. "That's good, since we've got at least nine hours driving ahead of us today. Assuming no accidents, blown tires, or missed turns."

"John! It's a straight shot down 95! I'm not sure how you got tenure if you can't follow the same road for 500 miles!" Jane looked at him playfully.

Did Phlox see a little bit of glee in her dad's eyes as Jane flirted with him? Maybe. As soon as she noticed it, though, it was gone.

"Never hurts to be prepared for inevitable delays. Murphy's Law and all that. We should eat our breakfast and be on our way." He glanced down at his watch. "It's 7:15. Assuming we can get out of here by 8:00, give us two hours for bathroom breaks, food, gas, and whatnot, that puts us in Miami around 7:00 tonight. Jane, when did you say the *Angel Princess* was leaving?"

"Tomorrow at 1:00 PM. Passengers can start getting on mid-morning, but no matter when we get on, we'll have a whole morning to kill if we get to Miami this evening."

"This whole trip is hurry up and wait," complained Chris.

"Better to hurry up and wait than not hurry up and miss the boat." John had spent the last seventeen years of his life killing time. He was an experienced temporal assassin at this point.

"Do you want to keep separating the boys and girls, John?" asked Jane. "It's like a middle school dance!"

"Phlox's call, not mine."

"Sure," chimed in Phlox. "It will be a nice change of pace riding in a different vehicle. And different company. Maybe Chris and I could switch at lunchtime."

"Great! Remember, no pillow fights while I'm driving, Phlox!"

Packing up their belongings and checking out of the RV park was faster than they had anticipated. Phlox and Chris were astounded by the plug on the side of the RV, which provided everything that its passengers would need for the next twenty-four hours, and disconnected itself, like a snake recoiling from a strike, after a swipe from Jane's watch.

"All Ethereum-powered," explained Jane, sounding like a proud aunt. "As soon as the payment went through last night, a smart contract was initiated. This put the plug under my control and it filled me up with electricity, automatically cleaned out the sewage system, checked my fluid levels, did everything but make me a nice cup of soup. I worked on something similar back in my glory days."

They bid their goodbyes to the Limehouse RV park and were on the road by 7:45. Ten minutes after that, they were driving south on Interstate 95. Phlox appreciated the roominess of the passenger seat in the RV. She wasn't exactly squeezed in her dad's car like Chris was, but here she could stretch out every inch of her 5'2" frame.

The ride through Georgia was uneventful, as Phlox listened intently to all of Jane's stories. About growing up in Tennessee with her little brother, going to New York for college despite not knowing a single soul there, dropping out after two semesters, and then single-handedly putting together one of the largest smart contract auditing firms in Philadelphia by the time she turned 25. Hiring a team and being the only woman on it... but still, the boss. Eventually landing in Pittsburgh as many of the early cryptocurrency people did. Meeting her dad, moving in with him, getting into fights about obscure blockchain decisions that would get so heated that he would storm out into the night, muttering that proof-of-stake was, mathematically and economically speaking, a fool's errand, and searching for a beer.

She told Phlox about faking her own death, just as so many other Old Bolsheviks had done. Writing up a will that specified a closed-casket funeral, cremation, no autopsy. Waiting for months after writing the will, so as not to arouse suspicion. Living a nomad's life in Canada, avoiding her old friends, but making new ones. She was always good at making friends. Keeping her mind sharp by learning to draw, and finding out that not only was she good at it, she loved it. Watching as cryptocurrency slowly took over the world, just as she predicted.

It felt weird to think that this woman could have been her dad's wife. Her mom, maybe, kind of. Not really, of course — she knew that any child they had would not have been her. Still, she felt like this was some strand reaching back to her father at around the same time that she was born. Her mom had been with her biological father, then. And John was Sam, and with this woman. She felt a little guilty thinking about it, but it was like meeting a potential, a variant, an alternate-universe version of her mother.

The miles flew by, and before they knew it, garish signs announced "Welcome to Florida — The Sunshine State — Governor Esteban Cruz." As they crossed the border, the clouds did in fact lift.

"Well, that sun has got to be a good omen," said Phlox. Jane had been telling stories of her life for miles and Phlox felt like she had to do a bit more to keep up her end of the social contract.

"Definitely, but I like to think that everything is a good omen. Life is more fun that way. Let me tell you a story.

"Once upon a time, a shepherd had a sick sheep, so he led the sheep off into the mountains so it would not get the other sheep sick. His neighbors all said to him, 'how awful! You lost a sheep!' The shepherd replied, 'we shall see.' A few days later, the sheep came back, recovered from his illness in the cool mountain air. And it had found several other wild sheep, who followed him back to the corral. The shepherd now had even more sheep, and his neighbors said, 'how wonderful! you have even more sheep now!' The shepherd replied, 'we shall see.'

"The son went to shear some of the wild sheep, but they were unruly, and he broke his leg. The neighbors said, 'how sad! His leg is broken!' and the shepherd said, 'we shall see.' Just then, a warlord came through the village, looking for all able-bodied men to come and fight in a war. The shepherd told them that he had to look after his son, who had a broken leg, and the warlord let them be. The neighbors said, 'how fortunate you are! The warlord did not bother you.' The shepherd said, 'we shall see.'

"The son grew up, but his leg never fully healed, and he had trouble shearing the sheep every season. His neighbors said, 'what bad luck! Your son will never be a great shearer.' The shepherd said, 'we shall see.' The son spent more time inside working on his poetry, which came to be known far and wide across the kingdom. His neighbors said, 'how proud you must be for this turn of events! Your son is a great poet!' Once again, the shepherd replied, 'we shall see!'

"I wonder sometimes what would have happened with my life if some things had turned out different. If I had married your dad. If I continued my business, which was doing great at the time. If I had not looked so deeply into Ethereum in those days. But all of those questions are fundamentally unanswerable. I don't know if it would have been a good thing, for me. Maybe I'd have ended up dead of a heart attack, stressed to the breaking point by the time I was 40. I probably never would have learned to draw. I might never have seen your dad again, or met you. So any omen I see, I think of it as good. It means that life is continuing and that, my dear, is intrinsically wonderful."

Phlox looked over at Jane, whose eyes were still on the road. She had such an inspiring outlook on life. Phlox knew too many people that wallowed in pity for the past, wondering what would have happened if they had talked to this person or asked that person out or whatever. Even she was guilty of it, sometimes. Here was somebody who literally threw her old life away, over the Birmingham Bridge into the waters of the Monongahela, yet refused to look back or think what might have been. It was pretty inspiring.

"Are you hungry?" asked Phlox. "I'm feeling like lunch might be in order soon."

"Too deep for you, huh?" asked Jane. "It's okay, sometimes I get a little deep and it's good to remember the basic things. Like lunch."

"It's not that," said Phlox, "it's just that I don't have anything to say to it. It's like... it touched my soul. That sounds cheesy, I'm sorry. I mean..."

"It's alright." Jane smiled, eyes twinkling, crow's feet crinkling. "You don't always have to put everything into words. Even if you are an English lit major. Sometimes trying to put ideas into words sterilizes them. Like a butterfly under glass. I'm glad you got something out of it, though.

"Besides, you're right. It's time for some lunch. I could go for some pizza, how about you?"

After a quick digression on whether or not pineapple on pizza was the best thing in the world or an abomination before God and man (Phlox being firmly on the side of the former), they pulled over to one of the innumerable pizza joints along 95. John and Chris stopped next to them on the cracked parking lot, the car tiny next to the RV.

Lunch was quick. Everyone ordered plain pizza, except for Phlox who got double-pineapple-and-spinach, and they watched a news show which was being displayed on an old-fashioned plasma screen on the wall. Life around the world seemed to be going on as normal — the standard political scandals and economic variations — until they were cleaning up their meals and preparing to leave.

"News out of Pittsburgh today," started the news anchor, whose grey hair and fashion sense placed him squarely in the last century. Everyone's heart skipped a beat as they stopped their pizza clean-up activities and stared at the television.

"Residents of that city's Oakland neighborhood woke up to an unusual site - teriyaki dinosaur. An unknown artist transformed the local museum's dinosaur statue into a dinner item."

The screen showed the famous dinosaur thickly covered from head to tail in a brown glaze, an artificial and obviously decorative fire underneath it. A professional-looking sign in front of it announced "Teriyaki sauropod — the latest flavor craze." Numerous people were milling around near it in the light rain, taking pictures with their watches.

"No wonder Brian needed so much soy sauce..." mumbled Phlox under her breath.

Soon enough, they were back on the road, with Chris and Phlox switching vehicles. Jane continued to drive the RV. She insisted that she was the only one who knew it inside and out. Chris rode shotgun, thankful for the legroom. Phlox hopped into the driver's seat of her dad's car, looking forward to a little less motion sickness now that she was the one in control. John also looked relieved that he'd be able to take a break and enjoy the scenery.

The drive through Florida was downright boring. The road was flat and well-maintained, especially compared to the hilly and pothole-filled roads around Pittsburgh. Phlox listened to ancient tapes on the portable cassette player, discovering the wonders of late 20th-century music that her dad still listened to. She occasionally tried the radio but there weren't that many radio stations between cities. Paying for the extra watts to transmit when there just weren't that many people outside the cities wasn't worth the cost. Ordinarily, she would have listened to a station on her watch, but her dad insisted that they keep their watches off unless absolutely necessary.

Her dad had been pretty quiet the entire ride, mostly staring out the window, watching abandoned housing developments being slowly overtaken by the swamp that was the natural condition of central Florida. There were rumors that you could buy houses like this for a few microbits. Some her friends had joked that they would work for a year, each buy their own tract house in the middle of nowhere, and retire.

When those suburbs were built, everyone wanted to live far from where they worked, spending a good portion of their lives commuting. But as jobs petered away, especially for those not in tech, it was as though a cloud lifted from the collective mind of America and people headed back into cities. Pittsburgh was a perfect example of this, but Florida reminded her that this was happening all over the country, if not most of the world.

They were on the road for about two hours when Phlox decided that it was time for a bathroom break. There were relatively frequent rest stops along 95, dating back to the big infrastructure push the Democratic Socialists were behind, thanks to President Rodriguez's "America for All" campaign. With ever-decreasing support from the federal government, though, they were mostly falling into disrepair, although still usable, just like the housing complexes.

Jane's RV pulled up next to them, close against the curb. Through the window, Phlox could see Jane talking in a very animated fashion. Across the parking lot, a maroon van pulled in and settled in the shade under a copse of trees and a run-off pond which Phlox assumed was full of alligators.

All four of them gathered around on the sidewalk, stretching their legs, enjoying the warm Florida sunshine. It was downright hot and humid this far South. Chris and Jane seemed a bit uncomfortable in the weather, Chris more so than Jane, but to Phlox and John, it felt like a vacation. They basked in the heat.

"How much longer do we have to go?" asked Chris after they all took care of the biological necessities.

"Maybe three more hours," answered John. "We're making good time."

"What were you all talking about?" asked Phlox. "I could see Jane here waving her hands around like a windmill all along the interstate."

"Ha!" answered Jane. "I was telling Chris here stories of the early days of blockchains. Back when the rest of the world laughed at us and we were the minority defending our vision of the future. A time of heroes, you know. The Golden Age. Even money that Chris hasn't figured out which stories were tall tales and which ones were true."

Chris blushed, although Phlox wasn't entirely sure if it was from the ribbing or from the heat, as Jane continued.

"Us old folk have to have our fun. Besides, every industry has to have its legends. Gauss adding up all the numbers from 1 to 100 in a minute after being given the problem as busy work in a class. Archimedes jumping up out of the bath and screaming 'eureka! eureka!' after realizing that displacement could measure the volume of an object of any shape. Why not Jane Virgil figuring out a recursion bug in an Ethereum implementation mid-coitus?"

Phlox laughed out loud in spite of herself, while her dad sighed. The way he did it, and the way Jane said it, made her think that this was a true story, and that her dad had direct knowledge of the incident. That made it even funnier, but it also grossed her out more than a little.

"*As I was saying,*" said John, "we were making good time, but if we wait around to hear all of Jane's stories, even the abridged versions, we're not going to be making good time any more. Let's get going. Just three more hours to Miami."

John decided that he was ready to start driving. Phlox called shotgun, even though she wasn't competing with anyone for the spot. As they got back into their cars and merged back onto the interstate, Phlox was filled with curiosity. She couldn't contain herself any longer.

"Dad, don't take this the wrong way or anything, but do you have any proof that people are after us? I mean, the way you raised me, I wasn't supposed to be, you know, running away from the police."

John looked a little hurt, but not really surprised.

"Daffodil, I wish I could give you some sort of document saying 'John Tseretelli is being chased by a shadowy conspiracy, sincerely, Shadowy Conspiracy,' but I can't. I have a feeling that if they ever showed themselves to me, that I wouldn't be alive to talk about it afterwards.

"What I can do is answer any question you have entirely truthfully. I shouldn't have lied to you when you were growing up, but I thought it was for the best, When we stop at the hotel tonight, I'll dump my brain wallet, show you that I have access to a ton of bitcoin that has been unused for seventeen years and that I'm the rightful owner. And I will swear on your mother's grave that I have been afraid for my life every single day of those seventeen years."

At that moment, John glanced up. His pulse seemed to quicken noticeably.

"Phlox, don't look back — look in the side rear view mirror — but is that the van from rest stop?"

A quick glance confirmed that it was. The ugly maroon paint job, the license plate on the front, the boxy shape which seemed deliberately anti-aerodynamic. She couldn't see how many people were in it, though, as the harsh Florida sun created reflections on the windshield, protecting the occupants from being identified.

"I think so." Phlox felt like she should have said it more confidently. "Yeah, it is." Still didn't sound very confident. Oh well.

"They stopped there but nobody came out to go to the bathroom," explained her dad. "I didn't think it was that big of a deal at the time. Lots of people stop at rest stops just to take a nap or whatever. But to stop for just as long as we were there and then get on the road just as we did... that seems fishy."

Phlox was no longer worried that her dad may have been telling her stories. It was circumstantial evidence, sure, but it seemed to confirm his story more than any statement he could utter.

"New plan," he said, "turn on your watch and message Jane. Tell her to slow down. Below the speed limit. Act like they've got some sort of mechanical problem. And we'll meet them... hmm..." He looked up at the green signs indicating the next several exits. "Three exits from here."

She typed the message in and quickly saw a response from her saying simply "ok." The RV, which had been in the process of overtaking a large self-driving truck, slowed, and was soon out of sight behind the truck. The maroon van was close behind them.

"Well, now the fun begins," said her dad, but nothing seemed to change about his driving.

"What are you going to do?" asked Phlox.

"This." John jerked the car over to the right to take the exit, without slowing down, at the absolute last possible second. Another few milliseconds and they would have ended up crushed against the concrete pylons marking the end of the exit. Phlox could feel adrenaline flood her system and her inner ear try to figure out what was going on. Beside them, the brakes of the maroon van screeched but rapidly faded as they took the side road off the highway.

John maintained highway speed for a little while, but soon slowed down. "No use getting pulled over by the state police for speeding," he said. "There aren't many, but why invite trouble?" They were on a two-lane road, winding around swampy land and the occasional small lake. There were few houses here, and fewer towns.

"Remind me never to doubt you again," said Phlox. "I don't know if my heart could take it. Literally."

John smiled, more broadly than Phlox had seen since he had shown up on her stoop back in Pittsburgh.

Guided by an outdated paper atlas that John kept under the seat, they eventually found a back way that ended up on the highway two exits later, where they said they would meet Chris and Jane. It ended up taking almost an hour, whereas they probably would have been there in five minutes had they just stayed on the highway.

They found Jane at a charging station, one of the newfangled ones which didn't even bother to support diesel or gas. Her RV was in a charging dock, and she was monitoring the charger. Chris sat on the steps of the RV, tapping his fingers on its side. No other vehicles were in sight, or any employees. This was an EtherCharge station, entirely automated, payments and problems handled by smart contract.

"Took you two long enough," said Jane nonchalantly, as if they were heading out for a walk in the woods and John couldn't find the trailhead. "RV's almost done charging up."

"With good reason," John said, and explained the maroon van and their avoidance of it.

"Oh John! What if it was all a coincidence! Maybe some driver pulled into the rest stop because his wife thought he heard something rattling, then headed back on to the road as soon as they realized it was just a loose piece of candy in the car. You just scared some couple in a van half to death with your crazy driving!"

"Better safe than sorry. You've been on the lam longer than me, you should know that."

"I also know not to draw attention to myself by driving like a crazy person and acting like every car is filled with assassins."

"Well, either way, I think we lost them. We hardly saw any other cars during our little detour, and it looks like nobody is following you here."

The charger beeped and Jane disconnected it from the RV.

"Onward to Miami!" called Jane. "And keep an eye out for any more spies on the road!"

It was evening by the time that they arrived at the Hotel Bird of Paradise. Leaving and re-entering 95 had taken more time than John had liked, but they hadn't encountered any other issues along the way. The ship wasn't leaving until the next day, so they still had plenty of time.

"This place is a favorite for Bulgarian and Macedonian nouveau riche," explained Jane. "Comfortable surroundings. Discreet staff. Luckily our alter egos are quite well-off. Remember, start acting like you burn bitcoin to light your cigar. There may be a few people booked on the *Angel Princess* staying here tonight, and we want to start cultivating the look of the mega-bourgeois who would get off a cruise midway through because they want to spend more time in Caracas."

Jane checked them in at the front desk, which required no human intervention whatsoever. It was quite slick. She finished the check in process by placing her watch against the screen, and almost immediately, four automatic carts rolled up. A screen on the front of each of the carts announced their rooms. A different room for each of them, Phlox noticed.

"Like I said, very discreet staff."

Jane showed them which cart was whose. The screens listed their aliases — "Janet Ivanova" for Jane, "Alexandra Kaganovich" for Phlox, "Zlatan Petrov" for John, "Georgi Stoyanov" for Chris. Phlox's and Jane's carts had the same pictures of an abstract beach on them, John's and Chris's, a little stylized city.

"I got us more realistic aliases, 'Chester Hammock.' Things have advanced a bit since Hollins-Babatunde. You two are on the city-facing side, but I sprung for ocean views for Phlox and myself. I figured you two wouldn't care about the views so much, and having us in two separate groups might be useful. Won't draw attention if they're looking for four people. Or three, if they didn't know I joined you. Or one, if they're just looking for me, now that I think about it. Good work, Jane."

"What kind of name is Zlatan?" asked John.

"Common Macedonian name. Come on John, I always thought you were a man of the world."

"Let's just do room service tonight," said John. "May as well take advantage of looking like we're wealthy."

They followed the carts up to their rooms, with John and Chris peeling off at one point for a different wing of the hotel. Phlox's room was right next to Jane's. The cart followed her in after she unlocked the door with her watch, and automatically unloaded her luggage — which consisted entirely of her school backpack — onto a piece of furniture which looked custom-made for the purpose of a temporary luggage holding spot.

The room was sumptuous. It was the only word she could think to describe it. The bed, bigger than any bed she had ever seen, was a good three feet off the floor and covered in a well-organized array of pillows, sheets, and comforters. She was positive that some combination of them would result in an absolutely perfect night of sleep.

She took off her shoes, kicking them toward the door, and fell backward onto the bed, which felt as soft and giving as a giant bowl of cotton candy. The room was elegantly decorated, beautiful thick curtains drawn against the fading light, paintings covering the walls, furniture solid and wooden. There was a television but it was demurely hidden in some sort of furniture, so as not to ruin the nineteenth-century grandeur with twenty-first century crassness, yet still allow people to rot their brains with it if they preferred.

Alexandra Kaganovich certainly has a wonderful life, she thought. This was quite a change from the Amaryllis Motel.

Phlox got up from the bed and crossed the room to the windows. She peeked out from behind the curtains in her room to view the busy streets of Miami bathed in the last remnants of the sunset. She technically did have an ocean view, as promised. Between two buildings, above the grey outline of the Miami Dikes, occasionally blocked by a branch of a swaying palm tree, Phlox was pretty sure that she could see a strip of flickering blue. It was either the ocean or a really large television showing an invalid channel.

Her eyes swept downward to the parking lot, which was filled with expensive cars. Latest models, all self-driving, all electric, all shiny and sparkling. People seemed to care more about their cars in Miami than they did in Pittsburgh. After a few seconds, something caught her eye and her heart skipped a beat.

Sitting directly across from her window, the maroon van from the rest stop three hours before sat quietly.

"The more identities a man has, the more they express the person they conceal."
-John Le Carré, *Tinker, Tailor, Soldier, Spy*

Banker Blues

An excerpt from an article in The Econometrician, *Volume II, Issue 5*

The bad news in the financial sector continues this week with another 12% drop in the financial services index. Leading the plunge was the 39% haircut taken by Third Swiss Holdings after its CEO, Franz Schnitzelmann, admitted that there was "no way that its 10-K could be released in a timely manner."

Traditional auditing firms have also seen their shares rocked as companies move to the blockchain, instead of traditional accounting records. "Double-entry bookkeeping has been a mainstay of business transactions for 500 years," says Haoniyao Mwangi, CTO of upstart firm EtherAudit. "However, there was still a necessity for CEOs, CFOs and auditors to examine records and sign off on them on a quarterly basis. By storing their financial records on the blockchain, it becomes almost impossible to 'fudge' them. All input and output are automatically verified, allowing no room for human error, intentional or otherwise."

So-called "triple-entry" bookkeeping — first proposed last century by Yuji Ijjiri — has been celebrated as the third historical change in accounting procedures. Although often seen as a dry subject, accounting has made large corporations and the modern world possible, and has a huge impact on all of our lives. Single-entry bookkeeping meant a quantum leap forward in how societies could be organized. Kings could determine who owed them money, or how much grain was in the silos in case of a crop failure or drought. Double-entry bookkeeping, where every input is matched with a corresponding output, and vice-versa, meant that errors within systems could be found easily. In single-entry bookkeeping, a scribe could smudge a paper and suddenly you owed 50 goats instead of 5; in double-entry bookkeeping, one could check to see if the number of goats that you took from the king matched the number he said you owed him. However, a scribe only had to do a little extra work to make sure that both entries matched up with the erroneous information. This was widely known as "cooking the books."

Triple-entry bookkeeping fixes this fatal flaw. The third entry is the blockchain itself, which provides an unchangeable record. Saying that you received fifty goats from the king could easily be checked against the king's records which showed only five goats leaving. A malicious accountant would be unable to change these values without unthinkable computing power.

Smart auditing — that is, moving records over to self-verifying contracts and immutable storage — has found numerous instances of embezzlement and fraud. In a recent study by Two Five Six Wealth Advisers, 53% of Fortune 500 firms have moved at least some of their accounting over to a blockchain solution. Of these firms, almost 78% have found some error in the process, and 24% have fired at least one person after discovering an error.

Chapter 17

What Evil Looks Had I

Phlox looked out again to verify that it was the same van that they had encountered earlier. There was no doubt in her mind that it was.

She raced out of her hotel room and knocked on Jane's door. A muffled "just a minute!" rang out. Every second felt like an hour, but Jane did come to the door after a minute, blouse halfway unbuttoned and a towel around her shoulder. She looked to be about to berate Phlox for interrupting her shower preparations but her body language changed quickly when she saw the look on Phlox's face. Phlox could feel her eyebrows moving up above her blue eyes.

"Phlox! What's wrong! You look like you've just seen Death himself."

"I might have."

She explained to Jane about the van. Jane buttoned her blouse all the way up, put down the towel, and peeked out of her window, barely moving the curtains.

"Maybe your father isn't paranoid..." she muttered. "I can't even begin to calculate the odds that the van stopped at the same rest stop we did, left at the same time, and ended up in the parking lot of the same hotel. I mean, it's possible, but so is me winning the Worldwide Ethereum Lottery ten times in a row."

"How did they find us?" asked Phlox.

"I don't know. Your friend Chris still messaging his would-be girlfriend Vera?" Seeing Phlox's reaction, she smiled. "He probably spent half an hour talking about her on the ride today. He still has it bad for her. Men!"

"All the same, we should probably get out of here. Hope you didn't like your room too much, dear."

Phlox felt a sinking feeling that she would not be spending the night on a beautiful cupcake of a bed piled high with various-sized pillows. She hoped that at least her night would not be spent on the ground. Funny how twenty-four hours ago she was looking forward to camping. A few minutes on a comfortable bed and she was suddenly spoiled.

She and Jane grabbed their backpacks and walked straight over to the other wing. Phlox knocked on Chris's door, but nobody answered. She put her ear up to the door and couldn't hear anything.

"Chris!" yelled Phlox.

The door to John's hotel room opened and Chris walked out, followed shortly by John.

"What's up?" asked Chris. Phlox explained the situation to them as both of their faces gradually darkened.

"Damn it," said John, visibly deflating.

"Now, now, no time for pessimism," chimed in Jane. "Be prepared, is what I say. Luckily for you. Now let's all stop yelling in the hallway."

Feeling a bit sheepish, they all headed into John's room. If anything, it was even more gorgeous than Phlox's room — probably to make up for the lack of ocean view. John and Chris sat in two identical overstuffed chairs, and Phlox and Jane on the massive bed.

"I told you the Hotel Bird of Paradise was made for discreet clientele. Whoever these people are, they're probably expecting us to head out the front door at some point."

"It wouldn't be hard for them to stake out all around the hotel," John brought up. "How many people could fit in that van? Six or seven, easy. Not to mention if they have local law enforcement helping them out, this building would be entirely surrounded. It's going to be hard to sneak past them no matter which exit we take."

"Well, sure, if we leave the building."

"What do you mean?" asked Chris. "What else could we do?"

"Chris, put yourself in a wealthy Bulgarian's shoes. A wealthy Bulgarian like you, if you remember your alias. Paparazzi find out you're staying at the Bird of Paradise, promised a full litecoin if they get a shot of you, and you'll be damned if you end up on the front page of the Candid Shots of Rich People site.

"The hotel had these kind of people in mind when they built the place. What would you do?"

"Hire a helicopter?" asked Phlox.

Jane smiled. "Good idea, but no. You'd escape via the catacombs."

"Catacombs?" came the exclamation from everyone in the room but Jane.

"Sure. When they put up the Miami Dikes to prevent the waters from rushing in, they also added some massive pumping stations below. The water table is incredibly high here. A few of the poshest places, like the hotel in which you are staying, were able to negotiate a few entrances of their own. As long as you're a guest here, you can spend your entire vacation heading to various casinos and other tourist destinations without ever seeing sunlight. The Bulgarians love it."

"How do you know so much about how Bulgarian oligarchs experience Miami, Jane?"

"You're not the only man I ever dated, John," she replied with a wink. "Let's go."

They spent a few minutes gathering their belongings — Phlox casting one more wistful look around where she would have been sleeping — and met back at John's room. Jane led them down the stairs in the main lobby, then through a confusing warren of back rooms until they saw a small sign with Cyrillic and Latin characters on it. Phlox couldn't read the Cyrillic letters — she assumed it was Bulgarian — but the English read, "AUTHORIZED ACCESS ONLY! For invited guests of the Hotel Bird of Paradise."

A quick scan of Jane's watch against a scanner was all it took for the door to swing open of its own accord.

"Non-Ethereum, entirely local," gushed Jane, "but still tied in to the room accounts, which are stored on the blockchain. Probably used some of John's handiwork for the cross-chain interactions."

Walking through the door, they found themselves in a dingy-looking, unadorned stairway heading down. It smelled damp and musty, reminding Phlox of the basement of her child home. The cinder block walls were adorned with nothing except the occasional caution sign.

"Anyone using this should know what they're doing," explained Jane.

After descending a single floor, they found another door, which clicked with recognition as they approached. Jane pushed open the second door and they found themselves in a large room, elevated on a black metal catwalk. The floors were covered in pipes and machinery, the great pumps which protected Miami from the rising seas. The pumping itself was only a low drone, but combined with the muted rushing of water and the occasional squeak of a component that needed oil, it was a cacophony.

"Why is it so hot in here?" asked Chris.

Jane pointed down at a particularly shiny piece of machinery below. A stream of water was running over, and steam rising, from it. "Bitcoin mining equipment. They put them in here, said it would help cover the cost of the construction, and the water would cool them down naturally. Turned out to be a bit of a boondoggle, but the Miami Municipal Authority turns it on occasionally when enough hashpower goes offline."

She continued to lead them across the catwalk to a concrete outcropping, covered with several barrels and boxes of equipment. Another catwalk led to another door. In front of them was a third door, this one with a sign reading "SERVICE TUNNEL — Please do not enter."

Pointing at the door, Jane explained. "This one is used by actual service workers. Mechanics and plumbers who have to come in and fix the pipes and pumps. The other door across the way leads to a few other hotels and casinos. You all feeling lucky? We could spend the night here, or we could try to stay awake all night in the casinos. Casinos here only take Bitcoin or Litecoin, but I'm happy to spot you some if you can't shift your Monero."

Phlox looked at the plain concrete floor and thought back longingly to her room at the Hotel Bird of Paradise.

"How busy are these tunnels?" asked Chris. "Are we likely to be seen?"

"Can't say. I don't know if I ever saw anybody else down here, but it's not like I was spending my days in Miami hiding in the sewers."

"We could set up the barrels to hide us from any cross-traffic," said John. "We should be able to fit behind here, get some shut-eye, be prepared for our trip tomorrow."

"I'm going to vote no on that plan, dad," countered Phlox. "One, if anyone does come here, we're going to have lots of explaining to do, and there's nowhere to run. Two, we're pretty well-rested, I think. At least I am. Three, even if we do pull an all-nighter, we're going to be spending the next few days on a cruise. We'll be able to recover. Besides, aren't we supposed to be wealthy? Don't rich people waste money on gambling? I say we spend the night seeing some Miami nightlife."

Phlox's plan made sense, and they all quickly agreed to it. They grabbed what privacy they could behind the barrels and boxes and looked through their backpacks for something appropriate to wear to go waste some money. Phlox half-considered her prom dress, wrinkled as it was, but finally decided to go with a t-shirt and jeans. She hoped that it looked like an expensive pair of jeans from across the room. She never could tell the difference.

Only Jane ended up with something at least somewhat dressy, a nice blouse and a circle skirt. John and Chris were also wearing jeans, with Phlox's dad wearing a red polo shirt and Chris a camouflage shirt that read "I WENT BEAR HUNTING AND ALL I GOT WAS THIS LOUSY T-SHIRT."

"You know, in the movies, people going to casinos are always wearing tuxedos and ball gowns," remarked Jane. "We look like an office worker and her interns... some interns older than others."

Jane led them over a few more catwalks, making the occasional wrong turn, until they found a door that read "Orange Blossom Casino." Using her watch, she once again opened the door and they went up a staircase that looked like a twin of the one that they had gone down earlier at the Hotel Bird of Paradise.

Emerging near a kitchen, they quickly found themselves out in the lobby, looking around at the polished veneer of opulence. People milled about, dressed remarkably like John, Jane, and Chris. They blended in instantly, while Jane felt slightly overdressed.

"I guess tuxedos aren't in fashion, anymore," lamented Jane. "Well, shall we play some games?"

After finding some rental lockers for their backpacks, they headed over to a counter and each of them shifted over some millimons to Litecoin. Casinos generally didn't accept Monero, and they made payouts only in Federal Reserve Tokens. Playing the games still involved physical tokens, clay chips. A millilite's worth of them felt pleasantly substantial to Phlox. She kept fiddling with a handful of the blue, green, and black chips as she and Chris looked for a table to play. After making plans to meet up in a few hours for the midnight buffet, Jane and John headed off by themselves.

Casinos never were Phlox's scene. English lit undergraduates with a side job at a waffle shop were not exactly high on the list of preferred customers for casinos, either. Still, the combination this night seemed to be magical. Chris seemed to be having much less fun.

They wandered over to an Ethereum Roulette wheel. About a decade ago, Phlox remembered, there were a series of scandals where roulette wheels were rigged by the casinos. They lost their accreditation by the state, a few low-level employees went to jail, high-level executives floated away on golden parachutes, the usual story. This story, however, continued to drag on as additional casinos were found to have fiddled the numbers in ways subtle and overt. Faith in the gambling world was at a low point, and people started to bet with local bookies instead. These were illegal, of course, and government authories wrung their hands, but more importantly, the stock price of major casino companies plummeted.

The fix, like so many other things in the last few decades, came from the world of cryptocurrency. One wag in a paper noted that the nonce values — the values that miners searched for when mining for Bitcoin — were, for all intents and purposes, random. Why couldn't the casinos just use those instead of an old-fashioned ball spinning around a wheel? The nonces were numbers used to secure the building blocks of a multi-trillion dollar financial system, and if anyone had been able to predict their frequency, they would have made more money than Croesus already. Balls and wheels were Stone Age inventions. Why not a more up-to-date source of randomness?

A few casinos took the editorial writer's article seriously. The distribution of hash values did meet the criteria to be considered random, or close enough to it. Nobody could accuse the casinos of cheating, as customers could verify the nonce values of the latest block on their own. There was one problem, however; Bitcoin blocks occurred, on average, once every ten minutes, an eternity for a casino. Ethereum blocks were calculated every 15 to 30 seconds. Much better.

Ethereum Roulette seemed to be a pretty popular game here. The board above showed the last twenty or so hashes. Chris remarked that they looked strange to him, as they were in decimal — base-10 — instead of hexadecimal — base-16. For the purposes of the game, only the last two digits counted, but most players had some superstitions about the rest of the nonce having an impact on the next. They tended to be more complex versions of the Gamblers' Fallacy, where red would be "due" if there were too many blacks in a row, or conversely that if there was a "hot streak" of reds then another red would be coming up next. "The last two digits of a nonce are never in the previous full nonce." "The last two digits of nonces are always related somehow to the first two digits of the nonce three blocks ago." Despite the widespread belief in these patterns, which, if valid, would mean an inestimable advantage on behalf of patrons, casinos were somehow still profitable.

Phlox looked at the rules for the game. Simple enough, except for some complicated exceptions about orphaned blocks which she skimmed over. You could bet on a specific two-digit number, from 02-99, being the last two digits of a nonce, or if the number is even or odd. If it were either 00 or 01, everyone lost their money to the casino. The house had to get their cut somehow. Somebody was paying for all the shiny gold and the ultra-fast network connection to get the latest blocks off of the Ethereum network.

They played for about two hours, mostly making minimum bets, and always on even or odd instead for the long-shot specific numbers. They were looking to maximize the amount of time playing, not their money. It was more fun than Phlox imagined it would have been, but she wasn't sure if it was going to keep her awake all night.

Coming back from a trip to the ladies' room, Phlox looked around and couldn't see Chris at the Ethereum Roulette table. Perhaps he had gone over to the Bitcoin Bingo or Litecoin Lottery tables?

No. She didn't see him anywhere. Nor her dad, nor Jane. The beeps and bloops coming from the various machines, the flashing lights, the murmur of the crowds... it all took on a vaguely sinister air. Calming herself down, she started pacing around the edges of the game room. All she saw was people she didn't know, machines she didn't recognize, fake indoor plants and fake gold, a whole room of unknowns and the unknowable.

She started to walk faster, nervous in spite of herself. Her mind quickly jumped to worst-case scenarios. Had the people in the van taken them? Were they being tortured in a back room at this very moment? Casinos always had massive surveillance systems, right? Why did they decide to spend the night here? Whose decision was it? Oh god, it was *hers*.

Just as she was feeling at her absolute nadir, she noticed another Ethereum Roulette machine through a doorway. There was an entire other game room there. No, scratch that. That was the game room she was in before. She must have made a wrong turn after leaving the bathroom and ended up here. Chris was clearly visible next to the other Ethereum Roulette table, talking with Jane and John.

Breathing a sigh of relief and composing herself a bit first, she headed over to talk to them. Jane saw her before she got to them, though, and directed the others in Phlox's direction.

"Hey, Phlox. Where have you been?"

"Uhh, nowhere, just got a little mixed up on the way back from the bathroom."

"Oh, good, we were worried about you! We were thinking of hitting the midnight buffet, you want to come or you want to stay here with the rest of the high-rollers?"

The buffet was impressive in the way that all buffets were, with nigh-infinite supplies of subpar food, quantity and variety overwhelming any hint of quality. It was a single table, covered with a sneeze shield, which folded over and around and back in on itself in a way that seemed vaguely four-dimensional and non-Euclidean.

It was filling, though, and the variety allowed Chris to have some spaghetti with plain tomato sauce, Jane some chocolate chip cookies, and John some more pizza (which led to some ribbing from Jane and protestations that pizza was basically the perfect food). Phlox took a cue from Jane and made an ice cream sandwich out of two double-chocolate cookies and a mix of strawberry, rocky road, and butterscotch ice cream.

"How's everyone doing at the tables?" asked Jane, crumbs flying from the cookie in her hand as she gesticulated in the general direction of the game room.

Chris counted his chips, quietly mouthing the numbers. "Up 517 microlites. Not bad!"

Phlox looked at her chips, started to count, then quickly gave up to focus more attention on her frozen dessert concoction. "I think I'm about even."

"John and I aren't doing too shabby, either. But don't play too conservatively, we're going to drop these in some lucky shlub's pocket by the end of the night."

Seeing the horrified looks on the faces of Phlox and Chris, Jane continued. "Oh, not literally. We'll just leave them somewhere where they'll be found. One, we are not going to shift them out into Federal Reserve Tokens. Don't want to take the risk. Two, these chips have RFID tags inside them. Near-field communication from them can be tracked, and while I think we've done a good job of mixing things up, the people after us do tracking for a living. Another risk."

Jane seemed to realize that they were less concerned with physically dropping the chips in somebody's pocket and more with the loss of a sizable amount of money. "I hear you found ten of John's bitcoin and you're concerned about microlites? I've heard of misers but that's pretty ridiculous."

Realizing that the amount of money that they had been gambling with was now a very small percentage of their net worth, they calmed down and ate, mostly in silence. All of them were tired, except Jane, who seemed like she could easily go another few nights without sleep.

As the night wore on, they all stayed caffeinated with various drinks provided by the casino — *gratis*, of course, as an awake gambler will tend to spend much more money than a sleeping one. Phlox started to slowly lose money, while Chris was on a hot streak, tripling his initial stake by 5:00 AM. They decided to head out for a little fresh air on a balcony which overlooked the oceans and the immensity of the great Miami Dikes which kept the Atlantic Ocean from the ground floors of most of the buildings they could see. They watched as a few albatrosses settled in at different spots on it.

There was still quite a while before the sun would begin to rise, but the ocean was filled with sparkling lights — reflections of the city of Miami. After the air-conditioned chill of the casino, the warmth of the air and the humidity coming off of the sea felt like a blanket.

"Phlox, I've been thinking. I'm not going to get on the ship tomorrow."

"Seriously? After all this, the maroon van following us down the entire Florida coast, tunnels under the city, you still think that my dad's just paranoid?"

"I think that all of those things you mention are facts, but I don't think that they necessarily mean that someone is after us. I know your dad *thinks* that someone is after him. Don't worry, I won't tell anyone where you're going. Your secret is safe with me. I'll just catch a bus back to Pittsburgh, try to explain to my professors why I've been absent for over a week and make up the work. Maybe even try to patch things up with Vera, although I think that will be a harder sell."

"You're going to just pretend like none of this ever happened?" Phlox couldn't believe it. He was the one who got them into this mess.

"No!" The intensity startled Phlox. Two men further along the balcony, who seemed deep in conversation, looked up and cast inquiring eyes at the shouted syllable. "That bitcoin is going to change my life. I'll be safe, shift it to Monero, shift some back to Litecoin, maybe use some of the weirder altcoins that probably aren't being monitored as much..."

"Chris, I don't think this is a good idea. Not even a little bit."

"I know, Phlox. Otherwise, I would have asked you to come as well. But I thought I owed you an explanation before I left. Your dad's great, he's really smart, but I haven't been able to convince him that he's jumping at shadows and coincidences. Trust me, I tried on the car ride. He was having none of it."

"If that's the way you feel, I'm sorry. There's nothing I can say to make you change your mind?"

"No. I'm sorry, too, Phlox. It's been a fun ride. And maybe I'm wrong, in which case this shadowy cabal will get me before I get on the bus. In which case, you have my permission to tell me 'I told you so.' Or at least you can tell my ghost."

"Don't even joke about that!" Phlox ordered. Again, the two men looked up at the raised voice. Chris's eyes said that he was sorry, although no words escaped his lips. Phlox leaned in and hugged him tightly.

"Stay safe," said Phlox, quietly, but meaning it sincerely.

"I will," said Chris. Phlox turned to open the door to head back into the casino and tell her dad and Jane that Chris was leaving. There would only be three people heading to Venezuela. Her heart was heavy, and not just for the fact that there was now a person who knew their destination out there on his own. Chris had been a good friend. He could have tried to get the bitcoin for himself. He could have tried to turn them in or left them at any point. He definitely had opportunities at the Amaryllis Motel, or the gas station in West Virginia, or even that night in her apartment when her dad first came to the door.

Was that only a week ago? A little more than that. It felt like ages.

As Phlox's hand touched the metal door handle, a conduit for the coolness of the air conditioned air behind it, she heard a muffled scream. Looking over her shoulder, she saw the two other men had become three.

The third was Chris, a black cloth bag over his head, being dragged to the end of the balcony where a maroon van was idling.

"Ah! Well a-day! What evil looks
Had I from old and young!
Instead of the cross, the albatross
About my neck was hung."
-Samuel Taylor Coleridge, *The Rime of the Ancient Mariner*

So, You Commit Here Often?

An excerpt from an article in The Econometrician, *Volume II, Issue 1*

Throughout history, finding a partner in life — or for the night — has been something on which humanity has spent a large portion of its energy. There have been difficulties throughout, from finding somebody you liked in your small village, to knowing the correct way to doff your hat when meeting a lady, to determing who would pay during the first date.

When dating applications took off in the early part of this century, many problems were solved, but new ones arrived. People were concerned about the safety of meeting somebody that they had met online. While there were some issues, customers soon found that they could be ameliorated by meeting in a public place, letting others know where they would be, and similar safeguards. What many did not foresee was that some matchmaking companies would deliberately do a poor job of connecting people. After all, people tend to drop their subscriptions if they find their soulmate. The longer the period of time you spent looking for him or her, the more you would pay in dues. Additionally, if you chose one dating platform and your ideal partner chose another, you would never connect. Each site or app was an island unto itself.

As in so many other fields, however, blockchain technology was able to provide a solution. Tying directly in with various authentication and ID mechanisms already running on the Ethereum network, security and safety were built into these new dating dapps. All of the major dapps supported the SEDI-1 (Standardized Ethereum Dating Interface, Version 1) standard, which allowed users to interact with users registered on other sites. It was the difference between the early days of isolated, company-wide networks and the Internet.

Finally, the fact that these self-running dapps were no longer interested in maintaining cash flow from users, but rather in creating long-term matches, meant that the effectiveness of matching increased dramatically. Several implemented advanced machine-learning algorithms to determine compatibility. A recent study by researchers at the University of North Haverbrook found that users of said applications were 33% more likely to be in a long-term relationship, compared to users of traditional matchmaking applications.

Chapter 18

The Struggle with Nature

Phlox froze, her brain failing to comprehend exactly what was happening. Then, within the space of a few milliseconds, it seemed to issue conflicting commands to run, to hide, and to find her dad. She ignored all of them.

Knowing even as she was making it that it was a rash decision, and one that she would likely regret later, she ran across the balcony — thankful that she was not the type of girl to wear high heels — and kicked one of the men from behind, as hard as she could, in the crotch. He let out a yell, which Chris took as a signal to fall down. Chris's bulk was useful here; the second man, who had a firm grasp on Chris's arm, fell on top of him, a victim of physics. Phlox quickly kicked the second man in the crotch as well, leading to a second yell of pain.

There weren't many people on the street at this time, but a few passersby noticed the commotion and started to head in their direction.

"Help!" screamed Phlox, dragging Chris, still with a bag over his head, back towards the door to the casino. The men had recovered from the unexpected attacks, and one glanced up at Phlox with hatred in his eyes. He started toward her, then realized how exposed he was — at least one person was jogging over from the street to see what the problem was. The man looked like the stereotype of a bureaucrat — pale face tanned only by computer monitors, horn-rimmed glasses, clothes professional but cheaply made. She could almost see the decision-making process happening behind his eyes. He quickly determined that discretion was the better part of kidnapping, and ran away from Phlox, toward the waiting van. His partner followed quickly behind.

It couldn't have been more than a few seconds from the time she started running, but it felt like an eternity. Chris was in the process of tearing the bag off his head. It was cheap canvas, like something used to carry bulk rice home from the grocery store.

"Jag-offs!" yelled Phlox at the rapidly receding van, as the man who was jogging toward them came up. She could feel the blood pulsing through arteries, veins, capillaries, all through her body. Her breath was coming in quick bursts. *What the hell had just happened? And what had she done?*

"Are you okay?" the jogging man asked, concerned.

"Yeah," lied Chris, "just muggers. Saw us coming out of the casino with smiles on our faces, must have thought we'd hit the jackpot. First thing they did was try to grab my watch."

Two security guards from the casino casually walked over, wrinkled uniforms brushing against muscles that hadn't seen real exercise in years. One was noticeably older than the other, but the younger one looked as though he was rapidly heading towards being the older one's twin.

"What's going on here?" the older one asked Chris, suspicion in his voice.

"Nothing. Just an attempted mugging, I think."

"Mmm. You wanna file a report?"

"No, probably more trouble than it's worth. I'm fine."

"You got it," said the younger security guard, walking back over to their guard post at the entryway to the casino and thankful that *that* excitement was over with.

"You sure you're not hurt? Either of you?" The jogger's voice was tender but also impatient. He reminded Phlox of an old uncle from a Chekhov story, middle-aged, his demeanor torn between the fact that these kids ruined his jog but also really caring about their safety.

"No, I'm fine, really, life in the big city, I guess," said Chris, trying to maintain a joking manner.

"Yeah, me too," Phlox chimed in. "Things like this happen. But we're both okay."

"Well, you two stay safe." A strange echo of what Phlox had told Chris only a few minutes before, and the man was back on his jogging route. They watched as he crossed the street and past the shadows cast by the neon lights of the casino.

"Go ahead, say 'I told you so,'" said Chris, breaking the silence. "I promise I won't doubt your dad any more."

"I'm not saying anything. That was scary."

Phlox paused, thoughtful.

"I'll tell you what. We need to tell him what happened, but... we don't need to tell him why you were leaving the balcony. If you want to say that you were just getting some fresh air, I'm fine with that. But you need to promise me — promise me — that you'll believe me next time. I mean it."

"Cross my heart, hope to die, stick a needle in my eye."

"I'm serious, Chris."

"I am, too. When we first met, that was the most serious promise you could make. I think that whatever counts as serious when you first meet should always count as serious."

Phlox looked at him thoughtfully, but he seemed sincere. It was almost like he was trying to wax philosophical, or at least literary. *Hmm*, thought Phlox, *there's hope for the boy yet. Maybe he'll read something other than textbooks and science fiction.*

"Promise accepted. Now let's get back inside. They must have been waiting for you to leave the property. There's always lots of cameras inside casinos to catch cheaters, card counters, that sort of thing."

"How do you know so much about casino security?"

"Uhh, because I read a book every once in a while?" Phlox smiled.

The air conditioning hit them hard across the face as they came back in to the casino through the side door. After a few minutes of searching, they found Jane and John at a Monero Mahjong Madness slot machine. Between the two of them, with numerous interruptions of one another, Phlox and Chris explained what had happened at the balcony. John looked thoughtful.

"They must have been waiting for one of us to leave casino property. Why the hell would you go outside?"

"We were just getting some fresh air," explained Chris, "and watching the water. It was getting stuffy in here, you know, having been, uhh, inside for so long, all night, and I was feeling a little claustrophobic, so Phlox said we should get some air —"

"It won't happen again," Phlox said, stepping in with an air of finality.

Jane looked more agitated than Phlox could remember her seeing in the days since they met. "Well, they definitely know where we are now. I still have no idea how they found us.

"Here's what we'll do. Once we're on the *Angel Princess*, it's only a few miles until we hit Cuban authority over the waves. It's not international waters, *terra nullius* as they say, but I'll trust the Cubans over the Americans at this point. We just need to get on board the ship without the maroon van guys finding us."

"We need a name for these people, even if we don't know who they are. We can't keep calling them 'the maroon van guys.' "

"How about the Chekists?" Phlox suggested. The Cheka, the Soviet secret police, had executed many of the Old Bolsheviks last century.

Jane laughed. "Way to go with the theme, honey, pessimistic though it may be. Chekists it is."

The breakfast buffet was just opening, and they were all starting to feel the effects of the all-nighter they had just pulled, so they decided to grab some food. Over pancakes, danishes, and most importantly, pots of coffee, they discussed how they were going to get to the *Angel Princess* without being spotted.

Ideas were thrown out but just as quickly shot down. There were about seven city blocks between them and the dock. Walking with the morning crowd was no guarantee that they wouldn't be pushed into an alley. Their vehicles at the Hotel Bird of Paradise were almost certainly being watched. Jane wasn't sure where else the tunnels led to, and didn't want to start exploring there if the people after them knew about them as well. That they did know about the tunnels was probable, if they figured out that they should be staking out this location.

They considered leaving together, but that would make them extremely obvious. They discussed leaving in small groups, perhaps even one by one, but that would make them vulnerable. They even contemplated various ways of leaving in sitcom style, hiding in linen baskets or garbage cans. There was a lull in the conversation, and Phlox had a thought come unbidden into her head, one where she just knew the answer was there.

"Wait a second! What if we didn't leave, but someone else took us?"

"What do you mean, peony?" asked her dad.

"EthShare. We call for a car, it comes and picks us up. We ask for a van or something else big, ask them to pick us up in the garage or something."

"There's a loading dock around back," said Jane, running with the idea. "Also a place where rich Bulgarians leave when they don't want to be seen. It's hidden from the road."

John agreed. "That's a good idea. Whoever these people... Chekists... are, they obviously want to stay away from the casino. There's been no further attempt to come get us and we are the definition of sitting ducks here. Unless they're still nursing the wounds that Phlox inflicted. Too bad you weren't wearing steel-toed boots, buttercup."

"Thanks, dad. I just remembered what you taught me. But let's back up a second. We still don't know how these people found us."

"It has to be one — or more — of our watches," said Chris. "We would have seen somebody else in the tunnels, even if they did know about them. We were extremely careful shifting our mons over to lites. It has to be the watches."

John agreed. "Falkvinge's Law. Anything that can be used to track you, will be used to track you. We're being as safe as can be, but I'm sure they have their own tricks as well. Maybe there's some sort of unique frequency or pattern that our watches are emitting. I don't know, I've been out of this game for too long. But it must be something to do with the watches."

"Could we just toss them out? Or give them to somebody else?" asked Chris. "We can just get new ones later."

"We're going to need them to board the boat. And all of us showing up with brand-new watches is going to look really suspicious to the authorities. The *Angel Princess* is Venezuelan, sure, but they do have some rules." Jane had been through this before, apparently.

"Turn them off? Take out the batteries?" asked Phlox.

John shook his head. "Modern watches have battery backup for emergency situations. Who knows if they're sending out a signal even though they seem to be off? I mean, if we had the proper equipment, sure. But unless one of you has an electronics lab in your backpack, we'd be trusting to luck. We need to be sure they're not emitting any signal. Or else we're going to end up in worse shape than Chris, there."

Chris actually didn't look to be in too bad of a shape from his ordeal, besides some mussed-up hair. Phlox felt like she might still be freaking out if it had happened to her.

"Aren't there things that block the signal, though?" asked Phlox. "I remember reading some spy story about buildings that had metal all around them to prevent signals from leaking out. A far-away cage or something. But I don't have any metal boxes in my back —"

John stopped her. "A Faraday cage! Of course! You're a genius, hydrangea. We just need to surround the watches in material that will block any electromagnetic signals."

"That's what I said, Dad, but where are we —"

John ignored her. A short, middle-aged worker was at the buffet, slowly taking out pancakes off of a tray he was holding and placing them on the buffet plate. John left the table and approached him, doing his best to look like a friendly but befuddled tourist.

"Excuse me, sir," he asked the short man, "but it looks like our eyes were bigger than our stomachs. Do you think we could get some aluminum foil to wrap up our breakfasts for later? I'd hate to waste the food."

The short man smiled, the forced polite smile that all service workers were familiar with, the one that always prefaced them saying 'no' to somebody's request.

"I'm sorry, sir, but no food is allowed to leave the buffet area. Casino rules, sir."

"No problem, just thought I'd ask. Have a good one."

Returning to the table, John looked pained. "No dice. Stupid buffet rules."

They all looked around the casino buffet for something small and metallic that could be used for their purposes, but only saw generic paintings on the wall, easily-cleaned knick-knacks on dining tables, and more customers coming in to take advantage of the buffet as the sun rose. After a few minutes, Jane smiled.

"Excuse me for a minute," she said. "I'm going to get something to eat."

When she got up, however, Jane left the buffet area entirely. Phlox was confused. Where else was she going to go?

Phlox did not have to wait long before her curiosity was satisfied. Jane returned to the table with a small bag of potato chips, which she opened and unceremoniously dumped on the side of her plate.

"Why would you pay for a vending machine when there's a buffet right here?" asked Chris.

"Oh, Chris, such a software guy," cooed Jane, sarcastically. "John, would you like to explain?"

John's eyes lit up, realizing Jane's plan. "It's a foil potato chip bag. Metallic! It fits a watch, and it won't look suspicious having some trash in our bags. This is perfect! Well, wait, let's not count our chickens quite yet. I'm not an expert on potato chip packaging, and it looks pretty thin. Let's check that it does in fact block the signal."

They tried a few experiments with putting John's watch in the bag, quickly retrieving it, and viewing the current signal strength. There was some protesting from John that it didn't have to be *his* watch getting potato chip oil on it, but Jane quickly shot that down. It turned out that the bag didn't block the signal entirely, but did do a pretty good job.

"That's fine, we'll just grab a few more bags and put them inside of each other. The effect should be cumulative."

A few more experiments and they determined that three bags was enough to entirely block the signal for all of their watches. The entire time, Phlox was thinking how ridiculous this all must look to other tables, if they weren't too engrossed in their own thoughts about winning or losing some microlites at the tables.

Jane looked at her watch. "The *Angel Princess* is docked now. We can head over any time we want. I think we're going to be safer there than anywhere in Miami. I vote we get there sooner rather than later. It leaves at 1, so we have plenty of time, though."

"Jane, let's also set off your decoy in Alabama," said John. "They may not believe that we got from Miami to Mobile so quickly, but maybe they'll think that one of us is there. At least it will keep them on their toes."

"I've been working on a few other decoys, a few closer to here in the city. Rented out some servers under false names. Probably not going to be as foolproof, but it might confuse them. While I was up, I also took the liberty of getting the addresses for some of the other casinos in town. I'll send a few millilites to each of them. If they're monitoring us over the Litecoin blockchain, with any luck they'll think we're already at another casino, or heading to one."

"You're pretty devious, Jane." John smiled at her for the first time, at least that Phlox had seen.

"I learned from the best," Jane said, mysteriously, leaving it unsaid whether or not John was the best.

"Well, when should we do this?" asked Phlox. "I'm feeling a bit antsy, now that we actually have a plan."

"No time like the present." Jane fiddled with her watch a bit. "There. Right now we're announcing ourselves on the Bitcoin, Litecoin, Ethereum, and FRT blockchains with all the subtlety of a fire engine racing down a city street."

Trying to act as nonchalantly as possible, they placed their watches in the empty potato chip packages and ensured that they were sealed tightly. John took the plates of leftover breakfast food and a small mountain of potato chips to the garbage can.

Jane then got up and asked the concierge to call them an EthShare van, biggest one possible, and oh, would it be possible to be picked up at the loading dock? She then asked to see his watch and said how nice it was. She noticed that it already had a QR code up. This guy was no dummy. Jane transferred over a sizable tip in Monero.

Sitting back down at the table, Jane announced, "Our ride should be here within five minutes. We could have ordered it ourselves on one of our watches, but I figure that using the hotel concierge would mean one less vector for them to track us. He promised me that he would get it here as fast as possible."

"What, did you use your feminine wiles on him?" asked Phlox.

"Oh, Phlox, always remember, feminine wiles are one thing, but if you really want to get things done, you use cold, hard cryptocurrency."

"Also, it's the concierge's job to get cars for casino patrons," said John, unimpressed.

"True," Jane admitted, "but I'm paying for discretion. Leaving by the loading dock is not something ordinary 'casino patrons' do. If he thinks that we may be coming back, he's not going to be talking, if he wants some more millimons. And they all want it. More millimons, that is."

As advertised, the concierge came over to their table within a minute, speaking with a slight hint of a British accent. "Excuse me, your van has arrived. Please follow me."

They followed him through the hidden hallways of the casino, a confusing warren that they never could have found their way out of alone. For a moment, Phlox was concerned that he was taking them to some sort of ambush. But then the concierge opened up a door to a cavernous indoor space. A massive, steel corrugated door was off to their right, and near it was a large car decked out in the orange and green logo of the Orange Blossom Casino. Directly in front of them was a large self-driving EthShare van, with dark-tinted windows and three rows of seats.

"You can key in your destination when you enter," said the concierge, implicitly pointing out that he had no way of knowing where they were going, "and I hope you have had a wonderful time at our casino. Please come again soon."

They thanked him and placed their backpacks in the rear of the van. Clambering in, Phlox and Chris got in the back row, and John and Jane in the middle row. Jane typed in the address of the cruise terminal and the van started to move, the corrugated door of the garage opening automatically as it approached.

Even through the tinted windows, they were shocked at how bright the sun was at this latitude at this time of day. It felt almost like a physical force trying to break into the car. They looked around at the alley in which they emerged and tried to relax. The car took a direct path to a road that ran next to the Miami Dikes, and they all stared at the massive walls holding back the Atlantic. It was a marvel of engineering — Phlox had seen pamphlets in the casino for tours.

Despite their nerves, the entire ride went off without a hitch, as far as they could tell. The traffic seemed extremely light for what should have been morning rush hour. Within ten minutes they were leaving the van and heading up the ramp towards the *Angel Princess*.

Phlox had never seen a cruise ship in person before, and was quite impressed. Although not nearly as large as the massive "cruise liners" of the previous generation, the ship held at least 80 passengers along with 20 or 30 crew, and had its own pool on the top deck. A line of lifeboats ran along the sides, which Chris noticed.

"Uhh, these things are safe, right?" asked Chris.

"Safe as houses," said Jane. "Well, I mean, not really that safe. But it's not exactly dangerous. I can't remember the last time one of these wrecked, and even if they do wreck, there are plenty of lifeboats and these are pretty well-traveled sea lanes. We probably wouldn't have to end up cannibalizing someone after drawing straws."

"That sounds ominous. Like, you know, really specific foreshadowing." Phlox had not been concerned, but this sounded an awful lot like something that an actor in a bad movie would say just before boarding the *Titanic*.

"Well, knock on wood if you like, I'm just saying that it's safe."

They walked up the gangplank to a reception desk, and a chain stopping their entry to the deck. The reception desk was obviously a temporary construction that was brought out during boarding. An officious, tanned man dressed in a white uniform stood behind it and a laptop computer sat on top of it.

"Welcome to the *Angel Princess*," the man said, with just a trace of a Spanish accent. "Can I help you?"

"I'm Janet Ivanova," said Jane, discreetly trying to pull her watch out of its collection of potato chip bags. She had considered adding her own Bulgarian accent, but wasn't sure if she could pull it off. "And three others."

She held out her watch for the man to scan it with a small device. He then typed a bit at the laptop.

"Ahh yes. We have you, Miss Kaganovich, Mr. Petrov, and Mr. Stoyanov booked for the cruise. Please come in and Maria will show you to your quarters." He removed the chain.

From out of nowhere, a young woman with dark black hair, wearing a similar white outfit, appeared. She had a sharp, angular face that made Phlox think that she had the heart of a businesswoman.

"Hi, I'm Maria," she said. "Would you prefer me to speak Bulgarian?"

"Uhh, no thank you," said John, "English is fine."

"That's fine, but please let me know if you ever change your mind. Between us, the crew of the *Angel Princess* speaks eighteen different languages fluently." She was obviously very proud of this fact. "I myself speak English, Bulgarian, and Spanish, but if you have a different request you can simply ask me if any of the other crew members speak the language you would prefer. You can follow me to your room. Would you like me to get a porter for your, umm, bags?"

The questioning tone was due to the fact that each of them, despite the long voyage ahead of them, carried only a single backpack.

"We're fine," said John. "We all like to travel light."

"That's no problem, less work for our porter, ha ha." She started walking down the deck and indicated the others to follow her. "I would like to quickly acquaint everybody with the safety regulations and jurisdiction of our ship. As you may know, we are Venezuelan-registered, but we do follow the International Convention for the Safety of Life at Sea, or SOLAS, which regulates and checks our life boats, crew training, and other aspects of the safety of our line. I would like to assure you that we have never had any accidents or major incidents aboard our vessel."

Phlox heard Chris breathe a sigh of relief, but she soon found herself drifting off, not paying attention to Maria's patter. She assumed Chris was also not paying her much mind since she was clearly not a redhead. Phlox would hear the occasional phrase coming from Maria about what the different horn soundings meant, where the life boats were, and the ship's itinerary, but none of it seemed to stick in her brain for more than a few moments. It had been a while since she had needed to pull an all-nighter, and her brain was definitely not used to it.

Maria continued her well-rehearsed welcome spiel as they stepped through a door and down into a long hallway. "I would also like to remind you that as we leave port, our network connectivity will only be via geosynchronous satellites. This may mean higher latency for your transactions. You are always welcome to shift whatever cryptocurrency you may be using to Princess Tokens, which along with faster shipboard transaction times, will also allow you discounts on meals, beverages and souvenirs."

Maria led them to their rooms, which were small and spartan, but clean and well-maintained. Nobody expected much more on a boat. They quickly threw their backpacks down on their beds and met in Jane's room to discuss the plan.

The mid-morning sun was shining through the porthole in her room, and Jane was reclining on her bed. John was looking out through the porthole, while Chris and Phlox stood near the door.

"Okay, everyone," she said, reminding Phlox of nothing more than an elementary school teacher starting class. "I'm not sure if you heard, but we are officially on Venezuelan territory. The Coast Guard can still come and board us, especially if they come up with a reason for an inspection for safety compliance, but I don't know how much influence the Chekists have with them. They didn't seem to have much pull with the Miami authorities. It's good to be reminded that they're not omnipotent.

"In other words, I think we can all get some shut-eye. I know I'm ready for some. Oh, one last thing. Forget what Maria said about shifting your mons over to 'Princess Tokens'. Exchange rate is going to be horrible both ways and half the ship won't take them. There is a little bit of lag, but Monero works fine here and everybody will take it. Oldest scam in the book. I have to admit, I feel a bit of nostalgia hearing that they're still playing that con."

They all went back to their own rooms. Phlox didn't even change out of her clothes, just took off her shoes. She collapsed into the bed, threw a sheet over herself, and was asleep in minutes.

"In countries where there is a mild climate, less effort is expended on the struggle with nature and man is kinder and more gentle."
-Anton Chekhov, *Uncle Vanya*

Drivers On The Storm

An excerpt from an article in The Econometrician, *Volume I, Issue 9*

Ride-sharing took off last decade with a variety of different companies. They were a much cheaper and more effective form of transporation than traditional taxis. Prices rose soon after venture capitalists decided that losing money by subsidizing the rides was not a viable strategy over the long term. Earnings were soon squeezed by the higher rates demanded by drivers and the lower prices demanded by passengers.

When this led to the high-profile collapse of a few ride-sharing companies, a group of open-source developers realized that this was a perfect use case for smart contracts on Ethereum. The product they developed, EthShare, provided contractually guaranteed rides, passenger and driver ratings, and the ability to pay directly in ether. A minuscule percentage of the revenue is automatically directed to the core development team, but this amount is several orders of magnitude less than that taken by management and investors of the large ride-sharing companies of the last generation.

Word of mouth quickly made EthShare an almost ubiquitous means of transportation in major cities in the United States. The lack of advertising, minimal management, and reliance on open-source technologies has meant that the company has conducted over a hundred bitcoins' worth of transactions in the last year, with only eleven full-time team members and no outside investment. Although officially supported only in the United States, it is trivial for others to download the software and run their own variants of EthShare. It is already estimated that over 25% of all rides in the Estonian capital of Tallinn are done via EthJagada, a fork of EthShare with minor changes adapted to the Estonian market.

Although this surge in ride-sharing servies has unquestionably made transportation more convenient, there is one group that is dissatisfied with it. Major car manufacturers have seen their share prices crater over the last few years, as revenue has dropped sharply. Personally owned automobiles that are not shared out were always a rather expensive proposition; they were used, at most, for an hour or two a day, or even less. Ride-sharing services have allowed more efficient use of these vehicles, meaning that the demand for vehicles has gone down dramatically. Despite an extensive, industry-wide marketing campaign extolling the benefits of owning your own car, personal automobile ownership shows no sign of stopping its downward trend.

Chapter 19

Between Thinking and Doing

Despite Chris's misgivings, the voyage of the *Angel Princess* was basically uneventful. Phlox bought a swimsuit and spent hours alternating between swimming in the pool and lounging around reading a translated copy of *Doña Bárbara* that she had found in the ship's library. After buying some clothes that did not reference hunting in any way, shape or form, Chris sat alone in his room most days, learning a new programming language that he had downloaded a guide for long ago, but had never had time to go in-depth. The guide promised that finally this was going to be the language which would allow you to easily create parallelizable code, not mentioning the history of other languages which had made similar promises over the last seventy years. John and Jane caught up, reminiscing about old times, both still in shock that the person that they had thought died years ago was not only alive and well, but in front of them. Every evening, they all drank margaritas on the deck and watched the sunset.

None of them left the safety of the boat at its various ports of call. Havana and Kingston beckoned, but they determined, unanimously, that the risk of leaving the *Angel Princess* was too great. Whoever the Chekists actually were, they definitely had some sort of government connection. Venezuela had just about the most anti-government government on the planet. A ship flying under the flag of the Rothbardian Republic of Venezuela was the safest place for them to be.

The crew on the ship were extremely accomodating, and Jane made sure that they were tipped well. They were friendly with the other passengers without making friends. Despite Jane's misgivings, they even converted some millimons to Princess Tokens to play poker in the small onboard casino (the one place onboard which *only* accepted Princess Tokens). All in all, they tried to act just like another rich group taking a vacation. Perhaps a little more private than most, but not everybody wanted to be chatty on their vacations.

The days started to blur together for Phlox. She was used to having a relatively rigid schedule. Classes were at certain times, work at other times — even her social events were usually planned far ahead. But now, there was no calendar at which to look. She would bump into Jane and they would talk for a while. Her dad would knock on the door and ask if she wanted to grab some coffee. She'd see Chris playing shuffleboard and ask to join him. She went to sleep when she was tired, and woke up when she was not. It would have seemed like a perfect existence to her only a few weeks ago.

Living through it, though, it was damned weird. Despite the fact that she found herself a multi-bitcoinaire, running from the police, living as a fugitive, finding out that her unemployed blue-collar father was actually a famous cryptocurrency researcher, and that they were traveling under assumed identities to the world's first (and so far, only) anarcho-capitalist republic, what seemed oddest to her was her *schedule*.

After eight days, though, the schedule shifted. Jane gathered them all up after breakfast to discuss the next steps of the plan.

"We're putting in at Caracas in about half an hour," she said, looking at her watch. Phlox noticed it was an old, hand-wound one. Elegant. "We're going to meet my connection Alejandro not far from the docks, but I just want to go over a few things before we do."

John spoke before she had a chance to enumerate said things. "Jane, before you say anything else, I want to remind everyone to be extremely safe. This is Venezuela. Life is cheap here."

Jane rolled her eyes. "John, if you take a look at the assassination markets, life's pretty expensive. It's probably over a quarter of a bitcoin to have someone killed. He's right, though, it never hurts to be careful.

"Venezuela doesn't have much of a government. They used to be socialist, and rebelled pretty hard against that when Herrera took over. I don't think it's possible for a country to do more of a 180 than they did. The free market controls everything down here — the court system, the police, everything. We're going to have to pay what we think of as bribes, but they consider just a normal and even ethical part of doing business."

"This counts double for the so-called police," said John. "We're heading through Venezuela because there's not much of a government there, but what government they do have does actually care about protecting rights, especially the rights of foreigners. Having some Americans killed would be bad for their image and thus for their business. But most of what looks like police are going to be 'private security forces' around some little block of property, no matter what their uniform, and they are going to care much less about the Venezuelan economy as a whole than shaking you down for as much as possible."

"Oh, John, you make it sound so dramatic. You shouldn't read the news so much. Thousands, maybe hundreds of thousands, I don't know, of Americans come to Venezuela every year with no issues. Yes, we're probably going to have to pay some people off. But it's no big deal. And remember, they don't want to hurt you. Venezuelans, barring a few Socialist holdouts, are some of the least ideological people in the world. They're just trying to make a living."

"Granted, I've never been there, but I've heard stories."

"And I could read you enough stories about the United States in the Venezuelan press to make you wonder how anybody survives past age 21 without getting shot or ending up in jail for violating some obscure municipal ordinance. No matter where you go in the world, remember that people are people."

John sighed and silently agreed, waving his hands slightly as if to say "sure, sure, now get on with it." He still looked slightly uncomfortable.

"I don't think any of you speak Spanish, so please let me take the lead. My Spanish isn't great, but it's passable, and I know the people we're looking for."

"I also know some Spanish," said John. "And I probably knew Alejandro just as well as you, if not more so."

"I know some Spanish," Chris tried to chime in, only to be verbally bulldozed by Jane.

"Did you have many opportunities to practice Spanish in Amsteco? You don't think you might be the slightest bit rusty? Rusty, like the Rust Belt, get it?" Jane giggled a little at her own joke. "Besides, you haven't spoken with Alejandro in years."

"We're going to head to the main market. That's the *Mercado Principal* in Spanish. If you get lost, say that that's what you're looking for. We'll wait for you there. It's big, but try to find the biggest banana seller you can and wait there. We'll find you."

They all heard a prolonged blast of the ship's horn. Phlox wished she would have paid more attention to Maria's description of the signals, but Jane translated for her.

"One long blast — looks like we're entering the port of Caracas. Last thing — remember that everybody here accepts Monero, Litecoin, Ether, probably a few more. Don't shift any money to the money changers at the docks. Those Princess Tokens we bought for the casino were enough of a waste of money for this trip."

They all packed their bags, then went up on deck to see the city skyline as they approached the port.

"It's not as big as I would have thought," said Chris.

"Caracas itself is about twenty miles away," said Jane. "This is La Guaira, the main port for the city. Kind of a suburb of Caracas. We'll take an EthShare over, shouldn't be a problem."

"They have EthShare vehicles here?" asked Phlox. "I always assumed that was an American thing."

"Why would it be? The same code can be run on cars all over the world. It's decentralized. People buy a car, set it up with the EthShare dapp, boom. Nothing to stop them. Sure, some countries, like France, outlaw it for various reasons, but generally you're going to see EthShare cars all around the world."

As they looked down at the Caribbean waves marching toward the shore, Maria came up from behind them. Stealthy as always, they didn't notice her until she was within a few feet of them.

"Is there anything I can help you with before you disembark?" she asked, sun glinting off the teeth in her wide smile.

"No, no, you've been very helpful," said Jane. "Although I did mean to tell you earlier, I think we are going to leave the cruise here. A friend of ours is here just for the next week and we haven't seen him in *ages*. Is there any paperwork we have to sign?" She knew that the odds of a Venezuelan ship having extra paperwork to sign were so low that they'd probably encounter an underflow error calculating them.

"I am so sorry to hear that you will be leaving us early, Ms. Ivanova. You do know that there are no refunds on incomplete cruises?"

Jane waved her hand dismissively yet politely. "Of course, I wouldn't dream of skipping out on paying you after I agreed to it. Also, I wanted to give you, personally, a token of my appreciation and thanks for taking care of us on this trip."

Maria's watch was out and displaying a QR code faster than Phlox's eye could follow it. Jane brought her own watch out and pointed it at Maria's. Maria, breaking protocol a bit, looked down at the amount. Phlox could actually see her expending willpower to keep her eyes from bulging out.

"Thank *you*, Ms. Ivanova. If you are ever considering another trip, please be sure to ask which ship Maria Hernandez is on. I would be honored to help you once again."

"But of course!"

They descended the gangplank and looked around at La Guaira. Most of the other passengers had already made plans to go on various excursions to parks, or to take in some of the sights in the capital. They wandered off in tight little tourist clumps toward waiting tour guides.

There was a small market set up next to the dock, which looked like it was only open for business when ships were in dock. Another ship — the *Caribbean Countess* — was also docked, but it appeared to be getting ready to leave. Jane called up an EthShare car to take them to Caracas, but they were warned that it would be slow going. There weren't nearly as many EthShare vehicles here as in Miami, and most of the available ones had just been rented out by the various tour groups. They settled for a small hatchback which would be a tight fit for all four of them, but would be there in less than fifteen minutes.

They killed time trying to find the tackiest tchotchke they could. Phlox had an early lead with a conch shell that read "Life is a beach," only to find herself in second place behind Chris's plastic crab reading "I am crabby! It is Monday!" However, the final winner was Jane's discovery of a dancing cat wearing a bikini atop a pedestal which read, in bold red letters, "ENGLISH TRANSLATION GOES HERE."

Finally, an extremely small self-driving automobile pulled up to their location with the EthShare logo on it. Chris sighed.

"If I had that car entirely to myself, I may have enough room to be comfortable."

"It's only twenty miles to Caracas," said Jane. "You can handle it. Think of the soldiers on the beach at Normandy, waiting in those floating tin cans to face almost certain death at the hands of German machine gunners!"

"How is that supposed to make me feel better?"

"Well, machine guns aren't very common in Caracas. They're more of a Southern Venezuela thing. So you'll see fewer machine guns than the soldiers at Omaha Beach did after your journey, uncomfortable though it may be."

Chris found that he could not argue with that logic. Besides, there weren't really any other options. He squeezed into one of the front passenger seats. The others stowed their backpacks and found seats themselves.

The scenery was amazing as they slowly gained altitude, and none of them could keep their eyes off it. La Guaira itself seemed to be poured into a small depression on the side of the mountains behind it. As they ascended the mountains, the buildings became rarer and rarer and soon they were surrounded by thick green vegetation.

The twenty miles flew by, and before they knew it, they were at the *Mercado Principal*. Phlox had been imagining it as some sort of massive building, but it was an extremely large open air market. Stands had been set up in some sort of complicated, non-linear pattern than made Phlox's brain hurt. Vendors shouted their wares, switching to English as they saw the pale faces of John, Jane, Chris, and Phlox.

"Sugarcane sticks! Best price! One microlite!"

"Lake Valencia coffee! Very delicious!"

"Bitcoin miners! Latest generation! Fresh from the fab plant!"

Phlox noticed a tall man in a blue uniform, slowly wandering around the plaza and looking at different stands. Jane noticed her interest.

"*Mercado Principal* security," she whispered. "Remember, you're just a tourist. Nothing to worry about, but don't make eye contact."

The security guard brushed past them without a second glance.

"He's not worried about us," Jane explained. "He's looking for thieves. They take property rights very seriously around here."

They spent half an hour looking at various fruit stands, coffee sellers, currency shifters, and miner dealers. John was complaining to Jane that the mining hardware advertised as "latest generation" probably didn't have the hashpower to justify the electricity they used back in *his* day when she shushed him. Chris and Phlox were listening to some sort of preacher type evangelizing. He was a young man, dressed haphazardly, with what looked to be a ragged burlap sack being used as a cloak. Even through the language barrier, Phlox could tell that he was a powerful speaker, with all of the right pauses, emphasis on just the right syllables. She assumed that the preacher was talking about Heaven, God, the *summum bonum* of human existence.

"He's trying to pump some new cryptocurrency," Chris translated. "He says that the one true hashing function came to him in a dream, and he will be announcing an initial coin offering in the next thirty days."

Phlox was a bit let down. No universal truths were to be found emanating from the mouth of a cryptocurrency pumper. Chris, though, seemed enraptured. He tried to explain to Phlox that he was saying that all hash functions were simply imperfect manifestations of the one true hash, mere shadows of this idealized function.

"It's ridiculous, of course," Chris explained. "A hilarious kind of ridiculous, though."

Phlox looked around and realized that they had somehow become separated from her dad and Jane.

"Have you seen the others?" she asked Chris.

"Huh. No. I guess I was too focused on that pumper. I'm not worried, though — remember they just said to head to the biggest banana seller and they'd meet us there? Let's go look for it. Not sure how we'll know it's the *biggest* banana seller here but maybe it will be obvious."

They spent at least twenty minutes searching through the various stalls with no sign of a big banana seller. At one point, they made a turn down what they originally thought was an alley between two rows of stalls that would lead them back to where they had been earlier. They realized halfway down, though, that it was a dead end. Sighing, they turned around.

All around them were the tall back walls of the stalls, making Phlox, at least, feel like she was in some sort of canyon of commerce. The noise of the bustling marketplace was muted. The sun shone down brightly but narrowly down the alley. She and Chris were alone on this little road in the middle of the marketplace.

And then they weren't. A female figure appeared in front of them, sundress rippled by the wind, red hair tossled, pale skin almost audibly complaining about the ultraviolet rays given off by the nearest star.

Chris gasped.

It was Vera.

"Pero es que hay personas que, entre pensar y hacer, le salen canas. (But there are people who, between thinking and doing, grow gray.)"
-Rómulo Gallegos, *Doña Bárbara*

It's Simple, Simón Bolívar

An excerpt from an article in The Econometrician, *Volume II, Issue 5*

The final collapse of the Bolivarian Republic of Venezuela would not have surprised its namesake. After all, he supposedly said, "Flee the country where a lone man holds all power: It is a nation of slaves." Nominally socialist, the history of the previous government had consisted almost entirely of increasing concentration of power amongst a small elite.

Although government forces held out for several months in the Pacaraima mountains, the success of the combined revolutionary forces had not been in doubt for at least the last year. Under the leadership of General Manuel Herrera, the charismatic young revolutionary whose books on the philosophy of liberty inspired a generation, other anti-government groups almost unanimously ceded power to his *Consejo de las Fuerzas Revolucionarias* (Revolutionary Forces Council).

None of this was surprising. What has been surprising is what has happened after General Herrera took power. Refusing to follow the script of one strongman overthrowing another and becoming the new strongman, he gave a speech which shocked not only his fellow Venezuelans, but the world as a whole. His "Palacio Municipal" speech, delivered shortly after the defeat of the remaining United Socialist Party forces, was short but indicated a drastic change not only in how Venezuela would be governed, but also in how a country could be governed.

"My fellow countrymen," it began, "we have been asked what kind of government we shall arrange. And I know better than most that the previous government was the cause of much misery. But my answer to you is not that the previous government caused misery, but that governments themselvescause misery. We plan to make as small a government as possible. All citizens have the right to be free. I do not, and shall not, ask you to follow me by pointing a rifle at you. I ask you to follow me because it is what you want to do."

Venezuela has since become the first declared "anarcho-capitalist" nation. This has meant a government whose sole focus is on ensuring free markets and private property, while minimizing its control of other aspects of society normally controlled by the state such as education, policing, and the court systems. There have been rumbles from anarcho-capitalist theoreticians that it is not true anarcho-capitalism. "I am not entirely convinced that Herrera entirely understands the *anarcho* part of anarcho-capitalism," sniffs Dr. Abraham Murphy, author of the anarcho-capitalist primer *From Each According to Their Ability, To Each According to Their Ability*. However, all of the major economic theoreticians interviewed by your correspondent agreed that Venezuela was the country which most accurately represents the philosophy, even if it is not an entirely ideologically pure.

Chapter 20

The Pleasure of Understanding

"You!" yelled Phlox. Chris just stared, at a total loss for words.

Vera held up her hands in supplication. "Wait. It is me, just me, and I want to explain."

"Explain?" Phlox was enraged. "You sent the police after us, your goons threw a bag over Chris's head and tried to kidnap him, you followed us to Venezuela and now have us cornered in an alley... what's there to explain?"

"Well, first of all, I can explain that the people who tried to kidnap Chris were not *my* goons." Vera seemed perfectly at ease, as though this entire trip had been some sort of misunderstanding that she'd be able to clear up as soon as they gave her a chance. "You seem to have a very elevated opinion of my status if you think that I have my own goons."

Chris smiled. Phlox glared at him.

"You two have gotten yourselves into something much bigger than you thought, and for which I am sorry," she continued. "I know you just thought that you had found some old bitcoins. You didn't know you were interacting with one of the most consequential terrorists of the twenty-first century."

"What!?" exclaimed Chris and Phlox simultaneously.

"Sam Chambers — yes, yes, we know he goes by John Tseretelli now — and his compatriots have caused more problems in this world than any politician you can name. The fact that it's hard for you to name any politicians any more is the main problem. Cryptocurrency has weakened governments around the world. Tax revenues have dropped precipitously.

"Sam was one of the people who helped cryptocurrency become mainstream. His work wasn't directly violent, true. But how many children died due to cutbacks in government medical programs? How many families were put out on the street because governments couldn't provide them affordable housing?   How many people couldn't pay their student loans because the Army and defense contractors aren't hiring?"

"That all may be true," said Chris. "Maybe the world is worse now than it would have been if we were all still using fiat currency. But couldn't you say it's been better as well? Wars are local affairs now. Governments can no longer afford to maintain massive nuclear stockpiles like in the twentieth century. It's not just governments that have lost power or the ability to harm. Large corporations can't overcharge people and lie without recourse when people have control over their own money. Cryptocurrency has taken the power from large organizations of all kinds and put it into the hands of people — of all kinds. And you call putting power into the hands of people terrorism?"

Vera responded with a venom that surprised Phlox. "The hands of people of all kinds, yeah! Like drug cartels and brothels, money launderers and arms dealers. The monetary privacy you care about so much when you use your cryptocurrency... do you realize that others are paying for it with their blood? Republicans and Democrats in the United States saw this and fought against it. We lost, but we didn't give up the fight."

"Wait, are you a Republican or a Democrat?" asked Phlox.

"Does it matter?" Vera responded.

A few moments of silence passed as they stared at each other, until Vera spoke again.

"Look, I'll answer any question you have. I want you to understand our position. I think that once you do, you'll join us willingly."

"Why did you send out the entire police force in Pittsburgh but you could only have a couple of office workers chase us in Florida?" asked Phlox.

"All politics is local, especially nowadays. The Pittsburgh government has lots of old-school politicians with whom we have good relationships. Florida is overrun with Democratic Socialists and Libertarians, none of whom really agree with our goals. These aren't the old days when we could send out teams to every state in the Union to do our work. We called in quite a few favors to get all those police in Pittsburgh. Even so, you were still able to get away — nice work, by the way — when all we wanted to do was question you. To help find Sam Chambers."

"And do what, take all of his hard-earned money?" asked Phlox. "Or kill him like you did so many others?"

Vera looked slightly abashed. "Look, our group doesn't like to hurt people. But sometimes it's necessary. There were definitely people in the early cryptocurrency world that we had to... disappear. Especially with the people who were developing cryptocurrency, we occasionally, and regrettably, had to use some extreme measures. That was before my time — I'm not that much older than you. But that wouldn't do us any good now. If Sam were dead, would that really change anything? Death is not our goal.

"What we need is to get people to denounce cryptocurrency. Talk about the problems with it. And if we can get some of the original researchers to come out against it, our job is halfway done. I'm sorry, I really am, if we were a bit rough in treating with you." She looked imploringly at Chris. "And especially you. I know that what I did seemed horrible and I feel just as horrible misleading you. But I promise you that it — all of it — was for the greater good. We want to be able to take care of our people again, and our job is made a million times harder when we can't control our own monetary supply."

"You have Federal Reserve Tokens," said Chris.

"Who uses those? We're not dumb. We can view the statistics. Commerce doesn't take place on that blockchain, just tax payments. Companies ignore any regulations we try to put in place telling them they have to use them."

"Let me try to, ahh, encapsulate all of this," said Phlox. "You've killed people, kidnapped people, pulled in favors with local government officials... all to try to get my dad and convince him that his life's work was actually, as you called it, terrorism?"

"But only for the greater good!" replied Vera. "Even if we can't convince your dad, we have to try. If one person's death could save a million others from the same fate, who would hesitate to pull the trigger?"

"I would," stated Phlox, "because I know enough to know that I can't say definitively that one person's death will save many others. You know, in your heart, that there are benefits to cryptocurrency, as well. I've heard stories about what it was like thirty years ago. The system was bound to fall eventually."

"That's where we disagree," said Vera, with more than a hint of fanaticism in her eye. "It wasn't bound to fall. It was forced to fall. But we can re-build it. And make it even better than it was."

"Vera, you had better believe that I am not going to give up my dad to you for any sort of political regression."

She seemed suddenly angry, her pale skin flushed. "You say it's a political regression, but people were hurt by this. Your family made out like bandits because your father got lucky. He just got into a technology early. Do you know what happened to *my* dad?"

For a moment, Phlox wasn't sure if it was a rhetorical question or if Vera actually expected them to answer. The glare in her green eyes, though, quickly made it obvious that Phlox should not try to guess.

"He lost everything. Everything. He never trusted cryptocurrency, even as inflation ate away at his savings. So what did he do? Went all-in on gold. He sold everything in his retirement account for what he thought would be protection from inflation."

Phlox gasped. She knew what had happened next.

"Right before the Bulgarians started asteroid mining?" asked Phlox.

The anger on Vera's face went away, replaced by long-buried sadness. "They flooded the market for precious metals. Overnight, all of his wealth evaporated and he was left with shiny rocks. Did you kow aluminum used to be more expensive than gold? The Washington monument is topped with a little over six pounds of aluminum, just to show off how rich of a country we were. Then the Deville process came along, and aluminum was so cheap that you could wrap your food in it and throw it in the garbage."

Vera stopped for a second, seeming to realize that she had gotten off-track.

"I came home from school one day to find him hanging from a door. No note. He just couldn't take it anymore, having lost everything. And I know your dad didn't mean to do it, but he and his friends caused it.

"Just think about it. I took a big risk talking to you like this because I thought you both should know what the score is. But there are other people here, with whom I am associated, that take a more... direct approach."

"Duly noted," said Phlox. "Come on, Chris."

Chris stared at Phlox for a moment, then over at Vera. He went over to Phlox and they ran past Vera without saying another word.

It took another ten minutes before they found what was quite clearly the biggest banana merchant in the *Mercado Principal*. Unlike most of the other stalls, it sold only a single product. The majority of stands had a few products for sale. Mangoes, plantains, and a few satellite dishes, or coconuts, blockchain analysis software, and a variety of coffees. The products on this stand consisted solely of bananas. Thousands of them.

Even more tellingly, Jane and John were standing in front of the stall, looking over the banana selection. Phlox and Chris walked over to them, with Phlox filling them in on Vera's story.

"Terrorist?" asked John. "That's how they see me? I was a researcher!"

"You can't always change how others see you," said Jane. "Trust me. I speak from experience. But if they know we're here, we should get Alejandro and get out of here soon."

She led them over to the stand and asked the vendor something in Spanish. Phlox silently lamented again that she had decided to take French in high school. Fat lot of good knowing that language had done for her.

The man behind the counter nodded and held out his watch. She paid for four bananas, then turned back to the other three, giving each one of them a banana.

"Alejandro's on his way," she explained. "Eat your bananas. The potassium is good for you. Also radioactive, you know. Not enough to hurt you, though."

"You're always the macabre one, aren't you?" asked Chris.

"Well, according to the U.S. government, I'm dead. And according to your girlfriend's weird government revivalist movement, they want to make sure I stay that way. You'd expect a dead woman to be a bit macabre, wouldn't you?"

Once more, Chris could not argue with Jane's logic. She took his silence for a conversational surrender and changed topics.

"Can't believe they want to bring back dollars and euros and whatnot. I'll tell you what I do not miss — exchanging money. Remember our Southeast Asia trip, uhh, John? Felt like we spent half the time trying not to get ripped off by the money changers..."

A man came out of the crowd and looked at Jane. He had dark skin and a small moustache, but Phlox thought that he was one of the few men that a moustache actually suited. He was about as old as John and Jane, but had a boyish look about him, and he clearly cared about his appearance. His clothes were well-maintained and looked expensive, and his face could have been on the cover of a magazine. He reminded Phlox of an actor or a pop star just a bit past their prime.

"Jane!" he said, hugging her tightly. "It has been far too long."

"Alejandro," said John.

"I assume this is Sam?" asked Alejandro, looking at him as his face moved diagonally. "Yes! I can see it in your eyes, past all of the pictures on your arms!" Alejandro hugged John as well, if anything tighter than he had hugged Jane.

"It's John now, and yeah, we've all made some changes."

Alejandro looked down at Sam's tattoos and grinned. "Indeed. Some of us more than others. Still, I see you again with Jane after all of these years. Some things do not change. But come! I am forgetting my manners. You must be tired from your journey."

"Honestly, we're pretty well-rested," said Phlox. "I mean, we were just on a cruise."

"Yes, but doing nothing is sometimes the least relaxing thing of all! I never understood the allure of sitting around on one of those boats. But once again I forget my manners! You are Alexandra, yes?"

"That's what my name was for the boat ride, but you can call me Phlox."

"Phlox! The daughter of Sam Chambers! Oh my. This is certainly something." He looked over at Chris. "And you are Georgi, yes?"

Chris nodded. "It's Chris." The rapid-fire talk of Jane and Alejandro seemed to exhaust him.

Alejandro noticed that Phlox was finishing off her banana. "Do you like the bananas? They are from my family farm. The soil around Caracas, it is not always good for bananas. But we have very good soil at our farm. You will all stay with us tonight."

"Have you been here the whole time, Alejandro?" asked John. "While the rest of us have been hiding?"

"Yes, I am the one Old Bolshevik who has stayed somewhat aboveground. This is because Venezuela is safe for people like us now. We have had our times of troubles already and people would like there to be peace. I do not advertise my presence loudly for other governments to hear, and they do not come here to find me."

"So are we going to start our new lives here?" asked Phlox. "Jane, I thought you said that this was just a stopover to our final destination."

Alejandro sighed. "I tried to convince her that this is the right place for all of you, but she would not listen. And I believe that John agreed with her. I have given up on arguing as she has her mind fixated on her idea.

"You can be the guests of my family for as long as you like, though. We have much farmland. Sam... John... you should meet my wife, Arianna. And my own three children. The countryside is beautiful, a small river runs right past our house, through a... how do you say?... a cleft in the mountains."

"We'd love to, Alejandro, we really would," said Jane, "but it's just not in the cards. I am looking forward to seeing your place, though, and catching up tonight. Maybe we can all share a little Venezuelan wine?"

A grin spread across Alejandro's face. "Of course. It would not really be a reunion without a bottle. Or two, perhaps! But you do not want to drink too much before your journey. I have heard that space travel unsettles the stomach."

"Don't worry, I know my limits. As does John, here. Can't speak for Phlox or Chris."

"I won't overdo it," Chris said, "I've learned my lesson before."

"I am sure you have," replied Alejandro, "but the travel is quite difficult. No more than a few sips for you! Even this may be too much, if your tongue is not used to our wine!"

Phlox was confused and a bit irritated that everybody seemed to know the plan except for her. "Can we all just back up a second, and tell me where are we going?"

Jane was happy to oblige. "Isn't it obvious? We're going where Mitesh said we should go — the place where people always said Bitcoin's price would end up.

"To the moon!"

" 'I have not the pleasure of understanding you,' said he, when she had finished her speech."
-Jane Austen, *Pride and Prejudice*

Blockchain of Command

An excerpt from an article in The Econometrician, *Volume IV, Issue 23*

Ensuring the validity of elections is a key factor in ensuring the functioning of a modern democracy. After several allegations of hacking and possible vote manipulation or even modification, several countries passed laws requiring paper ballots or at least paper ballot verification. While several non-governmental organizations pushed for paper receipts or other software-independent backup systems, even this minimal election anti-tampering measures were often met with skepticism by the vast majority of politicians then in power. In retrospect, it must be noted that these politicians were elected using these same insecure systems.

Thanks to blockchain technology, many of these problems have been reduced or even eliminated. Several state governments in the United States have started using simple Ethereum contracts for voting. All votes are secured by users' personal keys, meaning that it is impossible to see who has voted for whom, ensuring a secret ballot. Yet the results are publicly visible and verified to be correct. This method has been challenged several times in close elections by recounts, but in all cases, the final numbers were exactly the same as the initial numbers. Removing ambiguity and human intervention in voting has resulted in a much stronger and secure system. As anyone involved in the computer industry can attest, humans are often the weakest element in a software system.

Not everybody is pleased by the move to secure votes on the blockchain. Janice Klaaratz, a voter in the key battleground state of Pennyslvania, expressed the frustration of many voters. "How am I supposed to trust this software? I remember my computer crashing all of the time when I was a kid. Who's to say that some Democratic Socialist is modifying the numbers on my hashes? Or if one of them is a developer on the team and making the numbers come out their way, deleting my Libertarian vote?"

Still, researchers re-iterate that this is a safe and proven technology. "Do voters really understand how previous electronic voting systems worked?" asked security researcher Rawya Musa. "The entire security community agrees that these blockchain-enabled voting systems are orders of magnitude more secure than any electronic system in use, say, fifteen years ago. Is it possible that there are defects lurking in the code? Of course. There are issues that affect every manner of voting, as we do not live in a perfect world. The question, though, is not whether the system is perfect, but better than the alternatives. And the answer to that question is — indisputably — yes."

Chapter 21

Not Because They Are Easy

"The moon?" asked Phlox and Chris, in unison.

Jane nodded. "It's where most of the Old Bolsheviks are hiding. Moonbase Prime is beyond the reach of the governments of Earth."

"You knew about this, dad?" Phlox was dumbfounded.

"Jane and I talked about it at the Orange Blossom Casino. We're both going. It's your choice if you want to come, but it's the only place we're going to be safe. This isn't like the old days on the moon, living in a spartan airlock and surviving on tubes of food paste. There's over 5,000 people living there: men, women, and even a few children. The first baby was born on the moon three years ago."

"I will not join you," chimed in Alejandro, "but I will take you to the Caracas Spaceport."

Phlox felt like she was in a daze. This would be heading off into a true frontier. There were communication links between the Earth and the Moon, of course, but this was not something that she had ever considered. Moonbase Prime was a strange libertarian experiment, trying to survive in the airless void. She remembered chatting with her friends in high school, making fun of the geeks who would choose to live there.

"It's not my choice," said Phlox. "I'm following you, Dad. You haven't led me wrong yet."

Chris seemed to have no doubts about his decision. "I'm in. I've wanted to go to Moonbase Prime since I was in high school. I don't think my mom will be very surprised if that's where I end up, although I think she probably assumed I would have graduated first."

John smiled. "Glad to hear it, since we already bought the tickets for you both. Let's go, then."

Finding their way to the edge of the *Mercado Principal*, Alejandro led them like a tour guide through the maze of stalls. He would occasionally stop and chat with a vendor, or point out a particularly nice mango, or tell them details about a building in the distance. He also told Phlox and Chris his story.

Unlike John and Jane, who were interested mostly in the technology of blockchain, Alejandro considered himself its philosopher. Under the previous administration, when hyperinflation started rendering his savings and salary worthless, he used some of the subsidized electricity to became one of the largest Bitcoin miners in Venezuela. It was a stable store of value when everything else that you couldn't eat or drink became close to worthless.

When it looked as though Herrera's victory was inevitable, Alejandro started writing a semi-autobiographical series of essays, explaining, from hard-earned experience, why it was a mistake to trust in money issued by the government. The book was a best-seller in the United States and he became somewhat famous as a speaker there, which is how he met Jane and John.

As the remnants of the old Venezuelan order crumbled, he stayed in Pittsburgh, watching from afar as the others who had joined him in Bitcoin mining became the new elite. Those who had held on to the old, worthless Venezuelan dollars were now often destitute. He, and others like him, were unbelievably rich. After hearing Herrera's "Palacio Municipal" speech, he knew that it was safe to return to his homeland and start rebuilding it, and help those who did not have the foresight or capability to dabble in cryptocurrency earlier.

At the edge of the *Mercado Principal*, they found Alejandro's drab green van — old, dirty a few flecks of rust around the wheel wells. For somebody who talked of himself as the elite of the country, it seemed like a very modest vehicle. But, as Alejandro reminded them, he was never a big holder of bitcoin or any other cryptocurrency. He had enough to get by, and what he did not need, he used to help his country get back on its feet during the precarious times after their civil war.

Alejandro continued the tale of his life, with barely an interruption by any of the others. It seemed like he could talk forever without ever worrying about having nothing to say. Yet Phlox found his life interesting. Growing up in Western Pennsylvania, she could barely think of anyone she had met who hadn't been born nearby. Once she started university, of course, she had met quite a few. She still found the stories of others' lives, who did not grow up anywhere near the shadow of the decaying steel mills, fascinating.

He met a lovely girl with eyes that changed color from day to day, from green to blue to hazel, depending on her mood. Her blonde hair was like spun gold, her anger was like some primeval volcano god, her love was more than he could handle. She was born in Puerto Rico, but had worked in Venezuela as part of a charity organization. She fell in love first with the country, and then with Alejandro. Together, they built a new house on his family's ancestral land, not far from Caracas, where bananas grew fat and yellow while Alejandro wrote his books. They had one child, and then another, and then another.

Slowly, he lost contact with most of his friends in the cryptocurrency world, until they started coming to Venezuela to escape from shadowy people who seemed to be tracking them. It reminded him of the inverse of his time under the old regime, when he went to the United States to avoid being hunted down. Now his friends from the United States were coming here. Their stories were all the same. None of them knew who was looking for them, only that they were being tracked, friends of theirs were being killed, and other friends were disappearing.

"I do not know who these enemies are," said Alejandro, "but they have long memories and are quite dedicated to finding us."

"We've been calling them Chekists," interrupted Jane.

Alejandro laughed. "Of course! If we are the Old Bolsheviks, who else could they be? I have helped many of you — from the U.S., from France, from Canada, from China. I always give the option of staying here, but they all want to go to Moonbase Prime."

"There's nothing stopping the Chekists from coming here," said John, "but there's a pretty good chokepoint to get to the moon. There's no way to get up there without taking one of the shuttles, and there are only, what, three launchpoints? Here, Baikonur, and Jiuquan?"

"Yes, but I have heard that they may stop accepting shuttles from Jiuquan. This is just idle gossip, but there is some argument between the leadership of Moonbase Prime and the Party. Apparently some members of the Party believe that Prime's declaration of sovereignty violates the United Nations Outer Space Treaty. The Kazakhs never signed the treaty, and the Russians who operate Baikonur have never raised a fuss. We in Venezuela signed the treaty, many years ago, but have recently made a great show of publicly disavowing it. There is little gain for us to support it, you know, and much to gain by being allied with Prime. So the shuttles will continue to run from here, I am certain."

"You're disavowing a treaty that you signed?" asked Phlox. "Does that happen often? Sorry, I don't mean to be rude."

"Oh, Phlox," said Jane. "This is such a small example! Do you know that if you find an island with bird poop on it, you can claim it in the name of the United States if it's not claimed by someone else? The Guano Islands Act. Still on the books even today, almost two hundred years after it was passed. But nobody is expected to abide by it, and if you try, the U.S. government is probably not going to back up your claim. Ernest Hemingway's brother actually tried it once, didn't go well for him.

"The Convention Against Torture, the Anti-Ballistic Missile Treaty, all kinds of treaties with the Native Americans... they've withdrawn from or just plain ignored. The U.S. isn't even the worst of the bunch."

"That is one of the reasons that Herrera was against forming a traditional government," explained Alejandro. "Going back on promises is just something that states do."

Phlox was so enthralled that she barely realized that the van had stopped on a dirt driveway. A small but tidy house — "cozy" was the adjective that sprung to her mind — was in front of them. It was painted red, and capped by a large, blue barrel, apparently where water was stored. There were a few touches that showed that children lived there: a small bicycle lying near the door, a wooden jungle gym obviously made from leftover lumber.

The landscape in which the house sat was awe-inspiring. Large mountain peaks were around them in three directions, with trees and greenery covering the slopes. A small river — nothing compared to the Monongahela — flowed rapidly past them, off to their right. Behind the house, green bananas were slowly growing on their trees. Phlox knew that the plants on which the bananas were growing were actually very large herbs, but her mind insisted on referring to them as "banana trees."

"Welcome to my home," said Alejandro. "I am afraid that you will all have to stay in one room tonight. We have a room for my son Sebastián, and the girls share a room, but Sebastián will be spending the night with his sisters. It will not be luxurious, I am afraid, but it should do for the night."

Alejandro turned off the ignition on the van — internal combustion, Phlox noted, not electric — and they got out. As they did, three kids bounded out of the front door, a boy who looked to be about eight, followed closely by two girls who looked to be five or six.

"These are my children," said a beaming Alejandro. "Sebastián is the eldest, then Daniela, then Gabriela. Don't let her height fool you, Daniela is older than Gabriela. *Verdad, pequeña?*"

Daniela looked up at her dad with an annoyed expression, then smiled when he tousled her brown hair.

"Come in, come in," said Alejandro, and they all headed into the house. Within a few milliseconds, the children were off in another room, yelling at each other and sounds of their playing echoing through the rooms.

The house was filled with a delicious, savory smell, and Phlox half-expected to see a grandmother in the kitchen cooking. When she saw the kitchen, though, it was empty of people. There were only various pots boiling, and pans searing, and an oven heating.

"Arianna must be around here somewhere..." said Alejandro.

"I am here!" came a voice from another room. Phlox looked in to see a woman sitting at a table, papers strewn in front of her. She had a pencil in her hand, and occasionally tapped some numbers into an ancient calculator. Her blonde hair was cut short and stuck out at crazy angles, reminding Phlox, at least, of some sort of superhero.

"My anachronistic wife! Still using pencils!" said Alejandro cheerfully, and went over to give her a peck on her cheek.

"These must be your friends," she said in an accentless voice. Phlox was reminded that she was born in Puerto Rico, and was probably effectively bilingual.

"Indeed!" A round of introductions took place.

"I'm sorry to be rude, but I have a little more work to do here," she said, seeming to be actually contrite. Not so contrite that she didn't turn around without any more explanation and start scratching her pencil against the paper.

"Arianna is a banker," explained Alejandro. "Some still practice the Old Ways, double-entry bookkeeping and the like. She is an expert on this topic. She mostly helps interpret the finances of companies using the blockchain to old business houses in Switzerland."

They stayed for a massive dinner, *ensalada caprese* and *arepas* stuffed with cheese, *empanadas* with black beans, a creamy *bien me sabe* cake to finish the meal off, and all washed down with a dark red wine. After the meal, John, Jane, and Alejandro talked about their days together in Pittsburgh, while the kids played house on the floor. Phlox and Chris mostly chatted with Arianna about how she ended up in Venezuela and telling her about their own lives.

The evening ended relatively early, around 8:30 PM. John, especially, was quite tired. He was not used to this much socializing, and he had never been an extrovert. Jane, Alejandro, and Arianna were all for continuing the evening, but they were overruled by Phlox and Chris, who also felt like they would collapse at any moment. They also knew that they would be heading on to the shuttle tomorrow, and didn't want to have a hangover during launch. Flights to the moon had gotten more comfortable since the days of the Apollo missions, but they still were not *that* comfortable.

As promised, they all spread out in Sebastián's room, with Phlox, the smallest among them, taking the bed by default, as she was the only one who fit on it. She was a little bit put out that a nine-year-old's bed was big enough for her, but at this point in her life she was used to that kind of thing. The others slept on the carpeted floor, surrounded by a collection of soccer balls and pencil-and-crayon drawings.

The next morning dawned crystal clear, not a cloud in the sky. They all had a filling breakfast of leftover *arepas*, said goodbye to Arianna and the children, and packed up the van. They were all leaving by 8:00 AM, which seemed amazing to Chris and Phlox. Their internal clocks had shifted incredibly from their time in college over the course of their adventure.

"Let's go!" said Alejandro, turning the key in the ignition. The engine sputtered for a few seconds, then started running smoothly. Alejandro shifted into reverse and there was a sudden, loud bang.

"Just a backfire, nothing to worry about!" he explained. "I must check my spark plugs. But I can do this tomorrow."

They pulled out of the long driveway, already missing Alejandro's home and his family. The banana trees receded quickly out of sight, and the road turned from dirt to gravel to asphalt. The Caracas Spaceport, despite its name, was not in Caracas, although it was the closest major city. It had been built quite a distance away, as the shuttles landing and — especially — taking off were not exactly quiet. In a country where assassination markets were considered a viable way of resolving issues, none of the designers of the spaceport wanted to risk angering city residents.

As they drove, Alejandro continued his lecturing. It was easy to see why he had been a sensation on the talk circuit in the United States; he was an enthusiastic presenter on anything, even something as quotidian as spaceport history. The Caracas Spaceport had been built immediately after Herrera's announcement of Venezuela's new economic system, funded by the same crypto-barons that funded Moonbase Prime. Although many in the international press derided the project, saying that anarcho-capitalism as an economic model was fundamentally flawed and businesses should avoid investing in Venezuela, the project ran smoothly and was soon shuttling tourists back and forth to low-Earth orbit. After a few months of this, the first lunar mission was successfully accomplished. Nowadays, shuttles ran back and forth to Moonbase Prime every week.

Although there were other spaceports in the world, Alejandro continued, this was the most active for personal trips. Jiuquan and Baikonur both beat it in terms of actual tonnage carried into space, but, for various reasons which made sense to Alejandro, this was not the best metric to use in measuring spaceport usage.

He also noted that once they got to the spaceport, they would no longer be on Venezuelan soil. Venezuela treated Caracas Spaceport as a legal extension of Moonbase Prime, much like an embassy. It was well-guarded, as there were concerns about terrorism when it was first being built, although no attacks had ever taken place on it.

There were few other vehicles on the road that morning, and the weather was absolutely perfect, the clouds continuing their boycott of the sky. At least, the weather felt perfect to Phlox. Chris looked as though he would have preferred something a bit chillier, and judging by the way he was squinting, perhaps with a few clouds added to the mix. Jane and John seemed to not notice the temperature either way, but stared out the windows, looking pensive, as Alejandro rattled off statistics and anecdotes to prove his point that the Caracas Spaceport was, by far, the greatest spaceport on Earth, and possibly the solar system, although he lacked clear data on lunar or Martian bases.

An abrupt shudder of the van and a loud grinding sound broke the flow of spaceport information from Alejandro. Some sort of accident, thought Phlox, but then realized that Alejandro had suddenly hit the gas, instead of stopping. Another vehicle had hit them and they had swerved, but he had done a decent job of correcting.

The engine complained as Alejandro tried to get away, pedal pressed to the floor.

"Six kilometers! Come on!" he yelled. Phlox knew he meant it was that far to the spaceport.

Phlox caught a glimpse of two pale white men in a red pick-up truck to the side before the truck slammed into them again, pushing the van entirely off the highway. The van careened off a guardrail, the sudden change in direction causing pain in her neck. She lost sight of the truck, but looked over to see her dad slumped in the seat next to her.

"Dad!" Phlox yelled. He didn't respond.

Jane, sitting in the back seat, shook his shoulders. "Sam! Wake up! Damn it, Sam!"

Phlox was momentarily relieved that there didn't seem to be any blood on her dad. He must have hit his head against the unpadded insides of the van. That didn't mean everything was okay, she knew, but somehow it seemed less dangerous.

She looked back to see the two men, staring at her with a neutral hatred in their eyes, perfectly calm but all the more menacing for that. She locked eyes with the driver as it approached, noting the blue dress shirt he was wearing, the lack of stubble on his face, hair combed to the side in a perfect part, as the truck approached. It was significantly faster than Alejandro's van, with some sort of cow-catcher on the front to minimize damage to their own vehicle while maximizing it to any vehicle they happened to hit.

A third collision, this time from the back, pushed them forward. A spray of safety glass crescendoed around them all as the back window broke into thousands of tiny bits. As if from a great distance, she heard Chris scream in a mixture of shock and pain. Phlox felt her body jerked forward and then back, entirely of its own accord, a victim of physics.

When she regained control, the first thing she did was look over at her dad, still unresponsive. She reached into his backpack lying at this feet, digging through the clothes, the toiletries, the paperback sci-fi novels, and found it.

She pulled the revolver out of its case and, in the same motion, swiveled her head around to look for the truck. Before she saw it, she noticed a bridge ahead of them, crossing a deep canyon. She saw the truck next to, and slightly behind, them. They were obviously making another attempt to run them off the road, and if it happened on the bridge, there looked to be about a thousand vertical feet between where they ran them off and where the car would stop.

Glancing down at the revolver, she popped open the cylinder and saw that it was fully loaded. Her dad was taking no chances. She took aim at the truck out the back window, Chris and Jane ducking, and squeezed the trigger.

Nothing happened. The trigger didn't move. Phlox felt a surge of disappointment greater than she had ever felt before.

"Is there a safety or something?" she asked to nobody in particular.

"It's a revolver!" yelled Jane. "Squeeze harder!"

With a millisecond's worth of regret that she didn't spend more time working out, she squeezed with all of her might. The shot went wild, the recoil hurting her arm and forcing it up. Her ears rang from the noise, so much so that she couldn't hear anything else. This was nothing like in the movies.

The truck had backed off a bit when they realized that they were being fired upon, but was now making another approach at them. Phlox took aim again, squeezing the trigger so hard it felt like her fingers were going to bleed, then flinched right before the second shot was fired. She could sense the bullet flying off into the sky.

The truck veered away from them, less interested in ramming them off the road if they were going to fight back. Phlox could see the passenger pulling out his own handgun. The ringing in her ears was louder, her arm was sore from holding the revolver in front of her, but so much adrenaline was flowing through her that these feelings seemed insignificant. The passenger had opened his window and was aiming the handgun at them...

She pulled the trigger once more, pain shooting through her hand. One of the front tires of the truck popped, or exploded, she wasn't sure which, but the truck skidded sideways and off the road. The front of the truck collapsed into the pavement, sparks flying as metal scraped asphalt. One of the back tires of the truck fell off and continued moving forward down the road, another pawn of inertia.

Phlox suddenly noticed a quick burning sensation on her shoulder, followed a moment later by excruciating pain. Looking down at her left shoulder, she could see that her shirt was covered in blood and more was soaking through her shirt. A red area the size and shape of a light bulb was slowly growing as she gasped uncontrollably.

She started to say... something... then forgot what she was going to say... unable to concentrate due to the pain, she tried again... the pain lessened as reality seemed to flicker in and out... but she couldn't talk. She tried. One last time.

It was no use. She lost consciousness.

"We choose to go to the moon in this decade and do the other things, not because they are easy, but because they are hard."
-John F. Kennedy, *Address at Rice University, September 12th, 1962*

From My Cold, Dead Blockchain

An excerpt from an article in The Econometrician, *Volume V, Issue 22*

As the world increases its reliance on blockchain technology, one of the issues which was a major strength of Bitcoin and other cryptocurrencies is turning out to be a major problem. If you do not know the private key of an address, it is essentially impossible to access the bitcoin stored there. There are many ways of storing a private key, but most of these require some knowledge by the accessor. For example, physical ownership of a hardware wallet is usually not enough. You must also know a passcode or password.

This is an essential security feature. Sadly, though, this has caused many problems for the estates of people who owned cryptocurrency. Many would-be heirs have been disappointed to find that the bitcoin that their parents had been saving for years is inaccessible because nobody knows the password to access them.

A possible solution to this problem, multisignature wallets, has been known for years. A multisignature wallet, also referred to as an m-of-n wallet, requires some subset of people to agree to access the wallet. A common solution is to have a 2-of-3 wallet, including the future executor of the estate, the beneficiary, and the testator. Only if two of these people provide their private keys can the cryptocurrency be moved. For example, the decedent-to-be and the executor may decide to change the beneficiary or move the currency. They may do so without the consent of the heir apparent. When the decedent-to-be becomes the decedent-in-fact, the beneficiary and the executor can transfer the bitcoin. The loss of a single private key does not mean that the cryptocurrency is forever inaccessible, as it would be in a traditional wallet.

However, multisignature wallets also have their own issues. In at least one case, a rogue lawyer made off with a fortune after collaborating with an heir. The lawyer was only found out because he reneged on the offer and attempted to run off with the entire stash. Unless one is keeping an eye on their cryptocurrency holdings at all times, this can be difficult to detect. There are numerous "wallet watcher" companies and products, but buyer beware. Many of these are scams which trick you into entering your private key. If you do choose to use one of these services, know that since the blockchain is public, there is never any need to give your private key to them.

Chapter 22

If You Don't Believe It

The first thing that Phlox saw when she regained consciousness was a bouquet of blue flowers. Phlox, she realized. Funny.

She looked around the room groggily, seeing white all around her, and realized she was in some sort of hospital. Her dad was sitting on a chair next to her, reading a thin book, some sort of collection of essays, an expression on his face that seemed like he had been worried for so long. Phlox peered at the book to try to read the title, realizing even as she did it that it was a ridiculous and superfluous thing to be doing right now.

She stared up at the ceiling.

John noticed that Phlox's eyes were open and relief washed over his face. "You're okay, marigold," he said, "just a little banged up. You lost some blood and fainted. The bullet just grazed you. It might hurt to raise your arm over the next few weeks, but nothing vital was hit. You'll be fine. You're a tough little flower."

She looked down at her arm. She realized she was wearing a hospital gown with the sleeve rolled up. There was fresh white gauze covering her shoulder, but not that much. It must not have been a very large injury.

"Are you okay, Dad?"

"Oh yeah. I feel kind of embarrassed, honestly. Hit my head against the wall and lost consciousness. That's not really good for you, but I'm okay. Better than the alternative."

Phlox realized that nobody else was in the room with them. "Is everyone else okay?"

"Everyone's fine, rose. Tseretelli luck, we're the only ones to get hurt. Alejandro is back at his house, and probably buying a new car and a better home security system. There was even some talk of him, his wife, and his kids coming up to join us soon. Chris and Jane both just went out to get something to eat. We've all been waiting for you. They should be back soon."

"What happened to the people in the truck?"

For the first time since she had woken up, the smile left his face. "We're not sure. Spaceport security went after them, but looks like they left their truck by the side of the road and escaped into the wilderness. Security is still investigating the wreck, but the two men got away."

The concerned look on her face must have been clear. "Don't worry, though. We're safe here. As safe as we've been since you and Chris transferred that bitcoin back in Pittsburgh."

"Where are we?"

"Technically, the moon, I think."

"What? We already took the shuttle up?"

"No, no, no! Let me finish! We're at the Caracas Spaceport Medical Center. It's extraterritorial here, remember? Technically territory of Moonbase Prime. If they come here, they're invading sovereign territory. Whoever these Chekists are, there's no way they're going to try to start a war. We're going to head up in the shuttle tonight. Our lunar citizenship has already been registered on the blockchain."

Phlox nodded. She couldn't believe that they were this close. Or that this was real. She had wanted an adventure, she thought. Now it seemed like that adventure was over. A new one was about to begin.

The door to her room opened, and a tired-looking Jane entered, followed immediately afterwards by Chris.

"Phlox!" Jane positively burst with excitement. "Are you feeling up to a hug?"

"Of course." Jane embraced her tightly, being sure to avoid her left shoulder.

"I have to say I'm impressed, Phlox," said Chris. "You were like an action hero."

"Action heroes don't faint, and they don't end up in the hospital at the end of the show."

Chris smiled. "Maybe they just don't show it in the movies or talk about it in books. I'm sure it just happens off-camera."

A doctor knocked and then quickly walked in, without giving anyone a chance to say whether or not now was a good time. He held a tablet which he glanced down at, light from it reflecting on his wire-frame glasses. He looked friendly enough, the classic avuncular presence of a middle-aged medical practicitioner in that comforting white coat. Dispensing some hand sanitizer onto his hands and rubbing them in a well-practiced motion, a ritual ablution, he approached Phlox on the small hospital bed.

"You don't remember me, but I stitched you up. Dr. Vasquez." He held out his hand, and Phlox shook it. "How are you feeling?"

She did a self-assessment. A little pain crept out from under the gauze. "Overall, good. I mean, I've felt better, but pretty good."

The doctor nodded. "It's going to get worse before it gets better, I'm afraid, but you'll be fine. You're going to have a pretty sore shoulder for a while, and you shouldn't try lifting anything more than a few pounds. I'm going to prescribe some exercises for you, but I don't think you need any drugs harder than aspirin.

"All that said, I think you're good to go in regards to spaceflight. I've signed the necessary smart contracts that will allow you entry. May I be the first to welcome you as a new lunar citizen."

After a few pleasantries, the doctor took his leave and they continued to catch Phlox up on what she had missed. The truck was incapacitated after Phlox's shot. Wit the pursuers unable to follow them, the van left the truck and its passengers far behind. When they had arrived at the gate to the Caracas Spaceport, they told the guards what had happened. About six guards had gone out in a massive military vehicle, lights on the top and side flashing, while emergency medical techs took Phlox to the Medical Center in their own ambulance.

Since then, they had mostly been waiting for Phlox to regain consciousness and to hear the news from the guards. The guards came back, corroborated the story, and Alejandro went home. Much as he wanted to stay, his wife had a meeting and somebody had to watch the kids.

Phlox listened quietly to the story. It seemed strange to hear about all of this happening when it seemed as though only a few minutes had passed since she was shot. Out the window, though, she could see that it was late afternoon, the sun setting behind the mountains and sending glorious reds and pinks throughout the sky.

Dismissing the others, she gingerly removed the hospital gown, but the gentlessness seemed unnecessary. If she wasn't mentally looking for the pain, it was easily placed in the background of her awareness. She slipped on a comfortable pair of jeans and one of the t-shirts she had bought aboard the *Angel Princess*, the red one with an outline of a boat heading into the sunset on it. It seemed appropriate. Her James Joyce hoodie was tied around her waist.

She exited the room and met the others, backpack slung over her right shoulder. She usually carried it over her left shoulder, but this would be one of the most trivial changes occurring in her life. The others were waiting for her in the hall. They all left the small medical center, Chris saying his goodbyes in half-decent Spanish to the receptionist with whom he had apparently been chatting earlier. Her hair was dark black, Phlox noticed, but it did have a little bit of an auburn shimmer.

Ahead of them was the terminal, the shuttle docked behind it. The shuttle stood impressively over the small terminal, a weird sort of matte chrome color, like something out of one of her dad's science fiction novels. They walked across the broad expanse of pavement toward it.

Arriving at the terminal, they all verified their identities via the watch, showing QR codes which verified that they were now lunar citizens. A guide led them to the entrance of the shuttle, climbing up a long ladder to their seats. Before heading into the cabin, they stored their belongings in coded cubbies.

The shuttle fit 20 people, in five rows of four. Each row had two sets of two chairs, separated by a central passageway with a built-in ladder. The seats were also at a 45-degree angle to the ground, facing the top of the shuttle, extremely soft, yet still looking vaguely military. There were small portholes through which they could see the last vestiges of the Venezuelan sunset. The ladder was built in to the floor, and it was a little tricky transferring themselves from the ladder into their seats. They all figured it out within a few minutes, though.

They were the first passengers to board, but it soon filled up completely. The expense of sending a shuttle meant that every flight was fully booked. If it wasn't, the flight didn't go up. Phlox looked around nervously as each new group of passengers boarded, but none of them looked familiar. When the last two boarded, a grey-haired Asian couple, filling up the confines of the small cabin, she relaxed. The men from the van, from the truck, the people who followed her in Pittsburgh — none of them were anywhere to be seen.

A flight attendant came around and verified that everybody's five-point harnesses were correctly set, and checked them. Taking a spot in the front of the cabin, he gave a quick talk about the various safety features of the shuttle. He then informed them about "space sickness," which a majority of people experienced their first time in microgravity, and discussed the proper use of the space sickness bags hanging in front of them. A few minutes were devoted to discussing how to use the restroom while in microgravity, which seemed like it would be the most onerous part of the journey. Other than that, the passengers should just sit back and enjoy slipping the surly bonds of Earth. Concluding his speech, he went back to a special seat in the back and strapped himself in, just as a voice came over a hidden loudspeaker.

"Ladies and gentlemen, this is your captain speaking. Welcome to flight RS-981. We will begin the launch process in a few minutes. After launch, we should reach orbit at approximately T+8 minutes. Barring any issues, we will then initiate trans-lunar injection at T+91 minutes. We will enter lunar orbit at T+49 hours, and have you at Moonbase Prime at T+51 hours. Until then, sit back, relax, and enjoy the ride. If you have to use the restroom, I recommend you do so now."

Nobody got up. The flight attendant said something into a microphone, communicating with the captain, and Phlox felt the ship slowly rise, gradually changing its angle from 45 degrees to 90. It took a few minutes to do so.

As she looked straight up at what was the ceiling — or the front? — of the cabin, Phlox noticed for the first time a timer running. Its yellow-on-black characters read "T-00h 02m 54s." She stared at it intently, then realized that she was just making herself nervous. She looked over at Chris, who looked like he was about the enter the biggest candy store in the world. Jane was literally twiddling her thumbs and looking around the cabin. She caught Phlox's eye and smiled. Her dad's eyes were closed. He looked more relaxed than she had ever seen him.

Phlox felt her heart race as the countdown reached single digits. She reached out and put her hand in her dad's, who held it tight. Her nervousness must have shown in her blue eyes, but his face calmed her as he looked over.

"Come on, Phlox. Aren't you excited to meet Satoshi?"

"And if you don't believe it or don't get it, I don't have the time to try to convince you, sorry."
-Satoshi Nakomoto

Chapter 23

APPENDIX A: Currency Conversions

All ratios are valid at the time this story begins. However, note that none of these currency have any sort of fixed exchange rate, except the FRT with the U.S. dollar. Thus, fluctuations occur on a regular basis, although they are usually small (less than 0.1% per day).

When discussing the Bitcoin or Litecoin network as a whole, the word is capitalized. However, when referring to units of currency, the term is lowercase. For example, "I was using the Bitcoin blockchain", but "I inherited two bitcoin."

Denominations are usually given in terms of centis, millis, micros, or nanos. These are often followed by a shortened name of the coin, although this is sometimes omitted if the currency is obvious. Denominations of ether are almost never used in normal conversation, although specialists in smart contracts, dapps, and the Ethereum network in general do have jargon which they use for various amounts of ether, including finney, szabo, and wei.

- Centi : one hundredth : centibit, centilite, centimon

- Milli : one thousandth : millibit, millilite, millimon

- Micro : one millionth : microbit, microlite, micromon

- Nano : one billionth : nanobit, nanolite, nanomon

Federal Reserve Tokens (FRTs)

These are exchangeable on a 1:1 basis with the U.S. dollar. They are occasionally referred to simply as "dollars", especially by older people, due to this correspondence. They are rarely used on a day-to-day basis except when interacting with government agencies or for other legally mandated reasons.

Currency 1	Currency 2	Exchange Rate
FRT	Bitcoin	1 FRT : 0.00000053 bitcoin
FRT	Litecoin	1 FRT : 0.00000456 litecoin
FRT	Ether	1 FRT : 0.00001161 ether
FRT	Monero	1 FRT : 0.00000877 moneroj

Bitcoin

Bitcoin tends to be used for saving accounts and large purchases such as real estate. It is not commonly used for everyday purchases. It is the most valuable cryptocurrency in terms of value storage, but transactions are not as common as the other three major cryptocurrencies.

Currency 1	Currency 2	Exchange Rate
Bitcoin	FRT	1 bitcoin : 1,896,011.01 FRT
Bitcoin	Litecoin	1 bitcoin : 8.65 litecoin
Bitcoin	Ether	1 bitcoin : 22.01 ether
Bitcoin	Monero	1 bitcoin: 16.62 moneroj

Litecoin

Litecoin is used by most people in cities for everyday purchases, and occasionally for larger purchases. It is the most commonly-used cryptocurrency across the world in terms of daily transaction volume.

Currency 1	Currency 2	Exchange Rate
Litecoin	FRT	1 litecoin : 219,192.02 FRT
Litecoin	Bitcoin	1 litecoin : 0.12 bitcoin
Litecoin	Ether	1 litecoin : 2.54 ether
Litecoin	Monero	1 litecoin : 1.92 moneroj

Ethereum

Ether is used to purchase computing power on the Ethereum network. Although it is possible to use ether directly to pay for goods or services, it is generally considered more of a commodity or resource (like oil or lumber) than a true currency.

Currency 1	Currency 2	Exchange Rate
Ether	FRT	1 ether : 86,143.16 FRT
Ether	Bitcoin	1 ether : 0.05 bitcoin
Ether	Litecoin	1 ether : 0.39 litecoin
Ether	Monero	1 ether : 0.76 moneroj

Monero

Monero is a truly anonymous cryptocurrency, unlike the other three major blockchains. While Litecoin is used in most cities, the economy of the countryside and smaller towns is dominated by Monero, at least in the United States. Due to its anonymity, it is difficult to determine the exact size of the Monero economy, but most estimates put it at approximately one quarter the size of the Litecoin economy.

Note: The plural form of monero is moneroj (e.g., "two moneroj and six micromoneroj"), as the term was taken from Esperanto. However, nobody except the most pedantic (and the occasional Esperanto aficionado) actually uses this form. The vast majority of people use the singular form as the plural form (e.g. "six monero") or the abbreviation "mon" with the plural "mons" (e.g. "two mons and six micromons").

Currency 1	Currency 2	Exchange Rate
Monero	FRT	1 monero : 114,080.08 FRT
Monero	Bitcoin	1 monero : 0.06 bitcoin
Monero	Litecoin	1 monero : 0.52 litecoin
Monero	Ether	1 monero : 1.32 ether

Chapter 24

APPENDIX B: Further Reading

In writing this book, I extrapolated current trends in cryptocurrency forward a number of years. I did not think of all of this in a vacuum, but was informed by people who have thought about this much more than me. If you are interested in furthering your own knowledge of cryptocurrency — and I recommend that you do — I have included a list of books, papers, and other readings that were helpful to me in the writing of this book.

The Age of Cryptocurrency: How Bitcoin and the Blockchain Are Challenging the Global Economic Order by Paul Vigna and Michael J. Casey.

American Kingpin: The Epic Hunt for the Criminal Mastermind Behind the Silk Road by Nick Bilton.

Anatomy of the State by Murray Rothbard.

Bitcoin: A Peer-to-Peer Electronic Cash System by Satoshi Nakomoto.

Blockchain Revolution: How the Technology Behind Bitcoin Is Changing Money, Business, and the World by Don Tapscott and Alex Tapscott.

The Crypto-Anarchism Manifesto by Timothy C. May.

The Cryptonomicon by Neal Stephenson.

The Cyphernomicon by Timothy C. May.

A Cypherpunk's Manifesto by Eric Hughes.

Digital Gold: Bitcoin and the Inside Story of the Misfits and Millionaires Trying to Reinvent Money by Nathaniel Popper.

Ethereum White Paper by Vitalik Buterin.

Ethereum Yellow Paper by Dr. Gavin Wood.

The Internet of Money by Andreas Antonopoulos.

Introducing Ethereum and Solidity by Chris Dannen.

Mastering Bitcoin: Unlocking Digital Cryptocurrencies by Andreas Antonopoulos.

Chapter 25

APPENDIX C: Acknowledgements

First off, I want to thank my wife, Allison Fromm. Without her support, this book would have never been possible. I also want to thank my son, Calvin, for (mostly) understanding when I needed time alone to get some writing done. Without my parents, Bill and Kathy Laboon, I wouldn't have been the person I am today, so they also get spots in the first paragraph. It's a cliché to thank your family, I know, but they really were the ones who needed to be acknowledged first and foremost.

I would also like to thank everybody who reviewed early copies of the book, especially:

Naomi Anderson
Karen Dengate
Alex Hetrea Kelley
Jason Li
Dustin Martin
Nate Menge
Kate O'Dell

Finally, a special thank you goes out to Satoshi Nakomoto, wherever — and whoever — they may be.

Printed in Great Britain
by Amazon